CORRIGENDA

Phil Egner

Copyright © 2023 Phil Egner

All rights reserved. No part of this publication may be reproduced, stored in a retrieval system, or transmitted in any form or by any means, mechanical, electronic, recording, photocopying or otherwise without the prior permission of the copyright owner.

This is a work of fiction. All characters, organisations and events portrayed in this novel are either products of the author's imagination or are used fictitiously.

Cover Design
FrinaArt

For Steven and Christopher

Who, even this late in the game, keep me on my toes far more than they'd ever imagine.

Corrigendum is the gerundive form of the Latin compound verb corrigo -rexi -rectum (from the verb rego, 'to make straight, rule', together with the preposition cum, 'with'), 'to correct', and thus signifies '(that thing) which must be corrected' and in its plural form, Corrigenda, signifies '(those things) which must be corrected'.

Sellon's Annotated Latin Grammar
London 1865

I am a little world made cunningly
Of elements and an angelic sprite,
But black sin hath betray'd to endless night
My world's both parts, and oh both parts must die.

Holy Sonnet V
John Donne

Could it think, the heart would cease beating.

The Book of Disquiet
Fernando Pessoa

CONTENTS

Title Page
Copyright
August 1999
Prologue — 1
Chapter One — 7
Chapter Two — 41
Chapter Three — 77
Chapter Four — 97
Chapter Five — 125
Chapter Six — 153
Chapter Seven — 181
Chapter Eight — 207
Chapter Nine — 245
Chapter Ten — 277
Chapter Eleven — 307
Chapter Twelve — 337
Chapter Thirteen — 365
Epilogue — 385
Afterword — 391
About The Author — 393

AUGUST 1999

PROLOGUE

The church is Norman - *'Serving the community since 1125'* jokes the billboard by the gate - and so you're surprised there's space in the churchyard for yet one more burial. Most funerals you've attended have been at crematoriums on the outskirts of cities, low brick built buildings discreet behind tidy rows of trees and a thirty-minute slot squeezed between entering the main door and exiting via the Memorial Garden. So, a family plot you guess and also assume this is going to be a more leisurely affair.

The mourners wait by the front doors. There's no shock of a life taken too soon or the sense of release encompassing one that's lingered, perhaps painfully so, for too long. They are either grouped in small clusters and acknowledge new arrivals with subdued greetings or, like yourself, stand alone and exchange a polite smile on catching another's eye.

Fifty or sixty people have gathered by the time the cortege arrives. You all fall silent. Some of the older ones bow their heads as the coffin is carried into the church. Following the pallbearers through the door, her two daughters dab at their eyes with small lace handkerchiefs while her son stares stoically ahead. You attach yourself to the end of the procession and once inside are directed to a pew at the rear. The casket has been placed on a bier in front of the altar and the vicar is taking his place in the pulpit.

It's a simple service. Most here are of an age for the hymns to be familiar from childhood, morning assembly if not Sunday School, and are sung with gusto. There are several eulogies, a colleague for many years, a fellow member of the Women's Institute and finally her youngest daughter, who celebrates what a loving mother she has been and what a joyous family she created.

Well, you reflect, third time's a charm.

* * *

You surprise yourself by how easy it is to resurrect the remnants of a West Country burr. Perhaps no longer from around these parts, people will surmise, but was once.

True enough.

You slowly make your way along the floral tributes, reading the cards. Family, friends, colleagues, old pupils. It's the latter you've cast your role as and don't expect that to be problematic. Eight hundred kids at an all girls secondary modern, thirty-five years gone by, who's going to recall every face?

At the end of the pathway, her children wait. A handshake for some, a hug for others, a sad smile for everyone.

"Your mother taught me at Farnwood," you explain to their quizzical but not unfriendly expressions. "She wasn't someone you easily forget."

Their smiles widen at this and the eldest daughter asks if you'll be coming back to the house.

Your reply is calculatedly cautious. You wouldn't want to intrude, you understand what the family must be going through... But at that her son insists, recites the address for you to nod along to as if committing it to memory, as if it hasn't already been lodged there for a long, long time.

By now the casket is back in the hearse, being driven at walking pace to the freshly dug grave by the far wall of the churchyard. You follow the procession and join the mourners at the graveside. The vicar intones ashes to ashes, dust to dust... As the coffin is lowered into the ground, it seems the youngest daughter is about to break down, but her sister puts an arm around her shoulders and she gathers herself. Family members come forward to drop a flower onto the coffin or scatter a trowel of earth and then you are all moving away, heading for the row of parked cars just outside the gates.

You're reaching into your bag for your keys when the youngest daughter approaches, accompanied by an elderly lady.

"Sorry, I've forgotten your name...?"

"That's okay." Smiling, you remind her.

"Right... Look, could I ask a favour?" She gestures toward her companion. "This is Maureen, one of Mum's oldest friends, and she's stuck for a lift over to the house. I was wondering if you could…?"

"Of course," you tell her and smile at Maureen. "I'll be glad of the company."

* * *

The house is only a five-minute drive from the church, which doesn't really allow Maureen much of an opportunity to probe the skimpy details rehearsed in your head. For her part, you learn Maureen was once a neighbour and still lives on the other side of the city, two bus rides away.

As you pull up outside the tidy suburban bungalow, you tell her to come and find you when she wants to leave, that you'll give her a lift home. It's no problem, you reassure her slightly uncertain thanks. You've time on your hands and a day like this is already difficult enough.

No matter how old someone might be, the death of a parent, particularly the surviving parent, always bestows the air of a lost child. The daughters and the son may separate briefly, to welcome a mourner or deal with a query from the caterers, but are quickly drawn back together, needy for that sense of strength and comfort unique to familial bonds…

The food has been laid out on a table in the dining room. You fill a plate with canapes and quiche, more for appearance's sake than appetite. You doubt anything would get past that tight knot in your stomach.

Returning to the lounge, you take in the photographs lining the walls and covering most surfaces, the latter doubtless carefully curated for today. With the husband, who you know died two years ago, she is smiling at the camera in locations which suggest tourism rather than travel. You study the children's progression through academia, school jumpers and cheeky grins to mortar boards and beaming pride.

Suddenly nauseous, you put down your plate and find a WC, but as you slide the bolt shut the feeling passes. So, you check your makeup in the mirror over a small sink and satisfied open the door. There's nothing for you here, you decide, time to exchange…

"Oh God! It's you, isn't it?"

Standing outside in the corridor is Maureen, wide-eyed, hand to her mouth and absolutely aghast.

CHAPTER ONE

Amanda

"How can you be so certain?" asked DI Amanda Palmer, half turning from the row of Italianate town houses to stare at the figure seated alongside her. "They all look pretty much the same to me and we're talking thirty years ago."

"The lions," he told her, nodding his head towards number three. "I remember the lions."

Amanda followed his gaze to where the portico steps reached the front door, either side of which sat a small stone lion.

"Okay," she said, slowly. "Let's go through it once more."

Declan McKelvey sighed, but Amanda figured he knew well enough how this worked. You listened to their story, you picked at it, you made them repeat it and then you started all over again. Ad infinitum, until either they slipped up or you finally took them at their word. He'd probably been on the other side of this scenario more than once himself, she guessed, played out in dimly lit barns deep in bandit country and with outcomes far grimmer than his own current prospects, however this ultimately went down.

"You were in the pub on the Caledonian Road," Amanda prompted. "It was your mother's birthday and you'd just called home. With…?"

"Ronan Doyle"

"The workmate you shared digs with?"

"Aye."

"When your boss, Brendon O'Doherty, turns up?" asked Amanda. "With Liam Kennedy?"

McKelvey nodded. As a passer-by approached, he pulled the flat cap on his forehead low enough to almost touch the thick framed, clear glass spectacles

"And this was the first occasion that you'd met Kennedy?"

"It was."

"What happened next?"

"Brendon said he had a job for us, that we were to drink up and follow him to the van waiting outside."

"But you didn't know what for?"

"There were two shovels on the floor," McKelvey told her, dryly. "It wasn't rocket science."

"So, you drive over here." Amanda paused. "Whereabouts did you pull up?"

"Right there, in front of the house."

"No trouble parking?"

"This was a slum in those days, mostly Irish and West Indian with half a dozen to a room. You think they could afford cars?"

"You park," said Amanda. "What next?"

"Brendon and Liam get out. Brendon tells us to stay in the van for a while."

"But there's a problem with the door catch after he closes it?"

McKelvey nodded.

"It slips open again. Only a few inches, but enough to see and hear what was going on."

"Right," said Amanda. "Take me through that once more."

"Liam knocks on the front door. Aidan McShane opens it. He..."

"You're sure about that? You'd met him before?"

"A few months earlier," McKelvey shrugged. "Well, not actually met. He'd been in a bar when one of the lads from the site started mouthing off, not knowing who he was. Brendon... calmed things down, you might say. But no doubt it was him."

"And you could overhear the conversation?"

"Most of it."

Amanda flipped open her notebook.

"'*This is from Conell himself*'," she read out. "'*It's the only way if you want a man of your own on the inside*'." Amanda raised her eyes questioningly. "That's definitely what he said?"

McKelvey nodded again.

"And that's when they brought the body out?"

"Well, rolled in a carpet." He shook his head. "It wasn't the wild west, you know?"

"Then over to the building site you've been working on in Kilburn and into the foundations with it?"

"That's right."

There was a silence in the car. They'd spent the morning driving around Kilburn trying to locate the site, but with no success. McKelvey could have been stonewalling but Amanda doubted it, he had a free pass on just about anything that had gone down back then. Unlike Notting Hill, the area had undergone so much redevelopment over the last thirty years that it would have been more surprising than not for his memory to have led them straight to it.

"My flight..." McKelvey reminded her softly.

Amanda turned the key in the ignition.

"I'll drop you at Victoria Station," she told him. "You can get the Gatwick Express from there."

Jack

Jack Vanner hesitated as he approached Petroc, then flicked down the indicator stalk and turned into the campsite entrance.

Although 'campsite' didn't really do Petroc justice anymore. When Brian, Jack's father-in-law, started out in the fifties, this had been little more than a field with a standpipe, picking up trade from holidaymakers arriving in St Hannahs on spec. There was a lot of that in those early years, it wasn't an uncommon sight to see entire families working their way down a street, knocking at doors on the chance of a room to let. There usually was, money so tight kids doubled up to leave a bedroom free, sometimes the whole household moving into a glorified shed in the garden for the school holidays.

The field had been rented from a farmer, but after three years Brian had been able to buy it outright. And not long after, the one next to it, profits always ploughed back into the business, hard pitches for caravans, a toilet and shower block, a small shop. Word of mouth gradually filled the site with campers returning year after year and now the young couples who'd first pitched their tent in the postwar promise of a new Elizabethan age treated their grandkids to two weeks of Cornish summer in a Scandinavian lodge.

Instead of pulling into a parking space outside of Reception, Jack parked out of sight around the back. A jam sandwich didn't do much for a holiday vibe, Brian had once told him, and so unless he was here on official business - a punch up in the bar, a bounced cheque - and wanted his presence noticed, he did his best to keep a low profile.

Reception was empty, so he rang the bell on the counter. The office door opened and when the cursory, polite smile on his wife's face widened to one of genuine pleasure, Jack felt a warm rush as he returned it. His was the kind of job where few marriages still had this going for them, so many years down the line.

"Hello, love, everything okay?" asked Carol, although if it was an official visit she knew he'd have phoned ahead or at least have Tina at the station give her a call.

"The Travellers are back," he told her.

Once a year, a group of Travellers arrived in St Hannahs and found somewhere illegal to pitch up. It took about a week to get the warrants and the bailiffs sorted out and then they'd move on, further down the coast to start the same dance in some other town. And before heading out to see what they had to say for themselves, Jack had decided he could use a cup of tea with his wife.

"Come on through," Carol told him, stepping back into the office. "The kettle's just boiled."

"Is Sally about?" Jack asked her.

"She's at one of the Lodges," said Carol. "We had a cleaner not turn up this morning."

Their youngest daughter was home from university, picking up pin money with odd jobs at Petroc and waitressing around town.

"And she's working at The Barque tonight," Carol continued, "so I thought maybe I'd grab fish and chips after I finish, seeing as it'll be just the two of us."

"Sure," said Jack, then added, "Is everything alright with her?"

"Alright?"

"I dunno." He shook his head. "I get the feeling that something's a bit off."

Carol studied Jack as she handed him a mug of tea.

"I think," she seemed to choose her words carefully, "there might be boy trouble."

"Has she said anything?" asked Jack.

"No," said Carol. "But girls her age..." She gave a slight shrug. "It's always boy trouble."

"Perhaps you should..." began Jack, but Carol cut him off.

"She'll talk about it when she's ready," Carol told him.

"And if she wants to."

"Alright," said Jack, tiptoeing back out of that minefield of feminine interplay, everything so sweetly pastoral under the casual sweep of a masculine eye.

"And Ruth Weinstock rang to ask if Sally could do the gallery opening next week," Carol told him.

"She'll probably," said Jack slowly, "need to be vetted for that."

Carol flashed him an amused glance.

"So the rumours *are* true?" she smiled. "Emma Brownlow is going to be there?"

Jack hesitated. He'd been informed that the Secretary of State for Northern Ireland would be attending the opening only the previous day. Purely as a courtesy, security for government ministers was handled by Section Two of Special Branch and they didn't expect much more from local police than holding the crowds back and keeping the roads open. He'd planned on leaving it until next week before telling his own officers, so...

"It's alright." Carol read his expression with a grin. "But it's a good job you don't play poker."

"I know she was married to the artist," said Jack slowly, "but I'm still not exactly sure what her involvement in all of this is likely to be."

"'All of this?'" Carol shook her head in perhaps not entirely mock exasperation. "Look Jack, the gallery opening and the eclipse are a big deal for the town. It's not just about art, it's well known that he played an important role behind the scenes of the Good Friday Agreement."

"Seriously?"

"Aidan McShane's family had been staunch Republicans throughout the Troubles," she told him. "Between the two of them, they got a lot of people sitting down together at the same table."

"Right," said Jack, slowly nodding. Finishing his tea, he rose to his feet. "Point taken."

Also standing, Carol lent forward and pecked him on the cheek.

"You take care," she said softly, as she always did when he stepped out through the door in uniform.

"See you tonight, love," he smiled.

Walking over to the car, Jack reflected that it might not be a bad idea to pay the gallery a visit at some point over the next week. All things considered, it wouldn't hurt to have the lay of the land.

Amanda

McKelvey slipped out of the car in a nondescript side street behind Victoria Station and Amanda felt relief at no longer having to conceal her contempt for him. However much the term was sanitised these days - 'confidential informant' for God's sake - a grass was still a grass, the lowest of the low. You might need them, but you needed sewers too and there was nothing unhealthy about a sense of revulsion towards both.

This was old school copper's reaction she knew and guessed not something the Security Service officers she'd spent the last few days working with would share. Some of them had been almost joking with McKelvey on those drives around Kilburn and for Amanda that had really brought home the width of the gulf between them. Not that she had a problem with expediency, some blagger sent down for a job he hadn't done - rather than the half dozen he had - left her with few moral qualms, as far as she was concerned that was no more than she was paid to do. Shield society from the worst aspects of itself.

But hers was a world of fixed boundaries, separating those who enforced the law from those who broke it and ultimately they held fast. In this reality, Amanda was beginning to grasp, today's enemies could be tomorrow's allies before reverting just as quickly.

She drove north to Westway, then along Marylebone Road into Pentonville Road, where she turned into the underground car park of an office block whose exterior had seen better days. It was pretty much *de rigueur* for a task force probing internal matters to be based behind an innocuous facade, those on the team dropping into their usual offices frequently enough to manage any interest in their current activities.

Officially on a sabbatical from the Cold Case Unit she'd been promoted sideways into three years ago, she and the

Security Service were in the process of evaluating how good a fit they might prove for each other. How long a process had been left open ended, but she was starting to sense that this investigation could be the deciding factor for both parties.

McKelvey was scheduled to disappear into the US Witness Protection Program within days, firsthand knowledge of Middle East arms dealers and Al-Qaeda money laundering atoned for a wealth of past sins, it would seem. Whether his assertion, almost casually dropped into conversation, that a young Aidan McShane had been involved in an IRA killing was simply farewell mischief making had been the subject of intense conjecture. McShane himself had died the previous year, the problem was that given his family background McKelvey's account was disturbingly plausible, the disquiet compounded by his widow's role as Secretary of State for Northern Ireland.

Amanda exited the lift on the seventh floor and stepped out into an open plan area which appeared to be in the final stages of being furnished with desks and computer equipment. A glass walled office took up most of the far wall and Amanda saw Keith Venables, MI5's Assistant Director General, in conversation with a young Indian woman.

Entering the room, Amanda realised they were examining photographs from a cardboard file and one having the look of being at least a couple of decades old. In the CCU she handled such files daily.

"DI Palmer." Venables looked up. "How did it go?"

Amanda shrugged.

"Nothing new," she told him.

"This is Detective Sergeant Shravasti Sule," he said. "We have her on loan from the NCIS. Chief Superintendent Kendall assures us," he continued, "she's one of their star analysts."

DS Sule gave a self-deprecating smile and Amanda introduced herself over a handshake. CS Kendall from the National Crime Intelligence Service was nominally in charge of the task force, but if push ever came to shove, thought

Amanda, Venables would probably take some shoving.

The Met, NCIS and the Security Service, she reflected. *Well, Special Branch was definitely noticeable by its absence.*

"And we might have something here," Venables said, indicating the photographs spread over the desk and then looking across at DS Sule.

"At the time of the alleged... incident," said DS Sule, "the house in Pembridge Villas was already the focus of a surveillance operation." She gestured at the prints. "By Special Branch officers."

"An operation relating to what?" asked Amanda.

Venables shook his head.

"The file's rather patchy," he told her. "All we have is an arrest warrant for one Christopher Franklyn, who'd jumped bail on what looks like some significant drug charges. That had been his last known address."

"Since when did Special Branch concern itself with drugs?" Amanda was staring at him. "And where's the rest of the file?"

"Who was the officer who raised the warrant?" Venables asked DS Sule.

"A detective sergeant named Brian Maddox. He transferred over to the Branch at the beginning of 1970, from the Met where he'd been working undercover with a drug squad based at West End Central."

"Is he still around?"

"He retired a few months ago," DS Sule told him. "As a Chief Superintendent. Lives in Wimbledon."

"Ever come across him?" Venables asked Amanda, who shook her head as DS Sule passed him a sheet of paper with Maddox's contact details neatly printed on them.

Venables stared down at it and then over to Palmer.

"Any problem using your Met warrant card for this?"

Returning his stare, she gave another shake of her head. Venables handed her the sheet.

"Well, let's see what he has to say for himself."

Ted

The meal had been Faith's idea.

Ruth Weinstock was Director of the Senara Gallery and Fiona Shaw her partner, a relationship still capable of raising an eyebrow in certain circles. Faith tended to make early acquaintance with most new residents of St Hannahs and wasn't above taking those she considered interesting, but perhaps in need of a little social lubrication, under her wing.

Ted didn't mind, behind the rictus smile of the tourist trade St Hannahs could be every bit as parochial as the most inbred Dartmoor hamlet. Being seen clinking glasses in The Barque's restaurant with a local GP and the headmaster of St Anne's might not always open doors, but it did go some way to unlocking them.

Ted guessed Faith had also invited Dennis and Toni Nelson because he and Ted were on the interview panel for the new Head of English at St Anne's and she was hoping to induce a degree of *bonhomie* beforehand. Despite decades of friendship, when cast in their respective roles as headmaster and chairman of the board of governors they were frequently at loggerheads. And Toni came with a guarantee to have the ice broken at pretty much any gathering by the time the cork was out of the second bottle...

"So, these interviews start tomorrow?" Ruth asked Ted, almost spookily picking up on his thoughts.

Ted nodded.

"If it were up to me, I'd simply rubber stamp Gillian Brown," he told her. "As I think would the governors." He looked across the table at Dennis, who responded with a nod. "In the six months Gill's been doing the job, she's turned out to be probably the best head of department we've ever had - nothing against poor old Derek, obviously."

The others nodded sympathetically. Well into a course of chemotherapy after surgery that proved far more radical than his prognosis had suggested, Derek Keyworth had made it clear that whatever the outcome he wouldn't be returning to St Anne's. Life, had explained his letter of resignation, was now filled with other priorities.

"You've no idea of the bloody hoops we have to jump through," concurred Dennis. "Probably the same in any organisation grown bigger than one man and his dog. But in education, all the boxes you need to think about ticking have become a minefield." He took a sip of his drink. "And try sacking a teacher these days, however incompetent. Just about the only thing that'll get them out the door is kiddie fiddling."

"So what you're saying," said Toni, "is that all these poor sods are going to be traipsing down to Cornwall from all over the country to be interviewed for a vacancy the governors have already made up their minds about?"

"There's only one candidate from outside the county," Ted told her. "She's currently at a school in Shoreditch, with a very impressive track record according to her CV, but probably too young for the position." He shrugged. "So I don't think her own expectations will be too high. I daresay she's starting to get interviews under her belt more for a sense of how it all plays out. But essentially, yes, we'll be spending the next two days just wasting our bloody time. In an ideal world…"

Ted broke off as the waiter appeared and began clearing away their dinner plates. And after he'd departed, appointing the new Head Of English had the feel of a topic run out of steam.

"How are things with the gallery?" Faith asked Ruth.

"Still on schedule," Ruth told her. "But it's going to be tight."

"I heard that you actually knew Aidan McShane," Ted said to Fiona. "That you were down here when these paintings were created?"

Fiona smiled and gave a slight shake of her head.

"Aidan and I were both working at Joyce Kelly's studio, during the Easter week of 1967. But the paintings were completed back in London."

"What was he like?" asked Dennis.

"He could be a bit intense, even in those days," said Fiona. "We didn't really get to know each other that well. I was staying in a flat over the studio and Aidan had a chalet at Petroc. And he was spending most of his free time with Don Mayberry and Lee Munro."

"Less of the name dropping, dear," said Ruth primly and the others smiled.

"Did you know them, too?" asked Toni.

"We'd meet in the Harbour Lights occasionally. They'd eat there most evenings and it was also Joyce's favourite restaurant. But I couldn't say we knew each other well."

"And you'll be showing all the Cradle of Thorns paintings?" Dennis asked.

"First time they'll have been back together since they left his studio," nodded Ruth. "Between that and the eclipse, it's going to be a really big day for St Hannahs."

"Rumour has it," said Toni, "there's quite a VIP contingent heading into town for the opening?"

Ruth hesitated.

"I'd love to talk about it," she said slowly, "But the way things are these days..."

"That's alright," smiled Dennis. "We'll find out for ourselves soon enough."

Catching Toni's expression - which suggested this was a topic she felt still had some mileage remaining - Ted thought it politic to pre-empt her.

"So how was the cruise?" he asked, turning towards Dennis.

"Surprisingly, an enjoyable time was had by all," he smiled. "We're thinking of booking another one."

"Really?" said Ted.

"Believe it or not, he was affability itself," nodded Toni. "He said 'Good Morning' and 'Good Evening' to people and, on occasion, even chatted about the weather."

"I can pretend to be normal if I have to," said Dennis dryly, to smiles around the table.

"Where did you go?" asked Fiona.

"Budapest to Amsterdam," Toni told her. "I'd been worried it was going to be a bit 'If it's Tuesday it must be Nuremberg' but it wasn't at all. The whole thing was very leisurely paced. We even went to see *Die Zauberflöte* in Vienna."

"In German?" asked Faith.

"Naturlich," smiled Toni.

"How does that work?" asked Ted. "Is there a printed text you can follow or some form of subtitles?"

"No." Toni shook her head. "But it was no big deal. In fact, one of my old boyfriends used to say that going to the opera was a bit like watching porn. The plots are ludicrous, the dialogue absurd, what you're actually there for are the performances and so the less distractions there are to that the better."

"*Antonia!!!*" Faith's mouth literally dropped open, but both Fiona and Ruth were laughing.

"You'll have to excuse my wife," said Dennis, turning to them with a raised eyebrow. "Occasionally the social niceties pass her by completely."

"How did you two meet?" asked Ruth, still smiling.

"I was a chambermaid at Tregenna Bay, which has been in Dennis's family since the year dot," Toni told her. "It's not an unusual story, a bit like the European royal families freshening the bloodline with commoners every now and then. So the town doesn't fill up with congenital idiots." She took a sip of her drink. "Not that you'd notice."

"How many children do you have?" asked Fiona.

"Ah," said Toni, hesitating only slightly before placing her glass down on the table. "The best laid plans, as they say..."

There was only a moment's uncertainty before Faith turned to Dennis.

"I like the hair," she said. "Very Teutonic - what's the story behind that?"

"It was a bit blowy on deck," said Dennis, running a hand across his cropped skull, "and it was all over the place. So I decided to have a trim."

"There was a minor translation issue at a hairdresser's in Regensberg," smiled Toni. "Yvonne's not happy. We saw her yesterday and Dennis got a real dressing down for getting it cut somewhere else."

"I tell you," said Dennis, "I had less hassle playing fast and loose with girlfriends back in the day than I caught from Yvonne over this bloody haircut."

"Oh, she'll come around," grinned Toni. "How does it go with you men? 'Look, I was walking down the road, and yeah, okay, I'd had a few drinks, and I saw this hairdressers and it looked really nice in there. And though I knew I shouldn't, I went inside. Then, before I realised what was happening, I was in the chair and even as she was cutting my hair, I knew it was just so wrong. But what it also made me realise was what a good hairdresser you are, and how lucky I am to have you, so in a way this whole thing has actually brought us closer together...'"

Everyone was laughing as the waitress arrived with the dessert trolley.

"Hello Sally," said Faith. "Home for the summer?"

"Hello Dr Cantrell," she smiled, almost shyly. "Mr Cantrell."

"It was Mr Cantrell when I was marking your homework." He shook his head. "These days it's Ted."

"How's Oxford?" asked Faith.

"Great," said Sally. "It can all be a bit much at first, but you soon settle in."

"I've always loved Oxford as a city," Fiona told her. "I can't imagine what it must be like to actually study there."

"It's not all dreaming spires and sherry with a don, there's a lot of hard work involved." Ted paused and looked Sally straight in the eye. "And a lot of hard work getting there. We were all really proud of you, you know? And still are."

The beginnings of a blush started creeping up Sally's neck.

"Well," she began, hesitantly, "I…"

"Oh, stop embarrassing the poor girl, before she begins to realise how envious we all are of her." Toni reached out and squeezed Sally's hand. "But you make the most of it, Sally, young people have no idea how fleeting this time of their lives really is."

"Nor of how the nature of temptation changes with the passing years," said Faith. "My God, would you look at that Black Forest gateau!"

"No one's twisting your arm," smiled Ruth. "You could just pass."

"What this ritual involves," Ted told her, "is Faith sacrificing the most enticing item on the dessert trolley to somehow justify reaching for any of the others."

"Well, we all know about Faith having her cake and eating it," grinned Toni, to renewed laughter.

There really is nothing in the world, thought Ted, leaning back in his chair with a smile of contentment, to compare with the convivial company of good friends.

Well, almost nothing.

Toni

"I hear Claudia Pascoe's back in town," said Toni, sitting down at the dressing table and catching Dennis's eye in the mirror as he slid into bed. *Sans* pyjamas, she noted, but that was okay - he'd had enough to drink not to be making a major performance out of it, but not too much to take forever arriving at the finale. And who knows, if she slowed down getting the slap off, he might be snoring by the time she joined him.

"It's the inquest tomorrow," he reminded her.

A couple of months earlier, Claudia's husband Robert had been found slumped over the steering wheel of his car inside a garage filled with exhaust fumes. Speculation had been rife ever since and with Robert the proverbial big fish in a small pond, she imagined the courtroom would be standing room only tomorrow.

"What do you think?" she asked Dennis.

"Misadventure." He gave a sharp nod of his head. "Robert was too much of an arrogant arsehole to top himself and by all accounts he'd had a skinful that night. Rod Truscott took his car keys off him earlier in the evening before serving him anything more to drink, but apparently he had another set." Dennis shrugged. "He drove home legless and then passed out in his garage."

Toni screwed up the tissue she'd been using, dropped it into the waste bin and reached for the moisturiser.

"If he was too drunk to remember to switch the engine off, why wasn't he too drunk to close the garage doors?"

"Who knows?" Dennis gave another shrug. "Could be there was a fault with the remote or maybe he pressed it accidentally without noticing." He paused. "Are you going?"

"Probably." Toni worked the moisturiser deep into her forehead and then down to the corners of her eyes, where the distinction between laughter lines and crow's feet was giving serious consideration for a procedure. Only a *minor* one, she reflected, but wasn't that a slippery slope... "If only to support Claudia."

In the mirror, Dennis raised an eyebrow.

"Claudia and I get on," she insisted. "And I've known her probably longer than I've known you."

That was true enough. Although Claudia hadn't actually moved to St Hannah's until the mid-seventies, her family had owned a holiday home here for as long as anyone could remember. She and Claudia had met as teenagers, Toni sneaking off to the Burrows to be chatted up and hopefully turned on by the beats and discovering this impossibly glamorous creature down from London was doing the same.

"You can be pretty sure, given the circumstances, that some kind of dirt will get dug up tomorrow," said Dennis quietly. "Truth's always elusive and it's a winding road reaching it - marriages dissected, motives questioned, lives re-examined. Do you really want to be one more face in a crowd she'll probably believe is only there to be entertained?"

"Faith will also be giving evidence," said Toni. "So it's as much for her as Claudia."

Without comment, Dennis simply lay back and closed his eyes.

Toni returned her attention to the mirror and slowly reached for another tissue.

First memories are never more than residual impressions. They've stuck for a reason but that lack of context should always leave you wary of family narratives owing more to indulgence than veracity.

Take nothing at more than face value.

A bluebell field stretches as far as the eye can see. The sun is bright in your eyes, warm on your skin and you're being tickled with buttercup petals under your chin. The softness of your mother's body, a hint of Eau de Cologne, your cheek scraped by your father's stubble as he carries you to bed. Cod liver oil lingers at the back of your throat, metallic tinsel decorations, the rough cloth of a little Union Flag which you wave at the Queen as she drives by in that Coronation year.

Things coalesce. A sense of self snowballs, all you love, dislike, fear, accept, reject, is compressed into a tight core gathering downhill momentum, collecting the loose detritus which adds volume rather than mass. You learn from what passes and project into what's coming, to win smiles, avoid smacks, earn trust, sidestep disdain.

The rules are a minefield, but one that can be mapped.

Memory is now triggered more by cognition than resonance. A beach holiday and Daddy explaining the tides and how not to get caught by them. Blackberry picking and Mummy showing you the berries you must never pick, the ones that will make you poorly, despite them looking so pretty and their name so musical.

And then the dark cloud which settles over all of your lives.

Daddy has to go away for a while, Mummy tells you, and so you and your sister have to be good girls because Mummy has much more to do now. Almost every evening Mummy needs to go out, and so it's Cathy who gives you your tea, tucks you in and reads you a story. One night you awaken with the tummy ache and so you get out of bed to find Cathy, who'll know what medicine to give you. Cathy is in the living room, but she is crying and so you ask what the matter is. Daddy is poorly, she explains, very poorly, and when you ask if that's because he ate the wrong berries, Cathy cries even harder and pulls you towards her.

Then one morning, Mummy is sitting by your bedside as

you wake up. She is leaning forward and you realise she has been stroking your hair.

You're going to have to be a very brave little girl, she tells you. You're aware of other voices in the house, of people crying. Daddy's in heaven now, she explains. He was so special that God wanted him there all the while.

This is the first time she's told you something you don't believe and it won't be the last.

You never learn how Mummy met him, or indeed anything about his life, before he came into yours. But suddenly he is there all the time, one month simply a guest for Sunday lunch, the next sitting down with you all for dinner every evening.

Jim.

You're going to be bridesmaids, Mummy tells you and your sister. "Won't that be lovely?"

You and Cathy stay with Granny Vera while Mummy and Jim honeymoon, a week in Brighton. When they return, he is to be called Dad, you are told, not Jim.

"He's the provider for this house now," *she states.* "It's no more respect from the pair of you than he's due."

Aloud you call him Dad, but never in your head. In your mind this interloper is Jim, always will be, and it is incomprehensible how he has turned your life upside down and inside out.

We're moving to a new town, Mummy tells you. Dad's got a new job there. We'll have a new house - one with a garden - and you'll be going to a new school, where you'll meet lots of new friends.

New, new, new! A word which once had a freshness about it, conjuring expectations of surprise and excitement, now drips with if not menace then dark overtones. The house is bigger and brighter than the one you leave, with a large picture window through which to gaze at the bland uniformity of the other houses on the estate. An estate growing larger with each passing week to the accompaniment of hot tar, cement dust and fresh paint. But this house never feels like a home, never somewhere you are happy to run back to with the story of your day.

You sense Cathy shares your disquiet. Where once she was smiling and chatty, now she is sullen and withdrawn, almost secretive. Eventually Mummy orders her to snap out of it, to appreciate how lucky she is, but surprisingly Jim takes Cathy's side - she'll soon be a teenager, he tells Mummy, they should worry if she wasn't moody.

And that it's just a phase she's going through.

Mummy starts a job at the local Odeon, a couple of evenings a week as an usherette. It means they'll be able to afford a holiday, she explains, a fortnight in Weston Super Mare or Weymouth next summer. The nights she works, Jim treats them to a fish supper, sending you down to the chippy for two cod and a tanner's worth of chips, while he and Cathy get everything ready to divvy it all up between the three of you. And usually a fruit pie, cake or shortbread from Cathy's domestic science class, always delicious, but, and despite Jim's compliments, these are the occasions that Cathy seems to retreat even further into herself.

You've not really made many new friends at school. You arrived midway through the term, and those girls eager to engage with you have been left out of all the little cliques for a reason. But you enjoy Miss Tanner's class, you're better than the others with the Janet and John books and you know your times tables all the way up to twelve.

One morning, after quiet time, you all clamber up off the floor, take the cushions over to the cupboard and go back to your seats. As you sit down, Michael stands next to you, talking to someone on the other side of the table. Nina Thomas passes behind you both, casually moving his chair aside to make her way through. Michael lowers himself, catches only the edge of the seat as he sprawls backwards and then his head cracks against the sharp ridge of a radiator.

He screams.

Within seconds, blood is everywhere and all is chaos and

confusion. Miss Tanner comes running over, with an expression on her face which you've never seen before. This is one of the many details you'll flesh out in later life, as you replay this scene more times than you could probably count or would want to.

It's not only concern on her part, but fright. Whatever's just happened is on her watch.

She gathers Michael up in her arms, staring around the classroom wildly. Before she can ask the obvious question, Valerie Holmes, one of the girls who cosied up to you when you first arrived but who you've never felt comfortable with, extends her arm to point at you.

"She pulled the chair away, Miss." Her eyes are narrowed and her expression full of spite. "While Michael was sitting down."

"I didn't!" You shake your head disbelievingly. "Nina moved his chair to pass by and he sat down without looking."

But you're about to be introduced to mob mentality, that collective euphoric rush at the first sniff of blood. Someone calls out your name and then, almost in unison, it becomes a chant, everyone joining in and with fingers pointing at you.

It's quite terrifying.

Suddenly Mrs Cleaver, the headmistress, enters the room, the din must have reached all the way down the corridor. Miss Tanner stops to speak to her as she carries Michael out. She strides over, grabs you by the wrist and almost drags you out through the door.

You are taken to a small office and told to sit down. You're left alone for twenty minutes, perhaps half an hour, before Mrs Cleaver returns. Again, without a word, she takes you by the hand and leads you along to the staff room. Michael is sitting on a chair, visibly shaking, and she positions you behind him.

"Look at what you did." You cannot mistake the anger in her voice.

A chunk of skull is missing from the back of Michael's head. Through it - and although it can't be more than a quarter of an inch deep you seem to be staring into a chasm - you can see a pink mass. Its effect on you is immediate, you feel faint and nauseous.

Mrs Cleaver's fingers dig into your shoulder as she turns you around, her face swooping down until it is only inches from yours.

"You are a wicked little girl," she hisses.

At that moment, the doors open and two ambulance men appear. Mrs Cleaver goes over to them and another teacher, whose name you can't remember, takes you back to the office.

"Are you alright?" she asks, not unkindly.

"It was an accident," you tell her, shaking your head. "Nina moved the chair to get by."

Her expression is almost pitying, and at the time you think it's because she doesn't believe you. But she probably did, you later - much later - reflect. What she understood was that wasn't the issue here, that what mattered was backs being covered, integrity preserved.

The door opens and Mrs Cleaver steps into the room.

"Her mother's here," she says.

Back home, your protestations of innocence cut as little ice as they did at school.

And then he returns.

Events are a whirlwind, barely time to register them unfold. You are uncomprehending as he reaches for his belt buckle, pulls the thin leather free and loops it into his hand. But then he is sitting and you are picked up and placed face down over his lap. You squeal with indignation as your dress is lifted above your waist but your cries soon turn to screams.

The first lash is across your bottom and you've never known pain like it. It's a fiery sword, you're sure you've been cut open and it is quickly followed by two more. You become desperate to free yourself and, for a moment, you almost succeed. Pushing yourself up and away, you begin to slide towards his knees.

"Hold her still," he says.

Mummy leans forward and lifts you onto his lap once more. Fastening your wrists together behind you with one hand, she uses the other to press you down hard against him. Now he strikes lower, across the back of your thighs where the skin is even more tender, and despite the blinding pain you sense the precision with which he works his way down to your knees. For the next week, perhaps longer, the whole world will understand what happens to wicked little girls in this house.

When he is finished, there's nothing but a terse silence about him. It's Mummy who tells you to go up to your room and stay there, that there'll be no dinner for you tonight. Not that you could have kept any down. As the sharp pain subsides, a dull nausea rises from your stomach and your whole body is shaking. You tentatively feel behind you, but even the slightest touch reignites the agony and you spend the evening face down on the bed, the pillow wet with your tears.

You don't return to school until after the weekend, but you are a lone figure now and would be even if the stripes across the back of your legs didn't brand you a creature apart. A solitary presence in the playground and an invisible one when raising your hand in the classroom, you slowly accept this as the new norm and deal with it by retreating into yourself. A departure which nobody, at home or school, appears unduly perturbed by.

Jim is talking to you again. Initially, it's more acknowledgement by a series of grunts than a dialogue and the slightest infraction on your part, imagined or otherwise, sees you packed off to bed with no dinner. But after a month or so, he has an announcement.

"I want Cathy to go down to the chippy from now on," he says, one evening at the table. "You can stay here and help me get everything ready."

"What?" Cathy is staring at him, dead eyed.

He repeats himself.

"But..." Cathy is uncertain, shaking her head.

"She needs to be doing more around the house," he tells her. "Now she's growing up. To make things easier for your mother." He shrugs. "And learning how to set the table properly would be a start."

Mummy nods approvingly.

"Right," says Cathy, slowly. "But we'd better go down there together at first. Just to be sure I know what I'm doing."

Jim is impatient at this, but eventually concedes.

"Alright," he says, "although I don't see what there is to get wrong about it. But after that, I want you going down there by yourself."

The next evening, after Mummy has left for work, down at the chippy you introduce Cathy to Mrs Benson, fat and jolly and who always has a smile for you, explaining that from now on she'll be coming down here twice a week. Arriving home, Jim has set the table and is slicing a raspberry pie, which Cathy made today in domestic science.

Cathy plates up the cod and chips, then hands yours across to you. You reach for it but she's looking over at Jim, facing away from you both as he slides each slice of pie into a dessert bowl. Your fingers are perhaps an inch from taking it from her when she turns back to you, looks you straight in the eye and lets it tumble to the floor.

Jim whirls around at the sound of china crashing against the tiles.

"Jesus Christ!"

"She dropped her plate," Cathy tells him. "She wasn't looking at what she was doing."

You are shocked enough by this to be left dumbstruck. You're aware of your mouth dropping open as you stare at her disbelievingly, but Jim's fingers are already sinking into your shoulder and you're being violently shaken.

"What the hell's the matter with you!!?" The rage borders on apoplexy. For a second, you think he might strike you but then he seems to gain control over himself.

"Go to your room," he barks at you, "and I don't want to see you again before breakfast."

As you leave, you give Cathy one last uncomprehending look. Although her eyes meet yours, they somehow seem to be focused far behind you and her expression is almost serene.

At first you think it's a dream.

Then a nightmare.

The screaming is loud enough to raise you from sleep and you want nothing more than for it to go away. You bury your head under the pillow, pulling it tight against your ears and the sound does stop, at least for a moment. But then there are other sounds - doors slamming, voices shouting, the wail of a siren and however hard you press at the pillow, you can't shut them out.

There are heavy footsteps on the stairs. The door to your bedroom bursts open and the light switches on.

"She's in here." A deep male voice. You let the pillow fall away and slowly sit up.

"Oh, thank God." A female voice from outside. Mrs Atkins from next door enters the room and stares down at you. The figure beside her, you realise, is a policeman.

"Are you alright, love?" he asks, gently.

You nod and Mrs Atkins reaches down to scoop you up. She holds you tight in her arms as she carefully steps down the stairs and into the hallway. The front door is wide open, figures in uniform bustle through it in both directions. By the light of a streetlamp, you see that people have begun to gather on the pavement.

Overwhelmed by the incomprehensibility of it all, you burst into tears. Mrs Atkins pulls you closer.

"I want my mummy," you tell her.

"I know love," she says, softly. "I know."

You're approached by a policewoman and another policeman, this one wearing a peaked cap rather than a helmet.

"I'm taking her next door," Mrs Atkins tells them. "I'll look after her there."

"By rights, we should wait for Children's Services," says the policewoman. But after a second's reflection, the policeman shakes his head.

"We'll sort that out in the morning." He gives Mrs Atkins a brief nod. "Go on."

She carries you towards the street, where wide-eyed stares of strangers are waiting, and then out through a threshold you will never enter again.

You're gently shaken awake by Mrs Atkins.

"You need to get up, love," she tells you. "There are some people here to see you."

She places a carrier bag down on the floor as you pull the blankets aside and sit up.

"I fetched some things for you to wear," she smiles.

"Is my mummy here?" you ask and her smile falters a little.

"Not yet." The reassuring nod she follows this with seems forced. "Perhaps later."

Getting dressed all by yourself is something only recently managed, but there are no shoes with laces to tie - which you sometimes need help with - but within a few minutes you're standing up, tugging everything straight. There's no mirror in the room to check your hair, but last night you were too upset to take it out of pigtails and brush it fifty times like you usually do before going to bed, so it should still look tidy.

Mrs Atkins is waiting for you at the bottom of the stairs and, taking you by the hand, she leads you into the parlour. Two people are sitting on the settee, a policewoman in uniform and next to her is an older man in a suit and tie. On one of the armchairs opposite sits a lady dressed in a matching dark blue jacket and skirt, with a cardboard folder resting on her knees. All three are smiling at you, the man's lips perhaps a little tighter than the women's.

"Sit here, love," says Mrs Atkins, indicating the other armchair, and you pull yourself up onto it.

"I'll make you a cup of tea," she tells you, "and some toast. Would you like some jam on it?"

You nod and are aware of the brief stare she gives to the other three adults in the room before closing the door behind her.

The woman in the suit reaches for your hand and squeezes it.

"I'm Margaret," she says. "And this is Brian and Debbie."

"Where's my mummy?" you ask her. "And Cathy? Why can't

I be at home?"

"Your Mum's at the hospital," she replies. Then, reading your expression, quickly adds, "She's not poorly. She's..."

Margaret seems to struggle for the right words.

"Your Mum's had a bit of an upset," Brian tells you. "She just needs looking after for a while, but she's alright."

"Where's Cathy?" you ask.

All three are silent at this. After a few seconds, the policewoman leans forward, staring at you.

"Can you tell us what happened last night?"

"What do you mean?"

"Well, you didn't have dinner with your sister and dad, did you? We..."

"He's not my dad," you break in sharply. "Jim's my stepdad."

They exchange glances.

"Alright," says Margaret. "Your sister and your stepdad. Would you explain to us why not?"

You bite your lip.

"I was made to go to bed with no supper," you tell him.

"Why was that?" asks Brian.

In the end, you repeat what happened three times. Firstly, about dropping your plate, then everything between coming home from school and being sent upstairs, and then once more, with them asking questions rather than just listening.

But each time you're careful to leave out Cathy's fingers letting go of the plate when it was still inches from yours. Without knowing why, you sense this is really important.

Mrs Atkins comes back into the parlour.

"I've made her a bit of breakfast," she tells them. "Poor little mite hasn't eaten since I don't know when."

Brian nods and you let Mrs Atkins take you by the hand once again and lead you out of the room.

When you return to the parlour, Brian is gone and his place on the sofa has been taken by an older woman. She has silver hair and wears narrow spectacles perched on the end of her nose, which she peers at you over rather than through. Her name, she tells you, is Dr Gordon and she is looking at you with some concern.

"Are you my mummy's doctor?" you ask and she shakes her head.

"No," she says, adding, "I'm not that kind of doctor."

You've always assumed there's only one kind of doctor, but her expression doesn't encourage further questions.

"Last night," begins Margaret and inwardly you sigh at the prospect of going through it all again for Dr Gordon, "where did the pie come from?"

"Cathy made it at school," you tell her, "in domestic science."

"She made it yesterday?" asks the policewoman. There's something about the uniform that makes it impossible for you to think of her as 'Debbie'.

You nod.

"Cathy wasn't at school yesterday," says Margaret. "Didn't you know that?"

Wordlessly, you shake your head.

"Are you sure - you're not fibbing to us?" Margaret gives you a small smile. "You won't be in trouble if Cathy told you a secret."

"No. She said she'd made the pie in class."

"Did you and Cathy tell each other secrets?" asks Dr Gordon. "When I was a little girl, my sister and I did."

You hesitate.

"We used to," you say quietly. "But since things changed, not really."

"Things changed?"

"Daddy dying... Moving here."

"Did the two of you talk about that?"

"At first," you tell her. "But then she just got very quiet. I thought she was sad."

"Sad?"

"Yes," you nod. "Like I was."

"Before or after your mother met your stepfather?"

You consider.

"Sad before, quiet after."

Margaret appears to be about to speak, but the door opens and Brian comes into the parlour. He looks at Dr Gordon, raises an eyebrow and she rises from the settee and follows him out of the room.

"While your mummy's being taken care of," Margaret speaks slowly and carefully, "we're going to have to find somewhere for you to stay. A home with other children."

"I don't want to stay with other children." You begin to cry. "I want to stay with Cathy. I want Cathy to look after me."

"It's just for a while," she says, but the tears are really flowing now.

"Well, what we…" begins Margaret, but breaks off as Dr Gordon returns. She is stern faced as she comes over and kneels down beside your chair, but then her expression softens as she takes your hand.

"Did your stepfather," she asks, her fingers noticeably tightening around yours, "ever touch you in places where you thought he shouldn't?"

From that point on, everything is a whirl.

They're going to take you somewhere you'll be looked after, they tell you, but in the hallway you wrench your hand from Margaret's and rush to Mrs Atkins, who begins to cry as your arms are gently disentangled from around her leg.

There is an explosion of light as you step out onto the pavement. Flashbulbs are popping and you've never seen so many people jostling together. An ambulance with its rear doors open is waiting by the kerbside, but Brian leads you through a sea of curious faces to a police car, blue lights already flashing even though it isn't going anywhere. You and Margaret climb into the back and after Brian shuts the front passenger door, it slowly starts to pull away.

At first you're surrounded, the windows full of those same gawking expressions. Brian reaches out a hand to flick a switch and a sudden burst of the car's siren is startling enough to clear a path through.

You're too small to look properly out of the car, are only aware of the tops of buildings as they flash by, taller as you approach the city centre.

"We're going to the hospital," Margaret tells you, "just to be certain that you're alright."

"Is it the same hospital where my mummy's staying?" you ask. "Will I see her there?"

"It's a different one," Margaret explains. "But you'll be able to see her very soon."

In later life, you're never quite sure whether Margaret actually believed this or was simply placating you. You've always lent towards the latter, she knew well enough how the system worked.

There's the nylon gown which fastens up the back. Fingers in rubber gloves which - however dexterously they pull, prod and penetrate - are nothing less than a violation, as are the swabs and cotton buds which follow them. These same fingers trace along the fading hatch-work of Jim's belt and there are endless questions concerning the notions of discipline you've been subjected to.

They give you a tablet which they say will make you feel better, but it doesn't. It makes your legs heavy, so heavy it's hard to place one foot in front of the other and your thinking seems to be heavy too. Even when dealing with things you didn't understand, your mind always seemed swift and nimble, your thoughts quicksilver darts, but suddenly it's dull and foggy in there, with everything so far away.

Then Margaret is sitting down with you.

Cathy's gone to heaven, she tells you, God's looking after her now. And your mummy is so sad about this, that she'll need taking care of for a while, too.

You have to be a brave little girl.

You struggle to grasp this. You don't understand why whoever's taking care of Mummy can't take care of you as well, instead of Margaret and the doctor with silver hair and the glasses she doesn't look at you through. You try to ask her, but the words become jumbled up in your mouth and you wonder if that's why you're not able to cry. That if you can't explain how sad you are, the tears won't work properly and then you find yourself tumbling into sleep, where you discover that dreams have stopped working too.

Over the next few days, information arrives in scraps. Eventually you'll learn to peer behind what you are told, understand there's always something lurking just out of sight. To digest what you manage to grasp, cautiously hoard what you don't and have faith that, given time, all will become self-evident.

Later there'll be fishing expeditions into these dark pools of memory - words heard from the other side of a curtain, emphasis artfully positioned in a question, looks exchanged at your responses...

But now all is confusion.

The only thing you truly comprehend is that the part of your life which you understood has ended and another is about to begin.

CHAPTER TWO

Faith

As a GP, Faith regularly attended inquests, but this was the first time she'd given testimony in the case of someone she regarded as a friend. But any misgivings on walking the borderline between personal and professional appraisal were quickly laid to one side. The coroner merely questioned her as to Robert Pascoe's mental health, initially with regard to possible symptoms of depression she might have treated or discussed with him. Faith told the court, truthfully, that Robert Pascoe had never sought treatment for any issues relating to his state of mind and nor had there been occasion when she felt this was something that needed to be raised with him.

Mr Pascoe had been drinking heavily the evening before he died, the coroner informed her. Had his alcohol consumption ever given her cause for concern?

Anticipating this question, Faith thought long and hard about it in the days leading up to this inquest. It was a safe assumption that most people halved their weekly alcohol intake when discussing it with their doctor - and those who smoked probably divided their cigarette consumption by an even larger figure - but Faith never placed much emphasis on quantity.

Among her patients were farmhands who'd knock back a couple of pints at lunchtime, double that on their journey home in the evening, but when this was combined with the exertions of physical labour and a healthy appetite, she felt there was little to lecture them about. Far more worrying, in her opinion, was the solicitor needing a stiff drink before returning to the office in anticipation of spending the afternoon on the phone with a difficult client, or a housewife faced with yet another drawn out empty day steeling herself with the sherry decanter.

That Robert Pascoe was a nasty drunk was common knowledge, but he wasn't a regular one. And she'd known him long enough to be aware that his drink of choice was whisky. If you're a secret drinker, your tipple is likely to be vodka - odourless, colourless and unless you're constantly bumping into the furniture you'll probably get away with it. Robert might well have displayed a malicious streak after drinking, but she had speculation of her own regarding that, which is why she intended to remain in the courtroom after her time on the witness stand.

But meanwhile, she was unhesitating with her reply.

"Robert Pascoe wasn't an alcoholic," she told the court. "At least in my opinion. And as well as being a patient of mine, I also knew him socially."

The coroner acknowledged this with a small nod, thanked her for her testimony, and allowed her to stand down.

Faith made her way over to the public gallery, where Toni lifted her coat from the bench alongside her as Faith approached.

"Saved you a seat," she said softly.

Faith lowered herself down and turned her head towards the next witness entering the courtroom.

Rod Truscott was the landlord of The Barque who'd served Robert Pascoe in the hotel bar on the night of his death. The events of that evening had been gossiped about around town from the following day onwards and Truscott provided no surprises, other than the occasional hint that Robert could be a handful after one too many. But the essence of it was that Robert got into an altercation with two tourists who, for whatever reason, he'd taken a dislike to. The argument had grown heated, and while not becoming physical, Robert's choice of language prompted Truscott to escort him from the premises. Having earlier relieved Robert of his car keys as a condition of serving further drinks, Truscott offered to call him a cab, an offer declined. The last Truscott saw of Robert was of him making his unsteady departure along the pavement.

It was now common knowledge that Robert kept a spare set of keys in a magnetic container attached under the front wheel arch and had used these, even in such an intoxicated state, to drive himself home.

The coroner thanked him for his testimony and called Claudia Pascoe, Robert's wife.

Claudia was dressed sombrely, a business like two-piece suit, charcoal grey, the skirt falling just below the knee and the jacket over a black silk blouse. Faith found herself studying Claudia with an intensity she hoped her features didn't betray.

On the surface, Claudia's evidence was straightforward enough. The morning after Robert's run-in at The Barque, Claudia had been awakened by the newspaper delivery boy ringing her front doorbell. He'd heard a car engine running behind the closed garage door and banging on it elicited no response. Claudia had opened it using the exterior keypad, where they'd discovered Robert slumped at the wheel. As the fumes quickly cleared, Claudia sent the boy into the house to call for an ambulance and then ventured inside to open the driver's side door. She could find no pulse on Robert's wrist and the paramedics, who arrived within minutes, confirmed death had occurred several hours earlier.

Claudia gave her evidence calmly and clearly, already well settled into, thought Faith perhaps a little uncharitably, the role of stoic widow. Under the coroner's gentle interrogation, Claudia explained she hadn't noticed her husband's absence the previous evening. With increasing age she'd become a light sleeper and Robert prone to heavy snoring, a dilemma eventually resolved by separate bedrooms.

As the coroner delved further into the history of Claudia and Robert's marriage, Faith couldn't help her thoughts drifting back to earlier this year.

* * *

It had been Robert's fiftieth. Most of St Hannahs upper crust, as Faith tended to think of them, were invited and almost all had shown up.

The Pascoes' had really pushed the boat out, thought Faith as the evening moved along. The caterers had a hog roast set up on the patio, together with tables ladened with varied fare for more delicate appetites. A Beatles tribute band - a pretty decent one actually, Faith had to admit, both in sound and appearance - was belting out the soundtrack of just about everyone here's youth and good-naturedly taking requests called out from the crowd.

"I'm going to ask for Revolution Number Nine," said Ted dryly.

"Behave," Faith told him with a smile.

"Will do," Ted nodded. "And it looks as if Robert is, too. For once."

Faith glanced over to where Robert and Claudia were greeting a pair of late arrivals. The couple were new in St Hannahs, she recalled, and had bought Cliff Dene, an art déco clifftop chalet overlooking the entire town. *'I'd not only sell my soul to have that place, but yours as well,'* Faith had once told Ted as they'd strolled by the harbour, staring up as it caught the last rays of the sun. *'Okay,'* Ted nodded, *'but after we move in, I'd want separate rooms.'*

Robert was all smiles as he greeted the couple - Richard and Veronica, she suddenly remembered - and let's hope it stays that way, thought Faith.

"We should mingle," Faith told him.

"So we're not going to boogie?" Ted raised an eyebrow.

"Don't you dare." Faith shook her head, suppressing a smile. It was a long-standing joke between them that asking Ted if he wanted to dance was her litmus test of how much he'd put away. Five minutes after smiling, 'Yeah, sure' Faith would be packing him into the car.

"Okay, well - *Jesus!*"

Faith turned around to where Ted was staring.

There'd obviously been some kind of collision between one of the waiters and Claudia. A tray lay on the ground surrounded by broken glasses and Claudia's dress was soaked.

"You stupid fucking cunt!" Robert snarled at the waiter, who was little more than a boy. "Why can't you watch what the fuck you're doing?"

He started forward, but Claudia moved in front of him, laying a hand on his chest.

"Robert, *stop it!*" She took a deep breath. "It was my fault. I stepped backwards without looking where I was going." She turned to the waiter. "I'm so sorry. Are you alright?"

Ashen face, he gave her a nod.

Turning back to Robert, she stared at him silently. After a few seconds, he nodded.

"Okay," he said softly, and then looked at the waiter. "Sorry - I was just... concerned." He shrugged. "But maybe we could get this cleared away before someone steps in it." He gestured at the shattered glasses on the ground. "Come on through to the kitchen with me. I'll find you a dustpan and brush."

"Think I need to head inside myself," said Claudia with a rueful smile after they'd left. One sleeve of her dress was completely soaked, as was the long chiffon scarf wound about her neck and trailing down her back.

"I was holding my breath there," Ted murmured. "Looked like it was going south pretty quickly..."

"Poor kid," said Faith. "But at least Robert had the grace to apologise." She hesitated before handing Ted her glass. "Hold on to that for me, would you? I'll just pop indoors to see if Claudia needs a hand getting cleaned up."

Faith made her way into the house and up the stairs. Only one room leading off the first floor landing had a light showing, through a door that was perhaps six inches ajar. She moved towards it.

And then froze.

She could see through into the bedroom where Claudia was sitting at her dressing-table mirror, the sodden dress crumpled by her feet. All she was wearing was her underwear and the chiffon scarf, but that wasn't what had caught Faith's eye. Around each of Claudia's upper arms was a circle of bruises, almost purplish with blotches of yellow.

Faith stood still, holding her breath as Claudia reached up to the scarf and unwound it. Another band of bruises encircled her neck, if anything of deeper hues than the others.

If ever, came flashing into Faith's mind, Claudia could be said to have a signature item of clothing, it was a silk or chiffon neck scarf, loose and trailing or tightly wound as a…

Choker! As tightly wound as a choker.

Slowly, Faith stepped backwards and made her way down the stairs, her thoughts in a whirl. Okay, once in a blue moon, a black eye might be down to walking into a door, but the only explanation for what she'd just seen were fingers dug into the flesh…

Faith saw her hand was shaking as she took her drink from Ted.

"You alright?" he asked, staring at her.

"Sure," she told him, flashing a smile. "Fine."

Mercifully, the rest of the evening seemed to fly by, but Faith was careful to steer clear of both Claudia and Robert, leaving at the end of the night with the minimum of pleasantries.

And since then, she'd said nothing.

Not to Ted, if only because he already struggled to keep his antipathy towards Robert under wraps and God knows what this might lead to.

And not to Claudia either, but she intended to.

When the moment was right.

On a visit to the surgery perhaps, or if the two of them should somehow find themselves alone. But there had been no appointments in the aftermath of that evening, nor had their paths crossed socially, at least under circumstances conducive to the kind of *tête-à-tête* Faith had in mind.

And now, it seemed, this was a matter resolved.

* * *

It was the sense of a sudden rise in interest rippling through the courtroom that returned Faith to the present.

"Robert kept his business affairs separate from home life," Claudia was saying.

The coroner leant back in his chair and studied her.

"Isn't it unusual for a husband not to confide in his wife?" he asked.

Claudia explained that five years previously, her husband's business had come under financial pressure and that she had sold her share in The Grange to - reading between the lines of what she was saying - bail him out. Well, thought Faith, that clears that up. There'd been a lot of speculation - alright, gossip - at the time about a bust up between her and Lee Munro over the running of the hotel. That must have added a new dynamic to the husband and wife relationship, mused Faith.

Then shortly afterwards, continued Claudia, he'd gone into partnership with the town's only other estate agency, citing the benefits of pooled resources and cutting costs. Well, if that's how she needs to spin it, thought Faith, so be it. But everyone in town knew that Alan Bradshaw's expansion had enough momentum behind it for Robert's only options to be surrender on favourable terms or eventual annihilation.

Claudia seemed to hesitate for a second.

"Two years ago, Robert told me that he and Alan had been offered an exceptional business opportunity involving the purchase and renovation of a local hotel. They had a line of credit in place, apparently, but needed a guarantor."

"To be clear," asked the coroner, "a guarantor for what, in effect, would be a loan?"

"Yes." Claudia's smile was almost a wince. "I own an apartment in central London, which I inherited from my mother. Robert said that I needed to offer it as surety." She shrugged. "I refused."

"What was Mr Pascoe's reaction to this?"

"Oh, we had the full gamut of emotions at one point or

another. But the upshot of it was that I remained adamant. And from then on, Robert never discussed any of his business dealings with me."

Instinctively and almost without realising she was doing it, Faith's hand rose to her neck, and she rested it softly against her skin.

"So, you'd be unaware if your husband found himself under pressure during the last days of his life."

"Business pressure, yes. But..."

She let her voice trail off.

"Mrs Pascoe," the coroner encouraged her.

"About a week before Robert's death, we'd been visited by a reporter," said Claudia slowly.

"A reporter?" he prompted.

"Well, by profession. But the reason he wanted to see us, he'd explained on the telephone to Robert beforehand, was that he was working on a biography of James Carrington."

"The VC?"

"Yes." Claudia nodded. "It was strange, really. Both Robert and I had connections to him, although quite independently. I'd once owned The Grange - or half owned it, it was the hotel I mentioned earlier, which I'd sold my share of to re-finance Robert's business."

"This was the house Captain Carrington built in St Hannahs shortly after the First World War?"

"Yes. And Robert's grandfather, Arthur, had served with him, he'd been the regiment's Adjutant. Immediately after the war they were involved in several business enterprises together and when Carrington decided to build a house in St Hannahs, Arthur moved down here to oversee the project."

"And, presumably, when it was completed he remained in Cornwall?"

"Yes. During that time he'd met Robert's grandmother and they'd fallen in love. Mary didn't want to leave the village where she'd lived all her life and so Arthur began to look for business opportunities in the area. Eventually, the story went, with a loan from Carrington he started the estate agency."

Claudia paused for a moment, as if ordering her thoughts.

"Our assumption was that this visit was purely for research and initially that seemed the case. He was interested in anything that I might have come across at the house - photographs, old paperwork to do with tradespeople, shopkeepers and servants. And the same from Robert - had his grandfather kept a diary, was there any surviving correspondence between Arthur and Carrington?

"But then he asked Robert if his grandfather had ever talked about his war service. Or of his specific duties in the regiment. Robert said that - like a lot of old soldiers - Arthur had been reticent about his wartime experiences. The family had heard a few anecdotes about life in the trenches, but nothing reflective of the horrors he must have seen.

"One of Arthur's duties as Adjutant, the reporter explained, was to sort through the effects of soldiers killed in combat before forwarding them on to their families. To remove anything that might seem inappropriate or likely to embarrass. At this point the reporter produced a selection of photographs."

Claudia gave a wry smile.

"I imagine they'd be considered very *risqué* back then, nude studies of young women, but by today's standards they seemed relatively mild. In fact, the thing I found most shocking was that each one was bloodstained.

"This was quite an enterprise, the reporter told us. Arthur would remove these photographs from the possessions of dead servicemen and hand them on to his partner, a corporal who would re-sell them to freshly arrived recruits. And with the mortality rate being what it was on the Western Front, the same photographs could pass through their hands on an almost daily basis.

"This corporal kept a diary, according to the reporter. He took out a sheaf of what appeared to be photocopied exercise book pages and passed them over to Robert. 'Dates, names, times, and amounts,' he told him. 'And as you'll see, for the period the figures are substantial - certainly enough to get a fledgling West Country estate agency up and running.'"

"That is outrageous," bellowed Mrs Pascoe senior, rising to her feet incensed. "An absolute slander."

The courtroom was now in uproar and the coroner raised his hand for silence.

* * *

Well Claudia, thought Faith as she and Toni walked down the steps outside, you certainly made it back here with a bang.

Once the hubbub subsided, there'd been little more to Claudia's testimony. She accepted that the possibility of an upcoming family scandal could have preyed heavily on her husband's mind during the days leading up to his death, but dismissed the notion that he could have become suicidal over it. He'd been in a reflective mood during that period, she explained to the court, and after the events in The Barque that evening had perhaps taken time to gather his thoughts before going into the house. Then with the drink...

That was Faith's own view of what had happened, or something very much like it. Robert had never struck her as someone who...

Her train of thought broke off as Claudia emerged from the courthouse. She was ignoring a group of reporters scuttling alongside her and holding out dictaphones as they barraged her with questions. What may be tittle-tattle in a city, reflected Faith, can be earthshaking in communities where reputational kudos spans generations.

Indeed, Mrs Pascoe senior was staring daggers at Claudia, as were most of Robert's family, their eyes never leaving her as she made her way across the small courtyard to where Paul Chapman from The Grange held open the rear door of a Range Rover. She slipped inside, Paul followed and the car pulled away from the kerb before the door was fully shut.

"Fancy a coffee?" asked Toni.

"Sure," said Faith.

"I might phone Claudia later." Toni shrugged. "To check she's okay."

"She's staying at The Grange, I heard," Faith told her. "Cam Ryr's going on the market, apparently."

"There'll be a stampede over that," said Toni and Faith nodded. Property in the old part of St Hannahs rarely came up for sale and beachfront houses hardly ever. Cam Ryr opened up onto a vista of sand and surf and whilst not a private beach, it was far enough from the harbour for Faith never to have seen it crowded. However much Claudia might put it on the market for, Faith envisaged a bidding war...

Her thoughts broke off. They'd reached the other side of the square and were waiting at a pedestrian crossing for the lights to change. But the Range Rover that collected Claudia had followed the one-way system around three sides of the perimeter and now came to a halt in front of them as the lights turned red.

Stepping down from the pavement into the road, Faith glanced into the back of the SUV. Claudia and Paul sat side by side, both staring expressionlessly ahead, and suddenly Claudia was struck by the mutual neutrality of that expression as if by a thunderbolt. *That's not how you look after a morning you've just h*ad flashed across Faith's mind. Relief, resignation, anxiety... There was an entire wealth of emotions that should have been playing out here and in that instant, she just *knew*!

Over the years, Faith had learnt never to ignore gut instinct. In the surgery, faced with symptoms that didn't quite gel with what should be the obvious diagnosis, it could be lifesaving. Faith wasn't sure how - although she had a pretty good idea of why - but the quiet complicity she'd just witnessed came with an absolute certainty that those garage doors hadn't closed on Robert Pascoe by accident.

And whatever conclusion the coroner might reach, whatever verdict was passed down, Faith doubted she'd ever see Claudia wearing a silk choker again.

Amanda

There's a point in most investigations where everything plateaus. After the initial rush of accusations, suppositions and testimony comes the inevitable sifting of fact and fabrication, probing detail, examining motivation and all with the knowledge born of experience that whatever you needed to crack the case wide open was probably right there before your eyes, if you simply knew which direction to come at it from.

Amanda had learnt from ex Chief Superintendent Maddox that Christopher Franklyn had been working undercover for Special Branch back in 1970. He was a police officer's son who'd somehow gotten involved in the radical politics and counterculture of the day and - with the Red Brigades in Italy and the Baader-Meinhof Gang in Germany raining down mayhem and murder across mainland Europe - was seemingly given *carte blanch* as to how he got results. That arrest warrant had actually been a way of bringing him in whilst preserving his cover. But Maddox hadn't been in contact with him since the mid-seventies.

DS Sule concentrated on the surveillance photographs and records from back then, police missing persons reports and National Assistance Board claim files, building up a list of who was living in the house during that summer of 1970 and where they might be now.

Amanda moved on to picking holes in Declan McKelvey's story, based on the assumption that no one on the other side of the table in an interview room is ever going to be giving you the whole truth. That what's being held back, and why, is where you should be focusing your efforts.

She learnt that in the late eighties, Ronan Doyle, who according to McKelvey had helped bury the body at the building site, cut an immunity deal for his testimony at a number of prosecutions. He'd spent twenty years as an active member of the Provisional IRA and while pretty low in the food chain he did know - quite literally - where the bodies were buried.

Britain didn't have a witness protection program *per se* - although there were increasingly vocal and influential calls for that situation to be changed - but did facilitate new lives for those who'd put themselves and their loved ones at risk by aiding the justice system or the state.

And let's not make the mistake of assuming those two are mutually inclusive, reflected Amanda.

This was usually handled by the individual police force involved rather than any national body and in McKelvey's case that was Greater Manchester Police. Best not to jump to any assumptions to his current location based on that, thought Amanda. Given her previous experience with 'supergrass' witnesses, she knew that he was now most likely living abroad. Probably a Commonwealth country - the UK still maintained strong ties so documentation was more easily acquired and her money would be on Canada or Australia.

Precedent was that any request from the Security Service to regional police forces was funnelled via the Chief Constable of that particular force. On Amanda's behalf, Venables made such a request to interview Doyle, on the grounds of national security, the assumption being that his deal was one of ongoing cooperation.

Venables himself was less of a presence in the office now everything was up and running, calling each morning for an update and emphasising he was to be informed immediately of significant developments. Given the political implications of the husband of the Secretary of State for Northern Ireland allegedly caught up in an IRA killing, Amanda guessed he was holding back from informing the government - specifically the Cabinet Secretary - of the investigation until they were absolutely certain it went beyond hearsay. But it was definitely something of a tightrope he was walking there.

Amanda kept returning to Christopher Franklyn. As a Special Branch informant he'd be keeping tabs on just about everything and everybody in the house but, as DS Sule had discovered at the outset of this line of enquiry, he seemed to have dropped off the face of the earth in the mid-eighties.

Even prior to that, the files were particularly sparse regarding his activities, almost suspiciously so given the role he'd played in the early seventies. 'Pruned' was the term used back then for unofficially redacting a file and Amanda couldn't help wondering if someone had been wielding the gardening shears here. There was reference to a wife, Karen, but no marriage record could be found, which made it likely the ceremony had taken place abroad.

She placed a request with Interpol for information on both their names and consoled herself with the thought that, almost always, something eventually turns up.

Jason

Most of the staff didn't like Americans. *'Too brash, too demanding'* was bandied around a lot at break times or in the bar after the grill came down, but not by Jason. As far as he was concerned they knew what they wanted, were happy to pay for it and he'd take that over the petty snobbery of his own countrymen any day of the week... And don't even get him started on the French or Germans.

Jason hoped to move to the States at some point, although the visa restrictions were pretty tight. Getting a work permit for any job a US citizen could do was almost impossible, but a cousin of his had taken a course as a valet after learning that 'English Butler' met that criteria. Ken was now working for some big shot in computers on the West Coast, while he waited for his Green Card to come through and...

Jason's thoughts broke off as the lift doors opened and a guest stepped out, briskly crossing the foyer towards him.

Well, speak of the devil!

"Good evening, Ms Weaver," he smiled. "How may I help you?"

Jason made a point of knowing the names of all the guests. He got jibed about this occasionally by co-workers, but he knew they didn't pick up half as much in tips as he did. Make someone feel memorable and they'll remember you. He used a system of word association, learnt from a course he'd sent away for in the post. The first thing that came to mind with 'Gail Weaver' was a loom and so he'd imprinted an image of her in a nineteenth century workshop, creating a rug with a storm blowing around her. Sounds silly, and it was something he'd never confided in anyone else, but it always worked.

"I'll be checking out in the morning," she told him. "My business here finished earlier than I expected."

"Very well, Ms Weaver," nodded Jason, pulling her booking up on the screen and amending it. "I hope your stay with us met your expectations?"

"Yes, it did, thank you." Her smile seemed genuine, if slightly hesitant. "I was hoping to go on from here to St Hannahs, in Cornwall, but I don't have anywhere booked. Would you be able to help with that?"

"How long were you thinking of spending there?" asked Jason, switching from in house reservations to a UK based GDS system.

"I'm not sure."

Studying the screen, Jason slowly shook his head.

"There isn't a hotel room free for the next seven days along the entire south-west coast," he told her. "Because of the eclipse. It's possible you might find bed-and-breakfast or a guest house if you simply turned up there - I could give you a printout of some phone numbers - but I wouldn't bank on it." Jason shrugged and gave a rueful smile. "There've been stories on the news about residents renting spare bedrooms out."

"What's the closest you can find?"

"The north Cornish coast, but further east. A town called Bude. About an hour from St Hannahs, usually, but with the traffic expected next week..." He offered an apologetic shrug.

"Okay, just bad timing, I guess." She gave him a wan smile. "But thanks for trying."

She turned to walk away.

"Actually," said Jason thoughtfully, "there might be another possibility. If you were to widen your options...?"

"My options?"

"I've a friend," Jason told her, "who's in the process of setting up a rental business."

Dennis

"If you'd like to go into the restaurant," the waitress said to Dennis, "your table's ready."

"Actually," Dennis gave her what he hoped came across as an apologetic smile, "my wife's not here yet. Is it okay if I wait until she arrives?"

"Of course," the waitress smiled. "Just come through when she gets here."

As she disappeared into the restaurant, Dennis turned to the barman.

"Looks like I can sneak a quick one," he said, indicating his beer with a nod. "But best make it a half."

The barman grinned as he took Dennis's almost empty glass and held it under the pump. As the topped up drink was placed back in front of him, Dennis became aware of a figure arriving alongside and turned in that direction.

"Hello Dennis."

Like a lot of people in St Hannahs, Dennis had ambivalent feelings towards Alan Bradshaw. Although he'd arrived in St Hannahs less than ten years ago, he'd managed to - *inveigle*, seemed the appropriate word - his way into just about every aspect of St Hannahs' life. From setting up as a one-man band estate agent, he'd somehow got into partnership with Pascoes, the largest real estate agency in the area, while his wife ran what was becoming the biggest self catering holiday properties business in town. And though he wasn't actually on the council, two of his employees were and no prizes for guessing who was pulling their strings. If he'd had kids, reflected Dennis, he probably be on the board of school governors too, so be grateful for small mercies at least. Gillian Brown couldn't stand him and he already had enough bitching and backbiting to contend with as things stood.

"I don't know if you've met Richard Hanson?" continued Alan.

Dennis hadn't, but he did know of him. Richard and his wife had moved to St Hannahs a couple of years ago. They'd been pretty low key, having the appearance of one of those new age couples who'd occasionally blow into town to open a gallery, antique stroke curio shop or vegetarian cafe and then disappear a year later, leaving little behind other than unpaid bills and a bad taste in the mouth.

But initial impressions had been confounded. It turned out they were loaded and had bought Cliff Dene - probably the most impressive house in St Hannahs - for cash, apparently. Word also got around they'd been generous to local causes without making a fuss about it.

So they would seem to be the complete antithesis of Alan Bradshaw and as Dennis reached out to shake hands, he couldn't help but wonder what they were doing together.

"Dennis Nelson," he said to him. "You've Cliff Dene, I understand?"

"Yes."

"So, what brought you to St Hannahs?" asked Dennis.

"A friend owned a house here." Hanson shrugged. "We came to visit and fell in love with the place."

"A not unfamiliar story," smiled Dennis.

"Amongst other things, Dennis is Chairman of the Board of Governors at St Anne's," Alan Bradshaw told Hanson and then turned his attention back to Dennis. "We've just been chatting to one of your teachers," he said. "Gillian Brown."

"She's a friend of my wife," explained Hanson.

"That's right," Alan went on. "They were celebrating her promotion."

"Well," Dennis gave a disparaging smile, "there's nothing official yet. We've other candidates to interview tomorrow. But she's been Acting Head of Department for six months now and done an excellent job."

"I'd have said that's more of a reason to go for someone else," said Alan.

"I'm sorry?" asked Dennis, somewhat taken aback.

"If you already have someone who can do the job," said Alan "going for the most promising external applicant gives you the best of both worlds. Particularly somewhere like here."

Dennis was shaking his head.

"I don't understand?"

"The whole world and his brother would love to live in Cornwall," said Alan. "Whenever we advertise a job, the CVs from up country are way more impressive than you'd expect for what the position involves. We've had some real talent injected into the business over the last few years."

He took a sip of his beer.

"And if they don't live up to expectations, well, it's no problem getting rid of them after a three-month trial, because there's already someone to step straight back into their shoes." He shrugged. "I mean, they won't be leaving Cornwall for Birmingham or Leeds because they're pissed off at missing a promotion, will they? And it's not like there's anywhere else for them to go down here."

"That's a bit… Darwinian," said Dennis, dryly.

Alan shook his head.

"It's never a bad idea to keep your people on their toes, Dennis. And," he added, "I saw that piece in the Western Morning News about school league tables in Cornwall - probably wouldn't hurt to have some ammunition ready, along the lines of fresh ideas and broadening horizons, if St Anne's keeps on slipping."

Dennis was staring at him.

"Only a thought," smiled Alan. "Anyway, what are you doing for the eclipse?"

"We're having a barbecue, at the house," Dennis told him, then realising the inevitability of where that led, "Friends and colleagues welcome, why don't you and Safranka drop by?"

"I don't think we've anything planned," said Alan, "so we might well do that."

Alan gave him one last smile before he and Richard Hanson moved off into the restaurant.

Dennis barely had time to reflect on their conversation before there was a tap on his arm.

"Hello," said Toni. "You look miles away."

"I think," said Dennis slowly, "I just invited Alan Bradshaw to the barbecue next week."

"You think...?"

"Okay, I did." Dennis shook his head. "But I'm not sure he'll be coming."

"Well, if he does," Toni gave a tight smile, "it's your bloody job to keep him and Gillian Brown apart."

It's the last time you see Margaret.

You'll be staying in a lovely home, with lots of other girls and boys, she tells you. And looked after by people who really know how to take care of children.

You have a nightdress and a change of underwear packed in a small suitcase. When you ask about your other clothes she smiles and says not to worry, everything will all be sorted out.

You leave the hospital in a van painted the same colours as an ambulance, but in the back are bench seats and large windows to look out of. Margaret sits next to you, holding your hand. This time you can see where you're going, but heading into an unfamiliar area of the city you soon lose your bearings.

Eventually you come to a driveway leading to an archway set in a high brick wall, curving away in both directions. Initial impressions are those of unease, but as you pass underneath, you relax a little. Inside is what could almost be a small village green, surrounded by half a dozen houses, the kind you've always thought of as posh.

There is a sign on the grass verge just after the arch, 'Riddell Children's Cottage Home'.

You pull up at a gatehouse, the driver gets out and slides back the door for you. Clutching your suitcase, you step down onto the gravel driveway.

From the doorway of this building, a middle-aged couple walk out to greet you, both wearing kindly expressions. Margaret introduces you and the lady kneels down, so you're both at the same eye level.

"Hello," she smiles. "I'm Aunt Anne and this is Uncle Jim."

She reaches out a hand. As you take it, she rises and leads you into the building, Uncle Jim on the other side of her and Margaret following.

Inside, Margaret opens her briefcase, takes out a collection of forms and you all wait silently, you still holding Aunt Anne's hand, as Jim carefully signs each one and passes it over to her. When they are all shut away back in her case, she kneels down to look you in the eye.

"I know you're going to be very happy here," she tells you. "If you're a good girl, do what you're told and work hard, then you'll soon be able to put all the dreadful things that have happened behind you." She reaches for your free hand, gives it a squeeze. "And you will be a good girl, won't you?"

You nod, biting your lip.

She stands up, brushing down her skirt.

"Don't worry," Uncle Jim reassures her with a smile. "We'll take good care of her."

Aunt Anne leads you out of the gatehouse and along the driveway. There are six houses here, she explains, all named after plants. Rose House and Lily House are where the younger boys and girls live. Violet House and Lilac House are for older girls, Tulip House and Rowan House for the older boys. You will be living in Rose House, she tells you.

You pass through the hallway of Rose House and up a flight of stairs.

"This is where you'll be sleeping," says Aunt Anne, pushing open a door.

It's a large room, with two rows of five narrow beds along opposite walls. You're struck by how precisely they're made up, each top sheet folded back exactly the same length from the pillow, the corners squared away. A small locker sits by each bed.

"First of all, let's get you taken care of," says Aunt Anne and you follow her down to a bed at the far end of the room. She opens the locker and takes out a bundle of clothing.

"These should fit," she tells you.

You look at her, not sure of what to do next.

"Come on," she says, and you catch something in her tone that wasn't there before. "We don't have all day."

You quickly undress and pull on the clothes you've been given. Although clean, there is a sense of ... being used about them. If not exactly itchy against your skin, there's a coarseness that feels unnatural. Finally, over the dress goes a dull grey serge pinafore.

You follow her back out onto the landing, where she

indicates a doorway opposite .

"The boys' dormitory." Aunt Anne fixes you with a stare. "Entry for girls is strictly forbidden at all times, under any circumstances. And vice versa."

She pushes open a door between the dormitories and you step inside. Two large bathtubs sit side by side and along one wall are a series of deep, wide porcelain basins, each with a single tap.

"You'll have a bath every Wednesday night and Saturday morning," she tells you, and then indicates the washbasins.

"Are you incontinent?"

You stare at her uncomprehendingly and she sighs.

"Do you wet the bed?"

"No," shaking your head.

That sigh again.

"No, Aunt Anne." You find yourself the focus of her steady gaze. "Children here are expected to be respectful. You'll always address an adult as Aunt or Uncle, unless you don't know their name, in which case it's Miss or Sir. Is that clear?"

"Yes," you tell her, before quickly correcting yourself. "Yes, Aunt Anne."

"That's better." A smile touches her lips before she turns back to the washbasins.

"Incontinent children do their own laundry. If there's been a mishap in the night, you'll bring your sheets in here and scrub them clean. Together with your nightgown. Understood?"

"Yes, Aunt Anne."

She leads you down the stairs to the ground floor and in through a door on the left.

"This is where we have our meals."

Two rectangular tables run the length of the room, a third sits at right angles across the top.

"On school days, breakfast is at seven thirty, Saturday and Sunday at eight o'clock."

Every place is set, you notice, with a knife, fork and spoon arranged with the same precision as the bedding upstairs.

You follow her into the hallway and through yet another

doorway.

"The Common Room," declares Aunt Anne.

The far wall is filled with bookshelves, whose contents - at a glance - range from infant picture books through Enid Blyton on to hardback children's classics. The adjoining wall is taken up by floor to ceiling cupboard space, holding an assortment of board games, toys and miscellaneous sports equipment - cricket bats, tennis rackets, shuttlecocks. You also notice what seems to be a vaulting horse, although smaller than the one used in PT at your old school, sitting on spindly wooden legs and its padded top much narrower.

There is a further puzzle. On the third wall, facing the window, a large blackboard has been attached and on it is chalked a grid of rows and columns. The left-hand column is a list of names - Valerie B., Alan T., Gillian R. - perhaps twenty in total. There are six further columns to the right and against each name appear random numbers in the form of 5/6, 8/6, 12/6. Some names have only single or double entries against them, most four or five but none are completely filled in.

You're curious but assume it will eventually be made clear.

Back out in the hallway again, Aunt Anne gestures towards the rear of the house.

"The kitchen is through there, out of bounds unless you are assigned duties there. Food preparation or dishwashing."

Next are the lavatories, which are only to be used, you learn, during the day. Under each bed is a chamber pot and these are to be emptied first thing every morning, before bed inspection.

You wonder about 'bed inspection'.

Stepping outside, you see the driveway is now filled with a column of returning children. They walk hand in hand, the girls in pinafores identical to the one you're wearing, the boys in grey jumpers and shorts.

Even the older ones.

"Nina!" *calls out Aunt Anne.*

A small dark-haired girl lets go of her companion's hand.

"Nina will look after you for the next few days," *Aunt Anne tells you, as the girl walks over.* "She'll explain all you'll need to know about how things are done here."

Aunt Anne introduces you to Nina.

"Just follow what Nina does, and we'll have no problems," says Aunt Anne.

"Yes, Aunt Anne," you tell her. "Thank you, Aunt Anne."

You and Nina watch her departing back, and then she turns to you.

"Let's take a walk," she says. "I'll show you where you're allowed and where you aren't."

You're aware all of this is new, that it's bound to seem strange, but still can't escape the feeling of something being not quite right.

It isn't until you have almost circled the green that you realise what it is.

Although all around is now teeming with children, there's none of the shouting and laughter you'd normally associate with that.

Silence is everywhere.

"We're allowed out here until teatime," Nina tells you. "If it isn't raining or not too cold." She gives a little shrug. "It's best to stay outside, if you can."

Tea's at five o'clock, you learn. After tea, you may play in the Common Room until half-past six, when you get ready for bed. An Aunt comes into the dormitory to say bedtime prayers with you, then the blinds are drawn and lights switched off at seven o'clock.

After saying grace before the evening meal, you are introduced to the other children. There are a few curious glances towards you, but mostly the atmosphere is one of indifference. You pick your way slowly through the liver and mashed potato on your plate, but finish it after Nina explains that if you don't, you'll find it waiting for you the next morning.

"Waste is a sin," she says quietly.

After you all set your places ready for breakfast, you're allowed in the Common Room. You begin to ask Nina about the blackboard, but break off as you stare at it.

Your name has been added at the bottom.

"That's everyone's demerits," Nina tells you.

"Demerits?"

"When you've been bad," she says, and you realise that the numbers which had puzzled you earlier are actually dates.

Each demerit warrants a stroke of the cane, explains Nina. But it only lasts for the three Sundays after you've received it, then it's rubbed out. You're only given the cane when there are six demerits against your name.

"What do you get a demerit for?" you ask.

"Being naughty, being disrespectful, wetting the bed." She gives a shrug. "Being wilful."

"What's wilful?"

"Anything they like," says Nina.

Whenever someone's tally reaches six demerits, punishment is carried out in the Common Room before bedtime, with all the boys and girls present. "So we might learn from it."

"Does it hurt much?" you ask and for the first time Nina turns to look you directly in the eye.

"If it didn't," she says, "they wouldn't do it."

Nina's bed is next to yours and, after undressing and slipping on your nightgown, you mimic her motions, turning the top sheet down and then kneeling for prayers.

"Goodnight, Nina," you whisper, after the lights have gone out and the door closes behind the Aunt.

"Hush," she tells you softly. "They sometimes listen with a glass against the wall."

In the darkness a girl is quietly sobbing. Your last thought, before slipping into sleep, is a vow that will never be you.

After you rise the next day, Nina shows you how to properly flannel your neck behind the ears, which along with your nails are the prime focus of morning inspection. Two little boys and a girl, wearing nothing more than shameful expressions, are scrubbing sheets, pyjamas and a nightgown at the other sinks.

In the dormitory, Nina teaches you how to make your bed, which, after a couple of false starts, you manage to her satisfaction, although barely in time. Aunt Anne appears in the doorway and you all stand by the beds as she makes her way down one side of the room and up the other.

A girl is sent to the bathroom to 'scrub her nails properly', another has her sheets and blankets pulled onto the floor and is told to remake it. Tears are not entirely held back, you guess each transgression is a demerit.

After examining your neck and turning your palms over in her hand, she studies your bed.

"Did Nina help you with this?" *she asks.*

"Yes, Aunt Anne," *you tell her.*

"Very well." *She gives a curt nod.* "But tomorrow you will make it all by yourself - is that understood?"

The question is directed as much towards Nina as yourself, and you both respond with bowed heads and a 'Yes, Aunt Anne' given in unison.

Breakfast is porridge, toast and a boiled egg. Afterwards, Aunt Anne gives you a letter, which she tells you is to be handed to the teacher when you arrive in class.

You are lined up in twos for the journey to school, the younger children at the front, the older ones at the back. Two Aunts patrol each side of this crocodile, which - as strange a sight as it must appear - would seem to be invisible to any casual passerby, none of whom spare it a glance.

There are three classes in each year, Nina explains as you walk along. A is the top stream, C the bottom one.

"Do you think we'll be in the same class?" *you ask her and the look she gives you is almost pitying.*

"We're in class C," *she tells you.* "All of us."

In the classroom, you wait by the teacher's desk as the other children take their seats. She reads the letter Aunt Anne gave you and then, picking up a fountain pen, adds you to the register.

Everyone from the Home, you notice, is clustered together at the back. She points at an empty desk in the front row.

"For the moment, sit there," she tells you.

The boy sitting at the next desk shoots his hand into the air.

"My mum says I ain't to have anyfink to do with those kids, Miss Cox," he tells her, fixing you with an evil stare.

"It's just for this morning, Alan," she reassures him. "When Mr Cartwright has finished with the chairs in the hall, I'll ask him to move the desks around in here."

Slowly, you walk to your desk and sit down.

This apartheid persists into the lunch hour. Although you may mingle with the other children receiving free school dinners, there is a solid cluster of grey jumpers and pinafores in the far corner of the dining hall.

"Mrs Hudson's on today," says a boy and for a moment everyone looks at each other and smiles.

"Mrs Hudson's one of the dinner ladies," Nina tells you. "She's kind."

Once the other tables have queued up and received their meals, yours is sent up to the counter. The grey-haired lady serving the food has a twinkle in her eye.

"Haven't seen you before, ducky," she says. "What's your name?"

You tell her, as she piles your plate high.

"There you are," she beams. "Get that down you."

When you return to the classroom, an extra desk has been placed at the back.

In the afternoon there is a spelling test and you make the mistake of getting all the words right. Miss Cox calls you to the front of the class.

"Whose paper did you copy from?" she demands.

"I didn't, Miss," you insist, shaking your head.

"Do not lie," she almost shouts.

You consider.

"Because I'm new," you say carefully, "I don't know everyone's name." You look her in the eye. "So it must have been from one of the other children who got them all correct."

For a second Miss Cox is lost for words.

"You insolent girl," she barks.

Standing up, she snatches a wooden ruler from her desk.

"Hold out your hand!"

There is a stinging pain across your palm, which travels like fire down into your arm.

"And the other one."

If anything, this hurts even more.

"Back to your seat!"

As you walk to the rear of the classroom, everyone's eyes are avoiding yours except Nina's, who for the first time is looking at you with an expression almost approaching interest.

After the bell rings for the end of the school day, two Aunts are waiting in the playground. Once you're all paired up, the crocodile makes its way through the gates and back towards Riddell.

Nina's hand around yours is tentative, there for appearances' sake but barely touching. You guess she knows how it's feeling.

"Are you alright?" she asks, when both Aunts' attention appears focused elsewhere.

You nod.

"Don't be different," Nina tells you. "Doesn't matter how, just don't." She briefly squeezes your fingers, utilising the tenderness for emphasis. "They don't like different."

The two of you play skipping rope until it's time for tea.

Nina's been here eighteen months, you discover, after her mum ran off with a soldier and drink got the better of her dad. You're not exactly sure what's meant by that, but you guess any story that's seen someone in through these gates won't be an easy listen, and so simply acknowledge her account with a sympathetic nod.

Your own mother's poorly, you tell her. But when she's well again, she'll come and get you, and then you'll both live together in a nice house, just like you did before.

Nina smiles but doesn't quite meet your eyes, as if reflecting on a tale heard many times before and in no doubt of its outcome.

As unfamiliar as everything still may be, there is a definite sense of unease as you enter the house and make your way to the dining room. A girl from your dormitory speaks softly to Nina and as you go through the door, she turns to you.

"Angela has six demerits," she tells you.

You're not sure who Angela is, but once seated there's no mistaking her. The girl you noticed before breakfast, washing her bed sheets and nightgown, is biting her lip and tears are in the corners of her eyes.

The meal is exactly the same as the previous night, except the liver is now a little tougher to chew. It's easier to get down, you discover watching those around you, when cut into tiny pieces and mixed with the abundance of potato provided.

"There will be an Assembly in the Common Room before evening free time," an Aunt announces, as your plates are collected by one of the girls on kitchen duty. While waiting for the breakfast tableware to be brought out for you all to set for tomorrow morning, Angela rises to a tap on the shoulder from an Aunt and is led out through the door.

You and Nina are amongst the last children to enter the Common Room. The others are sitting cross-legged on the floor facing the blackboard, in front of which has been placed the small vaulting horse you wondered about earlier. Angela stands beside it, tears flowing freely.

Uncle Jim enters the room, carrying a long, narrow case and he nods to the two Aunts. As he clicks open the latches, one Aunt lifts Angela and positions her facing downward over the padded top of the contraption, which you now realise has nothing whatsoever to do with PT. A wide leather strap fastens around her waist, holding her in place. Other straps fasten Angela's legs to the supports of the device, just above her knees and tightly enough for the flesh to bulge either side of where they bite in.

Meanwhile, Uncle Jim has removed two sections of bamboo cane from the case and screws them together into a three-foot length, one end fitted with a tight rubber grip and the other capped with six inches of shiny steel. He turns to the Aunts and nods.

One of them lifts Angela's pinafore up and over her hips, until it almost hangs from her shoulders, and with a large safety pin fastens it in place, while the other rolls her thin cotton pants down into a narrow band across the top of her legs. Both Aunts then move to the front, each taking hold of one of Angela's wrists with both hands. They appear to brace themselves.

You expect some sort of address from Uncle Jim, some admonition on the evils of sin or a warning concerning future behaviour, but with no further ado he positions himself behind Angela and begins.

The first blow cuts across her buttocks and there's barely time for the scream to die in her throat before the second lands an inch lower down. The third and fourth strokes cut the back of her thighs, as her arms are stretched to their full length by the Aunts and her legs beneath her knees kick wildly. Two final strokes are placed diagonally across each cheek.

Uncle Jim steps away and the Aunts release their grip. Angela's hands start to move behind her, where blood is starting to seep through the broken skin along the visibly reddening weals.

"Still!" barks one of the Aunts.

With a whimper, Angela hesitates and then lets them hang down loosely. Uncle Jim has unscrewed his cane and after placing it back into his case, he gives the Aunts a nod and leaves the room. From a cupboard is produced a glass jar containing a thick, white unguent. The Aunts smear this over not just visible injury, but the entirety of Angela's buttocks and upper thighs.

When seemingly satisfied, one of them turns to you all.

"Dismissed," she says, "and an early bedtime tonight, I think. That we may all reflect on the nature of sin and its inevitable consequences."

As you all rise and file singly out of the room, she begins to unbuckle the contraption's straps.

The other Aunt turns to the backboard, picks up the duster and carefully rubs out all the demerits against Angela's name.

'The hours drag and the years fly by', is a saying usually attributed to old age, but experience has taught you otherwise. What it's really about is being forgotten, when any given day of your life is no worse and no better than any other.

Nina, your first friend in the Home, is soon gone. Many of the children are 'boarded out', sent to live with families in other parts of the city, so you don't even see them again at school. They are supposed to be treated as sons and daughters, but those who do return bring tales of being little more than unpaid skivvies.

And there are occasional whispers of things much worse.

You are neither boarded out nor caned. At first, this puzzles you, until gradually the rationale becomes apparent. Unlike other children, you receive regular visits from various representatives of officialdom - as a deep trauma survivor you can be regarded as both a bright star in the firmament of social research and a wasteland to be picked over for psychological analysis. But both involve interviews with no Aunt or Uncle present and they are obviously chary of providing you with ammunition locked and loaded.

And equally, any prospective family would learn of your history and most would find it difficult to dismiss the thought that where there was one bad seed, might well be two.

Throughout these years you manage to cobble together some kind of education. Even at school, this is almost a process of osmosis, but in the Common Room there's a set of Victorian Encyclopaedias and a Collins English dictionary. Mostly knowledge from an age when much was regulated in finding its way into the public domain and that which interests you is often infuriatingly ambiguous. But you are able to construct some concept of life beyond these walls, albeit the scrappy worldview of the autodidact.

You wake one morning, after a night of stomach cramps, to feel a sticky warmth between your thighs. You pull back the bedsheets to discover your lower body wet with blood and start to scream. The other girls gather around staring, until Kath, an older girl, sends them away. She tries to calm you, but the hubbub has attracted an Aunt, who takes everything in at a glance and then tells you to follow her. She asks Kath to bring the sheets.

In the bathroom, the bedclothes and your nightgown go into a tub and Kath begins to scrub them. As the Aunt soaps you down, rinses you clean and towels you dry, she is almost kindly as she explains.

You're a woman now, you discover, and ever since Eve listened to the serpent in the Garden of Eden, all women carry that terrible sin with them. As a punishment, God makes every woman bleed one week out of four and the only time this stops is when she carries a child, as God rejoices in all new life and so spares her confinement this burden.

She hands the practicalities of dealing with this disquieting development over to Kath, with an instruction to 'take her down to the sanitary cupboard'. Once there, Kath retrieves a bundle of pads and straps, instructs you in their usage and then gets you set up with them.

"Don't worry," she reassures you. "It might seem scary at first, but after a while it's second nature."

Like a lot of things, you reflect.

CHAPTER THREE

Sally

"There's a gas bottle needs changing for number seventeen," said Grandpa. "And a shower tap is sticking in twenty-three."

"Okay" Sally nodded and began loading the Rascal pickup. She counted off sets of fresh bed linen and towels against today's departure sheet and, satisfied, headed back inside.

She rechecked the figures against the departures board to make doubly sure. Seven leaving and twelve arriving, but she'd done the five empty ones yesterday afternoon, while things had been quiet. Half an hour per caravan, swap over the Calor Gas cylinder - twenty-three was one of the changeovers so she'd check the taps once she'd finished.

"I should be back about two," she told her grandfather. "If you've a list for Bowdens by then, I'll head straight over there."

Bowdens was their local wholesaler in Truro. Theoretically it shouldn't need more than a weekly trip to stock up the site shop, but it only needed a few days of rain to keep the visitors shut away in their caravans and lodges - and out of the town's cafes and restaurants - to have them descending on the shelves like locusts.

"Okay, but check on Esme first, right?" Grandpa handed her a flask and a foil-wrapped package, still warm from the oven. "And don't just knock and leave them by the door. Make sure she's alright."

"Of course," Sally told him. "I always do."

* * *

Sally had known Esme for as long as she could remember and, as a little girl, been completely enchanted by her. Esme's ornate Gypsy caravan was a common sight in this part of Cornwall and to Sally it was something out of a fairy tale. Esme would lead the white mare harnessed to the caravan along country lanes from farm to farm, where there was usually some kind of work to be found for her and the corner of a meadow to pitch up overnight.

Occasionally Esme would find herself in a lay-by for the night and that's how Dad first got to meet her, soon after his promotion and the move to St Hannahs. When the lay-bys along the coast road were widened into Viewing Areas back in the eighties and overnight camping came at the expense of a heavy fine, Dad turned a blind eye to the little caravan parked discreetly to one side and told his officers to do the same.

That's when Sally came to know her. Returning from Truro or some other family outing, Dad would always pull over for a chat whenever he saw her. Sally and her sister would be allowed to feed the mare sugar cubes and then giggle as it nuzzled their faces. Esme had been God knows how old back then and her features had barely aged in the years since, but now, with her gait stiffened, her movements were noticeably more careful and precise.

It was last autumn when Dad had a word with Grandpa and headed off to find her. Esme had finally flickered up on Social Services radar and Dad understood better than most what boxes would be left unticked for a twenty something social worker dealing with someone who'd possibly been born in the previous century and still skinned a snared rabbit over a cooking pot for lunch.

He'd spent the best part of a day following Esme's trail across north Cornwall, finally catching up with her to offer a pitch at Petroc for the coming winter.

There'd be a few hours work in the kitchen for her meals if that's what she wanted, he told her, steering clear of any notions of charity, but if she didn't that was fine too, she'd be left alone. And in the spring, she could move on again. Dad was ready for an argument, had all manner of carrot and stick strategies in his head to get her in through the gates. But Esme made no protest, simply held him under her steady gaze until he'd finished speaking and then quietly nodded.

"You've never seen such sadness in a single gesture,"

Sally overheard Dad tell Mum that night. "But she knew I was right."

Esme arrived at Petroc a week later and, ignoring the touring pitches, found a grassy spot by the stream that bordered the edge of the site, where the mare could graze.

And had been here ever since. The mare, which must have been as ancient in her way as Esme, passed away a month into winter. Her heart had just worn out, the vet told them, and Esme had walked over to the stream and knelt down by the waters while he supervised her removal.

Dad offered to take Esme to the auctions at Truro Livestock Centre, but she'd simply given a sad shake of the head and they both knew, without a word being said by either of them, that this was where Esme's journey would also end.

* * *

"Oh, I almost forgot," said Grandpa, as Sally was halfway out the door. "This came for you."

He reached under the counter and held out an envelope. Taking it from her, Sally recognised the handwriting and her heart sank.

"Everything okay?" asked Grandpa, catching her expression.

"Yes." Sally gave a brief nod as she stuck it in her pocket. "Just something I have to sort out."

"You sure?"

She nodded. Sally knew Grandpa worried about her and Grandpa wasn't one of life's worriers.

"Right," he said. "See you at lunchtime. And don't forget Esme."

"I won't," Sally told him over her shoulder, stepping out through the door.

Sally steered the Rascal along the narrow road towards the static pitches, but with impatience getting the better of her, she pulled over to one side and switched off the engine. She took the letter from her pocket, slit the flap open with her nail, but as she unfolded it, she couldn't help but catch the drift of what Martin had written. *'I thought we had something special'* and *'Can I come and see you?'* registered before she had the sheets properly straightened out. Without even a pause, she refolded them and slid them back into the envelope.

And all in his tidy, carefully spaced hand, she reflected. At least there's passion to a scribble, which only reinforced her belief that what this was really about was dealing with a role he'd never in a million years expected to play.

She stuffed the envelope into her pocket. That Martin came with rumoured caveats was one of the reasons she'd played easy to get with him. If she was going to 'do it' - and it wasn't just peer pressure which had brought her to the conclusion that it was about time that she did - then she could do worse than a fun guy who had a reputation for fresh fields and pastures new after carving another notch on the bedpost.

And that was fine with Sally. Once she'd checked out everything was functioning as it should and grasped the basics of what to do with it, there'd be opportunity enough in the future to put it all to more emotionally invested usage.

At best, thought Sally, slipping the Rascal into gear and pulling away, he was like a spoilt little kid who's been told no to a shiny new toy that had caught his eye in a shop window. And now it was less about that toy and all about not being able to have it.

* * *

Sally parked alongside Esme's caravan. Picking up the tinfoil package and flask, she stepped down onto the grass. She missed the mare, who'd meander over at her own sweet pace and gently nuzzle Sally's cheek, knowing there'd always be an apple in her jacket pocket.

She rapped on the door. Not getting a response, she tried again, but heard no signs of movement from inside.

"Esme? It's Sally."

Still no answer.

Sally hesitated. She'd never before entered uninvited, but given the circumstances...

It took a few seconds for her eyes to adjust to the light, but when they did she let out a sigh of relief, only at that point realising that she'd been holding her breath. Esme was at the table at the end of the caravan, sitting upright with a cup and saucer in front of her.

Sally strode towards her.

"Esme," she said. "Sorry, but I did knock. I've brought…"

Sally broke off, staring.

Esme was rigid and although her eyes were open, they were unseeing. Sally reached out to touch her arm.

It was cold.

She needed to fetch Grandpa! He'll know what to do, he'll…

Sally's thoughts caught themselves at she stared at the table where Esme was sitting.

It had been set for two.

In the centre was placed a samovar, alongside a loaf of black bread. At the seat opposite Esme was a china cup and saucer, identical to the one in front of Esme and both only held damp tea leaves.

Esme never had visitors!

Slowly, she reached out and touched the cup by the empty seat with her fingers.

It was still warm.

Sally turned and fled.

Ted

Ted sat back in his chair and smiled at the other members of the interview panel. Coffee had just been served and most were adding milk to their cups or stirring in sugar and he was optimistic about being out of here before they'd need a refill.

"So," he said, "I think we can all agree that we've been fortunate enough to have to make a difficult decision from a choice of outstanding candidates."

Around the table it was mostly nods and smiles. Although, noted Ted, Dennis Nelson's was barely perfunctory, his attention focused on what appeared to be a doodle he was creating in his notepad.

"But we've also been fortunate enough," continued Ted, "to have a candidate who's more than proved her ability to fill this role. In the six months since she stepped in to…"

"Prunella Pozniak," said Dennis Nelson, so quietly that for a moment it seemed Ted would simply bulldoze right over the interruption, but then he stopped and stared at Dennis.

"I thought she was most impressive," continued Dennis and a few others nodded. Linda Haversham the most vigorously, Dennis noticed.

"She's rather young," said Ted, pulling the slim, cardboard folder labelled 'Ms Pozniak' from the pile in front of him and flipping back the cover. The rest of the panel did the same, after sorting through their own copies of the candidates' files. Dennis simply had to lift his notepad away from the file already open on the table.

"Is that a bad thing," asked Linda Haversham, the first time Ted recalled her speaking during the entire interview process, "if she has the experience?"

"*'Ms Pozniak has proven to be an outstanding member of staff throughout a period of great difficulties for this school,'*" read out Dennis. "*'I consider her one of the major factors in Greendales's route out of special measures and whilst wishing her* every success in her career, I would be extremely sorry to lose her.'"

Dennis looked up from the file.

"I know we can sometimes take references with a pinch of salt," he said and around the table there were a few wry smiles at past experience of being used as a dumping ground for incompetence. "But not when they're that glowing."

"She seemed to me," said Ms French, the other governor on the selection panel, "someone the children would find it easy to relate to."

"I don't doubt Gillian's abilities one bit," said Dennis, "but she's always struck me as being a little... Rigid, is perhaps the word I'm looking for."

"My own niece," said Linda Haversham, "suffers from dyslexia. It would be fair to say that she's not found Gillian Brown over supportive."

Ted had the sensation of shifting sands beneath his feet, of a grip loosening.

"Well," he said, "if that were..."

"And of course we have to consider all the factors here," interrupted Dennis, still in that infuriatingly quiet but reasonable tone.

"All the factors?" echoed Ted, staring at him.

"This is the third year running St Anne's has slipped down the league tables." Dennis shrugged. "The Governors have been fielding increasingly tough lines of questioning. It would be nice to show evidence that we were engaged in some out of the box thinking to resolve matters."

Ted found himself beginning to bristle.

"If you're suggesting that my staff are less than competent..."

"No one's suggesting anything of the sort, Ted," Miss French told him. "Only that sometimes, for expediency's sake, appearances matter more than substance."

"The teaching staff at St Anne's," continued Ted, still unwilling to let this go, "is amongst the best in the county."

"I wouldn't disagree with you," said Miss French. "But

you know, it's also exceedingly white."

And that's when Ted knew he had lost.

"We'll make Ms Pozniak our primary candidate," he said, slowly. "And offer the position to Gillian Brown in the event of her turning it down. Agreed?"

Around the table, all heads nodded.

Ted reached for his coffee.

He'd been right. It was still warm.

Amanda

Amanda was still deciding what to do with the weekend when her mobile rang. She'd been toying with either going into the office and running through everything once more, without the distraction - she hoped - of other people, or maybe taking the polar opposite approach and driving down to Brighton for a couple of days. Let the sea breeze blow away the cobwebs for a fresh start on Monday.

"Amanda Palmer," she answered.

"Good evening Ms Palmer, this is Brian Maddox."

There'd been so many names in such a varied context lately that it took Amanda a second or two to place him.

"You came to see me the other day," he reminded her. "In connection with…"

"Yes, of course," she broke in. "Please excuse me, my head's really not where it should be right now."

"Did you get any further with Christopher Franklyn?" he asked.

"No." She almost let out a sigh. "We can't find anything after the mid-eighties. I put in a request to Interpol a few days ago that I'm still waiting on."

"You might try Amsterdam," said Maddox softly.

"Amsterdam…?"

"After you left, I thought I'd ask around. You know, a call to those who were in the job back then, plus a few others you'd get the occasional whisper from." He hesitated. "I wouldn't bet the farm on it, but word is, from two separate sources, that he's running a bookshop there."

"I don't suppose you've a name or address to go with that?"

"Sorry. But I'd imagine the local force will be keeping tabs on just about anyone in that line of business, given the city's reputation. Seems likely that if he is there, he'll be on their radar. And that would fit in with his history - his wife's

Dutch, you know?"

"That would be..." Amanda ransacked her mind. "Karen?"

"Carin," said Maddox. "C-A-R-I-N."

"Right." Amanda took a deep breath. "That's brilliant. I really can't thank you enough for this."

"Glad to help." Maddox hesitated. "And look, if there's a problem with Chris - and I think we both know how skittish some people can get at being pulled back into a life they thought they'd put well behind them - then give him my number and ask him to call me. We always got on."

"Thanks, Brian."

"Good luck," he said.

"This is Mr and Mrs Needham," the Aunt tells you.

Over the last eight or nine years, it's not been unusual for an Aunt to bring you along to this office to meet people. Sometimes they're from what are called Child Welfare Services and carry clipboards and cheap biros. Others are younger, with cardboard folders stuffed with newspaper clippings and shiny blue xeroxed copies of forms filled out long ago, on which they scribble notes with a fountain pen. All have questions, all look at you in a manner you know they don't employ with other children and you're careful never to confound their expectations.

But these two are different and you immediately sense what's happening.

Even though he's seated, you can tell that Mr Needham is shorter than average. You've learnt to be wary of short men, payback at life cheating them in this manner tends to be directed at the defenceless rather than those they envy. He is round and soft where his wife is thin and sharp. Some fat men have a solidity to them, the sense that were you to collide you'd bounce straight off, but watching Mr Needham wobble in his chair like a jelly, you believe he'd simply roll you up as if you were a piece of fluff. Collide with Mrs Needham, she'd cut you right open and you catch a glint in her eye which tells you she'd probably enjoy that.

The words everyone are speaking rush by in a blur of fake smiles and nodding heads as you try to adjust to this new reality. A suitcase has already been packed for you. Obviously there is no time for the goodbyes and farewells of friends, only a last fleeting image of Riddell from the back seat of the Needham's car.

You remain silent throughout the journey. 'Speak only when spoken to' is one of the few rules created to impose discipline which is also a pretty good maxim for life in general and this is a silence the Needhams seem to have no compunction to break. It's a quick trip, twenty minutes or so, to a semi-detached house in an area which would appear to define 'suburbia'.

The word that enters your mind at this point is tidy. The front lawn gives the impression that no daisy or dandelion would dare pop up into its neatly mowed lines. The mock Tudor facade *displays no chipped brickwork or faded paint. The hallway would epitomise the expression 'A place for everything and everything in its place', while the two girls sitting side by side on the sofa, waiting to greet you, have the appearance of being recently worked over with a scrubbing brush.*

It is, you quickly learn as you are escorted around, a house of rules. In each room they hang from a hook on the door - 'All books and toys to be tidied away before leaving', 'Dirty cups and plates to be washed and dried immediately after use', 'No more than six inches of bathwater', 'No talking after lights out.'

'Lights out', you discover, takes place in an attic conversion atop a steep flight of stairs equipped with two sets of bunk beds. Both top tiers have the rumpled appearance of possession and so you take one of the lower ones and hope for continence.

Barbara and Valerie, you learn, are the names of your roommates. You indicate the fourth empty bunk with a questioning nod of your head.

"That was Helen," Barbara tells you, and there is something about the tone of her voice that gets your attention.

"She caused trouble," adds Valerie. "So now she's gone."

'Shipshape and Bristol fashion' isn't an expression you've come across before, but its meaning soon becomes clear enough. Your name is added to a shiny whiteboard in the kitchen, where each morning the three of you discover the day's allotted chores. There is nothing arduous about these - errands to the shops, light housework, laundry - although they do take precedent over homework on your return home from school each day. Only once they're completed are you allowed to go up to the bedroom with your school books.

Mr Needham is rarely seen other than at the evening meal. He seems content to let Mrs Needham run the household and it is indeed her handwriting that designates each day's tasks. But your first Saturday with the Needhams, there is an entry on the whiteboard that's not been there before, and in larger, printed capitals rather than Mrs Needham's flowing hand.

'ALLOTMENT', it reads against Barbara's and Valerie's names.

You're looking at it with a puzzled expression when Barbara and Valerie walk into the kitchen. Barbara comes to a sudden halt, Valerie's face visibly blanches. Then, without acknowledging you in any way, they turn and leave the room.

Mrs Needham keeps you busy all day long - scrub this, fetch that, nothing completed to her satisfaction, little assuaging her brusqueness. Only when Mr Needham returns with the two girls does she address you with anything approaching civility, handing you the basket of vegetables he's brought back and asking you to wash them in preparation for dinner. She tells Valerie and Barbara to go straight upstairs and clean themselves up, while Mr Needham retires to the living room with his pipe and the evening paper.

You've long learnt to 'keep yourself to yourself', to 'stay out of what doesn't concern you'. Yet, you have a sinking feeling that this is about to very much concern you.

Valerie and Barbara remain subdued for the rest of the evening.

"They worked really hard today," Mr Needham jovially informs his wife, "so no surprised they're tired out."

Mrs Needham seems less than convinced, but he carries on unabated.

"An early night for the pair of you," he continues and suggests that you and 'mother' can clear away the dishes and manage the washing up. Folding his napkin, he stands and leaves the dining room.

The silence he's left behind is unlike any you've ever experienced. No one will meet anyone else's eye. You sense that if they did, the flow of recriminations would be unstoppable.

Eventually, Mrs Needham rises and indicates the empty dishes and plates to you.

"Lets get these out of the way," she says and then turning to the girls, "You should both be up to your beds."

Silently, they leave the room, closing the door behind them.

You attempt conversation as you dry the dishes Mrs Needham washes, but she is away somewhere else entirely. As soon as you're finished, you excuse yourself and also make your way upstairs.

Barbara is under the covers, on her side facing the wall. Valerie sits at the dressing table. You try to catch her eye in the mirror, but she won't meet yours.

You lie on the bed and begin to read.

"When it's your name on the board to go down to the allotment with him," says Valerie, in a voice so quiet it almost startles, "just do what he wants." She still doesn't meet your gaze. "If you don't fight, he won't hurt you. And it's over quickly."

She turns away from you.

It proves to be good advice.

The next weekend your name is on the board. The week after that, Valerie's. Then yours again. And again. And again.

"That's how it started with Helen," says Barbara, out of the blue one night as the three of you lay in the dark. Everyone knows what 'it' is. "Every week. Until she couldn't stand it any longer and told a teacher."

"And...?" you ask.

"The school reported it." Valerie's tone is weary. "But he's a special constable, isn't he?" Her voice is almost a sigh. "So, they took Helen down to the police station and ganged up on her, kept on and on at her to say that she'd just been making up stories about him. And in the end she did, but then they got a doctor to examine her and when he found out she'd been interfered with, they had her put away. 'In need of care and protection,' was what they called it."

Their empathy, you understand, has its roots in guilt. While you are the sole object of his attentions, they will be left alone.

But what you haven't realised - and perhaps should have - is that his obsession with you is attracting attention from elsewhere.

The next day, when you arrive back - you still can't think of it as home - at the Needham's house, there is quite the reception committee waiting for you. One of the Aunts from Riddell,

Miss Smith who you know from Children's Welfare Services, a uniformed policeman and a stony faced Mrs Needham are all gathered around the kitchen table.

On which is a brooch, a ten shilling note and two half crowns. You see the scene that's about to play out as if it were already written word for word in your mind.

"Here she is," Mrs Needham hisses, "the little thief!"

The policeman stares at you sternly.

"Can you explain how these came to be found under your mattress?" he asks.

'Because she put them there' is the obvious answer, but you know how well that's likely to play out.

Instead, you hang your head in shame.

"I'm sorry," you say, softly.

The flash of surprise which flickers in Mrs Needham's expression is gone in a second, but the looks of contempt on the Aunt's face and dismay on Miss Smith's appear to be settling themselves in for a while. The policeman's impassive grim countenance is unchanged, all this probably no more than grist to the mill of his daily grind.

"You nasty, spiteful creature," spits the Aunt. "To repay charity and kindness in such a way."

"I'm sorry," you repeat.

"Well, sorry's not good enough." The Aunt is really getting into her stride now. "Believe you me, you're going to find out what happens to wicked little girls like you."

You already know exactly what happens to wicked little girls like you. But biting your lip, you look up at the policeman.

"I want to give the other things back too," you tell him, contritely.

"Other things?" he asks. "What other...?"

"I've nothing else missing," Mrs Needham breaks in, perhaps just too brusquely. "Only the brooch and the money from my purse."

"From people's houses." Your voice is almost a whisper. "Where I went to play."

"Dear Jesus!" erupts the Aunt and Miss Smith is genuinely distraught as she stares at you.

"Where are they?" asks the policeman.

"I hid them down at the allotment."

"The allotment?"

"We have to help Mr Needham with his vegetables," you explain. "I put them in the shed there."

"We'd better go and collect them, then," says the policeman.

"That's Bill's shed," says Mrs Needham, and the blood has noticeably drained from her face. "He's the only one with the key to it, so you'll have to wait until..."

"That's the key, there," you break in, pointing to where it hangs on its hook by the kitchen door and the look Mrs Needham gives you is like thunder.

The policeman reaches for it and nods towards Miss Smith.

"Make sure you're holding her hand all the way," he tells her, probably assuming that you've little left to lose and given the opportunity could outrun all three of them. "Don't worry Mrs Needham, you can wait here."

You see she is nothing but confusion now, slipping the coat she'd reached for back onto its peg. But you're the sole focus of everyone's attention and so this doesn't register with them.

Miss Smith's grip is firm but not painfully tight. It's a silent procession to the allotment and once there, you guide them to Mr Needham's shed. The policeman unlocks the door and, one by one, you follow him inside.

"Behind that," you say, pointing at a deck chair leaning against the far wall.

The policeman moves it to one side, revealing a shelved recess.

"What the...?"

He reaches down and lifts a tangle of lacy underwear. The two women both give you puzzled stares but then catch their breath as he also discovers a pair of handcuffs and a braided leather tawse. They come closer as he takes out a 35mm camera and a short, broad plastic cylinder.

"What's that?" asks the Aunt.

"A developing tank," he tells her. "For film."

The Aunt and the policeman turn to stare at you, but something else in the recess has caught Miss Smith's eye, and she retrieves a large envelope. Reaching inside, she pulls out a handful of prints. As she examines them, her expression is initially one of bafflement. Then comprehension dawns and with a small cry she lets everything fall to the ground as her hand flies to her mouth.

The Aunt kneels down and gathers the photographs back into the envelope. On rising, she sees the policeman is now holding a plastic cylinder, perhaps six inches long, an inch in diameter and one end gradually curving inwards to a point. He presses the base and it begins to hum. Quickly, he shuts it off again.

Miss Smith turns away from them, leans forward and vomits. The policeman fixes you with an almost accusatory stare.

"I thought you said that..." he starts, but then breaks off with an uncertain shake of his head.

You give a small shrug.

"I know," you say, meekly, looking him in the eye. "But perhaps I was confused... Maybe it was all just a bad dream."

Everyone's back outside, fresh air is being gulped down.

Miss Smith has regained almost all of her composure, but there remains a pallor about her. Your hand is in hers again, the grip still tight but now more protective than custodial.

"There'll be no more talk of theft," she is saying. "This is a child in dire need of protection and I will be applying for a court order to that effect first thing in the morning."

"She should come back to Riddell for the..." begins the Aunt slowly, but Miss Smith rounds on her furiously.

"She is going nowhere," she snaps. "She is staying with me."

The Aunt falls silent under Miss Smith's stare.

"Exactly how many children, over the years, have Riddell entrusted to the Needhams?" continues Miss Smith icily.

Without waiting for a reply, she turns to the policeman. There's nothing indifferent about his expression now.

"And I believe you have a job of your own to be getting on with, officer?"

He stares at her, then down at you, before nodding his head.

Miss Smith fastens her grip on your hand even tighter and neither of you spare a backward glance as she leads you out of hell.

The courtroom isn't nearly as scary as you'd expected. There's no dock, witness box or judge on high, wigged and gowned. The three magistrates are at a raised bench, but you sit at a table with Miss Smith and there is no one else present. You're aware that Miss Smith has argued, because of the disturbing nature of the circumstances which have brought you here, that the public and press should be excluded from the proceedings, a condition to which the court has agreed.

The presiding magistrate is a lady in her early fifties. Her colleagues are two men, both perhaps a decade older. It becomes obvious she at least has spent time familiarising herself with the case, as her initial questioning of Miss Smith is solely concerned with the progress of the enquiry concerning the failure of various departments. Satisfied that all seems to be moving ahead in a satisfactory manner, she turns her attention to you.

"That you're a child in need of protection is in no doubt," she tells you, not unkindly. "And I find it appalling that the system tasked with ensuring that has failed you so dreadfully. I'm equally appalled that the options available today for us to remedy this are so limited and, to be frank, so inappropriate." She pauses for a second. "But we must deal with this as we must."

Miss Smith begins to speak, but the magistrate raises her hand, silencing her.

"I believe we need some kind of psychological assessment here, to both determine the degree of harm done and to establish a path forward. For obvious reasons, I'm reluctant to send you back into an institution which you'll most likely be testifying against in the near future." She pauses again. "I'm equally reluctant to place you in a psychiatric unit, on however temporary a basis."

She begins a low but earnest discussion with her two fellow

magistrates. After perhaps less than a minute, she gives a sharp nod and turns back to you.

"As an initial course of action, we're committing you to an Approved School. Do you know what that is?"

"No, Madam." You've been versed in the appropriate forms of address by Miss Smith.

"Essentially, it is a boarding school for young people who have been deemed, in some way, to have lost direction. This can involve breaking the law in a non serious manner or through a variety of circumstances finding themselves in need of care." She sighs. "I have my own views on a system which treats both victims and perpetrators in the same fashion, but that's by the by."

She gathers papers together in front of her.

"But I can assure you this case will receive the utmost priority, with a view to an early, and entirely appropriate, resolution."

You bob your head towards her.

"Thank you, Madam."

She smiles and all three magistrates rise from the bench.

CHAPTER FOUR

Amanda

Amanda was in the office, working backward through her notebooks. Five years ago, two Dutch drug squad officers were in London tracking down a Turkish dealer who'd shot dead a colleague during a drugs bust that went sideways at Rotterdam docks. Amanda had pulled out all the stops to help, turned a blind eye more than once to the finer points of national jurisdiction and they'd had their man in handcuffs on a plane to Schiphol by the end of the week. Their gratitude had been profuse and genuine...

She found the number.

"Goedemorgen," replied Amanda to whatever she'd just been greeted with. "Spreek je Engels?"

"Yes, good morning," came the reply.

"My name is Detective Inspector Amanda Palmer, I'm with the London Metropolitan Police and I'm trying to contact Boij Vissen."

"One moment, please."

Amanda could hear the woman speaking away from the mouthpiece and then she was back.

"I'm afraid he is out of the office right now," she told Amanda. "Is this matter urgent - could another officer help?"

No and yes were probably the honest answers to that, but she guessed things would run a lot smoother if Boij was on her case.

"Look," said Amanda, "I understand that you can't give his details out over the phone. But would you call him - I'm sure he'll remember me - and ask him to ring either my office or cellphone?"

There was just a moment's hesitation.

"Of course," she said. "Let me have the contact numbers."

After Amanda hung up, she considered calling Kendall but decided to hang on until she definitely had Franklyn in her sights. But God knows how long there'd be to wait and she'd been in such a hurry to get into the office that she'd skipped breakfast. Maybe slip out to that delicatessen along the street, she could…

Her mobile rang.

"Amanda Palmer."

"Amanda. Boij Vissen here. What can I do for you?"

"Bloody hell, Boij, that was quick."

He laughed.

"We are all slaves to technology now, Amanda. There is no escape for any of us, even on the golf course. You're keeping well?"

"Yes, thanks. And sorry about this, but I'm after some information in a hurry and I didn't want to get bogged down going through official channels."

"You were never really one for 'official channels' as I recall," said Boij dryly and Amanda could picture the smile on his lips.

"What do you need to know?" he asked.

"I'm trying to find someone named Christopher Franklyn," she told him. "He's not wanted, but we believe he may inadvertently have information relating to a case we're working. We've heard he runs a bookshop in Amsterdam. His wife, Carin, is Dutch and the wedding ceremony probably took place in the Netherlands, but we don't know her family name. And I'm afraid that's it."

"Right, I'll get someone on it," said Boij. "Keep your cellphone nearby."

The line went dead.

Amanda did have time to make the delicatessen before he got back to her, but only just. She was about to unwrap the grease paper from a salami sandwich when her mobile began ringing.

"Okay, Amanda. The guy you are looking for is the proprietor of a business called Gallery de Witt, on a street named Bloemgracht in central Amsterdam. That's a pretty smart address, a stone's throw from the Anne Frankhuis. He also owns an apartment near Vondelpark so he's definitely making a lot more than I am. We've phone numbers for both. I can tell you that he's not a person of interest to local law enforcement, so I'd guess he's either clean or clever. Give me the fax number where you are and you'll have all we've got in the next ten minutes."

"Thanks Boij, I really appreciate this." She read the number off the fax machine to him.

"Will you be coming over to interview him?"

"I... "Amanda realised she hadn't thought that far ahead yet. "I'm not sure."

"Let me know if you do," said Boij. "We'll have dinner and I'll show you a side of this city no tourist ever gets to see."

"In that case," smiled Amanda, "I'll definitely be twisting my boss's arm."

She rang off and immediately dialled Kendall's mobile.

"We've found Franklyn," she told him.

Jack

Jack pulled into the Viewing Area, switching off the lights and siren as he parked. Tom had already taped off a section large enough for the Air Ambulance to set down and Jack paused before getting out, taking in the scene.

Tina's first call had been routine, someone found collapsed by a car along the Truro road, paramedics were attending and Tom was about three minutes out. Initially, it looked a medical emergency, but she'd update him when she had more.

Her next call was more urgent. Tom had run a NPR check and the car came back registered to a Richard Hanson, who had a local address. Tom was waiting for ... Tina broke off for a second. The paramedics were calling in the Air Ambulance, she told him. And they'd also discovered a blow to the head, recent but they couldn't determine whether it was pre or post collapse.

"I'm on my way," Jack told her.

As far as Jack was concerned, justice wore a blindfold for all but some incidents you approached with a touch more caution than others. He'd never met Richard Hanson, but did know of him. Whenever anyone new took up residence or started a business in St Hannahs, Jack ran them through the PNC. It was the sort of place, his predecessor had told him, which attracts those needing to keep their head down or looking for a fresh start and it never hurt to have your card marked as to why.

The Hansons hadn't triggered any warning bells. The wife had a conviction for possession of marijuana going back thirty years, a West London magistrates' court, Jack noted, and the husband a few speeding fines. Cliff Dene, the house they'd bought, was one of the most expensive properties in town and over the following months he'd picked up - St Hannahs being what it was - that they'd made their money in computers.

He'd also learnt that they were friends with Lee Munro, the actress - actor, you had to say now days, he corrected himself - who'd had an interest in The Grange before her career moved from the BBC to Hollywood. Still did, apparently, although it was no longer a hotel but ran residential courses for business executives.

All of which meant that Richard Hanson was well connected enough for Jack to make doubly sure that everything went by the book here. If there was even a hint of foul play...

He let that train of thought go as Tom raised a hand in greeting, then opened the door and stepped out. The only vehicles not belonging to the emergency services were an old VW campervan, one of the earlier split screen models with a V shape on the front, and a restored sixties Jaguar saloon, which Jack recognised from around town but hadn't realised belonged to Richard Hanson.

A woman he'd put in her late forties was standing alongside the camper, watching the paramedics as they tried to resuscitate the figure on the ground. As Jack made his way over to them, Tom walked towards him.

"So, what exactly do we have here?" Jack asked him.

"The lady in the campervan had stopped to make a phone call," said Tom. "She saw the Jag pull in but then moved behind the van, out of the sunlight so she could read the screen in the shade. When she turned around, he was collapsed by the car. She went over, he was unconscious, she dialled nine nine nine."

"She didn't try to move him?"

"She told me that if he hadn't been breathing, she'd have tried CPR." Tom shrugged. "As things were, she just kept an eye on him until the ambulance got here."

Jack nodded towards where the paramedics were working.

"And that's definitely Richard Hanson?" In this job, you learnt not to make assumptions.

"According to the driver's licence in his wallet."

"And what about that bruise on his head?"

"He might have banged it going down, but there's blood on his collar and not on his face, so maybe he had a chance to wipe it off. Then again, how he was lying on the ground, that could have been the way it flowed. Plus, robbery doesn't seem likely - he had two thousand in cash on him."

That got Jack's attention.

"Really?"

"In an envelope, jacket pocket. Which suggests..."

Tom let the sentence trail off and Jack slowly nodded. Two thousand wasn't exactly pin money, even in the circle Richard Hanson moved in, and the envelope implied it being earmarked for a definite purpose. Finding out what for might go a long way to explaining what had happened to him.

"Has his family been contacted?"

Tom shook his head.

"No. Tina phoned the house but got no reply."

"Okay." Jack considered. "Tell her to hang fire, I'll..."

Jack broke off at the sound of the approaching helicopter and looked up.

The air ambulance came in fast and low. There was none of the slow hovering descent usually associated with a landing and the doors were open before it touched the ground. Two paramedics carrying a stretcher joined their colleagues and there was an urgent exchange as Richard Hanson was lifted onto it and strapped down. They were back in the helicopter before the blades had finished spinning and then, with a roar, the engine fired up again. In a whirlwind of dust and sand they were gone.

One of the paramedics from the ambulance walked over to Jack and they exchanged nods. During the holiday season it was a rare few days that went by without their paths crossing, generally down to ill-advised combinations of alcohol and rip currents or sea cliffs.

"They're taking him to Derriford," he told Jack,

confirmation of how seriously they were treating this. The Royal Cornwall at Treliske was their local hospital, Derriford at Plymouth was the major trauma centre for the entire southwest peninsula.

"What can you tell me?" asked Jack.

"Most likely a stroke," he said, "but we can't be sure. Hence..." He nodded in the direction of the departing air ambulance and Jack understood what he was saying. The quicker a stroke received treatment, the less serious the outcome. "Definitely not a coronary."

"There was also a head injury?"

"Could have whacked it going down, although I wouldn't have thought that would cause a concussion, so..." He shrugged. "I'd say that one's a mystery for you to solve."

"Right. Okay, thanks."

With a nod, the paramedic walked over to where his colleague was loading their equipment back into the ambulance. Tom was taking down the tape and so Jack headed over to the campervan.

"Thanks for your prompt action," he said. "Ms...?"

"Weaver. Gail Weaver," she told him, giving a self-deprecating shrug. "All I did was call nine one one."

American by the sound of her.

"Even so - where he'd fallen, behind his car, he wouldn't have been spotted from the road. He was lucky you were here." Jack paused. "You'd pulled in to use your phone, I understand?"

She nodded.

Jack looked pointedly over her shoulder into the camper, where both an unmade bed and a table with the remnants of a meal on it could clearly be seen.

"Nice van," Jack told her. "You don't usually see ones that age in such good condition. Yours?"

"A rental."

"You're on holiday here?"

Just the slightest hesitation.

"Yeah. And when I heard about the eclipse, I thought I'd

check it out."

"Have you anywhere to stay?"

She slowly shook her head.

"With this being August - and the eclipse - pretty much everywhere is fully booked." He gazed over her shoulder again, into the van. "And as you're probably aware, there's a hefty fine for staying overnight in a Viewing Area."

Jack reached into his pocket and took out his notebook and pen. He saw her expression tighten as he began to write.

"But head along the road for about a mile and a half, and you'll come to a holiday park and campsite called Petroc." He ripped the page out and handed it to her. "If you give them this and tell them Sergeant Vanner sent you, they'll see you alright."

"I..." She managed to get the confusion out of her voice. "Thank you, Sergeant."

"Enjoy your stay here, Ms Weaver," Jack told her.

He left her staring at the sheet of paper and walked back to the car. He clicked on the radio.

"I'm heading over to Cliff Dene," he told Tina. "If Mrs Hanson's not at home, there may be a neighbour with an idea of where she is. In the meantime, if you hear anything more about her husband's condition then let me know, okay?"

"Will do," said Tina.

Jack switched on the engine and pulled away towards the road.

Amanda

Venables was the last to arrive.

From the background sounds Amanda had picked up from his mobile, she guessed he'd been on the sidelines at a school soccer match and his appearance in a tracksuit seemed to confirm this. It was hard to think of him as a family man, switching back and forth between this world and the normality of dinner parties and parent teacher evenings. She knew how much police work took its toll - Amanda hadn't worked with many colleagues still on their first marriage - but the necessity of keeping dark secrets from even those you love had to come with a price. That alone, she reflected, could likely prove the thin end of a very insidious wedge...

"So, where are we?" he asked, sitting down.

They were gathered around the table in what had once been a conference room. Leaning forward and resting her elbows on the polished surface, Amanda brought everyone up to speed on Brian Maddox's phone call and what she'd learnt from Boij.

"The Dutch were pretty quick off the mark there, weren't they?" asked Venables. "Think they've an eye on him themselves - running an Amsterdam bookshop does suggest a shady line of work."

Amanda shook her head.

"Boij Vissen says not," she told him.

"And you believe him?"

"Yes." Amanda shrugged. "I've known him a while and he owes me from... From when he was last in London."

"Okay." Venables slowly nodded and then looked at Kendall. "How do you want to play this?"

"It seems we have two options," said Kendall. "We either call him or turn up on his doorstep." He stared at Amanda. "What would your slant on it be, DI Palmer?"

"If Franklyn is into something dodgy over there,"

Amanda's tone was cautious, "being doorstepped by the Met means he's more likely to clam up than cooperate. Plus, it's not like we have any jurisdiction. If we get off on the wrong foot and he tells us to take a hike, there wouldn't be a lot we could do about it."

"So...?" Venables was staring at Amanda.

"My instinct is to play it as straight as we can," Amanda told him. "I'll call, tell him I run a cold case unit and that I'm looking into something we believe happened in Notting Hill back in the seventies. That I can't go into details over the phone, but after speaking to Brian Maddox we think he might have information which could help us." She met Venables's stare. "I had the impression from Maddox that the two of them used to get on. If Franklyn starts getting cagey, I'll offer to give him Maddox's phone number to check me out. When we spoke, he told me he'd be okay with that."

"Maybe mention that anyway," said Kendall. "I don't see how it can hurt."

"I'll also emphasise that he's not a suspect, or even a person of interest, in our investigation. Then ask if we could meet in Amsterdam."

Venables looked around the table.

"We all happy with that?" he asked.

Everyone nodded and Amanda picked up the phone, read the number from Boij's fax and dialled.

"We'll try his home first." The dial tone filled the room as she switched to speakerphone. "If not, then..."

She broke off as a female voice answered.

"Goedemiddag."

"Goedemiddag," replied Amanda. "Would it be possible to speak with Christopher Franklyn?"

"Sure," said the woman. "May I ask who's calling?"

The delivery was fluent, but the slightest trace of an accent suggested she was Dutch. Probably Franklyn's wife, thought Amanda.

"My name is Amanda Palmer," she told her. "Mr Franklyn

doesn't know me."

"Okay... Give me a second and I'll try to find him."

"Thank you," said Amanda, but there was already a clunk as the phone was laid down. From a distance she heard, "*Kit!* Telephone."

After a short pause came the sound of approaching footsteps, then "Hello?"

"Mr Franklyn?" asked Amanda.

"Yes."

"I'm Detective Inspector Amanda Palmer. We've never met, but do have a mutual acquaintance. Brian Maddox?"

There was silence for a few seconds.

"Well," he said softly. "There's a name I haven't heard for a while."

"So I understand," said Amanda. "He sends his regards, by the way."

"Right..."

"Mr Franklyn." Amanda took a breath. "I run a cold case unit in the Met. We're currently investigating events alleged to have taken place in the early seventies. Our inquiries led us to ex Chief Superintendent Maddox, who suggested that we speak to you. I want to emphasise that we don't believe you've any involvement in what we're looking into, simply that your... situation at that time, shall we say, puts you in a unique position to be of assistance."

"I see," said Franklyn, hesitantly. "So, what exactly are we talking about here?"

"I'm afraid I can't go into details over the telephone." She hesitated. "I'd like to come over to Amsterdam to discuss this further." She looked over at Kendall. "If, for any reason, that's not feasible, then we'd be prepared to cover expenses for you to travel to London."

Kendall nodded.

"It must be pretty damn important," said Franklyn slowly, "for you to be fishing around in thirty year old memories."

Amanda allowed herself a tight-lipped smile.

"As I said, Mr Franklyn, I can't go into detail over the phone."

Another silence.

"Actually," continued Franklyn, "I'm in London tomorrow."

"Really!" Amanda tried to keep the surprise out of her voice as eyes widened around the table.

"I'm staying with friends in Cornwall later in the week," he told her. "For the eclipse. But I'll be in London for a couple of days first. There're one or two things there that need my attention."

"I doubt," said Amanda carefully, "this would take up more than an hour or so of your time."

"I've arranged to see people tomorrow afternoon and evening," said Franklyn, "but I could do Monday morning."

"Thank you Mr Franklyn, I really appreciate it. Do you have a mobile number?"

"I do, but I think it's unlikely to work in the UK." He paused. "I'm staying at the Russell, in Bloomsbury. Why don't I call you after I've checked in and we'll take it from there?"

"Sure. Do you have a pen handy?"

Amanda gave him her number and hung up.

"Right," said Venables, rising from his chair. "Let's see if I can make the second game."

"I'll walk out with you," Kendall told him. "I had a thought earlier today that I'd like to run by you."

"Is everything okay?" DS Sule asked Amanda after they'd left.

"Sorry?"

"You seem pensive."

"Hmm." Amanda shook her head. "I'm not sure. That all seemed a little too easy."

"Easy?"

"You get a phone call out of the blue from a complete stranger about a very dubious episode in your past and you're just... Oh, I don't know."

"Mentioning Maddox probably helped?"

"Perhaps." Amanda shrugged. "Let's see what he's like on the other side of the interview table. Anyway, how's it going with the missing persons files?"

"Slowly," DS Sule told her. "It really doesn't seem to have been a priority back then." She sighed. "At least, not unless there's actual evidence of foul play involved. Mostly the assumption is kids running away from home or women escaping abusive relationships, with little by way of coordination between different forces."

"And then a flurry of everyone covering their own arses if a body turns up."

DS Sule gave a tight smile.

"Exactly."

"You know," said Amanda, "there is another possibility. The Family Tracing Service, run by the Salvation Army. It's mainly for reuniting long-lost relatives rather than actual missing persons, but it might be worth a shot."

"Right," said DS Sule. "I'll get onto them."

"I've a contact there," Amanda told her. "We used them once or twice in the Cold Case Unit, I'll email you the details." She paused. "Are you staying?"

"Thought I'd go through the files one more time."

"Okay," nodded Amanda. "But if you find yourself going around in circles, take a break, alright?"

"Sure," said DS Sule.

Extract from unpublished B.Ed thesis, Bristol University, 1966.

A—— arrived at Fairholme under a care and protection order issued by a magistrate's court.

In terms of admissions to Girls' Approved Schools, this is by far the norm, with 65% of girls committed deemed to be beyond parental control or in moral danger, and only 35% guilty of an actual offence. The corresponding figure for boys is 95% offenders, but the fact that, regardless of the reason for their admission, almost all adolescent girls arrive with a history of sexual immorality, goes a long way to redress those statistics in the minds of those whom one might have hoped to have gained a more forward-thinking perspective. Rather than their being regarded as victims of societal circumstance, the prevalent view is invariably that weakness of character leans toward promiscuity as a lifestyle of choice.

Court papers and Department of Children's Services reports - made available to us prior to her arrival - revealed that at an early age A—— had been subjected to extreme emotional trauma. The nature of this I choose not to reveal in this paper, the circumstances involved were so unique as to almost certainly negate her anonymity should I do so. As a result of this, she was placed with the Cottage Children's Homes, where she resided for eight years before finding a placement.

It was subsequently discovered that there had been long-term incidences of sexual abuse in the household where she found herself. At the time of A——'s admission, the husband was in custody, awaiting trial at the Court of Assizes.

While medical examination revealed that A—— was still virgo intacta, photographs retrieved by the authorities suggested the husband had been insidious enough to satisfy himself in a manner which would deny potential accusations any tangible physical evidence. The presiding magistrate at A——'s hearing had requested a psychological assessment be conducted without delay and an appointment with the Visiting Psychiatrist was scheduled *for the day following her admission.*

In my role during this period as Relief Instructress, my official duties amounted to little more than filling in for other members of staff during annual leave, weekends, or periods of illness. However, the headmistress invariably tasked me with greeting and settling in all new arrivals, the thinking behind this doubtless being that my closeness in age to these girls would create a more empathetic and less intimidating impression of the world they were about to enter.

At this point, a digression into the typical nature of our admissions may prove instructive. Although they ranged from feral runaway to wayward grammar school girl, it would be more accurate to regard this a Gaussian bell curve rather than spectrum, the two examples cited more outliers than end markers in an equally measured series of distinctions.

The girls' ages ranged from fourteen to seventeen. Roughly twenty-five per cent were of the lower age, forty the upper, with the balance evenly split between fifteen and sixteen-year-olds. Most of these girls had made several court appearances prior to their committal and, as previously noted, the majority of these related to care and protection issues rather than criminal activity.

In terms of family history, it will probably come as no surprise to learn that they were from a predominantly working class background. To break that down more specifically, around thirty per cent were from what might be termed deprived homes (dependent on Welfare Services), twenty-five per cent from 'good' homes and thirty-five per cent from council tenancies. With six per cent of girls coming from rural areas, only four per cent of girls could be classified as having a suburban or 'middle class' home environment.

In my experience, those were the ones to watch out for.

The illegitimacy rate of the girls admitted was a fairly consistent fifteen per cent. While the number of girls who had grown up in homes with the father permanently absent was almost impossible to discover, I don't believe that twenty per cent would be an overestimate.

In terms of academic ability, only twenty-five per cent of the girls had a reading age equal to or above their chronological age, with sixty per cent one to four years below that and fifteen per cent at primary school level or lower.

With regard to sexual aberration, irrespective of age around seventy-five per cent of the girls committed had had sexual intercourse, with perhaps a further ten per cent having indulged in sexual activity during which actual intercourse was unlikely. Some twenty-five per cent of girls admitted - or returned after absconding - needed treatment for gonorrhoea, syphilis or trichomonas vaginalis, conditions invariably accompanied by scabies and pubic lice. The latter two infections could be dealt with by the nurse, but, with no visiting venereologist, treatment for venereal disease necessitated an escorted journey for the girls in question by public transport to the General Hospital. Every such group excursion during my time at Fairholme resulted in at least one further abscondion, somewhat defeating the long-term purpose of these visits.

For the most part, the girls lived up to the impression created by the preliminary reports we received from the probation services. We became depressingly adept at assessing which girls, with the right degree of help, had a realistic chance of getting their lives back on track and those to whom we would merely be an interim stop on the journey to a Mother and Baby Home or Borstal.

A——'s arrival was reassuring. The absence of indicators all staff learnt to keep a watchful eye for - belligerence, wariness, artfulness, ingratiation - always allows for, if not a moment of relaxation, then at least a dissipation of tension.

In appearance, she was of average height and slim build, conventionally pretty with small, regular features. She moved in a casual, easy manner which suggested confidence with no air of truculence - so many of our arrivals were more than ready to square up against the world. Other than when responding to questions, she kept her eyes downcast - not unusual in girls from an institutional background - but when she raised them, one did catch a definite glint.

I escorted her to the dormitory she had been designated. Based on the reports we had received, it was felt that she would settle in better with the few grammar school girls currently resident. I helped unpack her suitcase and informed her that should she be in need of any items of clothing to come and see me in the morning. Until recently, gymslips had been mandatory, but this rule had now been relaxed for the older girls, the assumption being that age appropriate dress would prove an aid to self-confidence. I showed her the bathroom and lavatories, explained how sanitary matters were dealt with, and then took her downstairs where dinner was about to be served. I introduced her to three of the girls she would be sharing the dormitory with, grouped together on one table, before taking my place with the other members of staff who were dining at Fairholme that evening.

There is inevitably a process of 'sizing each other' up whenever a new girl arrives, a situation which can prove a flash point if two girls perhaps have a history from a previous establishment. But A——'s integration passed without incident. I noticed a few looks in her direction that could have been taken as challenging, but which she chose to ignore, occupied with what seemed to be easy conversation at the table where she was seated.

After the evening meal, I took her to the headmistress's office for her initial interview. Cognisant of A——'s history, her manner was less brusque than I had known her to be in the past and was concluded by her wish that A——'s stay with us would be a productive one.

Escorting her back to the Common Room, I explained how the days here were structured.

The girls were woken at 7.30 am. Those with morning duties rose thirty minutes earlier, to lay the tables in the dining room and prepare breakfast for 8.30 am. The headmistress would hold an Assembly at 9.00 am in the Hall, comprising a hymn, prayers and the announcement of any changes to the day's work details. Every Friday, prefects for the coming week were selected, based on staff *assessments of demeanour or - where relevant - academic effort, this position being signified by a yellow ribbon.*

Schooling for girls aged fifteen and under began at 9.30 am and continued until 12.30 am. Girls who wished to study for their General Certificate of Education could apply to do so, but this was usually only granted to those who had arrived with a proven academic background, essentially a grammar school. Few elected to do so. To say this was a classroom of mixed abilities would be something of an understatement and most would find themselves nonplussed to be working through Latin declensions whilst seated next to an exact contemporary being coached through a Janet and John primer. A suggestion that perhaps our pupils should be grouped on the basis of ability rather than age was met with the observation that 'these girls are not going to become teachers or doctors'. Older girls were given duties in the kitchen, laundry and grounds, although one morning a week they would attend a Housewifery class.

Following lunch, their afternoons would be taken up with outdoor sport - rounders or netball - if the weather were clement, needlework or quilting if it were not. Dinner was at 5.00 pm, after which those girls not on that evening's twice weekly bath rota would read quietly or play board games. Interviews with the Housemistress could be held relating to issues raised by either party and the nurse was available in sick bay during this period until lights out.

There was no all night monitoring of the girls' dormitories. Experience had shown that if a girl wished to abscond for an evening's dubious pleasures, short of handcuffing her to the bed and installing bars on the windows, she would invariably find a way to do so. But duty staff were also cognisant that if homesickness were waiting to strike, then bedtime was the likeliest opportunity for it to do so. They would maintain a quiet presence on the landings during the cacophony of final settling down, one ear tuned for the more subtle tones of distress.

Before leaving A—— in the Common Room, I informed her that an interview had been arranged with the Visiting Psychiatrist for the following morning, as at the magistrate's request. Did she have any questions regarding this? I enquired, but she simply shook her head.

Wishing her a good night, I waited by the door until, with a tentative smile, she joined the girls she had been seated with during dinner.

Not many issues created as much division amongst the staff at Fairholme as the psychological assessment of our girls. It was an understandably difficult area, particularly before it became policy that the role of Visiting Psychiatrist should always be filled by a female. However lacking an education and social skills, few can demonstrate greater ability to disconcert an authoritative male than a wilful adolescent girl.

As well as interviews, conducted in the headmistress's office where the girl might have a sense of privacy, a variety of tests had been employed at one time or another with varying results. Least successful - and most derided by staff and girls alike - was the Rorschach inkblot test. Regardless of its supposed ability to gain insight into the deeper processes of the mind, in this setting it proved little more than an opportunity for the girls to amuse themselves at authority's expense.

'Looks like someone shat themselves, Miss,' or 'Is it a fanny, Miss?' are two of the more repeatable responses from girls who instinctively understood they would not be held responsible for the supposed workings of their subconscious. Whilst cooperation was not always necessary to formulate an accurate assessment - indeed, negative attitudes in themselves were often revealing - more constructive methodologies were sought.

Perhaps the most successful of those was sentence completion. The girls were given a list of fifty phrases, each beginning a sentence and then left alone with pencil and paper to continue them. The opening dozen or so were innocuous enough to have them scribbling away at a brisk pace before moving into areas such as 'My father - ', 'Love - ', 'I wish - ', *and* 'I am embarrassed by - '.

This proved to be remarkably insightful, occasionally quite movingly so. The conclusion was that a feeling of not being monitored as they worked through the questions to the beat of their own minds - even perhaps a sense that this wasn't actually a test at all - contributed to a degree of obvious honesty these girls would rarely have displayed in almost any other interaction.

The session usually concluded with a Stanford-Binet IQ test, generally regarded as no more than a depressing formality. Only around fifteen per cent of the girls scored higher than the median hundred, although one could qualify that by taking into account a lack of literacy, which in many cases impeded their actual understanding of the questions.

The Visiting Psychiatrist arrived at 10.00 am and I collected A—— from the laundry, where she was temporarily assigned duties. Unlike many of the girls who, when in the sole company of a member of staff, either blatantly crave attention or display sullen resentment, her demeanour was placid. I asked how she had slept the previous night and if she felt she was settling in well. She answered to both in the affirmative without elaborating further.

I was to remain in the office throughout A——'s assessment. It was not unknown for a process which inevitably drew sublimated trauma to the surface to turn confrontational and, on rare occasions, violent. The presence of a third party - as much to bear witness to how such a situation developed as to aid physical restraint - was, if not mandatory, then advisable.

The interview began with a gentle questioning of the emotional trauma she was subjected to as a young child, of which I alluded to earlier. I won't go into the details discussed other than to say that A——'s recollection of these events was vivid, yet accompanied by little evidence of the distress one might have expected to surface whilst reliving such experiences.

The psychiatrist then moved on to her life under the auspices of the Child Welfare Services. Did she consider herself to have been well treated? Had she made friends easily? Treated better than most, was her cautiously candid reply, the implication that her being a case study for students of both sociology and psychiatry - her history was the subject of at least one PhD thesis - her current welfare and state of mind were still being constantly monitored from beyond her immediate supervision. As regards friends... A—— responded with a casual shrug. You learnt not to get too close. Few people were in your life for any length of time. The psychiatrist and I exchanged glances, not because of any sense of self pity or regret in this observation, but at her offhand acceptance of it being simply the way things were.

The psychiatrist moved onto the case that brought her before the court. Perhaps she could tell us, in her own words, exactly what had happened?

At that point, we were interrupted. A fight had broken out in the kitchen between two girls, one of whom had discovered that the other had been sneaking out at night to see a local boy, who had led her to believe that she was the sole object of his affections. I knew the aggressor of this incident well and had calmed her down during previous altercations created as a result of slights, real or imagined.

The psychiatrist nodded towards the door and I rose, neither of us seriously believing that she would be put at risk by my departure. In the kitchen, this girl was now holding three others and the cook at bay, wielding a large carving knife and making all manner of dire, if unlikely, threats. I interposed myself between them and, based on previous experience, employed gentle reasoning whilst waiting for clockwork emotions to run down. After about an hour, she burst into tears and I was able to retrieve the knife and escort her to sickbay, where the cuts and abrasions on her fingers - the only actual victims of this affray - could be attended to.

On returning to the headmistress's office, I discovered that A——'s assessment had concluded. The headmistress was seated behind her desk, the psychiatrist sat facing her and upon my entry they broke off what appeared to be a muted, if somewhat serious, *discussion.*

I apologised for my intrusion whilst backing out of the door, but the headmistress motioned me inside and asked me to bring over another chair to join them.

Once I sat down, she inquired what my initial impressions were of A——. I explained that in our brief acquaintanceship she had struck me as somewhat introverted, polite without seeming obsequious. In short, not someone I would expect to prove troublesome during her stay.

The psychiatrist slowly nodded, exchanged glances with the Headmistress and handed me a half dozen or so sheets of paper, stapled together. On taking them, I realised it was the standard IQ test used for the girls, now completed and with the score written in blue in the top right-hand corner, heavily circled.

One hundred and forty-eight.

During my time at Fairholme I saw much that left me surprised, sometimes even shaken, but I believe that was the only occasion where I was conscious of gasping aloud. A score of one hundred and fifty was accepted as the gateway to genius, my own IQ had been tested at one hundred and twenty-nine.

A——, the psychiatrist continued, possessed a level of detachment she had rarely encountered. It was not unusual for people, particularly children, to deal with trauma by sublimation or blocking mechanisms, but A—— seemed to possess an ability to step outside of her emotions completely. She wasn't talking here about psychopathic or sociopathic behaviour - A—— had displayed typical emotional and empathetic responses during the psychiatrist's interview. However...

The psychiatrist moved on to A——'s abuse at her foster home. The headmistress and I were familiar with the case from the court papers and probation service reports. Although the molestation itself had taken place outside the house - in a shed on a garden allotment - it was believed that the wife, whilst not enabling her husband's activities, was certainly turning a blind eye to them. It is not unknown for wives to regard these aberrations as something they can countenance if all else in the marriage remains stable. It was the awareness that her husband had passed beyond what she could accept as an intermittent erotic spasm that she contrived to have A⸺ removed from the household by accusations of theft.

It had been during the police investigation of these allegations that evidence of the abuse was uncovered. The exact details of how this came to light were - here the psychiatrist seemed to choose her words carefully - somewhat sketchy, but reading between the lines of the various reports, A⸺ had manipulated the situation with a skill far beyond her years.

The psychiatrist paused here and then handed me another sheaf of papers. It was the sentence completion test.

'**I am embarrassed by** good intentions badly managed,' I read. '**My father** is a void which still somehow casts a shadow.' '**Love** would seem a virtue alibiing a multitude of sins.' '**I wish** for little and am rarely disappointed.'

The psychiatrist told us she had watched A⸺ complete this test whilst barely lifting pencil from paper.

Following a silence we all appeared reluctant to break, the headmistress asked what the psychiatrist's recommendations would be.

Her concern, she informed us, was that despite A⸺'s now obvious outstanding abilities, she had been too long excluded from the mainstream education system for them to be nurtured in any conventional manner. Her view was that while a child aged up to twelve or thirteen with barely a soupcon of formal schooling, could, with effort on their own part matched by those tutoring them, rise to find themselves amongst equals when taking O'Level examinations three years later, sixteen was deemed almost impossible.

But, with a shake of her head, we would have her full report in due course.

In the meantime, A⸺ was relieved of laundry duties and required to attend morning lessons. I felt - as I suspect did the headmistress - that this was no more than a sop to address the issues her assessment had raised, but in purely practical terms *there seemed little else we could do.*

In fact, this developed into a more than workable solution. A——'s education could be described as patchy at best and she obviously regarded this as an opportunity to plug some of its many gaps, particularly in the areas of modern history and politics which interested her the most. Although these subjects were not on our curricula - and not by a long shot, one might add - an eager pupil was enough of a novelty for the two full-time members of our teaching staff to construct a syllabus of their own, tailored around her unique situation.

She proved, as our American cousins would have it, a quick study. An area in which she displayed no interest was sports and games and so during the afternoon periods she was allowed access to the classroom where she could continue her studies.

As remarkable as her academic progress was over the following month, there was no escaping the Visiting Psychiatrist's conclusion that it was too late for her to follow a conventional scholastic route. The headmistress discussed with me - knowing of my intention to further my own education - what opportunities might avail themselves for her. Other than taking GCE courses at night school - no easy task whilst having to simultaneously earn a living - I had little by way of constructive suggestion to offer.

Finally, the Visiting Psychologist's assessment report was complete.

Much was made of A——'s inner self sufficiency, perhaps placing more significance on it than her remarkable IQ score. She also went into some detail regarding the circumstances she had already shared with the headmistress and myself, relating to the uncovering of sexual abuse at her foster home. She had obviously delved further into the details surrounding this and placed great emphasis on the role A—— had played, specifically in the way she had manoeuvred forces initially working against her to her own advantage. And it was from this standpoint that she concluded her report with a note of caution.

'Rules are rules and there are good reasons we follow

established practices,' she stated. 'But I do not believe this girl should suffer further, what is in effect, incarceration for something she is not responsible for. In such an environment, I think it inevitable she would become subject to pernicious influences, the most likely outcome of which would be a deep and lasting resentment at the circumstances in which she finds herself. That said, I have no practical suggestions as to what the correct way forward might be for her. I can only emphasise my belief that should society choose to make an enemy of this girl, she will prove a formidable one.'

A meeting was convened between Child Services, the headmistress of Fairholme and Lady S——, the presiding magistrate at A——'s original hearing, who was still following this case closely. As one proposal after another was raised, discussed and dismissed, it eventually fell to Lady S—— to forward a mutually acceptable solution.

As a patron of the arts and board member of a variety of trusts in that field, she had contacts at an establishment in County Durham named L—— Hall. Lady S—— explained this was once the country house of Lord K——, a renowned nineteenth century philanthropist and one much taken with the Arts and Crafts movement. On his death, toward the end of the Edwardian era, he bequeathed this house to a Trust established to create a haven for artists and writers, an opportunity for them to retreat from urban life and recharge their creative energies. It was also the aim of the Trust to broaden horizons for boys and girls of the lower classes and so a large section of the grounds had been made available for camping, by organisations such as the Woodcraft Folk, Boy Scouts and Girl Guides.

Another ambition of the Trust, continued Lady S——, was to provide opportunities of employment for young people whose abilities had not been allowed to flourish due to circumstances of birth and upbringing. The occupations were mostly menial - kitchen work, housekeeping, gardening - but it was honest labour. It put a roof over their heads and, more importantly, it brought them into direct contact with gifted individuals who might nurture fledgling talents. Over the decades, Lady S—— informed them, more than a few had found posts in the London households of guests at L—— Hall, some even going on to forge successful careers of their own in this field. She was sure, Lady S—— concluded, that this represented the best opportunity for A—— to move forward.

The decision was unanimous. Lady S—— made contact with the trustees of L—— Hall and a place was found there for A——. The headmistress herself elected to drive her to County Durham, being that part of the country where she had grown up allowed her an opportunity to spend a weekend with family, once reassured A—— would settle into her new surroundings with the minimum of fuss.

It has probably not escaped attention that the only satisfactory outcome to the case of A—— was facilitated by a member of the aristocracy's involvement with the legacy of a Victorian benefactor. In the second half of the twentieth century and during the third decade of the welfare state, this can only be viewed, I would suggest, with some irony.

Judith Temple

CHAPTER FIVE

Amanda

Amanda woke to the sound of ringing. At first she thought it was her alarm, before realising it was Sunday and she never set the alarm on a Sunday.

She reached for the phone.

"Hello," she answered sleepily.

"I think I've found him," said DS Sule. "The murder victim."

Amanda sat upright.

"Have you been at the office all night?" she asked.

"Yes." There was a slight pause. "I rang the Salvation Army and they offered to go through their archives for me. I spent a couple of hours on the missing person reports again and I was about to leave when they called to say there were a dozen or so cases which matched the dates I'd given them. Their records from back then haven't been computerised, but they'd photocopy the files if I wanted to come over and collect them."

Amanda swung her legs out of bed and stood up.

"Look, I'm going into the kitchen to put the kettle on. I'll pick up on the extension there, okay?"

"Okay."

After she'd filled the kettle and spooned coffee into a cup, Amanda glanced at the digital display on the front of the oven.

Six fifteen.

Suppressing a sigh, she lifted the handset off its cradle on the wall.

"Sorry." DS Sule's tone was contrite. "I hadn't realised how early it was."

"Don't worry about it," Amanda told her. "I know all about disappearing into a world of your own. But probably best to hang fire on getting Kendall out of bed just yet."

"Of course."

"So, you picked everything up from the Salvation

Army?" prompted Amanda.

"The thing is, all their files still had photographs attached, unlike the police reports. It didn't take long to check them against the surveillance shots and once I'd found him... Well, you know what it's like once things start coming together."

"So who is he?" asked Amanda.

"Do you think you could come in?" As Amanda hesitated, DS Sule added, "It's easier to show than explain and we're going to have to make some decisions about how we take this forward, right?"

Amanda understood what she meant. If McKelvey's story proved to be true - and from what she'd just heard, that now seemed more than likely - they couldn't put off notifying the Cabinet Secretary any longer.

"I'll be about an hour," Amanda told her.

* * *

Arriving in the office, Amanda found DS Sule in the conference room, the large circular table covered in photographs and sheets of paper. She put her bag down on a chair and stepped forward to study them.

DS Sule indicated around a dozen of the surveillance prints stacked together on the far left and Amanda began thumbing through them. The same individual was in each shot, a young man dressed in the fashions of that decade - flared jeans, suede jacket, collarless shirt - with longish, curly hair. He was mostly head on to the camera, coming down the steps from the front door, although a few were in profile as he walked along the pavement.

As she placed them back on the table, DS Sule handed her a thin cardboard folder. Opening it, she found a single sheet of paper with a colour photostat attached by a paperclip. There was no doubt it was the same person.

Peter Marshall, she read. D.O.B 21.10.1948. Initially reported missing by his sister, Susan, in September 1971, at Heavitree Police Station in Exeter. Last confirmed whereabouts was his home town of St Hannahs in Cornwall in 1967, although the sister believed he'd been living in west London. At least, she'd received the occasional letter from him franked with a W11 postmark. But in the previous year she'd heard nothing.

And that was about it. Amanda closed the folder and laid it back down on the table.

"Do we know anything more?" asked Amanda.

"It's really," DS Sule told her, sweeping a hand across the paper ladened tabletop, "confirmation by an accumulation of negatives." She took a breath. "Peter Marshall's never had a National Insurance number, never paid Income Tax. No passport issued, no bank account linked to anyone of that name with the same date of birth. Ditto for a driver's licence. Doesn't have a criminal record, never been married and no death certificate's been registered."

"Okay, that seems pretty conclusive," said Amanda softly. "What about the sister?"

"No CRO entries, no suggestion she was ever a person of interest to any of the usual agencies. Did a degree at Exeter University in the early seventies, after which she taught at a primary school in the city for a couple of years, before returning to teach in St Hannahs, where she still lives."

"I'd say she's definitely worth a visit, wouldn't you?"

DS Sule nodded.

"Okay, probably best to get a conference call set up." Amanda glanced at her watch. "Venables and Kendall should be out of bed by now. Let's see if we can catch them before they start making plans for the day."

Both were at home and both were in agreement that they couldn't delay bringing this before the Cabinet Secretary for much longer.

"Although, I would like to give it another twenty-four hours," said Venables. "To hear what Christopher Franklyn has to say, he was actually living in that house when all this supposedly happened. We should really get his take on things before hitting the panic button."

"There is one other thing," said DS Sule.

"What's that?"

DS Sule looked over at Amanda.

"According to ex Chief Superintendent Maddox, Christopher Franklyn became embroiled in all of this as a result of being arrested on drugs charges. After his father pulled a few strings to get him probation rather than a custodial sentence."

Amanda nodded.

"That's right."

"I checked it out." DS Sule paused. "Christopher Franklyn's arrest took place in St Hannahs, Cornwall."

"Well, isn't that interesting?" said Venables.

Jack

For as long as Jack had known Carol, there'd been family lunch at Petroc on a Sunday. These days, given the erratic pattern of all involved's lifestyles, 'lunch' could see them gathering around the table anytime between late morning and early evening, but gather they did.

When Jack first sat down with the Teague family, the young constable courting - and how ridiculously archaic that sounded these days - Brian and Mary's daughter, it had been a crowded and boisterous affair. Brothers, sisters, a couple of cousins, old Uncle Bryok who looked as though he was coming in through the front door from another century...

But those days were long gone. One generation in the Holy Trinity churchyard, reflected Jack, another scattered across the country and beyond in pursuit of a decent life. It wasn't the first time in its history the county had witnessed such an exodus, when the tin mines closed the young had taken what skills they possessed and struck out in their droves for the Cape and New Brunswick. But back then, Jack had gathered from the tales passed down via his grandparents, it had been a sense of venturing forth to seek your fortune. That wherever fate may guide your footsteps, you'd always know where home was. Little chance of that for today's youngsters, mulled Jack, priced out of the towns and villages of their birth by retirees from upcountry and second home owners who...

"More beef, Jack?" asked Brian, lifting the serving dish from the table and Jack nodded.

There was just the four of them, Brian, Carol, Jack and Sally. As Jack held his plate out, he turned to Carol.

"By the way," he said, "I sent an American lady over to you yesterday. Did you manage to sort something out for her?"

"Yes," said Carol. "I put her on Esme's pitch."

Jack looked at Brian quizzically, who shrugged.

"We've moved her caravan up behind Reception," he

said. "Any idea if it's likely to be claimed?"

"I doubt we'll come across a last will and testament," said Jack dryly. "Why, what were you thinking?"

"Perhaps an auction for charity," Brian told him. "And I might put in a bid myself. I could always find a spot for an homage to a lost age."

"What American lady?" asked Sally.

"It was her who found Richard Hanson in the Viewing Area and called it in. She'd probably spent the night there in her camper, but given the circumstances..."

He shrugged.

"You decided to do your bit for Anglo-American relations?" smiled Carol.

"What's the story with that?" asked Brian. "I gather he got into a fracas with that bunch of Travellers camped out in Belle Meadow."

Jack laid his fork down and stared at Brian.

"The paramedics thought it was a stroke," he said evenly, "and repeating that kind of speculation doesn't help matters."

Brian raised both palms as if in mock surrender.

"Just saying what I heard."

"Richard Hanson," said Jack carefully, "is a friend of Alan Bradshaw who owns Belle Meadow. From what we've gathered, Bradshaw had building work scheduled to start there tomorrow and Hanson visited Belle Meadows with a view of persuading them to move on." He hesitated. "When Tom turned up to get their side of the story, they were all packed up and ready to leave, so it doesn't really make sense they'd wish him any harm."

"Would that be the folding kind of persuasion?" smiled Brian and Jack nodded.

"They deny it, but we've good reason to think otherwise." Jack picked up his fork. "Look, I know I usually tell you all that anything I say at this table isn't to go any further, but in this instance, let's make an exception, shall we? If you hear any rumours about Richard Hanson being attacked by

Travellers, feel free to quote me."

"Point taken," said Brian softly.

"How is Mr Hanson?" asked Sally.

"They're keeping him in a medically induced coma," Jack told her, "until they get the results of the tests. I'll probably go over to Derriford tomorrow to see what the doctors have to say."

"His poor wife," said Carol.

Jack remained silent.

"Esme's funeral," said Brian. "I've had a word with Reverend Warwick. There's no room in the churchyard at Holy Trinity for her, but she'll hold a service there if that's what we want." He looked across the table at Jack. "Or we could just do the whole thing over at Penmount."

Penmount was the local crematorium on the outskirts of Truro. Jack recalled the small brass crucifix which always hung at Esme's neck.

"No," he said. "We'll have the service here. Then she can go to Truro."

"Okay, I'll get that all arranged," Brian told him.

Toni

"So does Gillian know it was you and Linda Haversham who ambushed Ted?" asked Toni, giving up on pushing peas around her plate and sitting back in her chair to stare at Dennis.

"Ambushed is a bit strong," said Dennis. "We simply entertained the possibility that things at St Anne's had started to become a little stale and... Well, suggested to the interview board that we should perhaps think outside the box."

"And I'll bet it was Linda who let you do the dirty work, wasn't it?" The thin smile on Toni's lips drew even tighter. "After a fair amount of whispering in your ear beforehand."

"That's unfair." Dennis shook his head. "As Bursar, Linda's voice wouldn't have carried as much weight as others in the room, but that didn't mean she was wrong - we all agreed Ms Pozniak was an outstanding candidate."

"Has anyone spoken to Gillian? Since stabbing her in the back, that is, or have they all gone scurrying away into the shadows?"

"Well, Ted obviously, to inform her of the decision."

"Ted obviously?" Toni shook her head. "As chairman, wasn't that your bloody job?"

Dennis hesitated.

"Ted's view was, given his relationship with Gillian, it should be him to break the news."

"At least one of you managed some integrity. And backbone. What was Gillian's reaction?"

Dennis was silent for a few seconds.

"Apparently, she hung up on him."

"I'll bet she bloody well did," said Toni, reaching across the table for the wine bottle and topping up her glass.

"I have to say," a touch of defiance now shoehorned into Dennis's tone, "that I'm surprised to find you sticking up for her. Remind me, how many years is it since you two last spoke?"

"Gillian and I don't see eye to eye on a lot of things," Toni admitted. "Okay, on practically nothing. But she says what she thinks and she's bloody good at her job." Toni shrugged. "And as she RSVP'd for Wednesday, I'd supposed she was planning on using the occasion to finally to bury the hatchet."

Toni raised the glass to her lips and stared over the rim at Dennis.

"Fat chance of that now."

* * *

It had been five or six years ago, a barbecue at Ted and Faith's. Toni couldn't remember what the occasion had been, birthday or wedding anniversary, she supposed. And yes, okay, she'd probably overdone the punch, but had been on her third glass before the realisation actually dawned that there might be more of a kick to it than you'd expect at one of these garden shindigs...

Returning from a visit to the loo, she picked up on an exchange between Gillian and Dennis that, whilst not exactly having the sense of a *contretemps* about it, was attracting attention from those nearby. Intrigued, Toni scooped up a refill - in for a penny - and walked over to join them.

"I just think it's highly inappropriate for an educational institution," she caught Gillian saying.

"That's really a decision for the music department," Dennis replied.

"I disagree," said Gillian. "Given the malleability of young minds, I believe that it's the Governors who should take action."

"What are we talking about?" asked Toni.

"Gillian thinks we should remove all of Nigel Kennedy's CDs from the school library," Dennis told her. "In view of his recent comments."

The classical musician, recalled Toni, during an interview with *The Guardian* newspaper had stated that he perhaps had a responsibility to get into heavier drugs to further explore his music, citing various groundbreaking musicians whose work, he claimed, had benefited by such experimentation. To say this had proved a controversial viewpoint would be something of an understatement.

Toni nodded.

"Yeah, I agree with Gill," she said, taking a sip of her drink. "Kids are impressionable and he has become very much an iconic figure."

She caught the flash of surprise on Dennis's face and it wasn't the only odd look that came in her direction as Ted, Faith, Gillian's husband Tim and a few others drifted over.

"Thank you, Antonia" said Gillian.

"I'm not saying he's wrong," continued Toni. "In fact, in his case, I daresay he's right." She shrugged. "But probably best to have kept his mouth shut and just got on with it."

"What!?"

Gillian was staring at her, wide-eyed.

"Well, I couldn't name a seminal musician of the last fifty years who wasn't into serious drug use at the height of their creativity," said Toni. "John Coltrane, Bob Dylan, David Bowie, John Lennon, Charlie Parker, Miles Davis..."

"I think that's a disgraceful statement." Gillian was staring daggers at her.

"Rolling Stones, Eric Clapton, Art Pepper." Toni shrugged. "I could go on for a while here, if you like, give you a chance to come up with someone who rocked the world while straight, but good luck with that."

"So what you're saying is that anyone who takes drugs can become a talented musician?" shot back Gillian.

"No, of course not. What I'm saying is that kind of creativity would seem to resonate, as Kennedy said, to chemically induced mind-bending. Usually at tremendous personal cost to themselves and their loved ones," she added, "but, however sanctimonious we might want to get about the nature of sacrifices made for art's sake, we're all hypocritical enough to keep buying the albums."

Tim reached out to rest a hand on his wife's arm, which,

without seeming to notice what she was doing, Gillian simply brushed away.

"I suppose you'd like to see them legalised too?" she said.

"No." Toni slowly shook her head. "I'm not in favour of that, but more for cultural reasons than anything else."

"Cultural reasons?"

"Yeah." Toni raised her glass and with a smile tilted it toward Gillian. "Does anyone seriously doubt that if this stuff had been developed by a research chemist twenty years ago, it would be one of the most controlled substances on the planet? But because we've centuries of ritual attached to it - taverns, toasts, buying rounds - it is, for the most part, socially manageable."

Toni sipped her drink.

"But when whisky was introduced to the American Indian tribes," she continued, "they called it firewater and drank it by the pint before setting out to rape, pillage and murder. Their own culture was passing around the peace pipe and mescaline fuelled spiritual vision quests. When psychedelics arrived over here in the sixties, kids were jumping off rooftops thinking they could fly." She shrugged. "Hard as it might be to accept, context frequently trumps content."

"Young people have been known to die after trying drugs only once." Gillian was now in a cold fury. "I haven't heard of anyone dying after just a couple of drinks."

"Well," said Toni, "during prohibition in the United States, back in the twenties, hundreds of people died after just a couple of drinks and for the same reason kids are dying taking drugs today - the stuff was being made in bathtubs by criminals who cared more about profit than safety."

Speechless, Gillian stared at her.

"Like I said," Toni told her, "I've no problem with pulling *The Four Seasons* from the syllabus while all this furore's going on, but let's not fool ourselves *why* we're doing it, right?"

Gillian glared at her for what must have been a full five

seconds before turning to storm away, leaving an icy silence in her wake as Tim trailed after her.

"Bloody hell, Toni," said Ted eventually, "I'd hate to see you lock horns with someone you *didn't* agree with."

And although their paths had crossed at various social functions at least a dozen times since, that had been the last conversation between them.

* * *

"So, do you suppose she'll still turn up?" Toni asked Dennis. "On Wednesday?"

"Most of the teaching staff who aren't away on holiday are likely to be there," Dennis told her. "As well as a few governors. She's not going to find it easy."

"And let's not forget Alan Bradshaw," Toni reminded him. "If he and Safranka do show up, that'll be the real icing on the cake for her."

Dennis sat back in his chair.

"Okay, I'll go and talk to Gill," he said quietly. "Tell her it was my decision, explain the factors that contributed to it and why I believed - still believe - it was the right one. But emphasise those factors don't diminish the value of her contributions to St Anne's, past and future."

"Might be a hard sell," smiled Toni, but putting her glass down, she reached out and squeezed his hand.

"I'll also tell her we're *both* looking forward to seeing her at the barbecue."

Toni nodded.

"And on Wednesday," continued Dennis, seemingly picking his words with care, "maybe give the punch a miss, just this once. There's going to be an awful lot of people walking on eggshells and it wouldn't take much for..."

Toni cut him off with another squeeze of her hand.

"Deal," she said and then smiled. "Be something of a novelty *not* to find myself living up to everyone's expectations."

The setting seems idyllic, but you've learnt not to go too much by appearances. Linden Hall sits in parkland - at the edge of which you can see deer grazing - and is approached by a long gravelled driveway. This eventually opens out into a circular parking area below an imposing flight of stone steps leading up to the front door. But Mrs Stuart does not stop the car here, instead following signs which read 'Tradesmen' into a narrow passage between the house and what appears to be a stable block. This emerges into a small courtyard of worn brickwork, in which are set dirty windows with scruffy wooden frames.

"And here we are," she tells you.

During the drive from Fairholme, Mrs Stuart has explained that Linden Hall once belonged to Lord Knowle, a renowned nineteenth century philanthropist and a patron of the Pre-Raphaelite Brotherhood. Mrs Stuart has gone into great detail regarding his charitable efforts and ensuing legacy and all related to you in an admiring tone. But from what you've learnt of Victorian industrialists, you'd view such benefactions being more down to concerns of an increasingly imminent meeting with their maker than altruism.

Your duties will probably include those of a housemaid, Mrs Stuart explains. It's not a demeaning position, she tells you, over the years many girls from Linden Hall have found positions in the households of guests - names you would be certain to recognise, she adds, but you wouldn't be so sure of that - and others have used it as a springboard to a variety of careers. Hard work brings its own rewards, she emphasises, and you dutifully nod, although you wouldn't be so sure about that, either.

As Mrs Stuart lifts your suitcase from the rear seat of the shooting brake, a door opens and a figure steps out into the courtyard. She is middle-aged and there is a no-nonsense air about her, both in appearance and manner. She stands ramrod straight as you and Mrs Stuart approach, her long dress starched enough to have the sense of a uniform and her greying hair is tightly pulled back into a bun. But as you draw closer, you see that her eyes are creased with fine lines and that the expression she regards you with is not unkind.

"No one there will have knowledge of your past," Mrs Stuart has told you, "but it has been emphasised to them you entered our care as a victim rather than offender."

"This is Miss Benfield." Mrs Stuart makes the introductions and Miss Benfield leads you both inside. Along a dimly lit corridor you reach a small office, where Miss Benfield lowers herself down behind a desk that, while covered in paperwork, still creates an impression of workmanlike efficiency.

Mrs Stuart opens her briefcase, takes out a single sheet of paper and hands it over to Miss Benfield, whose eyes appear to dart down the page rather than actually read it. You guess she's picking out the relevant details. Then, seemingly satisfied, she uncaps a fountain pen, signs at the bottom and gives it back to Mrs Stuart, who returns it to her briefcase and then holds you in a steady gaze.

"I hope you'll be able to put the past behind you here," she tells you. "And I wish you luck."

"Thank you, Mrs Stuart," you tell her.

One last smile and then yet someone else has signed themselves out of your life for good.

"This is a very egalitarian household," Miss Benfield explains, leading you up a curved wide staircase. "There are no separate staff quarters, facilities are shared and we all dine together at breakfast, luncheon and dinner. You'll mix freely with the guests, both during the course of your duties and recreationally." She paused. "It's not unusual for one of the artists to ask you to model for them or a writer to perhaps have some notes transposed."

At the top of the stairs she leads you along a dark corridor. Halfway down, she indicates two doors on the left.

"Bathroom and WC," she tells you. "There's a strict rota for bathing, everyone is allotted twenty minutes and each evening you'll find your scheduled time for the following morning, together with that day's duties, on a notice in your room."

She catches your quizzical expression.

"There are no fixed roles here. Positions in the kitchen,

household and grounds are rotated on a daily basis." Miss Benfield gives the slightest of shrugs. "The original trustees believed in allowing their charges the widest breadth of experience possible and nothing over the years has suggested that to be an unwise decision."

Miss Benfield stops at a door, opens it and you follow her inside. The room isn't large, but it is light and airy. A narrow wardrobe stands in a corner, a dressing table is placed against one wall and a chest of drawers sits under the window. The bed, while not a double, is wider than a single and will be the largest you have ever slept in.

There are no blankets, you observe, just bottom and top sheets under what appears to be a large, fluffy eiderdown.

Miss Benfield notices you staring.

"It's called a duvet," she says. "I take it you've never used one before?"

You shake your head.

"They're commonplace in Scandinavia," she continues, "where the nights are freezing. So rest assured, you'll be more than comfortable."

She hesitates and then looks you straight in the eye.

"There are no rules here." Her voice becomes flat, matter of fact. "Just a basic expectation of honesty, respect for those around you and the application of commonsense in all matters. If those protocols are confounded, there will be no second chances. You'll simply find yourself standing at the end of the driveway, with your suitcase and left entirely to your own devices. And the world - as I'm sure you've already discovered - can be a very cruel place." Her expression is unblinking. "Are we clear on this?"

Meeting her eyes, you try to make your tone as sombre as possible.

"Yes, Miss Benfield."

"Good." For the first time, there is almost the flicker of a smile on her lips. "I'll give you twenty minutes or so to sort out your things, then return to take you downstairs to meet everyone."

The door closes behind her and you begin to unpack.

There's been a lot of communal living so far in your short life and the thing which strikes you most about this is that whatever the institution, day-to-day practicalities run along exactly the same lines. Rotas for everything, mealtime gongs... The only difference here, having your own room, is an absence of secrets whispered in the dark. But plenty rise to the surface of your thoughts all by themselves, leading you by the hand into sleep.

Your duties are light and after the traumas of the last few months, you find a strange peace in their humdrum nature. You spend your spare time either in the library or walking the extensive grounds, exploring woodland and meadow.

Another house sits close by, less grand than The Hall but larger than a cottage. It's a private residence, you learn from Miss Benfield, belonging to Lady Georgina.

"Lady Georgina?" you enquire.

Miss Benfield's lips purse.

Lady Georgina, she explains, is the latest of the line descended from Linden Hall's original benefactor and as such is the current chairman - chairwoman, Miss Benfield corrects herself - of the Trust. You have the impression Miss Benfield believes this is a responsibility worn lightly. The house is her private residence and although her ladyship spends most of the year in Chelsea *- Miss Benfield lets the word fall from her lips as a clergyman midway through a Sunday sermon might speak of Sodom or Gomorrah - she is occasionally resident here.*

Whilst not exactly out of bounds, seems to be the gist of what she's saying, then best steered well clear of.

Time passes and the visitor influx swells. Campsites appear along the banks of the narrow river flowing through the grounds and the house itself grows busier.

Eventually you are asked to pose for an artist. Peter, apparently a noted author and illustrator of children's books, asks Miss Benfield if you can be spared for the day. After breakfast she leads you out to what was once a stable block at the back of the house, but has since been repurposed as a studio. It's deserted when you arrive, he's probably popped into the village, she tells you, and shouldn't be long.

After Miss Benfield leaves, you explore. It's very much what you expect an art studio to be, three half completed canvasses resting on easels, worktops littered with tubes of oil paints, palettes and brushes. On a wide workbench that runs the length of one wall are mockups for a book cover. 'The Secret Loch by Peter Matthews' you read on several versions of the same scene, two boys and two girls clambering into a rowing boat at water's edge, heather in the foreground and snowy peaks in the distance.

There are other drawings, pen and ink illustrations which, you suppose, are to accompany the story. One catches your eye, if only for the detail presented without making it seem crowded. A bunch of young boys are playing cowboys and Indians on the lawn of what you'd guess is a vicarage, a Norman church being the only other building to be seen. The Indians, carrying bows and arrows, wear just shorts and feathered headbands, while their opponents have cowboy hats and cap pistols in holsters.

A trestle table stands on a patio between the lawn and the house, plates of sandwiches and pastries are piled high between jugs of lemonade. A young woman, presumably the mistress of the house, smiles as she butters yet one more slice of bread.

A hedgerow separates the lawn from a small vegetable garden where a vicar, boyish enough to suggest he's the woman's husband, is pointing out a row of seedlings to his companion, a middle-aged scoutmaster.

On the opposite side of the picture, a group of what appears to be tinkers is passing by. An old man and woman each have a bundle on a stick, while another man in his twenties, perhaps their son, is carrying a snared rabbit. They pause to take in the scene before them, smiling benevolently.

You turn away at the sound of a car pulling up and walk over to the door. Outside, you see who you presume is Peter climbing out of a frogeye Austin Sprite.

"Hello," he calls over to you. "Sorry to keep you hanging

about. Had to pop into the village for some bits and pieces."

Unused to adults apologising, you simply smile and nod.

"Ever done any modelling before?" he asks, to which you shake your head.

"Easiest job in the world," he tells you. "All you need to do is stay still."

You're not really sure what to make of Peter. He looks to be in his forties, but there's something about him which suggests youth and vitality. His voice isn't what you'd think of as 'posh' - although he obviously is - but it's not regional either, just pleasant with no airs or graces about it.

"Sit there, for now," he indicates a chair in the centre of the studio, "and let's see what I can do with you."

Peter picks up a sketchpad, a stick of charcoal and begins to work. You find yourself flattered by this attention, even though aware you're probably no more to him than a bowl of fruit. But his conversation is easy and he does appear to be treating you as both an adult - rather than the child you still occasionally suspect yourself to be - and an equal.

He's curious to your background, the circumstances which have led you here. You're more cautious in your answers than you hope your tone conveys - you lost your parents at an early age, you've spent time in care, a bad experience in a foster home brought you to the attention of the trustees here.

He nods sympathetically as he listens, although never pushing beyond these carefully curated facts. He asks what your plans might be for the future and you simply shrug, less through nonchalance than an inability to explain to someone from this world the extent to which one's energies could be taken up purely by survival.

At this point you are interrupted by a knock on the door, which then opens before Peter can respond.

"Sebastian!" With an expression of delight, Peter puts down the pad and strides towards the young clergyman who's entered the room.

"Good to see you again, Peter," says Sebastian, as they

exchange smiles over a hearty handshake.

"You here with the troop?" asks Peter and Sebastian nods.

"Bivouacked on the other side of the stream." He gives a casual shrug and a wry smile. "Thought I'd try to put at least one obstacle between the randy little buggers and those Girl Guides who we couldn't miss doing very back to nature star jumps as we arrived."

Peter laughs and then seems to remember your presence.

"The two of us have known each other longer than I'd care to recall," he tells you, after making introductions. "And we usually seem to end up here at this time of year." He turns to Sebastian. "Is Susan with you?"

Sebastian shakes his head.

"Father-in-law's not too good at the moment," he says, "so duty calls. Looks like I'm den mother as well, this trip."

Peter laughs again and then gives you a slightly apologetic shrug.

"Look, let's carry on with this later," he tells you. "Sebastian and I have a fair bit of catching up to do. But in the meantime..."

He hands you an A4 cartridge paper drawing pad and a pack of charcoal sticks.

"Have a go yourself," he answers to your quizzical expression. "Take a walk around the grounds and show me what the world looks like through your eyes."

Somewhat nonplussed, you leave them to it, closing the door softly behind you.

You've settled yourself down by the edge of the wood and haven't been too impressed by your first couple of attempts. But the third one isn't bad. It would have been even better if you'd realised sooner how easily charcoal smudges, but then it dawns on you that this is a characteristic which you could exploit to artistic effect.

You become engrossed in this to the extent that you don't hear footsteps arriving behind you.

"That's pretty good," says a voice startlingly close, and you jump with surprise.

The girl looks to be in her late teens, early twenties.

"Jesus!" *she exclaims, catching your expression.* "I might just as well have crept up and yelled 'Boo!' in your ear, mightn't I?" *She stares at you, her face not unfriendly.* "Are you alright?"

You slowly nod, taking her in. What mostly grabs your attention is her cheesecloth dress, almost indecently short and which you definitely wouldn't want to be all you were wearing if caught out in the rain.

You're not exactly sure what to say to her. 'No trespassing' signs are all along the walls of the property, so however she came to be here, she must have seen them. But equally, you don't feel comfortable throwing your weight around on behalf of...

"Are you from The Hall?"

The girl breaks into your thoughts with a gesture towards the house.

"Yes," *you answer, if somewhat cautiously, and at this she seems amused.*

"Thought you might be," *she nods, then sticks out her hand.*

"I'm Georgie," *she tells you.*

Georgie! Could this possibly...?

If anything, her amusement deepens.

"I gather my reputation precedes me." *She gives a slight shake of her head.* "I'm actually on my way over there to see Benny. Fancy stretching your legs?"

"Benny?"

"Miss Benfield to you, no doubt, but don't worry," *she grins.* "I've a favour to ask, so I'll be on my very best behaviour."

During the short walk back to The Hall, she's the one doing most of the talking, curious as to where you're from, how long you've been here, what you make of the place. By the time you're climbing up the front steps, even you've begun to think of your answers as a masterclass in ambiguity.

You discover Miss Benfield in the kitchen, where the cook makes no secret of her pleasure at the discomfit our arrival ensues.

"Lady Georgina!" *Miss Benfield seems to be caught midway between a bow and a curtsy.* "I had no idea you were in residence."

"Got down here last night," Georgie tells her and then smiles over at the cook. "Hello Maisie - so how did Angela do in the end?"

"Five passes, three of them Grade As," beams the cook.

"See," nods Georgie. "Told you there was nothing to worry about."

She returns her attention to Miss Benfield.

"I'm here for a favour, actually," she says. "I've people over later for aperitifs and nibbles, but Tina couldn't make it this trip. Any chance of being able to borrow someone to look decorative with a drinks tray for a couple of hours?"

"Ah, well..." begins Miss Benfield, but Georgie gives a sideways inclination of her head in your direction.

"This one seems halfway civilised," she continues, "even if she's not too sure who she is, where she's from or what she's doing here. Could you have her kitted out and over to my place by seven sharp?"

Miss Benfield's hesitation is barely discernible.

"Of course, Lady Georgina."

Georgie turns to leave.

"See you later," she smiles at you and then, with her back now to Miss Benfield, slowly winks.

While much of what you've been required to wear throughout your life has left no doubt in the eyes of the world of your role therein, this is the first actual uniform you've ever worn.

The trim charcoal dress Miss Benfield laid out on your bed fits you surprisingly well, although when set off with black tights and a short, purely decorative frilly white apron, no one would mistake you for another guest, even without the ornate drinks tray you carry back and forth across the room.

A table against the far wall has been decorated with what you've learnt are called canapes and hors d'oeuvres and guests are expected to serve themselves. You gather that for the most part they are local worthies, conversations you pass through bristle with golf, hunting and a world going to the dogs.

Each time your tray accumulates more empty glasses than

full ones, you return to the kitchen to replenish them. On your second trip, you find a boy at the sink, busy with a tea towel. He is about your age, perhaps a year or two older, but in appearance he couldn't be more of a contrast with the company next door. His hair hangs over his shoulders and he's wearing what looks like an old suit waistcoat over a white T-shirt and faded denim bell-bottom jeans.

You see he has already filled another tray with drinks ready for you and so, exchanging nothing more than brief smiles, you carry it back out to the soiree, yet one more word you've learnt this evening.

Which has the feel about it of continuing late into the night, but Georgie obviously has other ideas. Just after ten o'clock, she clinks a spoon against the edge of her glass to attract everyone's attention and the room falls silent.

"I'd like to thank you all for coming," she says. "It's been a wonderful evening and delightful to see everyone again. But it was a very long drive to arrive here last night and one, I'm afraid, that's finally caught up with me." She pauses, letting that sink in. "Do have a safe journey home," she adds with a smile, "and bonsoir *to you all."*

A few seem somewhat taken aback, but most begin exchanging goodbyes and heading toward the front door. Within fifteen minutes, the last coat has been collected and Georgie is sliding the bolt shut behind them.

Turning towards you, she expels a long breath.

"Comes with the territory," she tells you, as you follow her through to the kitchen. "Have to do it every year, but like ripping off a plaster, best done sooner than later."

With a slight shrug, she pushes open the door. The draining board is empty of glasses and the boy is drying his hands on the tea towel.

"Have you two met properly yet?" she asks and after he gives an almost shy shake of the head, she introduces you, explaining that you're from The Hall.

"And this," turning back to you, whilst jerking a thumb

towards him, "is Jake."

You follow Georgie and Jake up a wide staircase, then along a passageway until you come to a narrower flight of stairs, which you climb to reach a small landing. An even smaller stairway, not much more than a steeply angled ladder, disappears through a hatch in the ceiling.

"Below is where the lady of the manor stuff plays out," she tells you, offering her hand to steady your last few steps. "This is where I actually live."

What you assume was once a series of garrets - probably servants' quarters - have been opened out into one massive attic space. What can be seen of the walls under an expanse of op art paintings, film posters and velvet drapes, suggest a colour scheme primarily of crimson and black. The floor is polished wood, mostly covered with what appear to be oriental rugs, and rather than chairs, large cushions are scattered throughout. The room is illuminated by a couple of Tiffany lamps and a light bulb which appears to be, somehow, at the centre of a giant ball of string hanging from the ceiling.

"Take a pew," she tells you and crosses to where expensive looking hi-fi equipment sits in a teak cabinet. She slides an LP record out of its sleeve, places it on the turntable and carefully lowers the stylus. Although you don't see any speakers, music fills the room, Indian by the sound of it, both rhythmic and gentle.

Coming back over to where Jake has sat down on the cushion beside you, Georgie hands him the album cover.

"Fancy skinning up?" she asks.

Jake nods, taking it from her and resting it on his knees as she lowers herself into a cross-legged position opposite you. He takes a metal cigar tube from his pocket, uncaps it and empties out a packet of Rizla tobacco papers, several strips of the thin silver foil used to line cigarette packets, a razor blade and what looks like an OXO cube. Georgie passes him a filter Silk Cut.

Jake quickly joins two Rizlas together along their length and then a third with a vertical join at one end. He takes the cigarette and draws it across his tongue before splitting the moistened side with his thumbnail. He spills the tobacco evenly into the - so that's why it's called a joint, *flashes through your mind.*

He lays it back down on the album cover, picks up the silver paper and carefully peels away the white tissue backing. Working deftly with his fingers, he fashions a small spoon, twisting most of the foil into a long handle and smoothing the surface of the bowl with his thumb.

Jake reaches for what you'd thought was an OXO cube and which you're now absolutely sure isn't and with the razor blade slices a sliver away and places it in the makeshift spoon.

You note Georgie is watching as intently as you are, but guess that her silent fascination is more down to anticipation than intrigue.

Reaching into his pocket, Jake takes out a lighter and holds the flame under the hash. Strands of black smoke begin to rise and he moves his head forward to catch them with his nostrils. With a smile, Georgie leans towards him and Jake raises his hand so she can do the same, as the room is suddenly filled with an almost sickly sweet pungency.

He crumbles the contents of the spoon along the length of the joint and then deftly rolls it up. Once sealed, he twists one end shut, rips a strip of cardboard from the cover of the Rizla packet and makes a tight cylinder of it, which he inserts into the other.

"You somehow get the impression he's done this before, don't you?" Georgie dryly observes and Jake grins.

He tears off the twist and raising the spliff to his mouth, lights it. Smoke billows everywhere and after drawing deeply, he passes it over to Georgie.

After a few puffs, it's your turn.

You consider and then shake your head.

"I've never even smoked a cigarette," you tell them.

"Don't try to take it down," says Georgie. "Draw it in and then blow it straight out of your nose."

Tentatively, you hold the joint and raise it to your mouth. You cautiously breathe the smoke in, attempt to exhale through your nostrils and suddenly there is an explosion of spluttering and coughing that has tears rolling down your face.

Jake and Georgie are both laughing as he retrieves the spliff from between your fingers.

"Told you," you manage to say, in between outbursts.

Still smiling, the two of them pass the joint back and forth until your composure has mostly recovered.

"Let's try this," says Georgie, moving to kneel directly in front of you.

"Open wide," she tells you, raising the joint to her lips. She draws the smoke in deeply and then leans forward to cover your mouth with her own. You feel the fumes fill your airways and this time there is nothing acrid about it. But it is all enveloping and as you try to pull away, Georgie's hand is on the back of your neck, holding you in place. You struggle for a few seconds, then as a warm rush flows up through your body and into your mind, you find yourself surrendering to this completely. And perhaps without being sure what it is that you're actually surrendering to.

After what seems an age, but probably isn't, Georgie releases you.

"You okay?" she asks, staring you directly in the eyes.

You nod.

And gradually, you become aware of a different quality about the world. You're not exactly clear what that might be, but as you lay back listening to the music, you are conscious of it being inside your head rather than listened to. Your thoughts are quick firing, some too fast to keep up with, but there's no sense of confusion. It is simply the pace at which they are travelling. Eventually, you give up trying and lose yourself in sounds that you may or may not actually be hearing.

You are aware of being gently shaken awake.

"We'd better get you home," says Georgie softly, "or Benny will be having my guts for garters."

"What time is it?" you ask, dreamily.

"Almost midnight," she tells you and that stirs you back

to awareness. Opening your eyes, you're conscious that the world still has an ethereal quality to it, but one that no longer feels unmanageable. Raising yourself to your feet is less of a struggle than you expected, but apparently appears shaky enough for Georgie to reach out a steadying hand.

"We'll walk you back over there," she says.

"That's okay," Jake tells her. "If you want to get your head down, I could do with a breath of fresh air."

Georgie nods at this and the two of them see you down the steps from the attic, Jake leading and Georgie behind. After that, the rest of the descent through the house is a breeze.

By the front door Georgie holds your coat open for you to slip your arms into and then, as you turn, she leans forward and kisses you on the cheek.

"Sleep well," she says with a smile, "and we'll be seeing each other again soon."

It's a cloudless, starlit sky and the night air has a chill to it. But strangely, you don't find this uncomfortable, simply another sensation to be experienced.

Crossing the field towards The Hall, Jake keeps a torch directed on the ground in front of you both.

"How long have you known Georgie?" you ask.

"A couple of weeks," he says. "I was hitching down to London from a commune where I'd been staying. She gave me a lift and we seemed to hit it off." He grins. "Particularly when she found out I was carrying."

"Carrying?"

"Hash."

"Oh, right." You consider. "Isn't it a bit risky, hitchhiking with that on you? If you get stopped and searched by the police, I mean?"

He turns to you with a smile.

"The thing about a cigar tube," he says, "is that you have a place to conceal it not really accessible to a quick frisk." His smile widens at your puzzled expression. "Technically speaking," he adds, "you'd have two places to hide it."

"Oh!" *you exclaim, as comprehension dawns.*

"Can I ask how you found yourself at The Hall?" *he continues, thankfully covering your confusion.*

"It's..." *You shake your head.* "It's complicated."

"Fair enough." *Jake nods.* "Only Georgie said on the drive up here that there was a girl staying at The Hall who she really wanted to meet. It struck me that anyone who's managed to pique Georgie's interest probably has a story to tell."

You consider this, recollecting Miss Benfield telling you that Georgie was head of the board of trustees managing Linden Hall. So, it's more than likely she knows exactly the route your journey here has taken.

You're not quite sure what to make of that and thankfully Jake doesn't push things any further.

"Okay," *he says, as you reach the front door.* "Goodnight and see you soon."

"Goodnight," *you tell him,* "and thank you for walking me back here."

"No problem," *he smiles. Turning, he disappears into the night.*

You half expect Miss Benfield to be waiting up for you, folded arms and a stern expression, but she isn't. The entrance hall is silent and deserted, as are the corridors leading to your room. You're careful to fold the dress neatly, laying it on a chair ready to be returned.

Earlier you'd left the window slightly ajar. After years of dormitories, a freshly aired bedroom is a luxury you think you'll indulge yourself with forever. Then, still indifferent to the night's chill, you leave your nightgown hanging from the hook on the door and slip into bed au naturel, *cotton sheets against your bare skin as you rock slowly back and forth, firing sensations in your nerve endings that, for the first time in your life, have become truly alive.*

CHAPTER SIX

Venables

"How's it going?" asked Venables, entering the office and folding his mac over the back of a chair.

"DI Palmer's with him," said Kendall, taking his eyes from the two monitors on the desk in front of him. One showed a closeup of Christopher Franklyn's features, the other camera was set high in a corner of the room, displaying a side view of both Franklyn and DI Palmer.

Kendall removed the headset and microphone he was wearing and turned to Venables.

"He's been here for a couple of hours," he told him. "First with DS Sule. She took him through the photographs, establishing who was actually living in the house and who was only visiting. Then we moved on to who was still around after the August Bank holiday."

"I'm not sure how reliable my own memory would be on something like that," said Venables, sitting down. "Thirty years on."

"That weekend," said Kendall, "most of the people in the house had been at the Isle of Wight Festival. So, what he remembers is who he spoke with about that after they returned. Plus, he was keeping notes on what was going on in the place."

"Does he still have them?"

"No." Kendall shook his head. "But if you've actually written something down and then taken someone else through it, there's more chance it's likely to stick."

Venables nodded, acknowledging the point.

"Did he come up with anything?"

Kendall gave a slow nod.

"It seems we have confirmation that someone called 'Pete' disappeared about that time. Says he can't remember his surname," Kendall shrugged, "which isn't implausible."

"So, you think he's playing straight with us?" asked Venables.

"It's looking that way."

"How are we getting on with the warrant for Pembridge Villas?"

"A magistrate issued it this morning and I've a team going in around now."

"Still no word on who actually owns the place?"

"Well, no one's been there for the last few days. All we have is a shell company registered in the Cayman Islands - Maybe Enterprises."

"Which sounds more dodgy than not," said Venables dryly, and turned his attention to the screen.

Franklyn wasn't exactly what he'd expected. *'Amsterdam bookshop owner'* arrived with its own dubious connotations, but Franklyn appeared neither disreputable nor seedy enough to live down to them. He was casually dressed, but the clothes were expensive and his manner was assured without seeming pushy.

Kendall flicked a switch on one of the monitors and the sound from the interview came through hidden speakers. He picked up the headset and spoke into the microphone.

"We don't seem to be getting anywhere fast here, Amanda. Let's rattle his cage a bit, see what that does, shall we?"

On the monitor, DI Palmer gave an almost imperceptible nod.

Amanda

Amanda was growing increasingly rattled herself, realised she had to do something about that, but having an audience didn't help.

And it was all her own damn fault. She'd waltzed into this interview with no preparation, just a set of assumptions about a one time grass who now ran an Amsterdam bookshop and then somehow was playing catch-up from the off.

It wasn't simply that he proved a whole lot smarter than she'd expected - she knew how to deal with smart. Or even the sense that he was holding back far more than he was letting on, when was there ever anyone on the other side of the table who wasn't? It was a growing certainty that behind his placid composure he was more amused than intimidated by her and the more she *'rattled his cage'* the more her own facade actually began to crack, until finally...

"Look," Franklyn said, leaning back and studying her, "have I wandered into some bizarre Alice Through the Looking Glass world here? I was asked to infiltrate extremist groups by Special Branch and I was thanked for doing it by the Home Secretary, so please, spare me the retrospective moralistic hand-wringing."

"Mr Franklyn!" Amanda was aware of her tone becoming increasingly terse. "We have credible intelligence that at least one murder was committed at Pembridge Villas during the time you were living at the squat there. No, we are not sure of exactly what happened and nor were we able to gain access. But today we finally obtained a warrant to search the property and that search will be immediate and forensic - cadaver dogs in the grounds and in the house we'll be going behind walls and under floorboards."

She paused.

"What I need you to be perfectly clear about is that if we were to uncover evidence which suggests that you have, either by intent or omission, hampered the course of our investigation, then I can assure you the consequences will be very serious indeed."

Franklyn's expression was impassive.

Kendall's voice spoke in her ear.

"Well, that seems to have given him food for thought. Maybe let him have a chance to digest it."

"I'm not exactly sure," Franklyn said slowly, "what would constitute 'hampering by omission'?"

Amanda stared at him.

"It would be withholding information which you knew to be pertinent to our investigation, whether directly asked for it or not."

"Right, got it," nodded Franklyn. "Well, I'm not sure how pertinent this is to the investigation itself, but you do seem to be under the impression that Pembridge Villas was an actual squat."

"I'm sorry?" Amanda couldn't keep the surprise out of her voice.

"It wasn't - the house was being managed by Lee Munro and everyone living there paid rent."

"Managed?" Amanda was shaking her head. "Managed for who?"

Franklyn smiled.

"Don Mayberry."

"The actor?"

"Yeah, he bought it as an investment when he first went over to Hollywood." Franklyn leant back in his chair. "Lord Mayberry now, of course. You know, the Queen's favourite thesp and long-term polo playing chum of the Duke of Edinburgh. And you've obviously checked that he doesn't still own it, haven't you? Because that would be a really interesting conversation the next time he was round at the palace for lunch or having a chat between chukkas - Special Branch ripping his home apart. Be a fair bet that whatever clown put a fiasco like that together would be spending the rest of their career checking ferry passenger lists at Immingham Docks."

"Shit!!" Kendall's voice.

Amanda stared at Franklyn speechlessly.

Staring right back at her, he tapped one ear with his finger.

"Cat got your tongue?" he smiled.

* * *

Venables looked up as Kendall came back into the room. "Everything okay?" he asked.

"They were actually pulling up outside," Kendall said dryly. "Another few minutes and there would have been a considerable amount of egg on our face." He gestured at the screen. "Any more surprises."

Venables shook his head.

"Lee Munro's going to be in Cornwall this week if we want to talk to her. She has a home in St Hannahs. Other than that, it's about wrapped up..."

He broke off as Franklyn, already on his feet, seemed to hesitate.

"DI Palmer..." he began.

"Yes," she said, sitting back down.

"I know I don't have all the facts here," he told her, "and I get why that has to be. But could I just talk for a minute? And ask you to bear with me?"

Palmer nodded.

"A couple of years ago, for my birthday, my wife bought me *'The World At War'* on VHS. I don't know if you remember it, twenty-six hours of Second World War newsreel footage cut with interviews and narrated by Laurence Olivier. It was a big TV event at the time, back in the seventies."

"Yes," nodded DI Palmer. "I was only a teenager, but I do recall it."

"And it's still pretty good. I was worried that twenty-odd years later it wouldn't stand up. Lots of things don't but this actually did. Anyway, episode ten is *'Wolf Pack, War in the Atlantic'*. You probably don't remember, it was about the U-boat attacks on the merchant fleet."

DI Palmer shook her head, seemingly bemused.

"I must have seen it but, no, nothing specific comes to mind."

"Well, exactly. But the thing is, we all know now that the reason the Germans were beaten at sea was because Alan Turing's team at Bletchley had cracked the Enigma code - British Intelligence knew everything that German Naval Command was about to do. But when the series was being made, that information was still classified. Which gave the Ministry of Defence the interesting challenge of coming up with a plausible explanation of how a handful of rusty old frigates, and a squadron of Swordfish torpedo biplanes, managed to almost annihilate a fleet of four hundred U-Boats that were spending most of their time submerged in the middle of the Atlantic."

Franklyn paused.

"And do you know what their solution was?"

DI Palmer shook her head again.

"Johnny Walker."

"I'm sorry."

"Captain John Walker RN." Franklyn gave a wry smile. "Every time I think about what must have happened, it puts a smile on my face. It's late at night, the top brass are sitting around a table at the Admiralty, scratching their heads over what the hell can they come up with here. The whisky bottle's being passed along, glasses are being refilled, then someone looks at the label and slowly says 'What if...?'

"And so that was the story they spun. Captain Walker, terror of the high seas, scourge of the Kriegsmarine. U-Boat captains only had to see his frigate on the horizon puffing its way towards them and they might as well scupper the boat there and then and have done with it. 'Captain Walker's tactics in submarine warfare' - and this was a really nice touch - 'were so revolutionary that aspects of them are still classified today'. And unfortunately, he couldn't be interviewed - he died of natural causes just before the war ended.

"And no one batted a bloody eyelid." Franklyn stared at her. "Look, I lived undercover for years and the first lesson you learn is that people will believe pretty much anything until you give them reason not to. That the most effective deceptions are about managing expectation by manipulating context." He shrugged. "And if you don't have the correct context, then any 'intelligence' can be made to seem credible."

He paused, as if choosing his next words carefully.

"I think you're being spun a line," he told her. "I think you've been convinced that Johnny Walker sank all the submarines. And I think that what you really should be doing here is finding out why."

Franklyn gave DI Palmer a final smile, shook hands and left the room.

She turned and, as she stared into the camera, her expression was inscrutable.

Jenny

The Reverend Jenny Warwick didn't spot her at first. It was her habit when entering the church in the evening to use the side entrance, not wishing to intrude on anyone's silent worship whilst passing through the nave. Usually she'd busy herself in the sacristy or around the altar, where there was always something to be tidied or straightened. Most got the message and she rarely had to approach someone to gently inform them that the building was about to be locked up for the night.

But the woman had been bowed so far forward she'd missed her completely and her straightening up in the corner of Jenny's vision had caused her almost to jump.

As if churches couldn't be spooky enough already...!

Jenny expected the woman would now rise and leave and so went into the oratory to give her a few moments to get herself together. But on Jenny's return she was still sitting there, staring blankly ahead. Adopting what she hoped was a purposeful yet friendly air, Jenny made her way towards her, but then slowed as she saw tears coursing down both cheeks.

"Hello," she said, softly. "Are you alright?"

Turning her head to Jenny was the first indication the woman gave of registering her.

"Yes, I..." The woman broke off, as if trying to gather her thoughts. "I guess I just lost myself for a while there." She stared around at the empty church. "Sorry, you must be waiting to lock up."

She lifted her bag and made as if to rise, but Jenny slipped into the pew alongside her and, sitting down, laid a hand on her arm.

"No, please," Jenny told her. "Take as long as you need."

The woman reached into her bag for a handkerchief.

"I'm okay now," she said to Jenny. Dabbing at her eyes, she managed a weak smile. "I usually only get ambushed at night, I guess there's," she turned her head and let her gaze sweep the church, "a lot of resonance here."

"And perhaps being far from home?" suggested Jenny. The American accent was unmistakable.

"That too," she nodded.

"Look," said Jenny, "I was just about to make myself a cup of tea. Would you care to join me? I have coffee, too," she added.

The woman gave another small smile.

"Tea's fine," she said.

"I'm Reverend Warwick," Jenny told her, rising. "Or Jenny, if you'd find that easier?"

"Hi," said the woman. "I'm Gail."

Amanda

It was with some relief Amanda that let herself in through her front door.

There're good days and there's bad days, she reflected, and somehow both were easier to deal with when drawing to a close than these mixtures of triumph and disaster, tugging your psyche this way and that until you weren't really sure what you thought about anything at all. Just found yourself at the drinks cabinet before even taking your coat off, half filling a tumbler with Johnnie Walker Black Label.

She'd been unforgivably sloppy when it came to Christopher Franklyn, knew she'd be beating herself up over that for a good while yet. 'Amsterdam bookstore owner' was almost a cliche in itself and she'd blithely gone along with it. But like Brian Maddox said, this tip-off was from those flitting around the edges of the underworld and how many times did she need telling that Chinese whispers were the *lingua franca* of that realm?

The bookshop Franklyn owned was actually antiquarian, dealing in rare volumes and prints. He and his wife inherited the business from his father-in-law who'd died the previous year, were just keeping it ticking over while probate was being settled.

Franklyn's *actual* profession, it turned out, was journalism, with occasional forays into ghosting autobiographies for minor celebrities and if Amanda had known *that* when she'd sat down with him, she'd have come at things from a very different direction. A hack with a nose for poking around the anecdotal nooks and crannies of someone's life would prove every bit as good as she was at going head to head and so it proved, with Amanda wrong footed from the start.

Yet...

Franklyn had filled in a lot of gaps, plus unknowingly

giving credence to DS Sule's conviction that their victim was Peter Marshall.

'It does seem like he's being straight with us' had been Keith Venables' verdict and that was Amanda's problem. Plausibility rarely flows so smoothly without at least a hint of being just a touch too well orchestrated. Wrong'un or not the jury was still out on, but every instinct she possessed told her Christopher Franklyn was playing some game of his own here.

The briefing with Sir Richard Milford went better than expected. Implications snap sharply into focus with the realisation that the person you're sitting next to will shortly be repeating your words to the Prime Minister, but the Cabinet Secretary reacted with a surprising amount of aplomb as the events of the previous week were laid out for him. Grasping the basic tenet that until there's actually a body all of this was little more than hearsay, he gave them *carte blanche* to venture wherever their enquiries might lead and assurances he'd use the full weight of his office on their behalf against any obstacles encountered there.

In the bedroom, Amanda changed into jeans and a sweater before pulling a suitcase out from under the bed. She'd intended to leave for the West Country in the morning, but Keith Venables cautioned her against turning up unheralded. Provincial forces had a tendency to get prickly about Met officers moonlighting on their turf, so let him have a word with the Chief Constable and set up some local support through official channels. She couldn't do the journey to St Hannahs and back in a single day, he'd pointed out, plus she'd be unlikely to find a hotel room because of the eclipse. So why not drive as far as somewhere like Taunton tomorrow, spend the night there and see what's what with this Susan Marshall first thing the next day? And as eager as Amanda was to get started, his logic was hard to fault.

The day's real bolt from the blue came after Sir Richard's departure. About to leave herself, Kendall had taken Amanda to one side and, almost as if he could read every doubt in her mind, offered her a job at NCIS. He'd then followed that up with an extremely persuasive manifestation of just what a smart move that might prove.

All in all, she had a lot to think about over the next few days.

Jenny

Jenny knew that the art of being a good listener was to actually listen. Sounds obvious, but so many people treat the other side of a conversation as little more than rehearsal space for what they were about to say next. *'Empty your mind, open your heart,'* had been a valuable mantra on her path towards ordination - but never use *that* word around the deacon - and it always served her dealings with parishioners well. It's all too easy to fill in the blanks of someone's life with preconceptions.

"It was a car crash about twenty years ago," Gail told her. "And considering the collision was head on, Mike thought he'd been lucky to get away with a fractured tibia and a couple of busted ribs." She paused, then let out a sigh. "But he'd lost blood and so the hospital gave him a transfusion before setting his leg."

Jenny remained silent.

"Nobody even knew what hepatitis C was in those days. Wasn't until Mike was diagnosed with cirrhosis of the liver - 'two beers Mike' - that alarm bells went off. But by then..."

Gail's voice trailed off.

"What about you?" asked Jenny, softly.

"Oh, it was no surprise I tested positive," Gail told her. "We'd never given up trying for a family, right until..." She shook her head. "But I was lucky, if you can call it that. A drug called interferon had been developed, too late for Mike, he had full-blown liver cancer." Her voice grew cold. "And the side effects of my treatment meant I couldn't..." Her eyes began to water. "At the end, when I should have been strong for him..."

She broke off.

"Can I ask?" Jenny reached out for her hand, gently squeezed it, "Are you over here all alone? Do you have someone to talk to?"

Gail wiped her eyes.

"After I got the all clear in June," she said, "I wanted to

get back to being busy as soon as I could manage. Just dreaded wandering around an empty house." She stared at Jenny. "I work in TV, for a true crime show called *Belladonna*."

Jenny shook her head.

"Sorry, I don't really watch much television."

"It only goes out in the States," Gail shrugged. "But while I was away, the studio's been in talks with the BBC about co-producing a series of specials. The show's been on hiatus, so I thought I'd come over to the UK and get the feel of things for myself. And mostly that's worked out." Gail gave a tight smile. "Wasn't till I took a breather that I got sideswiped."

"When are you off home?"

"Probably the weekend." Gail started gathering her things. "Pre-production for the new series begins at the end of the month."

"Are you going to be alright?" asked Jenny.

"Sure," said Gail. "Just talking was..." She gave Jenny a nod. "Thank you."

Both women rose.

"Look..." began Jenny.

"If I need another cup of tea," Gail told her, "I'll know where to come."

"Okay," smiled Jenny. "Let me show you out."

During your absence the previous evening, the duty roster has been updated to have you working in the gardens today. It's work you enjoy, trimming hedges and mowing lawns may be trivial tasks but that never diminishes the sense of achievement which always accompanies you back to the house.

Just before lunch, you receive a message from the Head Gardener that Miss Benfield wishes to see you in her office. Such summons rarely arrive without a touch of trepidation, irrespective of whether you've anything to feel guilty about, so it's with a sense of relief that you are greeted with a smile.

"I take it things went well last night?" she asks.

You nod and she motions you to sit down.

"Lady Georgina, as you've probably gathered, is usually accompanied by a maid. However," she makes a dismissive gesture with her hand, "for reasons I'm not entirely clear about, this has not been possible for her current sojourn. So," her gaze is steady, as if considering you, "she has asked if she could requisition you for a few hours each day."

Miss Benfield pauses, as if to gauge your reaction to this, but you're too surprised to do anything other than stare back at her uncertainly.

"The duties would involve light housework and preparing breakfast each morning," she continues. "Nothing I'd imagine you'd find too onerous and I doubt Lady Georgina is an early riser." *She stares directly at you.* "Would you have any objection to this arrangement?"

"No." *You shake your head slowly.* "No, of course not, Miss Benfield."

"Good." *She hesitates slightly.* "Additionally, you've spent some time with Peter Matthews? Posing for him?"

"Yes."

"It appears he enjoys working with you. He's asked that, if it wouldn't interfere with your other work, he'd like you to be available for the rest of his stay. Another fortnight, I believe. Shall we tell him that two to three hours in the afternoons would be possible?"

You nod, cautiously.

"As long as that won't cause problems with your own arrangements, Miss Benfield?"

"Your consideration is noted and appreciated," she says dryly. "But I'll manage."

Miss Benfield sits back in her chair.

"During your short time here," she studies you thoughtfully, "you've performed your duties more than adequately. It would also seem that you have a talent for arousing interest in others whilst being neither ingratiating nor obsequious."

She seems to weigh her words with care.

"I don't know the details of the circumstances which brought you to Linden Hall," she continues, "but you have a real chance to overcome the disadvantages which dogged your past. Both Lady Georgina and Peter are placing great faith in you. I urge you to do your very best not to let them down."

"I won't, Miss Benfield," you tell her, allowing your head to bow slightly. "Thank you."

And the road to hell, they say, is paved with good intentions.

Georgie's breakfast, you quickly discover, is rarely more than a pot of black coffee and an unfiltered Pall Mall, while 'light housework' is sweeping away the detritus of the previous evening's indulgences. You still wonder about the 'girl I'd really like to meet' comment Jake repeated to you, but most of the morning is spent chatting and listening to records whilst, Jake - having taken on an unofficial role of factotum - chops wood or mends fences. Most days prior to your departure, the three of you share a spliff, which sets you up nicely for an afternoon with Peter.

His chatter is incessant as he works, ranging from salacious gossip to the technique of artists he admires. He's not above breaking off from his work to make a point he thinks worth emphasising, opening one of the many art books filling the shelves to demonstrate Van Gogh's sleight of hand here or how Mondrian's style changes so abruptly there.

He also spends more time with the sketch pad you've handed back than you thought he would. 'You have a good eye,' he declares. 'With a natural instinct for making a composition work - it's only technique that's letting you down and that can be taught. You should seriously consider art college.'

You tentatively explain your lack of both qualifications and funds. Peter shrugs. He knows people, he tells you. And grants are easy enough to come by these days. He opens the desk drawer, takes out a cellophane wrapped, hardback notebook and, tearing the packaging away, hands it to you, together with a couple of pencils.

'A proper artist's workbook,' he smiles. 'Fill it with whatever you fancy and I'll pass it on to some people who could help you.'

A few days later, you've finished the housework before Georgie's returned from a trip to the village and Jake comes into the kitchen for a coffee. You get him to pose for a quick thumbnail sketch.

"Don't you have to be back at The Hall?" he asks.

"Peter's gone to Newcastle for the day with Sebastian," you tell him. "I've the afternoon free."

"Right," he says, looking at you in a rather odd manner. "So, fancy a trip?"

"Where to?"

He grins.

"Oh, places you couldn't even begin to imagine."

You stare at him, suddenly uncertain.

"Have you heard of acid?" he asks.

Of course you've heard of acid, it's liquid that burns. But something about the way he phrases the question suggests there's more to what he's saying and so you simply fix him with a questioning look.

"It's proper name is LSD," he eventually tells you.

"What does it do?"

"Well, it's a bit like opium, but not addictive. Colours get brighter, everything's very dreamlike but at the same time insightful. Psychiatrists have been using it to break destructive habit patterns, obsessive or compulsive behaviour. Some people hallucinate a lot."

"Okay," you shrug. Coleridge, Keats, De Quincey, they all used opium to churn over the darker reaches of the mind. Even Byron. So, why not give mad, bad and dangerous to know a whirl?

"Are you having your period?" asks Jake.

"No." You shake your head, looking at him quizzically.

"Probably best not having to be dealing with the messier aspects of life when tripping," he tells you. "It's surprising how fastidious cosmic consciousness can turn out to be. Usually a good idea to move your bowels first, too."

On returning from taking care of that detail, you find Jake sitting at the table unscrewing the top of a tiny, glass eyedropper bottle. Two sugar cubes are each standing on a square of metallic kitchen foil. You watch as he carefully lets the smallest drop of a clear, odourless fluid fall onto each of them.

He slides one over to you.

The liquid is tasteless, your mouth filled only with the tangy sweetness of moist sugar.

"Lick the foil as well," says Jake. "In case it seeped all the way through."

"So now what?" you ask, sitting back.

"So now," he smiles, "we wait."

You suppose twenty minutes or so have passed and you're beginning to feel bored. So bored, in fact, that you yawn.

And then suddenly stop, your hand flying to your chin.

The sensation was that of your lower jaw falling almost down to your stomach. But it's still there, you reassure yourself, still in place.

"Are you okay?"

You see Jake's lips moving, but the voice seems to be in your head, rather than outside.

You nod and risk speaking.

"I think so." You're conscious of the words forming in your mind before hearing them aloud. This strikes you as a novel concept, as if they've previously tumbled from your mouth of their own accord. "Everything's... strange."

"I'll put some music on," he says.

He rises, seemingly continuing upwards forever. Appearing to glide rather than walk over to the stereo, he kneels down by a collection of LPs. As he - endlessly - flicks through them, you become fixated by the play of light on the wall opposite the window, passing clouds you assume, but then looking out across the garden see only a clear blue sky.

There's a burst of static, a slow hiss as the stylus plays along a silent groove and then the room fills with music. Literally fills - silver and gold squiggles of sound rise from the speakers, languidly tumbling over themselves. You stare at the record cover Jake rests against the cabinet and recognise it as a Jacques Loussier Play Bach album, but, although you've come to know it well, the sounds you're hearing trigger no resonance in memory.

Turning back to the wall, the flickering shadows of only a few seconds ago - and how ludicrous is time, you reflect, it should be possible to extend or contract each moment to the exact length you need it to be - has now become a translucent diorama, playing out a scene from what appears to be a 17th century ballroom.

Ladies in extravagant gowns curtsy to bewigged gentlemen in elaborate livery. This slowly dissolves and reforms into a group of figures gathered around a bed on which a woman is sweating through the rigours of childbirth. It would seem to be of the same period, but the dingy attic lit by a single candle and shabby clothing reeks of poverty and deprivation.

You realise the room you are in has now taken on the same diaphanous quality of the scene you're viewing. There is the sense that you could walk from one straight into the other. You rise to your feet and move towards it. Perhaps too quickly, there is a rush of blood passing by your ears and you pause.

You shut your eyes for a second to reorientate. Opening them you find yourself entirely immersed in a latticework of light, joining myriad bright points and which you instantly understand to be the underpinnings of reality itself. And which is less a construct than a vibrating entity, of which each minute aspect is in *continual transformation and renewal.*

Yourself included... You grasp that we no more move through this world than a TV screen displaying the Taj Mahal has journeyed to Asia.

There is another rush of blood and you close your eyes. You open them to the room as it always was. The wall is just a wall and music no longer a visual spectacle.

You're not sure if the constriction in your throat is from relief or regret.

A large mirror sits atop an old sideboard and you carefully make your way towards it. You're curious to engage with whoever might be on the other side of the looking glass.

You don't recall having taken your clothes off and, for a moment, experience disquiet at the nude girl staring curiously back out at you. Then she smiles and so you relax. You turn around. Maybe Jake can explain how you've come to find yourself like this, but you are alone, the door to the room slightly ajar.

You shrug and return to the mirror.

You've rarely been capable of such genuine detachment. The legs could be longer, you decide, the boobs a touch perkier, but from the neck down you've no real complaints.

You lean in closer, to take in the features.

They sit well in the heart-shaped face, you conclude. You recall once thinking that your smile could be a little wider and your lips fuller, but on reflection - you giggle at the term - that'd probably be too much for such a pert nose. The eyes...

'Oh, you've been suckered in here' *flashes through your mind as you try to pull away from those deep, dark pools, but it's already too late. They've locked onto your gaze and are holding you fast.*

You succumb, ready to be immersed, half eager, half apprehensive to learn what might be down there. It takes a moment to realise that they really are just deep dark pools and that their function is simply to hold you in place.

The real show has been waiting in the wings.

Around those eyes in the mirror, the visage ever so slowly begins to change. At first it only ages, crows feet and worry lines deepen, features coarsen, greying locks hang lank. The skin tightens until the effect is almost skull like, but then appears the face of a young girl. She is fair skinned, her hair - 'flaxen' enters your mind - is braided in a manner that conjures longships, axes and battle cries. The hair darkens and thickens, as do the lips, the nose lengthens, curves and a tear courses down her cheek as she weeps and remembers Zion.

The transformations are now a whirl, a Chinese dowager with no knowledge of hunger or privation, a black wrinkled countenance which knows only of life on the plantation becomes the sunken cheeks, shaven head and haunted expression that daily watches smoke rise from the ovens. Pleasure, pain, ecstasy and terror stare out from the mists of time and all with the same message.

You know nothing!

You're aware of your name being called, softly at first, then in a tone more insistent, but it is impossible to tear your eyes away. Fingers closing around your wrist and gently tugging are equally inconsequential. Next there is a hand on each shoulder and you are being turned, quite forcibly, until the mirror passes out of your field of vision and you are back in the room.

Georgie and Jake are side by side, Georgie full of concern, Jake wide-eyed. You're careful not to meet either's gaze.

"Are you okay?" asks Georgie.

You take a while to consider this, probably long enough for that to be an answer in itself.

"What the fuck happened?" she demands of Jake.

"We were listening to music." He shook his head. "I had my eyes closed. When I opened them, she was standing over by the wall and her clothes were on the floor. I tried talking to her but there was no response… It's like she was catatonic."

"How much did you give her?"

"A single drop - around two hundred mikes… I took the same."

"Well, something's fucked up," Georgie tells him and turns

her attention back to you.

"Could be one of the crystals didn't completely dissolve," Jake says quietly. "I've heard of that happening."

"Everything's alright," Georgie reassures you. "We're going to stay here and take care of you."

You're still not entirely sure this is actually real and so you reach out to lay your palm on Georgie's arm. Dry and warm against your skin, you also become conscious of a miasma of scents and secretions about her that makes you want to draw her close, for reasons ambiguous enough to make that an impulse you resist.

"Just checking," you tell her.

"Go and fetch some orange juice," she tells Jake.

He nods and leaves the room. You're aware of a shimmering, of shapes beginning to coalesce along the wall.

You grasp Georgie's hand tightly.

"It's starting to happen again," you say.

"What's happening?"

You take a breath.

"Everything's connected," you explain. "That chair, the carpet, me, you. They're the same particles in constant transmutation..."

The room has become still.

"You can't experience it and define it at the same time," you continue, slowly. "That's why science and spirituality..."

Your thoughts are racing away faster than your voice can keep pace with.

"Okay..." says Georgie. "Well, shall we get your dress back on?"

"This is really important," you tell her, but are aware that even as you speak, this train of thought has already moved beyond the limits of comprehension.

Maybe if you close your eyes again, perhaps...

"Why don't you explain it all to me in a bit," Georgie is taking you by the arm, "but in the meantime, best not to be flashing your fanny at everyone passing by."

She leads you over to where your clothes still lay in a

crumpled heap and picks up your dress.

"Arms up," she tells you, slipping it down over your head and you take unexpected pleasure in being managed in such a childlike fashion.

"That's better," she says, tugging everything neat and straight as Jake comes back into the room carrying a pint glass of orange juice.

"Drink all of it," says Jake. "Vitamin C helps to bring you down."

You consider this.

"I'm not sure I want to come down," you conclude and then shrug. "Perhaps just a bit."

Georgie lets a smile play on her lips.

"Well, only half of it then."

It's possibly the most delicious drink you've ever tasted, giving you an idea of what the ancients had in mind when they spoke of nectar. So much so that you're eventually aware you're holding an empty glass in your hands.

"Oh dear," you say, staring at it.

"I wouldn't worry," says Jake. "It probably hasn't done more than take the edge off. If that."

Georgie reaches for the glass and places it on the table.

"Let's go through into the drawing room," she suggests. "I'll light a fire."

"Okay," you tell her.

Kneeling at the fireplace, Georgie fashions a construction of kindling, logs and coal.

"My first governess taught me how to do this," she tells you, sitting back on her heels as she lights a long taper with a match. "She'd been a scullery maid when she was a girl - literally a girl, I don't think she'd have been more than ten years old at the time - and she had to be up at five thirty every morning to light fires in the kitchen and dining room."

She carefully manoeuvres the full length of the taper through an outer gap and you hear only the slightest whoosh as the centre ignites. Smoke rises and then comes the crackling of dry wood.

You picture a young girl on her knees in a cold, dark kitchen, a slight figure whose plain, black cotton dress, white cap and apron which, however frequently starched and ironed, will always be as synonymous with poverty as any beggar's rags.

What were her dreams, what would have been the most she could have hoped for...? Before you realise it's happening - and can pull hard on the reins - the progression of humanity begins to unfold for you.

You're not exactly back to living in caves, but close. Earthen burrows, stone built hovels, timber shacks, then the birth of aspiration... Grasping that however shitty this existence might be, the world you'll eventually depart could be a better place than the one you entered. That despite how much pain and sorrow the future may hold, hope lies there too.

It is less the circle of life than unfurled propagation, hundreds of swollen bellies push out thousands more to become millions. A roaring torrent of flesh, blood and bone cascades down through the centuries, unstoppable - plague and warfare the occasional blockage but swiftly swept aside - while the fairy tales of religion and science bicker endlessly through the futility of making sense of the unknowable.

What a fucking mess!

"Sorry?"

Georgie is staring and you realise you must have spoken aloud.

You shake your head.

"Just... Running things through my mind," you tell her. "Trying to sort them out."

Georgie smiles.

"And how's that going?"

"It's... Better."

Which, in a way, is true. Whatever you're experiencing right now could, by no stretch of the imagination, be described as normal, but you no longer feel cast adrift from reality. You may *still be seeing what isn't there and hearing what isn't happening, but you are at a point where you know they're not there and aren't happening. You grasp that why this should be what you're seeing and hearing is what should be pursued.*

"Would you like a cup of tea?" asks Georgie and you nod.

The fire is well alight now. You lean forward and peer into the flames, never before having the need of psychedelics to see dramas unfold in the glowing coals.

But perversely all you experience is a dull red glow.

Georgie returns with a mug and you sit side by side.

"Jake is asleep," she tells you. "He must have taken some downers, I can never sleep after tripping."

Glancing at the windows, you notice it's now dark outside. Where did the hours go?

"He really likes you, you know?"

At your lack of response to this, Georgie studies you carefully.

"Do you mind me asking," she says, "but have you done it yet? All the way, I mean?"

Where to start? Although, in terms of what the guardians of morality would consider to be the definitive act, you remain undamaged goods, it's impossible to have been through what you have without the sense that you're at least a touch shop soiled.

But you simply give her a half smile and slowly shake your head.

"Come on," says Georgie eventually. "Let's get you back to the Hall."

You have a sleepless night, but not a disturbing one. It's not so much memories emerging from the shadows as the darkness itself retreating, events which once touched your mind like an electric shock are now strangely devoid of potency. Not that they are any less shocking, simply that your perspective on them appears to have been inverted. The only power sordid appetites and spiteful vindictiveness ever held over you was that with which your innocence endowed them and that time has passed.

This is a revelation of such magnitude that it feels anticlimactic - if not downright wrong - to be arriving without some degree of fanfare, but it doesn't. It's simply that in your deepest, inner self you are no longer cowering in a darkened room but standing on a sunlit plain, surrounded by clear horizons.

And, just before dawn, you slip into - for the first time in many, many years - dreamless sleep.

Woken by the alarm clock, you stretch your limbs like a cat, enjoying the tautness along the length of the muscles.

You half expect some morning-after settling of the bill to be paid, such as follows an evening's overindulgence with alcohol, but your head is clear. After slipping on your dressing gown, there is even a spring in your step as you make your way down the corridor to the bathroom.

Emptying your bladder and splashing cold water on your face, you seem more conscious of your body than usual, a tingling of the skin perhaps, or an awareness of inner activities about their daily business. There's a sense of physical lightness, particularly in your stomach, which you don't want to lose and so, after dressing, you decide to skip breakfast and head straight over to Georgie's house.

As you arrive, she's sitting at the kitchen table sipping black coffee, smoke curling up from the inevitable Pall Mall in an ashtray.

"How do you feel?" she asks

You consider

"Different," you tell her. "But okay."

"Things will settle down eventually," she tells you. "The thing about acid is that you never come back down to where you took off from." She lifts the cigarette to her lips and draws on it. "It takes a while to ease into a new normal."

"A new normal?"

"Acid is very good," Georgie's tone is cautious, "at keeping you distracted while the real work gets done in the background. While you're watching the firework display, there's a fair bit of *rewiring going on in the back of your head. The first time you drop it, at least."* She considers you carefully. *"And it's stuff you're more likely to stumble across casually than experience as a blinding light on the road to Damascus moment."*

The two of you sit in silence, but not an uncomfortable one. You've a lot to reflect on and Georgie, more than anyone, understands that's best done without distraction.

CHAPTER SEVEN

Shravasti

Shravasti knocked on Kendall's half opened office door.

"Do you have a moment, sir?" she asked. "I think I might have found something."

Kendall rose from his chair and followed Shravasti over to her desk, standing behind her as she sat down and began to tap at her keyboard.

"I decided to broaden our search parameters," she told him. "Looking at what was termed the counterculture back then in general rather than specific terms."

After a few seconds, a website appeared on the screen.

"This belongs to a Linda Thompson. She teaches at the Central London Poly - sorry, the University of Westminster these days - a MSc Contemporary History course. AltaVista came up with an article she'd written about the Notting Hill arts scene of thirty years ago and she mentions sharing a house with Aidan McShane and Lee Munro. But the really interesting thing was..."

Shravasti began scrolling down the page.

"...this."

A photo appeared. Half a dozen people were positioned on the steps leading up to the door of what they both now had no problem recognising as the house in Pembridge Villas. Three males and three females, all in their early twenties and the fashions and hairstyles suggested the late sixties. Kendall leant forward and began tapping the screen.

"Lee Munro, Peter Marshall, Aidan McShane," he said softly.

"The girl on the left," said Shravasti, "Franklyn recognised as Claudia Falcone, the other he knew only as Ronnie, I'm guessing a nickname."

The caption under the image read 'Housemates, 1970'.

Kendall pointed to the third male.

"So who's he?"

"Exactly. 'Housemates' it says," Shravasti turned to look at Kendall, "but he's not in a single one of those surveillance photographs."

"I assume," said Kendall, still staring at the screen, "that we have an address for this Linda Thompson?"

Tony

Tony Meadows climbed the stairs back up to his floor rather than use the lift. It was the accumulative effect of the little things in life, he believed, which ultimately made the big differences and took pride in fitting into the same size suit he'd worn twenty-five years ago.

Tony set great store in keeping fit.

He arrived at his room with a sense of relief. The last seminar of the day had dealt with revised pension regulations and after only half an hour he'd had to nudge his neighbour, who'd begun to softly snore.

"Sorry," the guy mumbled, embarrassed and apologetic.

"Don't worry about it," said Tony, quietly. "Another ten minutes of this and you'll probably be doing the same for me."

Back when he'd started at Midland Bank, things were simple. Banks were repositories of customer funds, which accountancy practices advised on and insurance brokers offered cover for. But the last twenty years had seen more than a degree of what Tony regarded as 'seepage'. Accountants no longer simply suggested that you needed a pension, they'd actually sell you one and frequently in collusion with a bank who'd more than likely tie your business overdraft to the conditions attached.

The days of bank managers sitting behind a desk, finger wagging at wayward account holders before being taken out for a three hour boozy lunch by prosperous ones, were long gone. Today they had targets and be prepared for a visit to Head Office if they were missed two months in a row.

And it wasn't as if there were any options to move on from here. Tony, like most bank employees, benefited from a heavily subsidised mortgage. That large, detached house in Highbury would be way beyond the means of most people on a similar salary and he could well imagine Anne's reaction to the prospect of downsizing.

Far as Tony could see, he was shackled for life.

One of the few perks to all of this was the need for continual refresher courses, two or three day jollies such as this and usually at some home counties golf club or south coast resort. He guessed St Hannahs had been picked because tomorrow's total eclipse could only be seen along the south-west peninsular. Most of the other delegates seemed enthusiastic about it, Tony thought it sounded a grim affair and a more than suitable backdrop to the bank's latest Machiavellian dictates.

The only talk today which really sparked his interest had been a seminar on cybersecurity. The speaker was both amusing and informative, leading Tony to believe he must have been a specialist consultant rather than an employee. The bank had recently issued all managers with laptop computers, through which Tony discovered the internet, something he'd previously thought solely the domain of geeks and freaks.

He hadn't been stupid enough to use it for personal web surfing. He'd guessed - quite correctly it turned out, as several colleagues received memos regarding *'inappropriate usage'* - that every single thing he was doing on there would be monitored and logged. But once he'd mastered the basics he bought a machine of his own, a cheap entry level model but more than adequate for what he had in mind.

There was a quarter of an hour before dinner. Tony sat down at the desk stroke dressing table in front of the mirror, took out this laptop and opened it up. The PCMCIA card he slid into the slot on the side looked identical to the modem his business one used, but it wasn't. Firstly, it had cost a great deal more, secondly it was only available via word-of-mouth introductions in very select circles and thirdly, just switching it on was highly illegal.

What it actually did was to search the ether for nearby unsecured internet connections - people were almost unbelievably lax about passwording their online presence - and then piggyback them onto the World Wide Web.

'Unless you start downloading masses of data,' the nerdy looking kid in the Islington pub had told him, exchanging the card for a roll of used fivers, 'no one'll know you're there and anything you get up to is gonna have their digital fingerprint on it, not yours.'

Tony waited, watching the slowly circling graphic in the centre of the screen. Then a box popped up, listing four connections and each with a zero against them, signifying they'd not previously been utilised.

Which, considering he was three hundred miles from home, came as no surprise.

He clicked on the top one and after a few seconds his Netscape browser loaded. Tony typed an address into the search bar and then his username and password into the website that appeared. He navigated to the page he needed, posted a short message and then exited back to the Windows 95 desktop to log out. Flipping the lid closed, he stood up.

Hopefully, by the time he could extricate himself from the inevitable post dinner drinks session, he'd have something sorted.

Andy

The thing was not to panic.

Andy tightened his grip on the young Traveller's arm - thank Christ he'd got the cuffs on before all hell broke loose - and took in the situation once more.

Three other Travellers, holding pickaxe handles, stood between him and his car. Surrounding this scenario was a crowd of about twenty, a mixture of angry locals and curious tourists it looked like. He knew that if the Travellers went for him the townsfolk would pile in on his side, but there was no way he could see a fracas like that ending without someone getting their head busted open and that was the last thing St Hannahs needed right now.

Trouble had been brewing all week. Since Richard Hanson had been found unconscious by his car, the rumour mill was insistent the Travellers were behind it and tensions were ratcheting up by the day. Jack got Harry Thomas to block the gateway to Belle Meadow with one of his skips so they couldn't leave, but in the meantime the town had reached its own verdict and so they weren't getting served in the shops and pubs, either.

Jack had been doing his best to calm things down - even been on the verge of letting them move on, judging by what he'd been saying earlier - because everyone knew this had become a powder keg just waiting to blow. Thing was, you could never be sure where the spark would come from...

Andy would never have guessed the new art gallery.

But this Traveller had gotten inside and thrown paint or something over one of the pictures. He'd made a run for it, but a student working there started chasing him and was joined by a couple of farmhands leaving a nearby pub. They'd caught up with him in the square and had him down on the ground when Andy'd arrived on the scene. He'd just finished cuffing him when a battered old van pulled up and these other three got out. Meanwhile, word's obviously been flying around town because the crowd surrounding them was growing larger by the minute.

Then, from a distance, came the faint wail of a siren.

Halle-bloody-lujah, was Andy's first thought, but knew he was being unfair. This standoff might have felt it was dragging on forever, but time had its own box of tricks in these situations. It probably hadn't been more than a couple of minutes since...

Jack's car screeched to a halt on the other side of the square. Andy struggled to keep a determined expression in place as a wave of relief rushed over him and heads turned to watch Jack pushing his way through the crowd until he stood between Andy and the three Travellers.

"You have to leave," Jack told the eldest of the trio. "If this goes any further, you'll be leaving me with no options here."

"That's my son," one of the others said angrily, but the elder motioned him to silence, staring at Jack.

"The doctors at the hospital," Jack continued, "reckon it was a medical condition which put Mr Hanson into intensive care." He paused. "So, I was about to let that go when..."

He gestured behind him to Andy and the Traveller in handcuffs.

"He's being arrested on suspicion of breaking and entering and causing criminal damage," he said to the boy's father. "We'll be keeping him in custody at least overnight, while we investigate those charges and," with a nod towards the still gathering throng, "for his own protection."

The elder appeared to consider this and then nodded. He turned to study the crowd..

"So many art lovers," he said dryly.

Jack gave only the slightest inclination of his head, Andy could imagine his wry smile.

"You'll be able to see him tomorrow," Jack told him. "Just check with the duty officer by phone first."

"As you say, Sergeant."

The three of them walked towards their van, the crowd silently parting for them. Jack gestured for Andy to put the young Traveller into the back of his squad car before turning his attention to everyone still gathered around them.

"Okay, folks," he said. "Show's over."

Tony

Tony Meadows had the act of disengaging from jovial company, without actually being missed, down to a fine art. The trick, he'd learnt over the years, was mobility.

A gathering of thirty or so people in a hotel bar inevitably splinters into much smaller groups and so moving from one to the other every few minutes creates an impression of being ever present, one further bolstered by their copious imbibing and his not actually saying goodbye to anyone prior to slipping away.

In his impatience to return to his room he was tempted to break habit and take the lift, but the lobby was between the bar and the Gents and there was a good chance of being confronted whilst waiting for it to descend.

"Oh, the night's still young," he could imagine a cheery voice cajoling. "At least have one for the road."

He compromised by taking the stairs to the next floor and then the lift up to the third. Letting himself into his room, his first action was opening his laptop and bringing it out of sleep mode. He kicked off his shoes, hung up his jacket and then sat down at the machine.

Pecking at the keyboard, he went through exactly the same sequence as before, albeit selecting a different connection, and eventually arrived at the notice board he'd posted on earlier.

'Bi, 48, looking for meet, St Hannahs, can accom, msg for details.'

Tony clicked on it to discover seven replies listed. Clicking on each displayed the text, while at the bottom of the screen were options to view the sender's profile, message them or delete. Tony started to work his way through them.

No.

No.

Definitely no.

Maybe.

Maybe.

Bloody hell, no!

Maybe.

Of the three maybes, only one was still online

'hi, where r u' tapped out Tony on the keyboard.

'st hannahs' came the response, a few seconds later.

'u visiting or local' asked Tony. It was unlikely to be someone else at the seminar, but best to make sure.

'local' appeared on screen. 'u'

'visiting' Tony added the name of the hotel. 'u know it?'

The reply took longer this time, an interval which struck Tony as having an air of consideration about it. Then:

'20 mins away.' And before Tony had a chance to respond, 'u up for it'

It was Tony's turn to hesitate. He reread the potted resumé, which managed to be both elegant and licentious. Knowing what to do with an apostrophe told you a lot about someone...

'room 326' he typed.

A message appeared onscreen.

'User logged off.'

Indeed, as easy as falling off an actual log, reflected Tony, sitting back in the chair and folding down the lid.

Actually, 'easy' strikes the wrong note, but what term would embody a lifetime of ventures into a hinterland of obsession and serendipity? Wanderlust, perhaps, if not already co-opted for more innocuous recreation.

But since a long ago initial spark ignited a flame whose embers are never wholly extinguished, when has there ever been a problem rekindling them? However prosaic the occasion, however mundane the location, it's a rare set of circumstances that at some point doesn't offer an exchange of glances followed by a flicker of acknowledgement. Never losing the ability to take in a room as if through a polarised lens filtering out the glare of banal social interplay, revealing the stark clarity of an underlying reality which passes most people by completely.

Most people.

Not the hotel waiter serving a table for one, carefully repeating the room number the meal's being billed to. Not the teenage hitchhiker, who feeling a hand brush his thigh when changing gear, spreads his legs wider rather than drawing them together. Ad infinitum... Looking back across the years, it's hard to recall any scenario that at some stage or another didn't find itself charged with opportunity.

And if not, there were always the pubs and clubs whose names are exchanged in the aftermath of trysts or listed in those magazines picked up in Soho, along with haunts for cruising and cottaging, where anonymity stirs a boldness which even after all these years can still surprise...

Because this was never the search for a soulmate. Indeed, enveloped in a freemasonry that trumps class, occupation interests, age, allure, politics and just about anything else we all sit in judgement on each other with, it all eventually comes down solely to that rush of blood from the brain to the groin, rarely with much by way of introduction and seldom an au revoir.

And likely to become even more so in a future of technological marvels. Mutual coy interrogations and a quid pro quo of peccadilloes will surely soon have a feel of antiquity about them, as sheltered behind usernames in internet chatrooms vices are shared at the click of a mouse and consummated in anonymous hotels barely a stone's throw away. There's almost a sense of loss about it.

Nostalgia, as the wags would have it, isn't what it used to be.

A rapping on the door snapped Tony out of his reverie. Who'd think a knock could convey much other than boldness or timidity, but over the years Tony has learnt to discern far subtler tones and cadences - caution, discretion, anticipation, wariness, excitement. So, he's aware it's not room service out there and also knows better than to leave someone hanging and exposed in a hotel corridor.

He quickly crossed the floor and answered the knock. The tracksuited figure - as an alibi, the evening run has become almost a *cliché* - standing there fixed him with an expression of frank appraisal. An expression, Tony had no doubt, mirrored on his own face.

Then the man began to slowly smile.

Tony opened the door wide and stepped backwards.

"Come on in," he said.

Jack

At the station, Jack left booking the Traveller to Andy and got on the phone to Senara Gallery to try to determine the extent of the damage.

Pretty superficial, he learnt from Ms Weinstock. He'd used ink - and soluble ink at that - rather than paint, but the insurance company wanted a report from a specialist restorer ASAP. Jack relaxed a little at that. If this were heading for the local magistrates' court instead of the County Assizes, the rent-a-mob 'Do Gooders' were unlikely to consider the consequent downplaying worth their efforts.

Ms Weinstock also confirmed there'd been no actual break-in, simply a door left open by one of the cleaners taking time out for a smoke. The Trustees had arranged on site security from tonight onward, she added and Jack bit his tongue regarding stable doors and horses.

Given the VIP list for tomorrow night, queried Jack, would it be okay if he came over first thing in the morning to check things for himself? And although both of them knew this wasn't really a request, she was amiable enough to say that she'd look forward to seeing him.

As Jack sorted through the paperwork that inevitably arrived on his desk during any absence - you let it accumulate at your peril - the phone rang.

"Hello," he said.

"Sergeant Vanner?" Tina's voice was raised that extra octave she used for official business.

"Yes, Tina?"

"I have the Chief Constable on the line for you, sir."

Jack held in a sigh. That hadn't taken long.

"Put him on."

"Hello, Jack," said the Chief Constable. "Heard you had a spot of bother in town tonight?"

"Yes, sir." Jack tried to keep his tone steady. "But in the

end, it died down as quickly as it flared up."

"But all taken care of? No repercussions for tomorrow?"

"No sir."

"Good." The Chief Constable hesitated. "Look, you'll be getting a visitor in the morning."

"Sir?

"A Detective Inspector Amanda Palmer. From London."

"Would that be the Met, sir?"

"I believe it's in connection with a cold case enquiry?"

"Which couldn't wait an extra day or two?"

"I'm aware the timing could be better." The Chief Constable did almost sound sympathetic. "But this request comes from the highest level. The very highest." He paused. "Do you understand me?"

"Yes sir," said Jack and he did. Political and way further up the food chain than a local MP. "Is this in connection with the visit tomorrow, or-?"

"You now know as much about it as I do," interrupted the Chief Constable."

"Yes sir," said Jack.

"She is to have your full cooperation." The Chief Constable's tone was measured. "And to be offered every consideration."

"Understood, sir," said Jack slowly.

"Thank you, Jack" said the Chief Constable and the line went dead.

Jack stared at the silent phone in his hand and then placed it carefully back on the cradle.

Tony

Tony closed the door and then crossing the room sat down on the edge of the rumpled bed.

Picking up his mobile, he saw that there'd been a call from Anne about an hour ago. It was unusual for her to phone while he was away, he guessed there must be some problem or other. He considered calling her back, it wasn't that late, but then worried she might catch something in his tone. The usual aftermath of emotions was already starting to wash through him, that familiar potpourri of regret, recrimination, guilt and disgust, but Tony'd long ceased to be disturbed by it. He understood this was as much a part of the process as the excitement of anticipation or the fire of consummation and the passing of the years had taught how to detach from it.

And once passed, the whole caboodle was ready to be battened down until the next time, sealed away from the pangs of conscience until a pointed look across a room became an itch impossible not to scratch or whatever might be simmering on the back burner of his psyche needed taking off the boil yet once again.

But in the meantime, he was emotionally vulnerable and Anne wasn't stupid. You didn't live with someone for twenty years without your antennae starting to twitch when something's off.

He tossed the phone down onto the bed and headed for the shower.

You stumble quite a bit during the next few days.

The effect at times is similar to the well known two-faces-in-profile or candlestick illusion - you're aware of the duality, but still can't visually perceive both simultaneously.

One always wins out.

In the same manner, you discover fresh perspectives on long held certainties without being conscious of any path that has led you to this new viewpoint. Neither swayed by well-reasoned argument or startled by emotional resonance, it strikes you that this is also possibly how the first steps to madness are taken, unjustified belief. The instinct is to cling to old precepts, but each time you revisit them, those same precepts have the feel of a skin about to be shed.

And here comes a candle to light you to bed.

You're intrigued by the emergent new you. You've always thought of yourself more survivor than rebel, slipping through the cracks rather than fighting unwinnable battles. You've still no interest in joining the fray - even on the opposite side you're playing the same game and never trust a figurehead - but passing through those cracks on your own terms could define your future in ways you hadn't before envisaged.

Eventually, your psyche runs out of surprises to ambush you with and you turn your attention to Jake.

The more time you spend with him, the more you realise that behind the hip, cool facade exists a far more fractured persona. He hasn't volunteered his story and you, better than most, know not to pry. But you guess somewhere along the line he's wandered from the path and not yet found his way back.

Over the next week, you road test feminine wiles and chicanery to encourage his pursuit and your eventual capitulation. As a lover, it's not like you have a solid yardstick to compare him to, but a potpourri of passion and tenderness - with just a touch of dominance stirred in - lives up to expectations, leaving you physically sated and emotionally gratified.

Pillow talk is mostly Jake reaching into the future.

He's going down to London soon, he tells you, to get some

money together. A friend has some scam involving paintings, he can make a lot of bread in only a few weeks. Once that's sorted, the idea is to score hash and acid and head down to Cornwall for the summer. It's a really cool scene, down there.

"Why don't you come along?" he asks, tentatively.

Why don't you?

That you can't stay here forever - or even for that much longer - is a thought you've been brushing aside with increasing frequency. But lacking both skills and qualifications, the chances of a job paying enough to put a roof over your head and food in the larder are remote.

You are, you've begun to realise - and surprised this hasn't dawned on you before - in terms of abilities needed to navigate the world out there, almost totally institutionalised. You've never so much as bought a bus ticket or ordered a meal in a restaurant. You have no idea how to rent a bedsit, write a cheque or even use a telephone kiosk.

But Jake does. Fractured soul he may be, there is the air about him of someone who knows his way around.

"Is there much hotel work down there?" you ask. From somewhere, you recall that accommodation and meals are often provided for staff at seaside hotels. Breathing space...

"Sure," he tells you. "Lots of the chicks who head down there take jobs as chambermaids or waitresses. But you wouldn't need to. We'd make enough selling dope to more than get by on."

With a smile and complicit nod, you listen once more to him outlining the road ahead, one you can at least start out along as companions.

Walking back to The Hall after spending the morning at Georgie's, you spot a commotion. Two police cars are parked on the forecourt, Sebastian's scout troop are milling around but there is an oddly subdued air about them. Miss Benfield's expression is sombre as she speaks with the officers. As you approach, their conversation comes to an end and she motions you over.

"What's the matter?" you ask.

"One of the scouts has gone missing." She gives a slight shrug. "He's probably run off home... It's happened before. They get homesick or have been ganged up on." She sighs. "But the police want us to search the house before they start on the fields and woods, in case he's hiding inside for whatever reason. Would you check your floor for me?"

"Of course," you tell her.

You make your way down the corridor, knocking on doors. If someone's in, then you explain what's happened. If not, you use the master key Miss Benfield gave you, checking under beds and in cupboards. You're halfway along when the door to Peter's room opens and he steps out, followed by Sebastian. Both are half turned away from you, but there's something about the look which Sebastian gives Peter - who returns a hard stare and a shrug - that freezes you in your tracks. Then, conscious of not wanting to be caught staring, you give a soft cough and begin moving towards them.

"Miss Benfield asked me to check the rooms," you say as you draw close. Peter's expression is now neutral and Sebastian is tight-lipped.

"I suppose the outbuildings are being checked?" he asks and you nod.

"I imagine he'll turn up at home in a few days, right as rain," says Peter, shaking his head. "But we have to go through the motions."

You acknowledge this with a brief smile and pass by to knock on the door of the next room. But you have a very definite sense of both pairs of eyes boring into your back.

But he is not found and neither does he turn up at his home. By the following day, a full-scale search is under way, with police tracker dogs and volunteers from the nearby village.

You watch this on the lunchtime local news with Georgie and Jake.

"Miss Benfield reckons he got homesick," you tell them. "Or ran away because he was being bullied."

"Doesn't look the hardy type, does he?" says Jake, as a picture of the boy flashes up on screen and it's hard to disagree. Cherubic - almost angelic - features suggest church choirs rather than campfires in the wild.

"Let's just hope he's found safe and well," says Georgie. "God only knows what his poor parents are going through."

But two days later the search is called off, after the body of a young boy is discovered on the riverbank five miles downstream from Linden Hall. Arrangements have already been made for the scout encampment to break up early and you've learnt from Miss Benfield the only reason they are still here is because of difficulties arranging a coach to take them home earlier than planned.

"I'll be leaving myself," Peter tells you. "Probably in a few days. The place has kind of lost its lustre, you might say. But let me have that notebook and let's see what I can sort out for you."

You've only a few sheets left, and you spend a couple of hours in your room sketching self portraits from the dressing-table mirror.

Satisfied, you close the pad and make your way along the corridor towards Peter's room.

But halfway down the corridor, through a window you see Peter and Sebastian climbing into Peter's Sprite, Sebastian behind the wheel. As they pull away along the driveway, you experience a totally unexpected, yet extremely intense, flash of envy for that kind of freedom.

What must it feel like, *you wonder*, to turn onto an open road and set out towards wherever that might lead you?

With just the slightest shake of your head, you watch the Sprite until it is out of sight before stepping away to return to your room.

Afterwards, you're never sure whether it was a trick of the light, or perhaps a slight unexpected breeze, which makes you stop and glance back over your shoulder. But there is definitely a sense of otherness, the awareness that this journey along the corridor is somehow different from all previous ones.

And then you spot it.

The door to Peter's room is slightly ajar.

Cautiously, ears pricked for the slightest sound out of the ordinary, you make your way slowly towards it. The gap is only a few inches, but still enough to change the pattern of light along here and after a moment's hesitation you press your palm against the upper panel - for some inexplicable reason you're reluctant to touch the brass handle - and push. It opens with a creak, but it's noise that won't escape the corridor and standing at the threshold you see the room is empty. With a last glance up and down the passageway, you step inside, carefully closing the door behind you.

It's spacious and airy. French doors lead out onto a balcony and large picture windows are set either side, through which streams a flat north light. It's a strange combination of studio, office and bedroom. A draughtsman's drawing board faces an easel, palette, tubes of oil paints, brushes soaking in a glass jar all sit on a small table beside it. A similar size bed to your own is pushed against one wall. Opposite is a desk with a swivel chair, alongside which stands a filing cabinet.

You walk over to the drawing board.

A sheaf of drawings has been gathered together and moved over to the edge, a large cardboard backed envelope placed on top of them. Taking note of the envelope's position, you lift it away and pick up the drawings. There are ten or so sheets, all studies of a young girl bathing - standing and soaping herself, sitting in a tub with her knees drawn up before her, intimately dousing herself... You turn them over, laying each flat in the sequence you go through them. On coming to the last one - stretching sideways, reaching for a towel - a sense of familiarity which has been growing stronger suddenly clarifies.

You pick up the envelope and tip it open. At least two dozen Polaroid prints and perhaps half as many strips of 35mm negatives tumble out. You reach for the photos, but, as you register what you are staring at, the realisation leaves you stunned and breathless. They are all of you, taken - you assume - from behind what must be a two-way mirror in the first floor bathroom. Slowly

- your hands are not actually shaking but almost - you lay out the sketches, overlapping and still in order, and then you match the photographs with each drawing. After placing the last one in position, you stand back and study them.

Peter has taken some artistic license, but not much. Your breasts are smaller and your hair is in a loose chignon, a style you've never worn, but - crazily - realise actually quite suits you. And your pubic hair, not exactly luxuriant to begin with, has been further depilated to conceal almost nothing.

You hold a negative strip up to the light at the window. Scouts, you guess, diminutive figures and very much out of uniform... Some of the shots feature adults, a black band at the neck you presume would be a clerical collar.

About half of the drawings have only a single Polaroid counterpart, some others as many as three. You select a print from two of these and put them to one side, along with six of the negative strips. You gather the rest of the prints together and return them to the envelope. The sheets of paper you collect back into a sheaf, repositioned where they originally sat and then you carefully place the envelope on top as best as you can remember.

As you take your hand away, it brushes across the surface of the drawing board and in the short distance it travels, you register a change of texture. On closer examination, you discover that what you assumed was a large backing sheet is only actually attached along the top, the thirty degree tilt keeping it in place and that what you've just sensed is something underneath. With ears straining for the sound of footsteps outside, you once again move the collection of drawings aside and lift the backing sheet upwards.

An A3 sheet of very heavy cartridge paper is revealed. At a glance, it would appear to be the illustration from Peter's book that you came across in the studio the day you first modelled for him, but further examination reveals that it isn't.

Not by a long way.

All the elements of the original are here, and in the same setting, but what is now unfolding tells a very different story. While the central focus of the scene is still the skirmish between the boy scouts playing cowboys and Indians, in this scenario all the Indians are wearing nothing but a headband and their underpants. A minor detail, you might think, until the eye wanders to the fringes of the illustration.

An Indian taken prisoner now stands pressed forward against a tree trunk, his arms tied at the wrists around it and he is blindfolded. A hedgerow separates him from the rest of the scene, as it does the family of tinkers grouped behind him. But gone is any sense of obsequious fawning, their expressions drip with menace. The younger is holding out the snared rabbit for the older man to take and, as he starts towards the boy, his free hand has fallen to his crotch. The old man's attention is entirely directed at the bound figure, and while the woman's gaze is pure malevolence, her thin smile is one of indulgence.

In the small vegetable garden, the vicar leans his back against the wall. Directly in front of him, the scoutmaster's left arm is outstretched, with the palm pressing against the brickwork by the vicar's head. The other is down in the space between them, obscured by the scoutmaster's body. The vicar is staring out over the scoutmaster's shoulder as if seeing something in the far distance.

In the centre of the drawing, the vicar's wife remains at the trestle table, but she is no longer buttering bread whilst smiling fondly at the boys in front of her. Her stance is now hesitant, her expression querulous, her eyes narrowed and, although still holding a knife in her hand, the impression is that of her grip on it tightening...

As fraught as life with Mr Needham might have been, you had the sense that was the gnawing and scratching of a disturbed mind at the bottom of some deep pit he had chosen to dig for himself.

And himself only.

But this... Without understanding how, you realise this speaks if not of conspiracy, then complicity. You are not yet old enough to have the vocabulary to articulate exactly what you feel nor to have the experience to understand the full implications of what you've discovered here today, but you instinctively grasp this is far beyond one man's dark cravings.

Carefully, you rearrange the drawing board as you found it and slip the Polaroid prints and 35mm negatives into your pocket. You turn to leave but hesitate as the filing cabinet comes into view. Slowly, you cross the room and are almost relieved to discover that it's locked.

There's only so much you can take in at one time.

Only when you're outside in the corridor, the door pulled shut behind you, do you realise your clothes are soaked with sweat.

"You're leaving? Tomorrow?"

Georgie can't keep the surprise out of her voice.

You nod.

"With Jake?" She studies you. "So what's the plan?"

"Head down to London." You shrug. "He's an idea of how to get some money together. From there, perhaps spend the summer in Cornwall."

"So, you two are...?" She lets the question drift away, whilst looking at you quizzically.

"We'll see how it goes." You give another shrug. "Early days yet."

"You don't think," choosing her words carefully, "you might be rushing things."

You study her for a few seconds and then reach into your jacket pocket. Keeping your eyes fixed on hers, you pass over the two Polaroid prints you took from Peter's room.

Puzzled, Georgie stares down at them and then her hand flies to her mouth.

"On balance," you tell her, "I'd say the sooner the better, wouldn't you?"

You didn't really have any doubts, but her ashen expression dispels even the slightest lingering suspicion.

She sinks down into a chair, still staring at the photographs. "Where did you..."?

She breaks off shaking her head.

You sit facing her and begin to talk. Peter's door ajar, the illustration unlikely to find its way into the proofed copy, the sketches, the prints. You make no mention of the 35mm negatives, you've learnt it always pays to have at least one ace up your sleeve...

"I want you to stay here tonight," she says quietly and you nod.

"Have you told Jake about this?" she asks.

"No."

"Can we keep it that way?" Catching your stare, her expression hardens. "I will get to the bottom of this," she tells you, almost vehemently. "But I need to be careful how I go about that, at least until I know what I'm dealing with." She sits back in her chair and sighs. "So at the moment, the fewer people who've seen these, the better."

"Okay," you say.

"How are you and Jake planning on getting to London?"

"Thumbing it, apparently."

"I'll run you over to the A1 first thing. And I'll give you my London contact details. We'll need to keep in touch."

She stares down at the photographs once more and slowly shakes her head.

"Oh, bloody hell!"

CHAPTER EIGHT

Sally

This wasn't the first time Sally had waitressed at The Grange, but the previous occasions had been in the main house, instead of out here on the terrace, and it didn't take long for it to dawn on her just how much more hard work this was going to be.

Every refill of her drinks tray meant a return trip to the kitchen, at least twice as far from here as the dining room. And, rather than methodically topping up glasses at the tables, she was required to circle the gathering with tray in hand, allowing the guests to help themselves as and when. Heavy on her wrists, heavy on her ankles and she had the gallery opening to look forward to tonight...

On the plus side, this was a pretty star studded affair. Sally hadn't spotted many local faces but recognised quite a few from the silver screen. She'd overheard Mr Chapman say earlier that some guests would be arriving from London by helicopter and then be whisked straight back once the eclipse was over. What it must be like, thought Sally, to live that lifestyle, would you ever really get used to it?

One local face Sally did recognise was walking across the terrace towards Ms Munro. But the vicar was wearing jeans and a blouse, probably for the same reason Dad never wore uniform off duty, guessed Sally. Nobody likes to feel they have to be on their best behaviour.

Sally made her way over to the small group the vicar had joined.

"Jenny," Ms Munro was saying, "I was beginning to think you weren't going to make it."

Then she lent in close to her and Sally couldn't catch what she said. The vicar's reply was equally *sotto voce* and Lee began to laugh.

"This is Jenny," Ms Munro explained to those around her. "We're involved in a project together." She turned again to the vicar. "I've mentioned Sy to you before, he's my American agent. And this is Chris Franklyn - Kit." She shook her head with a mock weary smile. "Kit and I go back so far it actually frightens me."

Smiling, the vicar took a glass of wine from Sally's tray.

"Any idea how long we've got?" Ms Munro asked Kit.

"A couple of minutes," he said, glancing at his watch.

"Okay, back in a sec." Ms Munro, put her drink down on the table. "This stuff always goes straight through me."

"Have you come far to be here today?" the vicar asked Kit.

"I live in Amsterdam, so yes," he smiled and then acknowledged Sy with a nod, "but not as far as some people."

"Lee said that you two have known each other for a long time?"

"Over thirty years," he nodded. "We were both involved with a street theatre group in London, back in the sixties."

Realising her tray was almost empty, Sally turned and headed towards the kitchen for refills.

Venables

Venables showed his ID to the WPC by the tape, who, after making a meal out of comparing him to his photograph, let him go on through.

"The back bar," Kendall had said and Venables made his way down a dark corridor to the rear of the pub. At the entrance to the room, a SOCO handed him a pair of elasticated plastic overshoes and purple nitrile gloves. Although Venables guessed that forensics had finished up here hours ago, he slipped the booties over his shoes and pulled the gloves on without comment. The Met really did like to milk the few occasions they could pull rank on the Security Service.

Suitably attired, Venables stepped into the room.

He was surprised to see the two bodies still in situ. Catching his expression, Kendall nodded.

"A busy morning," he told him. "Be another half hour for the coroner's van."

"What do we know?" asked Venables, turning his head to take in the scene.

Declan McKelvey was sat upright on a bench seat, at a table just inside the door. There was only one visible bullet wound, slightly off centre in his chest, exactly where you'd find the heart. Lent back against the wall, he should have tumbled over to one side by now but death scenes had peculiar characteristics all of their own, reflected Venables, where sometimes it seemed not even the laws of physics held sway.

"The shooter knew what he was doing," said Kendall. "A single shot for McKelvey was enough, two," he indicated the second body slumped over a table by the opposite wall, "for Denham." He shrugged. "Looks like he was on his feet for the first round, high in the chest, which sent him backwards and down. Then another to the head to make certain."

"Any shell casings?"

"No." Kendall gestured to bullet holes in the wood

panelling behind Denham, tagged and numbered. "Forty-five calibre bullets, the forensic guys think a revolver, but they'll confirm that later. From the entry angles and splatter patterns, they reckon the shooter was standing at the bar. Probably walked in, appeared to wait at the counter, then turned and opened fire."

"There wasn't anyone serving?"

"Ring for service." Kendall indicated a large brass bell.

"And no one heard anything?"

"Possibly used a silencer. Maybe subsonic rounds. At this range, it wouldn't make much difference."

Venables considered.

"So, who was he exactly?"

"Barry Denham, ex Special Branch. Left the force about ten years ago, been working as an enquiry agent since then. Almost exclusively divorce work, some low level corporate security."

"Ex Special Branch?"

Kendall nodded.

"It probably won't come as much of a surprise to learn that he spent time with Chief Superintendent Franklyn's team."

"The thing I don't get," said Venables, "is why they were at separate tables." He stared at Kendall. "There are way too many connections here to believe they didn't know each other, so why were they on opposite sides of the room?"

"Maybe waiting for someone?" suggested Kendall. "To head off somewhere together, but in the meantime wanted - needed - to appear incognito?"

"Someone who arrived and then..." Venables gestured at the bodies with his hand and Kendall shrugged.

"You can't help but have the feeling," continued Venables, "that there's some serious covering of tracks going on here. If the Irish caught wind of what..."

Venables broke off as Kendall's mobile rang.

"Hello." As Kendall listened, he raised his eyes to meet

Venables'.

"Okay," he said, eventually. "We're on our way."

He pocketed the phone.

"Forensics are into Barry Denham's computer," he told Venables, pulling his gloves off. "They say there're things we need to see."

"Right."

Venables followed him to the door, before pausing to take one last look around.

"The yanks are going to bloody love this," he said softly.

Sally

Everything, thankfully, broke up pretty quickly after the eclipse. Ms Munro had retired to her room citing jet lag, the VIPs all ferried off by a fleet of Range Rovers and the caterers were almost finished packing away the tables and chairs.

"Thanks Sally," said Mr Chapman, handing her an envelope. "I know this was short notice, you'll find something extra in there for you."

"That's alright, Mr Chapman," said Sally, surprised. "You didn't have to do that."

"You put yourself out for us," he told her. "That doesn't go unappreciated. And please, Paul."

He hesitated.

"How did your dad get on last night?" he asked and to Sally's look of surprise added, "He was here when the call came through about what was going on in town."

"Things calmed down pretty quickly, from what I understand," said Sally. "Only one person was arrested."

"What about the painting?"

"I don't think it was badly damaged, but it's been withdrawn from the exhibition. I..."

She broke off as Lee Munro's friend Kit came out of the house to join them.

"Everything sorted out?" Paul asked him.

Kit nodded.

"Carin's flying to London on Saturday," he told him. "Then we're going over to Los Angeles with Sy, probably next Monday."

"Well, congratulations," said Paul.

"It's far from being a done deal." Kit shrugged. "But with Lee's weight behind it, there's a realistic chance that it could actually get off the ground."

"If you don't need me any longer...?" asked Sally.

"Of course, sorry," smiled Paul. "Do you have a lift back

into town?"

"One of the caterers is dropping me off," she told him.

"Well, thanks once again," said Paul.

"You're welcome."

Making her way towards the house, Sally caught the two of them in a window's reflection over her shoulder. It was probably just a trick of the light, but it did strike her that their shared posture seemed to have acquired the rigidity of statues.

Tina

Over the years, Tina had proved herself pretty competent at reading Sergeant Vanner's moods. And she did always think of him as Sergeant Vanner rather than Jack, even though he'd never been one for putting on airs or pulling rank, not like some of the officers who visited St Hannahs. She'd not needed long in the job to learn that it was often a lot easier to deal with the position than the person, that chain of command exists for a reason.

But this afternoon was a first.

Sergeant Vanner had spent the day out of the station with the detective from London who Tina understood - she wasn't above listening in on calls, the more she knew the better to manage - was down here with the Chief Constable's blessing. Tina'd monitored their progress around the town, initially over at The Grange where this DI Palmer was hoping to interview Lee Munro and then she'd had to track down Sue Marshall for them, who Tina was friends with from the choral society and had taught her daughter in year four.

By now Tina had enough pieces in place for her to realise this was a cold case enquiry with the heat suddenly turned up. So, when she'd finally got hold of Sue and arranged for Sergeant Vanner and DI Palmer to call at her house this afternoon, Tina'd suggested Sue might want to have a family member or a friend present, purely by chance of course.

St Hannahs looked after its own.

With an hour or so to kill before seeing Sue, Sergeant Vanner decided to investigate the damage done at the Senara Gallery last night. Tina spoke to Ruth Weinstock to check that wouldn't be a problem, then confirmed it was okay for him to head over there.

Halfway through a belated lunch break, as ever taken at her desk, there was a phone call from a lady in London trying to contact her husband. There'd been some kind of family emergency, he was down in St Hannahs for a banking seminar and when it came to finding out where that was being held, nobody at the bloody bank he worked for seemed to know their arse from their elbow. Could she help?

Tina took her number and said she'd get back to her. There were half a dozen possible venues, but Tina doubted she'd have to try them all. If not the first hotel she called, then most likely they'd have an idea which it was and so it proved. Probably the Atlantic View Motel the receptionist at Tregenna Bay told her, who indeed confirmed they had a Mr Tony Meadows booked in there. Tina left a message asking him to contact his wife and then rang Mrs Meadows to give her the motel's details.

While she'd been sorting that out, there'd been an emergency call, an ambulance for a suspected case of food poisoning. Andy had responded - police presence was mandatory for all 999 shouts - and he came back over the radio to confirm that it was Mr and Mrs Carstairs, together with their young niece who was staying with them on holiday.

Tina knew Mrs Carstairs from the WI, couldn't say she'd ever really gotten on with her, a bit too full of herself if you asked Tina, but she closed her eyes for a few seconds to let her mind fill with something between good wishes and a prayer.

Opening them, she saw Sergeant Vanner together with DI Palmer come in through the front door and it didn't take Tina more than a glance to realise all was not well.

When they'd left this morning, Sergeant Vanner had been polite, if somewhat prickly, probably down to nursemaiding a visiting officer on what was likely to be St Hannahs busiest day of the year, supposed Tina. But his mood now struck her as quietly subdued, his expression almost reflective. And to be honest, DI Palmer didn't look too happy with herself, either.

"Everything alright, sir?"

Sergeant Vanner slowly nodded.

"Did Tom release the bloke from last night?" he asked.

"About an hour ago," Tina told him.

"And made it clear that we wanted the lot of them gone from St Hannahs by this evening?"

"Yes, sir."

"Okay. DI Palmer's going to need somewhere to stay tonight. I've explained that because of the eclipse, that could be a problem, but..."

"Actually, sir," interrupted Tina, "I think there might be a cancellation at the Atlantic View, a family emergency we were asked to help out with. Do you want me to try them?"

"Okay, let's go through to the back and get it sorted out. Tom," he called out, "would you cover the front desk for a couple of minutes?"

"Sure." Tom appeared in the doorway of the interview room as they made their way through to Sergeant Vanner's office. Tina reached for the phone, but before she picked it up, it gave a sharp buzz. She stood back as Sergeant Vanner shrugged and lifted the receiver to his ear.

"Tom?" He listened for a second or two before offering the phone to DI Palmer. "It's your office," he told her.

"Oh, right," she said, with what to Tina seemed a meaningful look around. "Is there anywhere I can...?"

"Don't worry." Sergeant Vanner nodded towards the door. "I could do with Tina bringing me up to speed with what's been going on while we've been out."

They left DI Palmer in the room and stepped out onto the veranda which ran across the back of the building. It was the last place in the station where officers might still sneak a ciggy and probably the only spot other than a cell where you could also be guaranteed privacy.

"Did DI Palmer find out what she was looking for, sir?" asked Tina.

"Not really," he said. "Sue Marshall had a tale to tell, but it wasn't the one she wanted to hear." He patted his jacket pocket as he spoke, noted Tina, a leftover trait from the days when there'd be a packet of Navy Cut in there. "Not a tale anyone would, to be honest. And Lee Munro," he continued, before she'd a chance to react to that, "won't be available until the morning, jet lagged after a flight from Los Angeles apparently, hence..."

He gestured with his thumb back towards the room.

"So, anything I need to know about what's been happening here?" he asked.

Venables

DS Sule rose from her chair as Kendall and Venables entered the room.

"So, where are we?" asked Venables, as she followed them both into his office.

DS Sule opened the file she was carrying.

"From what was on Denham's PC," she began, "it looks like McKelvey and Denham have been in each other's pockets for years."

"If we're talking computer records," said Kendall, "I assume that's not going back much further than the mid-eighties?"

"True," said DS Sule. "But Denham was still a serving police officer at that time. And McKelvey only lived in London during the early seventies - that was probably when they first met."

"Do we know what McKelvey was getting from Denham?"

DS Sule shook her head.

"What they've found are encrypted email drafts. Tech says we're unlikely to crack it anytime soon - they did suggest asking the NSA to try."

"I don't think we can count on much by way of transatlantic cooperation, given how this has played out so far," said Venables dryly. Then he looked at her sharply. "Sorry - email *drafts*?"

"Instead of sending each other emails," DS Sule told him, "they both logged into the same account and left draft messages for each other." She shrugged. "So there's no chance of them being intercepted."

"How is that a problem if we can't decrypt the bloody things, anyway?"

"Electronic communications are scanned for encrypted files as a matter of course," she said. "Could have sent up a red flag."

"I'm getting too old for this game." Venables slowly shook his head. "So, all we are left with is this Susan Marshall's brother, Peter." He let out a sigh. "Have we heard from DI Palmer?"

"She was seeing Ms Marshall earlier this afternoon, sir," said DS Sule.

"Try to get hold of her, would you?"

"Yes, sir."

"So what do you reckon?" asked Venables, as DS Sule closed the door behind her.

"We can pretty much take it as given that Denham and McKelvey were set up to stop either of them talking and we don't need to guess who by. The real question is, where did the leak come from?"

"The other side of the Atlantic, I'd say, considering how few people over here knew about it."

"Possibly. But we're still left with the conundrum of whether the whole Aidan McShane line was only a farewell up yours from McKelvey." He shrugged. "It's looking more than likely, but then why does every strand in this enquiry seem to...?"

He broke off as the telephone rang. Venables pressed the speaker button.

"I've DI Palmer, sir," DS Sule told him. "She can't get mobile reception where she is, so she's on a landline from the police station in St Hannahs. An unsecured landline," she added.

"Put her through."

"I just need to check something with DS Sule," said Kendall. "Back in a sec."

"Hello."

"Hello, DI Palmer." Venables hesitated. "Before we start... Just to bring you up to date, the impending deal is off. Curtailed by a third party."

"I.. I see."

"There were other factors in play, it would seem, including a Barry Denham, an ex Special Branch officer. Ever come across him?"

"The name doesn't ring a bell."

"He would appear to have had an agenda all of his own, going right back to the early seventies. He knew McKelvey and so I'd say we can be sure that he was in deep with this, probably from the beginning. The techs found some damning stuff on Denham's computer, it seems they kept in touch using an email account but not actually sending emails, however the hell that's possible. Anyway, McKelvey arranged a meet with Barry Denham last night, but when he turned up, there was somebody else waiting, someone who didn't want either one or both of them talking. No prizes for guessing who that might be, given the M.O."

"What exactly happened?"

"Not on an open line, Amanda." He hesitated. "So how did you get on? Have you spoken to that Marshall woman yet - do we have a positive ID for her brother?"

"It's definitely her brother," said DI Palmer slowly, "but she says he's still alive."

"*What!!?*"

"She claims he stumbled across something in 1970, which forced him to change his identity. He must have got a fake ID from somewhere and has been using it ever since."

"What name is he using?"

"She won't tell me... It's a long story - and not a very pleasant one. So..." She let the sentence trail off.

"Do you believe her?"

"Yes." DI Palmer sounded almost contrite. "Yes, I do."

"So, we've been played for bloody fools all along." Venables struggled to keep the exasperation out of his voice. "It would seem our Mr Franklyn was right after all, with his little Johnny Walker homily."

"I haven't spoken to Lee Munro yet. I'm seeing her in the morning."

"Just get back up to London."

"The thing is, the one person I don't trust in all of this is Christopher Franklyn - I don't believe a word he's told us." She paused. "If I were to put pressure on Lee Munro, then we might..."

"Coppers instinct?" interrupted Venables. "Amanda, we're not coppers."

Venables softened his voice.

"We're not in the justice business. We're in the containment business. We had a major problem. That problem has disappeared and so now we move onto the next problem and there will always be a next problem. We leave the detritus behind - it's no longer our concern."

DI Palmer was silent.

"Please don't think I'm doubting your instincts," he told her. "I'm not, you may well be right. In fact, you probably are. So, let's be clear here - what I'm doing is disregarding them, for expediency's sake." Venables paused, staring out through the window of his office to where Kendall and DS Sule were engaged in conversation. He sighed. "And if that's something which doesn't sit right with you, then perhaps you should consider Chief Superintendent Kendall's offer."

"I'm sorry?"

"Oh, please..." He hesitated. "You've a lengthy drive ahead of you, Amanda, regard it as an opportunity for some serious thinking."

He placed the handset back down on the cradle.

Amanda

Amanda stepped out of Vanner's office and closed the door. So, it seemed the decision had just been made for her. Never one for leaving a job half done - and probably never would be - she suddenly felt very weary and that wasn't entirely down to the prospect of a three hundred mile drive home.

Vanner was at the front desk chatting with the civilian receptionist. Tina, she recalled.

"Everything okay?" asked Vanner as she approached, perhaps catching something in her expression. Forcing a smile, she nodded and laid her briefcase flat on the counter.

"I won't be seeing Ms Munro in the morning," she told him. "Things have moved on, apparently." She turned to Tina. "But if it is possible to find a hotel room, I'd sooner be setting off back to London after a good night's sleep."

"Of course," said Tina, picking up the phone.

"I'm sorry to have thrown your day into turmoil," Amanda said to Vanner. "But it really did need to be done." She held out her hand. "I appreciate your help. Thank you."

"I'm only sorry you had a wasted trip," said Vanner, shaking it.

Tina finished speaking into the phone and hung up.

"Okay, you're booked in for tonight," she told Amanda. "Follow the signs for Truro out of town and the motel's by the roundabout where it crosses the A30. You can't miss it."

Amanda smiled her thanks, lifted up her briefcase and turned to leave.

"Safe journey home," added Tina.

* * *

The motel belonged to a nationwide franchise, next door was its own brand pub restaurant and Amanda didn't anticipate venturing much further than there this evening. Dinner, a couple of drinks and an early night seemed on the cards, followed by departure at first light so she could...

So she could what?

There wasn't really anything to rush back to, Amanda reflected, redoing her makeup after washing her face. The investigation regarding Aidan McShane was being closed down - to the relief, she supposed, of just about everybody in the hierarchy above her - but they wouldn't be able to sweep away the murder of an ex Special Branch officer. If there were any way of getting to the bottom of what Christopher Franklyn was covering up - and every instinct told her he was - that would be the route to take.

Satisfied with what she saw in the mirror, Amanda switched off the light in the bathroom, slipped on her jacket and left the room. If she took Kendall up on his offer, and right now it wasn't like her future was brimming with options, she'd at least have NCIS resources to follow any *sub rosa* enquiries of her own.

Making her mind up, she dialled Kendall's office line. It rang four or five times before a female voice answered.

"NCIS. Chief Superintendent Kendall's phone."

"DS Sule?"

"Yes," slightly surprised.

"It's Amanda Palmer. I was hoping to catch him before he left."

"You just missed him. Do you need his mobile number?"

"It's okay. It can wait until morning."

"I suppose you've heard what's happened?"

Reaching the entrance to the restaurant, Amanda stepped to one side of the doorway to continue the conversation, away from curious ears.

"That it's being wound down?"

"Probably."

"What about...?" Amanda was suddenly conscious of being on an open line. "What about last night's developments?"

"Likely to be handed over to anti-terrorism."

"DS Sule..." began Amanda, then hesitated. "Shravasti.

Those surveillance photographs of Pembridge Villas. I don't suppose that...?"

"I've digital backups of the originals, together with the rest of the old file." She paused. "Anything else you want me to do?"

Amanda smiled.

"No, that was it."

"I heard that Peter Marshall is still alive?"

"According to his sister, which puts us right back to where we started."

"Perhaps not."

"Sorry?"

Amanda listened as Shravasti explained Linda Thompson's website.

"So what we have," Amanda said slowly, "is a photograph of someone identified as a resident of Pembridge Villas, but who doesn't appear in any of the surveillance photographs?"

"It didn't seem that relevant when we had Peter Marshall in the frame," said Shravasti. "But now..."

"Do you have an address for her?" asked Amanda.

"Yes."

"Any chance you being able to go around there first thing, find out what she has to say? Before the plug gets officially pulled?"

"I was thinking the same. If we can get a positive ID on him, it's possibly a game changer."

"Okay," said Amanda. "This may not be as dead and buried yet as some people would obviously like it to be. We'll talk when I'm back in London."

"Have a good journey home."

Amanda snapped her phone shut.

Jenny

Whenever Jenny needed quiet reflection, this was usually the time and place she put aside for it. The seat by the Lych Gate just outside the church offered an uninterrupted view out across the Atlantic and with the sun barely above the horizon, everything around was suffused in a golden red glow. It was as much here as inside her church that Jenny gave herself over to the glory of creation.

'Whatever kind of day you've had, watching a sunset always seems an apt conclusion.' Those words, spoken to her by Lee Munro when they'd first met, often came back to her when she sat here, stark in their simple truth.

She'd gotten to know Lee well in the years since, couldn't say they were friends exactly - Jenny was careful to keep in mind the admonishment of never mistaking friendliness for friendship when dealing with those touched by fame - but they rubbed along together easily enough, she thought, for an acolyte and an atheist.

Lee had bankrolled Jenny's Sure Start program for young mums, got it off the ground with her cheque book and wasn't above using a little celebrity arm-twisting when it came to local fundraising. She was in town at the moment and this morning they'd arranged for her to come over to the Church Hall tomorrow, for an update and to meet some of the mothers.

An event which the rest of Jenny's day had firmly pushed to the back of her mind and which she was till turning over when her mobile phone began ringing. *She really must get into the habit of leaving it in the vestry when she came out here.*

"Hello," she said.

It was Tina Farlow, from the Police Station.

"Sergeant Vanner thought you should know," she said. "There's been a case of food poisoning at a barbecue." Tina's voice faltered. "It's bad, at least one death and several others are seriously ill." Tina hesitated. "We've heard the fatality is a child, but that's not been confirmed yet."

Jenny stood up.

"They're at the Cottage Hospital?"

"No, Treliske. The Sergeant asked if you needed a car?"

"It's okay, I'm on my way."

Jenny kept the phone to her ear as she almost ran towards the Rectory.

"What's exactly happened?"

"There was a 999 call this afternoon about Mr and Mrs Carstairs, been taken ill, along with their niece." Tina paused. "You know them, right?"

"Of course," said Jenny.

Margaret Carstairs was Chair of the local Women's Institute, had been something of a *bête noire* for Jenny when she'd first arrived in St Hannahs, although things had smoothed out between them since.

"About an hour later, there was another call. Gillian Brown and her husband."

Jenny had almost reached the front door, but that stopped her in her tracks. Gillian, a teacher at St Anne's, was also a volunteer at Sure Start and Jenny had come to regard her as a friend.

"How is Gillian?" she asked.

"I'm sorry. All I've been told is that she was taken to Treliske." There was a catch in Tina's voice which suggested she was putting a lot of effort into controlling her emotions. "It's pretty chaotic right now, there have been at least four other emergency calls."

"You said something about a barbecue?" Jenny had the front door unlocked, all she had to do was grab her handbag. She'd learnt long ago to keep an overnight case in the car.

"At Mr and Mrs Nelson's house," Tina told her. "From what we understand, everyone who's ill had been there."

"Tell Sergeant Vanner," Jenny reached for her bag and headed to the door, "that I'll be at Treliske as soon as I can."

Tina had already hung up.

Amanda

Amanda was walking back to the motel from the restaurant when her mobile rang.

"Hello."

"DI Palmer?"

"Yes."

"This is Detective Chief Superintendent Ray Thomas, Greater Manchester Police. I'm contacting you in connection with your request to interview Ronan Doyle."

Amanda came to a halt.

"Okay."

"Can I ask what your interest is in Doyle?"

Amanda thought fast. The obvious thing was to inform him the operation was being closed down, apologise for leaving him out of the loop and tell him to forget about it. But then again...

"I run a cold case unit that's currently part of a multi-agency investigation into allegations of a homicide in 1970. We're confident Doyle wasn't involved in the killing, but we're pretty sure he knows who was. Thirty minutes with him should just about do it."

"You're going to have to come up with more than that," said Thomas. "Names, dates and I'll need to corroborate those with Doyle before authorising a meeting."

"This is a national security matter," Amanda told him. "I'm afraid that's all I can tell you."

"Sorry." Thomas sounded anything but. "In that case, I've no choice but to veto your request."

Okay, decided Amanda, *in for a penny...*

"Right," she said. "I'll pass that along to the Cabinet Secretary."

"What!!?"

"As I explained, this is a multi-agency investigation. Sir Richard Milford, as Cabinet Secretary, oversees the Joint

Intelligence Committee and is keeping the Prime Minister updated on developments. Thanks for your time, Chief Superintendent Thomas."

There was silence and for a second Amanda thought he wasn't going to fall for it. Then:

"Thirty minutes, you reckon?"

"If that."

Another silence.

"Could you be in Liverpool, say tomorrow lunchtime?"

"I could."

"Look, DI Palmer," said Thomas, "I'll need to give Doyle at least a hint of what this is about."

"You can tell him," said Amanda, "to cast his mind back to Notting Hill Gate in the summer of 1970 and that I want to talk to him about a carpet."

There is more, you learn, to hitching a lift than initially meets the eye. You've noticed hitchhikers before, of course, figures by the side of the road with their arm extended and a raised thumb cocked backwards, but always from a car speeding by rather than stopping.

You're impressed by the etiquette most travellers display when arriving at a pickup spot. If others are already waiting, new arrivals move along past them to wait their turn. And this seems to be a practice motorists respect, pulling up at the first in line and everyone shuffling forward as they pull away. In England, you reflect, the notion of the queue is far more deeply ingrained than we might imagine. But occasionally a car will pick up the second or even last in order, presumably not liking what they saw in the initial figure or suddenly struck by something about the other.

Usually the shortness of a skirt.

You quickly grasp that hitchhikers fall into only a few categories. By far the most common are teens like yourself and Jake, long-haired and easily recognised as a definite subculture. Then there are students, still young but cleaner cut and with a college scarf prominently displayed. Older men who carry car licence plates, Jake explains, are delivery drivers, transporting new vehicles around the country and pocketing the train fare home. And finally servicemen, squaddies and ratings in uniform, heading home on leave.

But if your fellow travellers are an archetype, the lifts are anything but. And like Jake - together with the other hitchhikers you meet at curbsides and cafes - that's how you'll come to regard them, regardless of age, gender, predilections and prejudices.

Lifts.

Jake insists you wear a skirt rather than the jeans you'd be more comfortable travelling in. He even has you roll the waist, so the hem hangs well above your knees. And as you wait there, he positions you to the fore and emphasises the need to both smile and make eye contact with the approaching drivers.

"If it's a bloke," he tells you, before you set out, "you sit in the front passenger seat. If it's a woman, then I will." He shrugs

at your quizzical expression. "If he's getting an eyeful of your legs, he's more likely to be generous if we stop at a transport cafe. And she'll feel less uncomfortable with a guy alongside, rather than behind her."

And never, he emphasised, take anything to eat and drink offered in the car.

"I've heard of people being Mickey Finn'd," he says. "Took a coffee from a flask and the next thing they know, they're waking up on the other side of a hedge with their pants around their ankles."

Your route is down the east side of the country, an area not yet covered by the expanding motorway network, but you learn from Jake that makes it ideal for hitchhiking.

"You're not actually allowed to stand on a motorway," he tells you, "so the only place you can wait is by the exit from a service station or at the top of a slip road. They're all about fifteen, twenty miles apart, which means they become pretty crowded and that puts drivers off."

But on the Great North Road, he explains, there are lay-bys every couple of miles and frequent roundabouts.

"If we're lucky, we'll get a lorry heading all the way south," he continues, "but even a short ride is getting you there."

However, you're not lucky and playing back this journey in later life it's a struggle to keep the lifts in chronological order rather than by residual impressions. People, you discover, in the company of transient strangers perceived to be in their debt, are not the least bit shy about what's really going on in their heads...

There's the insurance salesman who rages against the politicians who've betrayed the great heritage of this country with immigration. That retired headmistress with a granddaughter suspected of dabbling in drugs and whose entire conversation is a gentle interrogation about a world sprung on her with little warning and of which she has no comprehension whatsoever. A tight-lipped solicitor who seems to have stopped only for an opportunity to rail against the immorality of modern society, the two of you obvious prime examples of this.

An off-duty policeman takes you ten miles out of his way because he's long believed that hitchhikers are disappearing along this stretch of road and so patrols it most evenings in his own time. The smiling but stoic young widow who makes you a bed up on her living room floor, whose quiet sobbing in the darkness might not be loud enough to keep anyone awake but is impossible to sleep through.

Next morning it's a lorry driver who's sure his wife is taking him for a fool behind his back, but on this trip he'll be arriving home twenty-four hours early and he can't wait to see the expression on their faces when he kicks the bedroom door open. A BOAC pilot regales you with tales of near misses and hints at aircrew debauchery in exotic locations. A university lecturer, mocking the notion that Shakespeare is the author of the plays attributed to him, buries you under expositions both obscure and detailed enough to be impossible to either grasp or care about.

And let's not forget the magistrate returning from a morning in court, whose initial offer of redemption - by accepting the lord Jesus Christ as your personal saviour - is eventually followed by one of a fiver each, if you'll sit on his face while Jake blows him.

Then finally does come that lorry all the way south, the last hundred and twenty miles covered in half a day. The driver drops you in Camden Town, a mile from his depot, and, before pulling away, points you in the direction of the tube station.

You think you'll be familiar with the London Underground from films and TV, but, as with most assumptions not based on direct experience, it's always the minutiae that gets you. Descending the escalator, one hand tightly gripping the smooth rubber handrail as people brush by, your nostrils fill with the pungent fusion of oil and electricity. It's a miasma you will encounter nowhere else and is seemingly impervious to the sudden blasts of air that blow through the rounded, clinically tiled passageways.

The platforms are crowded and you're careful to stand well back against the wall, although other people seem happy to totter almost at the very edge. There's a roar as a train exits the tunnel and for a second you think it won't stop, but suddenly it has and the doors are sliding open.

"It's the one after this we want," Jake tells you and you watch passengers being impatient with each other in the doorways. Then, after a cry of 'Mind the doors', the carriages seal themselves, the train pulls forward into a smooth momentum and is gone.

Jake takes you by the hand to lead you onto the next train. You sit facing each other, but as nobody else - even couples it seems - are engaging in conversation, you study the map over his head, actually little more than a linear display of station names.

"We change at Embankment," he says, which you acknowledge with a worldly nod, as if this were just one more settled routine of everyday life. There is a flurry of movement at each stop, but between stations all eyes are focused on magazines, newspapers and advertisements.

At Embankment, Jake leads you through another maze of tunnels to the platform you need and this time you board the first train that arrives.

"It's not worth sitting down," he says, taking hold of the pole by the door. "We're only going a few stops."

The journey back to the surface already has a sense of familiarity about it, as if the smells and sensations of this new world you've entered have now seeped through to your core. You step onto the escalator almost casually and adopt a nonchalant air to all around you. You instinctively understand it's important not to stand out.

Emerging from South Kensington tube station, you realise this is a very different London from Camden Town. Other than the red buses, Camden could have been the centre of pretty much any city in Britain with its shabby housing, dingy cafes and corner shops. But here...

For the first time, you can find meaning in the term 'cosmopolitan'. It's the architecture that's most striking, a turn of the century elegance in the intricate cream facades of terraced houses or the glazed red brickwork of mansion apartments, their covered balconies overlooking what could almost be described as a boulevard.

Queens Gate you discover it's called, as you pass the road sign at a junction.

After a ten-minute walk, Jake pauses in front of a house which you notice has multiple doorbells set into the wall by the entrance, each with a name tag alongside. Gazing upwards, you count four stories and there's probably another one hidden away behind the balustrade running across the top of the building, but it's the steps down to the basement that are holding Jake's interest.

He takes a piece of paper from his pocket, studies it for a moment and then gives you a nod as he pushes open the wrought-iron gate leading downwards.

"Come on," he says.

"Nice pad," Jake tells the boy he's introduced as Skip. "How did you find it?"

"From this bloke next door, Nigel." Skip finishes rolling a joint and tears the twist of paper away from the end. "He got left both places a couple of years ago, by some aunt he'd never even met." He shakes his head. "The lives some people lead, hey?"

The question seems rhetorical, but you nod anyway, as does Jake.

"The first thing he does is turn this place into flats, so he can live at the other one in the manner to which he intends to become accustomed." Skip reaches for a box of Swan Vesta, lights up and billows out a great cloud of smoke. "Thought he was a bit of a woofter to begin with, but he's shacked up there with these two Chinese birds and a right little pair of crackers they are too."

His eyes are on you as he speaks and you realise that, if not actually up for comparison, you are being assessed. You're torn between staring him down and letting your skirt, still furled up from your role at the roadside, ride even higher.

"Is he going to mind us staying here?" asks Jake.

"Nah!" Skip gives a dismissive shake of the head. "I know how to keep him sweet."

"So, these 'velvets' you were talking about?"

"Right." Handing the spliff to Jake, Skip stands up and crosses the room to where a large A3 art folder is leaning against the wall.

"Like I said, this is a really nice little earner."

He carries it back over, lays it down flat on the floor and opens it up. It's packed with artwork, cardboard backed prints is your initial impression, but then realise they are creations of pastels on flock paper. Skip hands one to each of you.

"You go door to door," he continues, as you both study them. "Telling people that you're art students, trying to raise money to put on an exhibition of your own."

You replace the piece in the folder and sort through the others. About two-thirds are A4 size, the rest A3. The artwork isn't actually too bad, given that the subject matter is occasionally a little twee. Some pieces have obviously been created to complement each other - you hold a portrait of an elderly Aboriginal man in your left hand, a second of presumably his wife in your right, and study them.

Skip looks at you and nods.

"Get them interested in the first one and then pull out the other," he tells you. "Double the sale."

"So how exactly does it work?" asks Jake.

"They give you an area that hasn't been worked yet, mostly in the suburbs. You pay a quid for each of the small pictures you sell, thirty bob for the large, and you charge whatever you can get away with." He shrugs. "I usually ask between two to three quid for the smaller ones, a fiver for the others, although I once got," he indicates the pieces you're still holding, "twenty-five for that pair."

"Bloody hell!" exclaims Jake.

"That was an exception - some old queen who had the hots for me." Skip flashes a tight smile. "But I'm disappointed if I don't make a tenner a day."

"Right..." says Jake slowly.

"Anyway, come along with me tomorrow and see what you think. But I'd guess the two of you," you get that look again, *"would do really well at this."*

He shows you around the flat.

It's obvious the basement had once been just one large space, probably a kitchen. But now it's partitioned off into a living room, bedroom, the box room where you'll be staying, bathroom and kitchenette, all still as gloomy as the original configuration must have been. The conversion appears to have been done in a hurry, stud walls with skimmed plasterboard and offering little by way of soundproofing.

But not something you're uncomfortable with, and indeed, take the opportunity that first night to noisily emphasise exactly who it is that you belong to here.

'Studio', you learn the next morning, is something of a misnomer. The building at some point had been a factory, manufacturing what was uncertain, but, for all the artistic ethos, the production line mentality is still in full play.

Just inside the entrance is a row of maybe a dozen easels, each with a velvet composition in progress. You'd imagined the artists would be students, but none of them are under forty, all are female and in appearance look more suited to a typing pool or shop floor. On a stand in front of each easel is the design they're copying. Two of them are working on the aborigine you saw yesterday. As you pass by, one woman raises her arm and a completed piece is removed by a young girl who replaces it with a blank.

That's carried forward to a bench, where several other pictures have been laid flat and are being carefully sprayed with what you assume is some kind of fixative. The next stage is a drying rack, allowing the sealant time to do its work. Each slot has a clock face with a movable hand above it, presumably set to the hour it was placed in there.

And finally, taking up half the length of the studio, are racks upon racks of finished product.

You walk through into another room, perhaps only a third

the size of the first one, where the sales teams are reloading their art folders. The boys are dressed mainly in denim and have hair hanging over their collars, the girls wear theirs mostly long and straight, set off with kohl'd eyes and pale lipstick. There seems an equal balance between tight jeans and skinny tops or loose shift dresses, short enough for the hems to flutter barely inches below their hips.

You guess you'll quickly discover what works best for you.

They all exchange nods with Skip, as he leads you and Jake across the room and into a small office.

"This is Ken," Skip tells you, introducing the figure seated behind the desk. "He runs the place."

Your first impression of Ken is of a jobbing actor miscast in a low budget production cashing in on Swinging London. You'd guess in his mid-twenties and although his hair is worn long, it still manages to be suggestive of regular attention from a barber, as does an extremely precise Fu Manchu moustache. The oriental theme is continued with a mandarin shirt and even before he stands, you know his jeans will have creases in them.

"Hi." He gives you both a wide, well practised salesman's smile and extends his hand. "I'm guessing Skip filled you in on how this works, but let's go through it again, shall we?"

He indicates a sofa pushed against one wall and sits back down himself.

"We give you a folder full of velvets, ten small and five large. You can sell them for what you like, but you owe us a quid for the small ones and thirty bob for the large. And so we're clear on this, we expect you to make at least two sales every outing." He pauses. "That shouldn't be a problem, although everyone has a glitch occasionally. When that happens, we suggest you buy a couple yourself and then swap them back in on a good night. But if that becomes a regular thing..." He shrugs. "I've got a waiting list of those wanting a chance at this - I'm giving you a shot because you're friends of Skip here and he reckons you'll do okay." You get a frank stare from him. "And he's probably right."

"Thanks," says Jake.

"We'll find you a different area to work each evening," Ken continues. "Always suburbia, new estates where possible but not council ones. You'll start out with a team travelling by Tube, but if you do alright we'll move you to a minibus, working the Home Counties, and that's where the real money is."

He leans forward.

"You need to be in here by two in the afternoon at the latest. To settle up what you owe from the previous night, load up with new pictures and find out which area you'll be covering today. And then split up the streets with the rest of your team. Do you have an A to Z?"

"No." Jake shakes his head. "But I'll get..."

"It's okay," Ken interrupts. "We've plenty, you can pick one up outside." He sits back in his chair. "Any questions?"

"What time do we start knocking on doors?" asks Jake.

"You're working mainly from seven to nine," Ken tells him. "Most people have finished dinner by then, after nine's a bit late to be letting strangers into their house." He shrugs. "Typically, around one household in five will let you in. Once you've got the folder open, you'll get a vibe pretty quickly as to whether they're serious about buying or not. If not, don't waste time trying to persuade them - pack up and move on." He hesitates. "These things actually do sell themselves to anyone who's interested. There's no need to play the tough salesman, neutral works better than pushy."

"Okay," says Jake, nodding.

"Anything else?" smiles Ken, and you both shake your head. "Right," he says, standing up. "Let's go and get you sorted."

You follow him out of the office and over to where two girls and two boys are drinking coffee and chatting.

"Where are you working tonight?" he asks one of the girls.

"Acton," she tells him. "That new Wimpey estate, off the North Circular."

"Should do well there," nods Ken, and then introduces you both.

"Show them the ropes, okay?" he says.

"'Course." The girl smiles at you. "I'm Maggie."

In many ways, knocking on doors isn't much different to hitch-hiking. Once inside a house, that same prurient curiosity frequently becomes more the focus of attention than the paintings. And you both quickly learn that as long as it's the husband or wife who initially ventures into this territory, taking them by the hand and leading them in deeper doesn't hurt the prospect of a sale.

"Straights are weird," Maggie agrees, at the end of that first night.

You're a team of six, Maggie nominally in charge if only because nobody else can be arsed and she's naturally a bit of a bossy boots. She and her boyfriend Mick also work as a couple, Barbara and Alex by themselves. You can't decide if Barbara is stand offish or shy, not that the two are mutually exclusive. Alex is equally quiet, but in a sweet-faced, little boy lost sort of way - you imagine housewives wanting to put an arm around his shoulders and ask him what the matter is.

The six of you take the Tube to Acton Town and mingle with the early evening crowd in a pub just across the road from the station. Maggie gives you and Alex the roads you'll be working, which you pencil along in your London A To Z. Barbara gets two blocks of flats. Meet back here when you're done, she explains, and ink in how far you got with a ballpoint. From the way things go tonight, she'll decide if it's worth returning tomorrow or to ask Ken for a different patch.

You start out on the road Maggie's given you. The plan is to work up one side and then down the other.

Initially, the signs aren't good. You do six houses, two doors are slammed shut with no response, three polite smiles and a shake of the head, then a confused old lady who doesn't speak English.

But the seventh is opened by a cheery-looking housewife, who listens to your pitch and then gives a big smile.

"We've just been saying that the place needs brightening up," she tells you, opening the door wide. "Come on in."

The living room floor is carpeted with toys and she clears a space for you to lay your folder down, while Jake runs through the sales patter with her husband, who is spoon feeding a toddler in a high chair.

As you go through them, you can see that they're impressed. The wife picks one up, a more draughtsman like version of a Van Gogh wheat field - sans ominous crows - and holds it against the wall beside the chimney breast.

"What do you think?" she asks the husband.

He studies it and nods.

"Actually," you say, "that has a companion piece."

You take another composition from the folder, a similar theme but with a church in the background, and position it on the other side of the fireplace.

The wife looks at the husband inquisitively and he turns to Jake.

"How much are they?" he asks.

"A fiver each," Jake tells him and his face screws up.

"We'd also have to pay to get them framed," he says to the wife.

"We've been careful to make them standard sizes," you say and both of them turn their attention to you. "You can pick up a couple of frames in WH Smith for ten bob each and do them yourselves."

"Even so..."

"Tell you what." Jake's expression pantomimes reaching a decision. "We'll knock off the price of the frames, so the whole thing will only be a tenner - nine quid for the pair."

The husband looks over to the wife, who smiles, nodding.

You're back out on the street in five minutes.

Three doors further down is keen on one of the aborigines. You try to pull the companion routine again, but these two aren't having it and so Jake ups the price to eight pounds and lets them haggle him down to seven.

There's a dry spell of six houses, then a couple who invite you in but obviously have no intention of buying anything. Jake cuts short a polite but insistent interrogation on free love and drugs and you move on again.

The street, you slowly gather, is a mixture of old people who bought their house when these were first built back in the thirties and young families recently moved in. You learn to recognise which is which by the exterior décor and skip the elderly couples, who only want to ply you with cups of tea and chat.

By the last pitch of the evening, you have your routine down to a tee. Suss out who wears the trousers - when it's the husband let Jake do the talking, man to man, but flash him a smile while the wife's distracted by what she's being shown. And if she leaves the room, brush against him as you point out some aspect of a composition. If it's the wife, you come over equally in control as she is, instructing Jake to pull out a particular piece that might have caught her interest and directing him to where it would be best positioned on the wall.

They buy a large oriental harbour at twilight, junks silhouetted against a setting sun, for a tenner.

Walking back to the pub, you share your exhilaration. Whatever low opinion you may have formed about Ken, his assurance that 'these things sell themselves' would seem to be spot on.

Maggie and Mick are already there, and she greets you with a smile.

"How did you get on?" she asks.

"Yeah, okay," Jake tells her, and gives a brief recap of how the evening went. As he finishes, Alex appears and seems to have done equally well. But by the time you've finished your drinks, there's still no sign of Barbara.

"Another?" Without waiting for a response, Mick reaches for the glasses and Alex says he'll give him a hand. Jake asks where the Gents are and heads off where directed.

"Should we perhaps...?" you ask Maggie, nodding towards the door. "If she's this late?"

Maggie raises an eyebrow.

"She's usually the last of us back," she tells you, and then glances over at the bar. "Barbara," she says slowly, "prefers to do the flats because they tend to be mainly single people. And mostly blokes."

You digest this.

"So...?"

"She does really well out of this," smiles Maggie, "one way or another. But I'm guessing her pad is a treasure trove of velvets."

You nod, as Mick and Alex return from the bar.

Definitely not shy then.

Returning to Skip's place that first night, with the prospect of getting some real money together looking a reality, Jake outlines his plans. The idea is to pool what you both earn, he explains, although half of that will still be yours, even though Jake's going to cover living expenses, etcetera, for as long as you're staying in London. But you'll lend him your share to score with, which he'll repay you down in Cornwall from what he makes dealing. After that you can decide what to do - find work in a hotel like you originally thought or return to London with enough cash for a bedsit or flatshare. Plus, now there are always velvets to fall back on, you wouldn't be stuck working in an office or shop.

In the meantime, he continues, they need to keep Skip sweet. Or rather, you need to keep Skip sweet. The job and somewhere to crash is down to him, so quid pro quo, right? This is the way the world works, he tells you, and it's better to play it than fight it.

As if you didn't already know that. As if you hadn't done worse.

Anyway, your call, he concludes.

Is it?

So, you move into the main bedroom and, for the first week, which of them slips under the sheets with you plays out to a steady rota. But then it's Jake for two successive nights, followed by Skip for three. Have they been spicing this up with a hand of cards or a roll of the dice you wonder?

Then one night, after you'd left them in the living room not only well stoned but most of the way down a bottle of Pernod, you're startled out of a light slumber by the realisation that you're sandwiched between the two of them. But the thing is, as passions *rise you can't escape the notion that your presence seems little more than an alibi for what's happening here, that you've become more conduit than receptacle.*

There's what men need, you remember hearing once, and then there's what men want. And maybe, offers post coital reflection, desire is rarely truly sated without at least a glimpse into the abyss.

Over the next month, you and Jake have become so good knocking on doors that Ken is genuinely sorry to see you move on. Normally he doesn't put people onto a minibus team until they've been there three months, he tells you, but even though it's only been four weeks he'll give you a shot at that.

"You'll make some real bread there," he assures you, but Jake is adamant. The 'real bread' is going to be made selling dope to the beats and weekend ravers down in Cornwall and between the two of you, you've now done enough to bankroll that. Although he doesn't explain this to Ken, who, for all the Carnaby Street schmutter, is pretty straight underneath. There're jobs waiting in the West Country, Jake explains to him, with people you don't want to let down.

"Well, if ever you're back in London," says Ken, "and need a few bob, come and see me. There's always a job for you here."

Jake assures him you will.

CHAPTER NINE

Amanda

As with most coastal cities, the journey through the suburbs seemed interminable. But eventually the thirties council estates gave way to Victorian terraces and sixties high rises, which then dropped Amanda down into an inner city confusion of multi-lane options that almost railroaded her into the Mersey Tunnel.

Amanda found herself in the old docklands area, now refurbished as residential apartments sitting atop boutique stores, restaurants and coffee shops. She turned into the first multistory car park she came to and with a sigh switched off the engine. It had been a six hour drive from Cornwall, with only a brief call of nature at motorway services near Birmingham, and she really needed to do something about her sugar levels.

As well as getting her head back in the game.

Walking briskly, Amanda followed signs for the city centre and eventually came to a Starbucks. She took her coffee and Danish over to a seat away from the window - old habits - and glancing at her watch ran the rest of the day through her mind.

The meet would probably last less than thirty minutes, Doyle's case officer had been adamant about that. They had no intention of giving her any clue to the identity he was living under or even the general area of the address he'd been found. Amanda debated whether to head home after seeing Doyle or find a hotel for the night and decided on the latter. If she left this afternoon she'd hit the school run and early commuter traffic, not the perfect start for a two hundred mile drive and it would be well after ten before she'd reach London. Not something her younger self would have balked at, but these days...

Amanda finished her coffee, dabbed non existent crumbs away from her lips with a paper serviette and rose to leave. She enquired at the counter for directions to Marks and Spencer and, with another glance at her watch, set off down the road.

Shravasti

The house was nondescript, one in a row of a dozen nineteen thirties semis whose architect had seen no reason to buck that era's fascination with mock Tudor. When first built, assumed Shravasti, they would have been identical, same paintwork, same windows, same front door and that uniformity must have been far more aesthetically pleasing than the culmination of half a century's worth of idiosyncrasies.

"You can't miss it," the husband had told her on the phone. "It's the horrendous green one."

He'd gone on to explain that the previous occupant had been a vicar who apparently painted whatever house he moved to green, so 'my parishioners can always find me.'

"I know," the husband had continued. "Where do you start? We'll get it sorted eventually, but right now, plumbing and a new boiler are the priority."

And it was the husband who answered the doorbell, a chubby, cheerful looking man in his early fifties.

"DS Sule, is it?" he asked, and when she nodded, opened the door wide. "Come on through," he smiled. "The missus is out back."

Shravasti followed him down a narrow corridor and then out onto an expanse of wooden decking which separated the house from the garden. A large woman in dungarees knelt tending to a flower bed. Laying her trowel down on the grass, she rose and, brushing loose soil from her hands, walked over to greet her.

"Hello, I'm Linda," she said, and then indicated a table and chairs. "Please, have a seat."

"Thank you."

"Would you like a drink? Tea, coffee? Something cooler? Something stronger? Something both? Assuming that 'Not while I'm on duty', is only for the telly."

"Coffee would be great," Shravasti told her and Linda

looked up at her husband, who nodded and headed back into the house.

"Thanks Tony," she said after him.

"So," Linda continued cautiously, "you're investigating...?"

"I'm with a cold case unit in the Met," said Shravasti, the lie practised enough in her head on the journey over here to roll smoothly off her tongue. "Occasionally things surface in a current investigation that we're asked to look into because, well, that's our turf." Shravasti shrugged. "We know our way around the old filing systems and are likely to have more of a sense when something's off."

"And my name's come up in an investigation?"

"No." Smiling, Shravasti shook her head. "Not at all. But we're checking out something alleged to have happened in the house where you were living in Notting Hill, in 1970, and so we're keen to talk to any of the tenants from that time. You've nothing to worry about."

"Must be pretty serious," said Linda, "if you're looking into it after almost thirty years?"

"I can't really go into details," Shravasti told her. "But yes, if the information we've been given is true, there would be implications."

"The artist, Aidan McShane, was living there at the time." Linda fixed Shravasti with a knowing look. "There were always rumours that his family was something to do with the IRA?"

"Did you know him well?" asked Shravasti, keeping her tone neutral.

"He had a studio in the basement," said Linda, "and I lived in an attic room. So it's not like we were forever knocking on each other's door borrowing cups of sugar."

"I understand that," said Shravasti. "But your paths must have crossed at some point?"

Linda seemed about to answer when Tony reappeared, carrying a tray with three mugs of coffee on it.

"Do you mind?" he asked, sitting down. "I'm as eager to learn about my wife's wild child years as you are."

"I think you're both about to be 'wildly' disappointed." Smiling, Linda gave a disparaging shake of her head. "The swinging sixties only actually swung for a very noisy few."

"How did you come to be living in the house?"

"An old schoolfriend of mine had a room there. When I decided to move to London, Kath offered to put me up until I found a place of my own." She shrugged. "In the end we finished up sharing, cheaper for both of us."

"Was she an actress?" asked Shravasti, adding, "I understood that most people living there were involved in the arts."

"No, but her boyfriend worked at the National Theatre, which is how she got to hear about the place. She'd been in some really creepy bedsit - spyholes in the walls kind of thing - and he wanted her out of there. But yes, you're right. Don Mayberry had bought the house as an investment, renting rooms out to pay for doing it up."

"Was he around much?"

"Hardly ever, he spent most of his time in America. Lee Munro managed the place at first, but then when her career started to take off it was Paul Chapman who handled any problems that came up."

"Sorry...?" Shravasti stared at her. "What was that name again?"

"Paul Chapman."

"An actor?"

"No - quite the opposite, in fact. He was ex army."

"Really? So, how did he end up there?"

Linda hesitated.

"To be honest, I'm not that comfortable repeating rumours about people," she said. "Particularly after all these years."

"I knew there'd be juicy bits," smiled Tony.

"This is simply a conversation," Shravasti reassured

Linda, picking up her coffee. "I'm just trying to get a sense of what was what in the house during that summer."

"Well, there was a lot of stuff going on in the place that..." Linda shrugged. "The kind of thing that wasn't really discussed back then, but did find its way into gossip, if you catch my drift?"

Shravasti nodded.

"So Don Mayberry and Paul Chapman were...? More than friends, shall we say?"

"That wouldn't have raised many eyebrows," Linda told her. "We're talking theatre and the arts here. Lee Munro had installed her PA in the house and we all knew what was going on there and that's another story I could tell you. But no, the word was Don was into some really kinky stuff, even if no one was exactly sure what."

"And Aidan...?"

Smiling, Linda shook her head.

"Sorry to disappoint you," she said. "All Aidan seemed obsessed by was his painting. We all knew not to disturb him when he was down in his studio and I don't recall ever seeing him with anyone other than as friends. There were a couple of girls who used to come around to the house - Emma and Claudia they were called and the three of them would have coffee together and go out for the occasional meal, but you never got that frisson from it, you know?"

"Actually," said Shravasti, "Aidan married Emma."

Linda stared at her.

"What! You mean that was... The politician, Emma Brownlow."

Shravasti nodded.

"Sorry." Linda shook her head. "It's just that in my memory she looks nothing like..." She gave a wry smile and a shrug. "Well, so much for my take on things."

"They weren't involved at the time?"

"No. Emma was in one of those on off relationships with a boy called Kit. I don't remember his surname."

Shravasti reached into her bag and laid a printout of the group photograph from Linda's website down on the table.

"The only people we're not sure of here are her," she pointed to the girl Christopher Franklyn knew as 'Ronnie', "and him." Shravasti tapped the boy absent from the surveillance photographs.

"That's Veronica, she was Lee Munro's PA at the time."

"Do you remember her surname?"

Linda shook her head.

"Sorry."

"What about him?"

"Jake."

"Jake...?"

Linda gave another shake of her head.

"I don't think I ever knew his surname. Or whether that was just a nickname." She shrugged. "A lot of people were into reinventing themselves back then."

"What can you tell me about him?"

Linda considered.

"What I mostly remember was that he definitely had a thing for Emma."

"They were involved?"

With a smile, Linda shook her head.

"Involved is a bit strong. Like I said, he certainly had feelings for her, but you never had the sense they were reciprocated. And it all got rather messy in the end."

"Messy?"

"During one of Kit and Emma's 'Off' spells, Kit had taken up with a Dutch student, who I don't think realised exactly what she was getting into. When it ended badly - and nobody was surprised about that - Jake caught her on the rebound. They went away together for a while. He worked as a roadie or something for a rock group, as I recall, and I've got it in my head that they were at the Isle of Wight Festival. Anyway, a month or so later, apparently, she turns up at Pembridge Villas trying to find him. She's pregnant and he's disappeared."

"Apparently?"

"Kath and I had moved out by then." Linda shrugged. "It was pretty obvious that with the work on the house almost finished, Don Mayberry would either be moving in himself or looking for more upmarket tenants. Kath's boyfriend found a house share in Islington and so we moved out. Kath heard about it all when she went back to settle up the rent with Paul."

"And this would have been..."

"The beginning of that September. I remember because we assumed we'd have to pay for the whole month, you know, with not giving notice. But Paul told her not to worry about it, Don had said that anyone who moved out by the end of October would have their last three months rent refunded to use on a deposit for another place, which we all thought was pretty cool of him." She smiled. "Of course, by then he could afford to be magnanimous."

"That was the month Aidan moved to Boston?" asked Shravasti, making a point of checking her notes again.

"I'm not sure," Linda told her. "After that, we sort of lost touch with everyone there."

"So you've no idea whether this Dutch girl ever found Jake?"

Linda shook her head.

"Kath mentioned the band he was a roadie for had gone to the States. Maybe he went with them. Sorry, I don't know what happened to her... Real life's just full of unresolved stories, isn't it?"

Shravasti remained silent, flicking backwards through her notes.

"You were talking earlier about Lee Munro," she said. "And her PA. There being some kind of story there?"

"Oh yes," grinned Linda. "It was supposed to be all 'free love' and everything back then, you know? It was obvious that Lee and Veronica had a thing going, but Veronica also had an art student boyfriend who was around a lot at the time, so you can imagine the speculation that went on. Anyway, one night

Veronica arrived home a couple of days earlier than expected from a promotional trip abroad with Lee and found Rick in her bed with some woman. My God, you should have heard the row that exploded... We were in the next room, but they probably knew about it two streets away." Still grinning, Linda slowly shook her head. "'So much for free love', said Kath, after Veronica had booted him out."

"Rick?" queried Shravasti. "As in short for Richard?"

"I suppose so."

"Can you remember his surname?"

"Sorry. Again, I'm not sure I ever knew it."

"Did they get back together, do you know?"

"Seems unlikely. Veronica was pretty wild that night. But it was a couple of weeks before we moved out, so who knows what happened? Is it important?"

Shravasti gave a nondescript smile and continued to question Linda for the next twenty minutes, without discovering anything more than she already knew. Eventually, she folded her notes and slipped them back into her bag.

"Thanks for your time," she said to Linda. "I really appreciate it."

"I don't see that I've been much help," Linda told her, as they rose from the table.

"Well, you've certainly given..."

"Hewitt," broke in Linda suddenly.

"I'm sorry?"

"Her surname - it just came to me." Linda smiled at Shravasti. "I remembered something from a newspaper, a photograph in a puff piece... *'Actress Lee Munro and her PA Veronica Hewitt arriving at Heathrow yesterday'.*" Slowly, she shook her head. "God," she said. "Memory's weird, isn't it?"

"Yes," said Shravasti. "Yes, it is."

Amanda

Amanda wouldn't have recognised Doyle from the photographs in his file, but no surprise there. He'd definitely had work done, a typical upturned tip of an Irish nose had been straightened and the gaunt cheeks of his twenties were now filled out. A grey buzz cut completed the new persona.

It was the woman sat facing him who pinged Amanda's radar. A blonde wearing a red leather jacket, she appeared casual enough at first glance but her eyes were everywhere at once. Amanda knew that if she'd been tasked with her job, she'd be over at the table by the mirrored wall and sitting with her back to the room. Twitchy's always a giveaway.

The cafe in Marks and Spencer was still busy with the lunch crowd and after collecting her coffee, Amanda made her way to where they were sitting. Two single tables had been pushed together and each of the free chairs had a shopping bag on it. Amanda indicated the seat next to the case officer, whose name she'd not been given.

"Is this taken?" she asked.

"Help yourself," the woman said, reaching for the bag. Then, looking over at Doyle, she stood up.

"I'll be about half an hour, no longer," she told him rising, to all appearances a wife parking her husband while she hit the fashion floors, but all three of them were aware who the words were really directed at.

Doyle nodded, watching her walk away. As she disappeared around a corner, he moved his gaze across to the main store and slowly smiled.

"Something strike you as funny?" asked Amanda dryly.

"I was simply musing," he said, "on what the world would look like if every single item of Marks and Spencer clothing were to suddenly vanish from the planet."

Amanda stared at him.

"I know," he continued. "I've more than once been

accused of a fanciful imagination and it is the kind of observation that might be regarded as trite." He shrugged. "Then again, it's also the kind of observation Stephen King could get eight hundred pages out of and wouldn't we all love his bank account?"

It was also the kind of observation, reflected Amanda, that you didn't expect from someone who'd few qualms over leaving a briefcase packed with Semtex under a table in a crowded pub, but kept that to herself. She'd long been used to having expectations confounded by confrontations with those on the other side of the law. The trick, Amanda had learnt, was never to let the impression they created leave a thumb resting on the scales of what they'd actually been proven capable of.

She stared at him coldly.

"Pembridge Villas, Notting Hill," she said. "Nineteen seventy."

"Yes," he nodded, "I heard that had piqued your interest."

"I know *what* happened." Amanda spoke softly. "You and Declan McKelvey were driven over there in a Transit by Brendon O'Doherty at the behest of Liam Kennedy. A body, wrapped in a carpet, was placed in the back of the van and taken to the building site you'd been working on in Kilburn, where it went into the foundations." She paused and fixed him with an even stare. "And all water under the bridge now, as far as I'm concerned," she told him. "But what I am interested in is who that was, who killed him and why."

"I never saw the body," said Doyle, matching her quiet tone. "As you say, it was parcelled up head to toe in a tatty old carpet."

"But there must have been talk about it?" persisted Amanda. "Even given the circles you were moving in back then, this wasn't exactly what you could call a run of the mill sort of day, was it?"

Doyle stayed silent.

"I assume," continued Amanda, her voice hardening, "that your immunity deal is dependent on *continual* cooperation." She gave it a few seconds to let that sink in. "So, if our subsequent enquires reveal that you've been less than forthright here, up shit creek without a paddle is going to seem like a Caribbean cruise compared to where you'll be sailing off to."

"As I said, I didn't see the body," insisted Doyle. "This affair was nothing to do with the Cause. Word was that there'd been some ruckus in the house that had gotten out of hand. And that Aidan McShane used his family connections to get it taken care of."

"McShane was overheard saying to Kennedy, 'It's the only way, if you want a man on the inside'. How do you square that with it being purely a domestic that unravelled?"

"I didn't hear that," said Doyle. "But I don't see Liam Kennedy helping out from the goodness of his heart." He shrugged. "No doubt there'd have been a payoff of some kind in it for him and Aidan's family did have the connections to make whatever that might be worthwhile."

Maybe, thought Amanda. Or perhaps it was something else entirely...

"But there was no talk about what had actually happened in the house?"

Doyle seemed to consider.

"A couple of nights later, we were all having a drink down at the *Black Horse*. I was at the bar getting a round in for the boys and Liam and Brendon were sitting at a table close by. 'So it's all sorted now?' I heard Brendon ask Liam. 'Aye,' said Liam. 'Hell hath no fury, right enough.'"

"So... It had been a woman who killed him?" asked Amanda, staring.

"This wasn't a line you'd be tempted to pursue," said Doyle, dryly. "Not if you had any sense." He hesitated. "But shortly afterwards McShane had moved to the States, Boston I believe it was. I'm guessing the family wanted him well out of the way of any potential fallout."

He stared across the table at her.

"And that really is all that I know."

"Just one more thing," said Amanda and Doyle sighed.

Reaching into her bag, she took out two of the surveillance photographs of Peter Matthews. Carefully, she laid them side by side in front of Doyle.

"Recognise him?"

He nodded.

"He was one of the lads who helped Aidan McShane carry the carpet out of the house."

"Are you certain?"

"Absolutely."

Amanda slipped the prints back into her bag.

"Okay," she said, rising to her feet. "That's about it." She hesitated. "And I'll make sure your case officer is aware that you made a valuable contribution to an ongoing investigation."

"Aye," was Doyle's languid response. "Anytime."

* * *

Once out into the street, Amanda checked her mobile. There was a missed call from Shravasti, stepping into a shop doorway she dialled the number straight back.

"It's Amanda," she said. "How did things go this morning?"

She listened as Shravasti related her meeting with Linda Thompson.

"This Jake," said Amanda, slowly digesting what she'd just learnt. "Do we have any idea who he might be?"

"No." Shravasti paused. "I did get a few more names to track down. The girl Christopher Franklyn remembered as 'Ronnie' is a Veronica Hewitt. Don't have any more on her other than she was Lee Munro's PA, but she'd be worth having a word with if she's still around. How about you?"

Amanda spent the next few minutes bringing Shravasti up to speed on her conversation with Doyle and the conclusions she'd drawn from that.

"Possibly the most significant thing you learnt," said

Shravasti, "is that Doyle didn't hear McShane talking about 'a man on the inside'."

"That's my take on it too," nodded Amanda. "I think we can be pretty certain that someone died at Pembridge Villas that day. But the only involvement the IRA had with it was cleaning up the aftermath."

"To protect McShane, do you suppose?" asked Shravasti.

"Unlikely," said Amanda "'Hell hath no fury', Doyle overheard Liam Kennedy say, remember? My guess is a domestic that got out of hand."

"And it definitely wasn't this Peter Marshall?"

"Not according to his sister."

"And you believe her?"

"Yes. Plus Doyle confirmed he was alive when they collected the body from Pembridge Villas. Although he would be someone worth talking to." Amanda considered. "So, what we really need to do next is find out exactly who this 'Jake' was and Carin Franklyn has to be our best shot at that. From what Linda Thompson had to say, there's a good chance he's the father of her daughter."

"She's also," Shravasti pointed out, "a Dutch citizen."

"I know," Amanda acknowledged. "Even with a solid contact in the Amsterdam police we need to tread lightly. Let's give it some thought and see what we can come up with."

"Okay, talk to you soon."

Walking back towards the Dockland area, Amanda tried to reconcile what Shravasti had learnt from Linda Thompson with what she'd gleaned from Ronan Doyle.

'If you want a man on the inside,' had puzzled her since she'd first heard it from Declan McKelvey. The assumption had always been that Conell McShane, Aidan's grandfather, would be making an existing informant available to Liam Kennedy, but what if that wasn't the case at all? What if this was someone new to both of them? This would have been about the time that Christopher Franklyn was working undercover for Special Branch. What if he were the man on the inside?

Wouldn't so much just fall into place?

So rearrange the pieces.

Christopher Franklyn and Carin break up. Jake catches her on the rebound. They have an affair. She falls pregnant. Jake disappears. The supposition at the time was that he'd taken off to escape the consequences of that fling, most likely to the States with the rock band he was a roadie for.

But what if he hadn't?

According to Linda, Carin had turned up at the house looking for Jake. What if she'd found him? 'Hell hath no fury,' Liam Kennedy had said. 'A ruckus that got out of hand' was what Doyle had heard and Amanda knew better than anyone how little it could take for entire lives to unravel in an instant of anger - a push on the stairs or the nearest heavy object snatched up in a blind rage.

And then afterwards bound together in complicity. A husband and wife couldn't be forced to testify against each other and Aidan McShane spirited three thousand miles away.

With Christopher Franklyn to all intents and purposes inside Special Branch and Liam Kennedy dangling the sword of Damocles over his head...

* * *

Amanda headed back the way she came. She'd noticed the usual hotel chains along the waterfront and decided her next move would be to check into one. Then dinner in a dockland restaurant, followed by an early night, ready for a predawn start. If she could get out of the city before the first commuter traffic started moving, she'd be in London by lunchtime.

Collecting her overnight bag from the car, checking into the Holiday Inn and freshening up took less than an hour. It was still only late afternoon and so she decided to take a stroll before dinner, hopefully to clear her head.

Because thoughts were all she had, Amanda kept reminding herself. It was entirely circumstantial, she didn't have a shred of evidence and that's what she needed to start working on as soon as she got back to...

"Excuse me."

Amanda turned to see an elderly couple smiling at her, the man holding a camera.

"Would you mind taking our photograph?" he asked. "In front of the statue."

He indicated a bronze figure, wearing what looked like battledress, gripping a pair of binoculars and positioned as if staring out at sea.

"Of course," Amanda told him, reaching for the camera. Keeping them steady in the centre of the viewfinder, she clicked the shutter.

"Thank you," said the man, as Amanda returned the camera to him.

"You're welcome," she smiled.

"Arthur served with him, you know?" the woman couldn't resist telling Amanda, which prompted an almost shy smile from presumably her husband. As they moved away, curiosity got the better of her and she stepped in closer to view the inscription.

Then gave a sharp intake of breath.

'Captain F. J. (Johnnie) Walker CB DSO' she read.

A submariner.

Jack

It felt to Jack like he was spending more time at bloody Derriford these days than the station.

Controlled chaos would seem to sum up what was happening around him, grim faced doctors moving from cubicle to cubicle, a determined demeanour about them and one definitely not encouraging interaction. Duty nurses were fielding questions from local reporters, whilst simultaneously engaged in urgent conversations on the telephone. A young trainee, with a handset to each ear, looked to be on the edge of tears. Then he spotted, sitting alone on the far side of the room, Reverend Warwick.

He hesitated.

To say that he and the Reverend had history would be stretching things, thought Jack, it was more that circumstance seemed almost wilful in pitting them against each other. He knew they'd started off on the wrong foot, Jack's natural antipathy towards those he considered 'do-gooders' - Christian charity he had time for, working the system he hadn't - would seem to have been interpreted as downright misogyny, which consequently was proving a hole seemingly impossible to climb out of. Combine that with the inevitability of professional encounters shoehorning them into diametrically opposed roles, well, Jack hadn't seen either of them making the other's Christmas card list anytime soon.

Unless...

Jack crossed the floor and lowered himself down into the seat next to her.

"Are you alright, Vicar?" he asked.

The expression in her eyes as she turned to him was that of someone coming back from far, far away. Then she slowly nodded.

"Yes," she said softly.

"Is there anything I can get you? Or anything you need

me to do?"

Silently, she shook her head.

"I was hoping to talk to one of the doctors," Jack continued. "For an update." He hesitated. "Do you know if there have been any...?"

"Dennis Nelson died during the night," she broke in, her tone somehow managing both pragmatism and tenderness. "I was just trying to arrange a taxi to take Mrs Nelson back to St Hannahs, but Veronica Hanson was visiting her husband and she's offered to... To look after her."

"How's Mrs Hanson's husband doing? They were keeping him in an induced coma the last time I was here."

"They still are, but..." She looked at Jack and shrugged. "I gather from his wife there are complications. The doctors were hoping to bring him out of it this morning, but there's been a decision to delay that for twenty-four hours."

"Possibly because they more than have their hands full today?"

"Well, fingers crossed on that one." She gave a sigh. "It's the most serious cases that have been transferred here, they've a more experienced toxicology team. The ones still at Treliske are only suffering mild symptoms, non life-threatening."

"Other than Dennis Nelson..." began Jack and then broke off. These were people who, even if he didn't know them well, were woven into the fabric of his life. Faces he saw on the street every day, part of a community that would struggle to comprehend, let alone cope, with this.

"Christine Bailey, Alan and Safranka Bradshaw, Leslie Stuart, Gillian and Tim Brown." Reverend Warwick's voice faltered. "Margaret Carstairs, her husband Harold and their niece Vicky, who'd come down to stay with them for the eclipse. She was thirteen."

"Have they any idea what it was?"

"No. Or if they do, they're not sharing it with me." She hesitated. "From what I understand, the symptoms didn't start until five or six hours later, which meant that all the plates and dishes had been washed and leftover food thrown away. It's something of a challenge, forensically, to separate it all back out for analysis without the risk of cross contamination."

"Can't they examine the stomach contents of...? Of the victims?"

"Apparently, there isn't a single procedure to identify a source. They have to carry out specific tests for pathogens and it seems there's a fair list to work through."

Jack stared at her.

"When did you last sleep?" he asked.

"I'm staying here," she told him, evenly. "Until..."

She gave another shrug.

"Let me see," said Jack, "if I can get them to find somewhere you could lay your head down for a few hours. You'll be no good to anyone if you're exhausted," he continued, as she appeared to be about to protest, "and they'll be able to come and wake you if there are any developments."

She seemed to consider this and then nodded.

"Thank you," she said.

Amanda

"The statue only went up last year," the sales assistant in the bookshop told Amanda. "It was unveiled by the Duke of Edinburgh."

She reached under the counter and passed Amanda a photocopied page from the *Liverpool Daily Echo*, reporting the ceremony.

"I keep these for people who are interested," she explained.

"Was he from Liverpool?" asked Amanda.

The sales assistant shook her head.

"No, but he was stationed here all through the war and so we do tend to think of him as one of our own." She beamed proudly. "He sank more U-boats than any other captain, you know?"

"Yes, so I understand," said Amanda, dryly. "Although I have to admit, I'd only recently come to hear about him."

"Well, life's just full of unsung heroes, isn't it?" said the sales assistant.

"I suppose it is," nodded Amanda. "Do you have a biography?"

"We do," said the sales assistant and Amanda followed her across the room to a shelf crammed with military volumes. She reached up and, taking one down, handed it to Amanda.

'*Relentless Pursuit*', she read, 'by D.E.G. Wemyss'.

"Actually," said Amanda, "it's for a friend. Would it be possible for it to be sent directly?" Then added, "He's in Amsterdam, I'm afraid."

"No problem," said the sales assistant. "We send books out all over the world. I'll just need a minute to work out the post and packing."

"That's okay," Amanda told her, "I can inscribe it while you do that."

She wrote carefully opposite the title page. Then, almost

as an afterthought, folded the photocopy from the *Echo* and slipped it inside the cover.

"Do you want it special delivery?" asked the sales assistant. "We've discovered packages sent to Europe can take a while to arrive otherwise."

"That's alright," Amanda told her. "There's no rush."

The sales assistant gave her a receipt for the total cost. After reading out Christopher Franklyn's address from her notebook, Amanda paid by credit card.

"Enjoy the rest of your day," smiled the sales assistant as Amanda left the shop, closing the door behind her.

"*You cocky little bugger,*" thought Amanda, "*I'll have you yet!*"

On the Tube journey over to Notting Hill, Jake explains the economics of it all to you. An ounce of dope costs eight quid and from that you cut around fifteen generous - 'you want your customers coming back' - quid deals. But bulk buying brings the cost right down. A 'weight' - a pound - can be had for sixty quid. You quickly do the math, which converts the street price into a clear profit of a hundred and fifty.

You have a hundred in cash now. Jake's plan is to buy a weight of top quality hash and twenty-five quids worth of acid, leaving fifteen for expenses - the train journey down there, 'You don't want to be hitching with that much gear on you', and somewhere to stay when you first arrive in Cornwall. Jake's heard of a campsite called Petroc with converted barns you can bed down in and kitchen and shower blocks on site.

"Are you sure it's okay for me to come along?" you ask Jake, leaving the station. "If he's this big time dealer, he won't be happy about someone he doesn't know turning up at his place."

"This guy we're seeing," Jake tells you, "is more of a fixer than a dealer."

"Fixer?"

"David sorts things out for people who aren't on the scene."

"What things?"

"Drugs, mainly." He shrugs. "Generally for showbiz types. Actors in town for a while, maybe politicians." He hesitates. "And to take care of anything else they might be into."

You consider.

"You mean girls?"

There's that shrug again.

"Sometimes. Usually boys and occasionally that very blurry area between the two."

"How did you meet him?"

"Scored from him at clubs and parties. He'd always do you a good deal, but..."

He lets his voice trail off.

"There was a catch?"

"I wouldn't call it a catch. You'd be invited along to some," *he raises an eyebrow, "scene giving his punters a taste of Swinging London - mods, dolly birds, weekend ravers. There'd be a few couples there, signed up for the night but acting like part of the crowd, who'd kick things off by putting on a show. You didn't actually have to do anything, but the thing is, after a while..."*

"You did?"

"Yeah." *He gives a slow shake of his head.* "Easy money, good times, getting off with someone you saw on the telly last week."

"So...?"

"I'm guessing he'll have a scene planned for the weekend. He usually does." *Jake pauses and then turns to look at you.* "If it sweetens the deal, would you have a problem with that?"

"With what?"

"Could be serving drinks, could be..." *He shakes his head.*

You consider.

"Let's see what happens," *you tell him,* "but the decision's mine."

"Sure," *he smiles.* "'Course."

The once grand house you arrive at in Ladbrook Grove has a dozen buzzers set into the wall by the entrance and Jake presses the lowest one. You're initially startled by the voice that crackles out of what you suddenly realise is a speaker grill rather than a decorative panel, but after Jake identifies himself the front door springs open with a loud click.

Jake leads you through to the back of the house and into a large kitchen.

"Hi, man," *says the figure rising from an oak dining table.* "Good to see you again."

"You too, David," *nods Jake and after he completes the introductions, the three of you sit down. Offered a spliff that's been smouldering in a glass pub ashtray, you take a couple of hits to establish your bona fides and then pass it to Jake.*

David's a bit of a surprise. You'd expected yet one more beatnik type, but he strikes you as more of a mod than bohemian, although there is a definite old world air of decadence about him.

He'd be easy to imagine sipping absinthe in a Montmartre dive.

"So, a weight, you said." *David takes the spliff back from Jake.* "I can do you Lebanese Red for sixty quid, eighty for Paki Black."

Jake winces.

"Seems a bit steep for the Black," *he tells him.* "I was thinking more the lower side of seventy."

David shakes his head.

"Two, three months ago, maybe." *He draws on the joint and the smoke comes billowing out of his nostrils.* "But there's been a couple of big busts lately, and now this stuff's like gold dust. Seriously, eighty's doing you a favour."

"What's the Red like?" *asks Jake.*

"Red's red." *David shrugs.* "It won't blow your mind, but if you're dealing it in Cornwall, I'd have thought they'd be grateful for whatever they could get."

"At eighty for the dope," *Jake shakes his head slowly,* "I'm going to have to forget about the acid."

David appears to consider him carefully

"I'm putting a scene together tomorrow night," *he says.* "At the place on Wigmore Street, you remember that, right?"

Jake nods, a trifle cautiously, it seems to you.

"The usual crowd..." *He turns his gaze towards you.* "Thing is, a couple of people have let me down. If you two wanted to step in there, I'd do you the Black for sixty and throw in twenty-five blotters of acid."

"Blotters?"

"Came in from San Francisco last week, that's how they're doing it over there these days. No more buggering around with eye droppers and sugar cubes. Now it's squares of impregnated blotting paper."

"What's it like?"

"From Owsley, so fucking mind blowing." *He shakes his head with a smile.* "Five hundred mikes a blotter, which means two of you can easily get off on just one of them. Dissolve it in a bottle of coke, shake it up, drink half each."

"Step in?" you ask quietly. "How, exactly?"

"Meet and greet with drinks as people arrive and, once things take off, a ten-minute spot as part of the scene."

"Scene...?"

David turns and reaches behind where he is sitting. There's a stack of glossy magazines on a shelf there. He retrieves the top one and thumbs through it. About halfway in he stops, gives a nod and, folding the magazine back at that point, hands it to you.

You're staring at a full-page photograph of a couple engaging in what's usually dubbed the 'doggy' position. The difference here is that it's definitely the bitch calling the shots - she's mounted him from behind, presumably with whatever's attached to the tight leather straps biting into the skin of her thighs and waist. With one hand she's gripping a belt, looped around his neck and restraining him from pulling away on all fours. Given this scenario, the expression on his face is open to a wealth of interpretation, but you'd guess it's most likely down to recent attention from the riding crop gripped in her other hand.

You take in the image silently for several seconds, as Jake - on the other side of the table - stares at you quizzically.

Then, passing the magazine across to him, you raise your gaze to meet David's and give a slow nod.

"Okay," you tell him, aware of Jake's stunned expression as his head jerks up from the page at this. "But fifty quid, not sixty."

David's eyes narrow, but after a few seconds he gives you a smile and nods.

"Done," he tells you, then turns to Jake as if for final confirmation. The hesitation is barely fractional.

"Sure," he agrees.

"Come round to Wigmore Street at six tomorrow," says David. "I'll have your gear and we'll sort the bread out once everything's wound down. Usually about three in the morning. Probably best to crash there afterwards. It's none too clever wandering about the West End in the middle of the night with a weight on you."

On the street outside, the hesitancy returns.

"Look," says Jake. "I know this was pretty much sprung on you... So, if you've any doubts at all, we could still do okay with the Lebanese Red. Even if we have to..."

"No," you break in, giving him a beaming smile. "It's fine. We got a really good deal." You let the smile widen. "This is the way the world works, right? And it's better to play it than fight it."

The hesitancy on Jake's face flickers into uncertainty.

The house is more impressive than you expect, tucked away behind Oxford Street and next door to an African embassy. As soon as you arrive you're separated from Jake, who's led off to 'help sort out the slides and screens'.

David explains how tonight's going down. The first part of the evening you'll be mingling with the guests, a drinks tray balanced on your right hand. Be tactile with the other one, touch their arm or shoulder while speaking, don't be shy about encroaching personal space. You'll find yourself being stroked or caressed most of the night and your role is to personify enticement, but if that turns to outright groping, then switching the tray to your left hand is a signal for David to sort it out. That's unlikely, everyone knows what's what.

He runs once more through the scenario you and Jake will be playing out and then introduces Nikki, a pert brunette who's maybe five or six years older than you. He explains it's your first time here and asks her to take care of you.

The pair of you get acquainted whilst lacing each other into identical silk and leather basques. For all her Sloane drawl and louche manner, she's friendly enough as she adjusts the straps for you. "Too much, too little or just right," she tells you with a final tug, "upwards and outwards never fails." And for the first time in your life, your bosom appears to have gained a presence all of its own.

She then busies herself with your makeup. "Tarty works better with age," she observes, applying pale lipstick. "Like you've seen it all before and whatever's up next is just grist to the mill. But," finished, she stands back and studies her efforts, "wayward waif is definitely your best look."

Her eyes meet yours.

"Nervous?" she asks.

You hesitate only for a second before biting your lip and nodding.

"Well," she smiles, "that we can fix. And quite literally..."

Nikki reaches into a large handbag, rummages around and eventually retrieves two thin, almost flimsy looking, plastic syringes and you blanch.

"Only a couple of jacks of H, love," at your hesitation, "and half an amp of meth. Just enough to take the edge off." Her expression becomes quizzical. "Done junk before?"

You shake your head.

"I'm not sure..." you begin, but she cuts you off.

"Honestly, darling," she holds the syringe upright and taps at a few bubbles clinging to its side, "you don't need to worry. If skin popping could get you hooked, half of bloody Chelsea would be registered."

Seemingly satisfied, Nikki turns her attention to you.

"Bend over."

You lean forward across the dressing table and feel her pull at the waistband of your knickers. There's a sharp stab on your buttock, followed by a playful slap after the elastic snaps back in place.

"There you go. Now bear with me," she says as you rise, "while I get myself sorted out."

The drugs you've done previously have mostly been cerebral, working their alchemy on inner reflection and the perception of the senses. So nothing has prepared you for a physical rush which almost knocks you off your feet.

You'd swear you can actually feel it moving through your bloodstream, in its wake a glorious golden diffusion, expanding outwards through membrane and tissue until it hits the nerve endings of your skin in a surge of pure sensuality.

You hold on to the back of a chair gasping, aware that Nikki is removing a syringe from the inside of her upper thigh and then *this torrent comes flooding into your brain, where the physical and emotional combine in a cascade of almost unbearable ecstasy.*

It seems to take a while to subside - although time is a pretty subjective concept right now - and then Nikki is holding you by the shoulders.

"Alright?" she asks and you nod.

"Make the most of it." She raises an eyebrow and smiles. "Because it won't ever feel this good again."

The initial rush has almost entirely subsided, but in its aftermath comes a strange peace. Your body has never felt so alive, your skin hasn't lost that tingle and catching a glimpse of yourself in the mirror, it seems that you've never cut such a purposeful figure. Your back is straight, shoulders square, head held high and there's no one out there in that room that's better than you, nothing in a look or a word that won't bounce right off you.

"Okay?" asks Nikki and you nod.

She leads you not to the grand staircase you saw on your arrival, but a narrow one at the back of the house. Originally constructed for servants and underlings, you assume, ensuring contact with the masters and mistresses who ruled these upper levels never exceeded the functions they were here to fulfil.

You arrive at a landing where circular trays are waiting to be collected. 'Drinks trays' would be a misnomer, although each is loaded with half a dozen small tumblers filled with an amber liquid, a silver cigarette box contains skinny joints the length of a Players king size and a fine china bowl, no more than two inches in diameter, holds triangular blue tablets.

Nikki picks up a tray and you do the same, taking a moment to balance it on your upturned palm.

"Make eye contact," she tells you, "without staring. And never look down."

You follow her into a room which must occupy the entire width of the building and most of its depth. Perhaps once a ballroom or library, it's also of an impressive height. Three of the walls are covered with paintings, erotic depictions of some form of pederasty ranging from the intentionally explicit to those - mainly biblical scenes - which have taken on that connotation largely by the context they've been placed in.

And consequently strike you as the most unsettling.

A makeshift white screen covers the far wall. A centre square is showing an example of early cinematography, from the nineteen twenties you'd guess, set in a nunnery and unlikely to have featured on the bill of a local Odeon. Either side of this, a carousel of smaller images from two slide projectors click ever onward at ten second intervals.

The people milling around, mostly male, are in various states of undress and you keep in mind Nikki's 'Never look down'. *As you circle the room, you can't help but wonder how you would manage this without the electricity crackling along your limbs or the rush between your ears. But a hand brushing the inside of your thigh as you move by or the contempt in the eyes of a woman you recognise as the presenter of a BBC TV arts magazine, are as water off the proverbial duck's back.*

In the centre of the room is a circular carpet, six feet or so in diameter, scattered with cushions. On it, the attentions of two youths to each other have gathered a curious throng, although figures are peeling away towards the sofas and chaise longues placed along the walls, in search of their own entertainment.

You're suddenly aware that David is standing to your left and Nikki has appeared on your right.

"You're up," he says quietly. "Nikki will help get you sorted."

"Ready?" she asks.

You allow yourself a deep breath, and then follow her out of the room.

It's closer to five than three before the front door has closed behind the last straggling guest. Jake and David are fiddling with an old-fashioned set of scales, brass weights and all. The Black is moist and sticky, but eventually Jake is handed a block the size of a small paperback, wrapped in kitchen foil. The acid blotters have cartoon characters printed on them, Donald Duck, Mickey Mouse, Olive Oyl.

"Best keep them dry," David tells Jake, and so they also get a silver wrap. All is then carefully packed away in your bag.

"Let's sort the bread out," says Jake and counts the notes onto the table by the scales.

"You shouldn't have a problem getting a cab on Oxford Street," says David, as he folds and pockets the notes. "But you're welcome to hang on here until the Tube starts."

Jake looks over at you questioningly.

"We okay?"

"Sure," you tell him. "Good to go."

CHAPTER TEN

Amanda

Amanda arrived back at the Kings Cross office to find half of the desks removed and only Shravasti waiting for her.

"Well, that didn't take long," said Amanda, staring around after exchanging greetings.

"Orders from on high."

"Why doesn't that surprise me?"

"Apparently," Shravasti said slowly, "pressure to close the investigation was more down to the Security Service than Downing Street." She shrugged. "At least that's the impression I got from the boss."

"Milford could have leant on them," said Amanda. "The Cabinet Office carries a lot of clout."

"Possibly. But that did intrigue me enough to go through the files one last time. Including," she added, "those surveillance photographs, the ones that Christopher Franklyn ID'd."

"Okay...?"

Shravasti opened a folder on her desk, took out a print and passed it to Amanda. An extremely attractive young woman - late teens, early twenties - was coming down the steps of 3 Pembridge Villas. Amanda turned the photograph over.

Claudia Falcone, she read.

"Italian?" she asked.

"No." Shravasti shook her head. "But her father was. Her mother's family name was Beaumont."

Amanda stared down at the print again.

"She's Sir Alexander Beaumont's niece," Shravasti told her.

"What!!?"

Until his retirement a few years ago, Beaumont had been Director General of MI5 and Amanda took a few seconds to digest this.

"I've been on quite a paper chase," said Shravasti. "You might want to sit down."

Amanda pulled a chair over from the neighbouring desk and lowered herself into it.

"This actually is the thread that starts to bring it all together." Shravasti began ordering sheets from the folder across her desktop. "The Beaumont family has owned a holiday home in St Hannahs since before the war. I'm guessing they were staying there in sixty-eight, when they met Aidan McShane. Lee Munro and Don Mayberry were down there too, McShane used them as models for his paintings. As he did Emma Brownlow, who was a scholarship girl at St Catherine's in Westminster, where Claudia was a pupil."

"Okay," said Amanda, nodding. "This is all starting to make a little more sense. So they got to know each other in Cornwall and then stayed in touch after returning to London."

Shravasti indicated the last sheet of paper.

"Claudia Falcone - Claudia Pascoe as she is these days, was in a business partnership with Lee Munro until about five years ago. A hotel in St Hannahs called The Grange."

"It's now the centre for residential training courses Christopher Franklyn told us about," said Amanda. "I was there on Wednesday, but I never got to meet Lee Munro."

Shravasti gathered the sheets of paper together and put them to one side.

"That girl Ronnie who I mentioned yesterday, Lee Munro's onetime PA, didn't prove that hard to find. She married a Richard Hanson in September 1970 and I'm sure it will come as no surprise where they're now living."

"St Hannahs," said Amanda.

"Where else?" said Shravasti dryly. "So, I did a routine search, internet as well as the usual agencies. What I wasn't expecting was this."

She handed Amanda a photocopied newspaper clipping.

"*Western Morning News*, three days ago." She paused, staring at Amanda. "Last Saturday Richard Hanson was found collapsed by his car, in a lay-by on the outskirts of St Hannahs. Brain aneurysm, apparently. He's still in a coma at Derriford Hospital in Plymouth." She paused. "I was intrigued enough to pull all copies of the *Western Morning News* for last week. And guess what I found in Wednesday's edition?"

Without waiting for an answer, she passed Amanda another photocopied press cutting. An inquest into the death of a St Hannahs businessman named Robert Pascoe had returned a verdict of misadventure. His widow, Claudia, expressed her gratitude to all of those who had been so supportive through this difficult time.

Finishing the piece, Amanda raised her head to stare at Shravasti. Silently, she handed Amanda four sheets of A4 pages stapled together.

Skimming down the first sheet, Amanda saw it was a series of extracts from the coroner's report on Robert Pascoe's death. She learnt that Pascoe had been found dead of carbon monoxide poisoning in his garage. Shortly before his death, Amanda read, Pascoe had been visited by a journalist, supposedly researching a biography of some local luminary Pascoe's grandfather served with during World War One and who subsequently managed various business interests on his behalf.

During this visit, the reporter claimed to have evidence that the real estate agency his grandfather had established in the nineteen twenties, and which Pascoe now owned, had been financed if not illegally, then at least unscrupulously. The details appeared scandalous enough to have caused an outburst in court from Pascoe's family, although the coroner's only interest had been the effect these revelations had had on Pascoe's state of mind. Presumably on the assumption that dirty linen takes a while to wash clean in small communities.

The inquest learnt from Pascoe's widow that the reporter offered to keep his findings out of the proposed biography for what would, to all intents and purposes, have been a bribe. Pascoe had then thrown him out.

Claudia Pascoe was unsure if the reporter made further contact with her husband, but agreed to give the coroner his details so he could be called as a witness.

Finishing the last sheet, she added it to the pile on Shravasti's desk.

"That seemed worth looking into," Shravasti told her. "Considering Claudia Pascoe, nee Falcone, would definitely have been on our list of people to talk to if the Security Service hadn't been in so much of a hurry to shut this down."

"What did the journalist have to say for himself?" asked Amanda.

"He was never called," said Shravasti. "But his details were in the coroner's report and so I followed it up."

"Okay... Do you think he's someone worth talking to?"

Shravasti simply handed her another photocopied newspaper clipping, from *The Guardian* and dated two weeks after Robert Pascoe's death.

It was an obituary.

'Respected Journalist Who Lost His Way', read the headline.

Slowly shaking her head, Amanda studied the accompanying photograph. A sandy-haired man of around thirty, classic good looks and the smile he offered the camera seemed more knowing than relaxed. Checking his date of birth at the bottom of the page, she calculated the picture had been taken in the late sixties, early seventies... When obituaries used a photo from a subject's youth, she'd learnt over the years, it was usually indicative that their ageing had little of a fine wine about it.

Amanda started to read.

* * *

Colin Savage, who has been found dead in his Nottingham home, was, during the 1970s, one of Britain's most feted journalists and a familiar face on the nation's TV screens. A series of articles in 1970 for this newspaper's sister publication, The Observer, *were regarded as groundbreaking. The seeds of* the industrial unrest which the UK was plunged into in the late seventies, and the effective annihilation of the trade union movement in the following decade, were there for all to see.

Colin did not have an auspicious start in life. Born in St Annes, a notoriously deprived area of Nottingham, at the beginning of the Second World War, his father was one of those who did not return from Dunkirk. His mother never remarried and although there followed a succession of men in her life, none could be said to have filled the role of father figure.

Leaving school at fifteen with no qualifications, Colin found work as an office boy at the Nottingham Evening Post. Taken under the wing of one of the senior reporters, he was soon researching background for breaking stories, before covering weddings, funerals and church fetes under his own byline.

Colin relocated to London in 1962 to join the Daily Mirror's newsroom and from there his progress was rapid. He joined The Guardian in 1965 and rapidly developed contacts at the very heart of government. The offer of his own regular column took him to the Observer at the end of the decade, where he remained for ten years, throughout which he was a much sought after political commentator for news shows such as Weekend World and This Week.

It was during this period that I first met him, as a freelance journalist attempting to get a foothold in Fleet Street after a fiery apprenticeship with magazines such as Black Dwarf, Frendz and IT. He was invariably generous with his time and if his criticism of your efforts could sometimes be abrasive, there was always the sense this was for your benefit rather than his hubris.

In 1982, his investigations led to the sacking - and ultimate disgrace - of a member of Mrs Thatcher's cabinet, discovered to have been a frequent visitor to a boarding house in south London whose true purpose was facilitating liaisons with underage boys. He confided in me shortly afterwards that he believed his telephone was being bugged and that he was under scrutiny by the Security Service.

A second story followed, a similar theme on a grander scale.

This time the allegations concerned a children's home in Essex, and that the participants included both prominent politicians and well-known show business personalities. When the lawyers became involved, his informant - an ex resident of the home - promptly vanished and rather than accepting that he'd been duped and issuing an apology, he insisted he was the victim of an establishment setup and fought the case through the courts.

These were the first steps down a long and dark path. Bankrupted by legal costs, increasingly resentful of what he believed to be persecution by the state and betrayal by those he'd placed his trust in, he descended into a world of more and more outlandish conspiracy theories, in later years the emergence of the internet providing an unfortunate echo chamber.

Speculation regarding the circumstances of his death has been the subject of much lurid reporting over the last few days. It would seem circumspect to put such matters aside until the inquest.

Colin Savage.
Born Nottingham 21 July 1940, Died 2nd June 1999.

* * *

"I remember this now," said Amanda. "Wasn't there some kind of scandal...?"

The next few sheets were, again, photocopies of newspaper reports, but this time from the tabloid red tops. First was a page four, single column announcement that the journalist Colin Savage had been discovered dead at his Nottingham home. The cause of death had not yet been revealed, it went on, but at this stage the police were not seeking anyone else in relation to their enquiries.

By the following day, the story had made the front page. Colin Savage's body had been found by his landlady and the circumstances were such that she'd had to be treated by the attending paramedics for shock and then taken to hospital herself. His death, the story continued, appeared to be the result of a bizarre sex act gone wrong. Various paraphernalia was recovered at the scene together with evidence of illegal drug use. The police were refusing to comment.

The next morning's headlines were *'Savage Death Kink'* and Amanda guessed they'd now got at least one CID talking, probably in a bar after an exchange of banknotes. Well, so much for looking after your own, she thought, but they'd certainly got their money's worth.

Colin Savage was found on his living room carpet dressed in women's underwear, including stockings and a garter belt. His hands were fastened behind him by a cord tied in a slipknot and his ankles were also bound together with a cord which ran from a loop around his neck. *'A device consistent with self satisfaction'* managed to be both coy and lurid and by noting that amyl nitrate - known as poppers - retrieved from the scene was a muscle relaxant used to facilitate anal sex, left little to the imagination as to what that device might be. Traces of cocaine and a half smoked *'marijuana cigarette'* seemed almost anticlimactic following that.

There were sidebars aplenty. Statistics on the yearly number of deaths from autoerotic asphyxiation, a list of previous victims, speculation that many more cases - particularly of teenage boys - have the scene of death manipulated by family or friends to appear a suicide.

The report finished by saying that although Savage had no known links to the BDSM community, the circumstances of his death would inevitably steer investigations in that direction.

In other words, look forward to another few days of salacious speculation.

Amanda stared at Shravasti and slowly nodded.

"I do remember it," she said. "I just didn't connect him with..."

She paused, trying to collect her thoughts.

"So within a month of Colin Savage visiting the Pascoes in St Hannahs, Robert Pascoe is found dead in a garage filled with exhaust fumes and Savage..." She broke off, shaking her head, then raised her eyes to meet Shravasti's. "Has there been an inquest yet?"

"Done and dusted," Shravasti told her. "And not exactly what you'd call in depth."

She passed over another sheath of stapled pages.

* * *

Shravasti had gathered court transcripts together with further newspaper articles. Given the attention the case had commanded, the inquest itself lasted no more than a day. Medical reports confirmed death by strangulation, the drug residue left in his body being nowhere near high enough to have caused an overdose. The police report detailing how he'd been found contained little - unsurprisingly - that hadn't already been revealed by the tabloid press.

Few of those who knew him well were keen to testify to his state of mind at the time of his death. Given the circumstances, reflected Amanda, there'd be an understandable reluctance to be tainted by association, but the ones that did were vociferous. Whatever peccadilloes Colin Savage may have indulged, he was not noted for being shy or repressed about them and this certainly wasn't anything he'd ever shared in the strikingly candid gossip of the circles he moved in.

And while all were careful not to venture into the realms of conspiracy theory - correctly assuming they'd receive short shrift from the coroner on that score - they were equally adamant that there was something very much awry here. However, a fetish not finding its way into barroom conversation didn't render its practice impossible - or even unlikely, if one read between the lines of the coroner's take on Colin Savage's lifestyle - was the judgement that held sway.

Last to testify was Savage's agent, who'd lunched with him on the day prior to his death. The mood had been buoyant, Savage had recently embarked on a new project and had been full of assurances all was going well. Savage spent much of his final days in newspaper archives and shortly before his death, his researches took him to Cornwall, where he'd stayed for over a week. He'd been greatly excited on his return, apparently confident of both getting his career back on track and justifying his previous allegations.

'But we'd heard all this before,' continued his agent, 'and with scant justification.' An examination of his papers afterwards contained not much more than wild speculation from fringe websites, and no references at all regarding his journey to the West Country. 'Colin wasn't above dangling bait,' he concluded, sadly, 'when fishing for an advance.'

The coroner brought the proceedings to a conclusion later that same day. A verdict of misadventure was inevitable, a stern lecture on the dangers of perverse sexual practices unsurprising. His old paper, *The Observer*, was the only Fleet Street newspaper that gave more column inches to the achievements of his life than the manner of his death.

* * *

Amanda sat back in her chair and stared at Shravasti.

"Savage was actually in Cornwall for a week... Do we know what he was up to there? Who else he saw?"

Shravasti shook her head.

"So," said Amanda, "have we wandered into a series of bizarre coincidences or is this directly related to what happened all those years ago at Pembridge Villas?"

"That's the line of thought I was taking," said Shravasti, "before going through it all again."

She gave a nod toward the pile of paper on her desk and smiled at Amanda's quizzical expression.

"I missed it the first time, too," she said. "The obituary."

Amanda worked her way back to *The Guardian's* piece on Colin Savage, staring bemused until:

Jesus!

'By Christopher Franklyn' read the byline.

"I had an idea that would get your attention," said Shravasti, still with a smile on her lips.

"Everywhere I turn in this case," Amanda said, "there he

bloody well is."

"It gets even more interesting." Shravasti took the last sheet of paper from her folder and offered it to Amanda. "Guess where Savage was living at the time of his death? And who found him?"

With her eyes fixed on the sheet in front of her, Amanda slowly shook her head.

"You have to be kidding me!"

Jenny

"Hello, Vicar," said the constable behind the desk. "What can we do for you?"

"I don't want to be a pain," began Jenny, "and I know that with everything else you have on your plate right now..."

She broke off as Sergeant Vanner came into the room.

"Is there a problem?" he asked.

"While I was at Derriford," she told him, "we had a break-in at the church. The insurance company says I need to get a crime number from you, before they'll pay out for the repairs."

"What happened?"

"When I walked up to the vestry after getting back, I saw that the wood around the lock was splintered. The door just pushed open."

"You went in by yourself?"

She nodded.

"You should have called us." Sergeant Vanner shook his head. "Anyone might have been waiting inside."

"Well." Jenny shrugged. "No one was."

"So, what was taken?"

"Nothing."

"Any vandalism?"

"No."

"And you're sure nothing's been stolen?"

"Absolutely. Everything's in its place, I've checked the Roof Repair donation box and it's untouched. In fact," she added, "they'd have done alright if they had jimmied that open, because there were two fifty pound notes in there."

"Is that usual?"

Jenny shook her head.

"A fiver's pretty much par for the course, perhaps the occasional tenner, but someone was obviously feeling generous."

Sergeant Vanner stared at her.

"Maybe I should come up and take a look around," he said.

"You think someone broke in to make a hundred pounds donation?" smiled Jenny.

"What I think," said Sergeant Vanner, "is right now I'm well past taking anything out of the ordinary in this town at face value."

* * *

"So when did you get back from Derriford?" asked Sergeant Vanner, as they pulled out of the police station carpark.

"This morning." Jenny gave a small shrug. "Whatever this is, it appears to have done its worse. A few people are still in intensive care, but their condition's no longer believed to be life-threatening." She turned to stare out of the window. "And there's work I need to be getting on with here."

"I heard there'll be a memorial service next week-" began Sergeant Vanner, but Jenny swung her head back around to cut him short.

"No," she said to him. "The Bishop told the media that, but..." She paused. "I'll hold a separate funeral service here for each of the victims, if that's what their families want, before a cremation at Penmount." She gave a sigh. "Unless they've a family plot at Holy Trinity. We'll have the memorial service perhaps in a few months, when... When some of the sting's gone out of this."

"I'm sure the town will appreciate that," Sergeant Vanner said quietly.

"And I really shouldn't be taking up your time like this." She shook her head. "It's probably just kids messing around or..."

"A while ago," Sergeant Vanner interrupted, "we had a flasher over on The Burrows. Targeted either single women or young girls out in pairs. After a couple of weeks, when it became obvious this wasn't someone down here on holiday who'd be disappearing back upcountry, we really went to town on it. Policewomen decoys, officers camouflaged in the undergrowth, the whole shebang. Took about a week to get him, but when the scale of the operation came out in court we walked into a real shitstorm, if you'll pardon my French. 'Couldn't police resources be put to better use, a sledgehammer to crack a nut, more in need of help than this level of persecution.'"

With a tight smile, Sergeant Vanner glanced sideways at her.

"And not a little of that was from your predecessor."

"I don't..." began Jenny, but Sergeant Vanner ploughed on.

"You see, what we know is that most serious sexual offenders start small. Flashers, peeping toms, quickly discover - rather like drug addicts, I'd imagine - that each time they indulge they need just that little bit more to get off on it. So, our priority is not only finding out who these people are, but letting them know we know who they are. To make sure they understand that whenever someone kerb crawls a schoolgirl on our patch, they'll be the first getting their collar felt."

Jenny was silent.

"I know it's sometimes difficult to grasp why we act in the manner we do," said Sergeant Vanner, "but there is reason behind it and those reasons are rooted in a whole world of experience."

"I understand," she said, softly.

"If someone broke into the church and we can rule out theft or vandalism, well, there's not much left by way of motive. We've no idea when it happened, but I'm guessing you're in there by yourself most evenings, when the place is empty. And that it wouldn't be difficult for just about anyone to know that."

The blood seemed to drain from her face in an instant, leaving her ashen.

"Oh, dear God," she said.

"So," Sergeant Vanner told her, "wasting my time's the last thing you're doing."

* * *

"Well, one thing I can tell you," shrugged Sergeant Vanner, "this wasn't a professional burglar."

They were staring down at the lock, now exposed behind splintered wood.

"I'm sorry?" answered Jenny.

"My teenage daughter could have picked that with her nail file," he told her. "And a lot quieter than..."

He gestured at the broken door.

"I'll get a Crime Prevention Officer up here," said Sergeant Vanner, glancing around as they walked through into the nave. "And I'm guessing he'll have his work cut out."

Jenny remained silent.

"In the meantime," he continued, "I'll arrange for someone to fix three or four dummy CCTV cameras. One round the back, another by the front entrance and a couple inside. You can't tell them from the real thing and they should prove enough of a deterrent in the short term." He paused. "Until then, I don't want you letting yourself into the church by yourself - is that going to be a problem?"

She shook her head.

"I'll sort something out with Malcolm. The verger here."

Sergeant Vanner indicated the row of pews.

"Make sure he checks those before leaving you alone," he said. "Together with any cupboards big enough to hide inside of."

Jenny nodded.

"If there's ever an issue with that arrangement," continued Sergeant Vanner, "phone the station and they'll send someone up here. I'll let them know what's what when I get back there."

He paused.

"I'd like to say," he told her, "that I don't want to frighten you, that you shouldn't worry. But until this is sorted out, frightened and worried are your best friends, believe me. For the next few days, I want you jumping at every bloody shadow."

Jenny managed a weak smile.

Sergeant Vanner took one of his cards from a pocket, scribbled on the back of it and handed it her.

"My mobile number." He shrugged. "Day or night, any worries don't hesitate to call."

She slowly nodded.

"I might as well lock up now, while you're here," said Jenny. "Save bothering Malcolm later. If you wouldn't mind waiting a few minutes."

"No problem."

"I usually have a cup of tea about this time," she told him. "Over at the rectory. Can I tempt you?"

"Seeing as how you're twisting my arm," he said.

This will be your first railway journey and you arrive at Paddington with almost childlike excitement. You're struck by the bustle of the station, a sense of embarkation which resonates with fresh beginnings of your own. Sipping coffee, you become fascinated with the giant destination board - every few seconds it rattles an updated piece of information into place and passengers scuttle off on their way or dejectedly shake their heads. How does it all work, you wonder, who controls it and from where?

The train is longer than you imagined, snaking away out of sight along the platform. And rather than a series of compartments, familiar from the films of your childhood, a central aisle runs the length of each carriage with seats either side facing each other across a tabletop.

There's a false start as you mistake the carriages on the next track pulling away for your own departure, but then you really are moving. Your eyes are glued to the window as the train gathers pace past tenements and terrace rows, all scruffy backyards and washing lines, an occasional stretch of industrial wasteland. But by the time you reach suburbia you're travelling at a fair enough rate of knots for the tidy uniform houses set in leafy avenues to be flying by and then the world is nothing but green fields and rolling hills.

"Let's go for a coffee," says Jake, rising. You follow him cautiously, the side to side swaying and clickety-clack over the rails leave you far less steady on your feet than you're comfortable with.

You pass through a dining car and a bar, both not yet open, before arriving at the buffet. You each take a coffee and a KitKat over to seats by the window and silently watch the world fly by.

"We'll have lunch in the restaurant later," eventually says Jake with a smile. "Won't be cheap, but it's going to be early evening when we get to St Hannahs and we don't want to be buggering about trying to find somewhere to eat."

You return his smile and then silence returns.

It's unspoken that the previous night has forever shifted the boundaries of whatever this relationship once was. Mercenary piece of theatre it might well have been, but the act itself will be permanently imprinted on both your psyches. A spectre with icy breath, waiting for just the hint of an erotic charge between you before pursing its lips...

You've never seen the ocean before, never been faced with a vista so wide and empty. You stand by the harbour wall transfixed, while Jake checks the sheet of paper on which he's scribbled the details of where you'll be staying.

"About fifteen minutes, I reckon," he tells you, folding away the directions into his pocket. "We should be there before dark."

Sea salt in the air has actually made you heady, the freshness all enveloping. You want to walk down to the beach, feel sand between your toes and paddle through the surf, but there's an urgency to Jake's tone and so don't push it. Hopefully, it will prove an experience rendered all the more exquisite by anticipation.

Jake's right, you take the footpath over a hill at the outskirts of town and from the crest you look out over St Hannahs to where the sun almost touches the horizon.

"We should get a move on," he tells you. "It'll go down really quickly now."

But it's still twilight as you arrive at the campsite.

"Touring pitch, chalet or camping barns," asks the receptionist, a girl no older than yourself.

At Jake's hesitation, she smiles.

"The chalets are paid for weekly in advance," she explains. "The camping barns are five shillings a night each, six bob with bedding. So, if you're not sure what your plans are, that's probably your best option." She gives a little shrug. "Plus, you'll have one all to yourselves, at least for tonight and I daresay for the rest of the week. We don't usually get busy until the Bank Holiday weekend."

"Okay," Jake nods, fishing out a ten shilling note and a florin. "With the bedding."

"Blankets or sleeping bags?" asks the girl, and there's just the slightest twitch to her smile as she adds, "We've only single sleeping bags."

"They'll do fine," you tell her, giving a questioning sideways glance at Jake, who slowly nods. As she goes over to a cupboard and takes out two sleeping bags, you add, "It still gets pretty chilly at night."

"Do you have a torch?" she asks and when Jake shakes his head, places a plastic flashlight next to the bundle on the counter.

"Campsite map." She hands over an A4 sheet of paper. "Feel free to use the shower block and the kitchen. There's a shop on site for food and other basics and there are a couple of supermarkets in St Hannahs. But if you need something for tonight, it closes in half an hour."

"Right," says Jake. "Thanks."

"And if you do want to stay on, let us know by twelve noon tomorrow," she adds. "Just come in and settle up for however long you've decided."

"Okay," smiles Jake. "And the barns are...?"

"Turn left out of here, follow the path to the end and you'll see them on your right, pick any one you want." She shrugged. "We got all three ready because there was talk the soldiers might be billeted there, but in the end they used the Town Hall."

"Soldiers?"

"They've been drafted in to deal with the oil spillage on the beaches. From the Torrey Canyon," she added, in response to Jake's blank expression.

Neither of you pay much attention to the news cycle, but you do recall hearing that an oil tanker had run aground off the Isles of Scilly.

"Oh right," you say and, gathering everything together, wish her goodnight.

As you walk along the pathway you pass a campfire, surrounded by a dozen or so people. Both the sound of a strummed guitar and the aroma of frying bacon come drifting over.

"We'll get settled in," says Jake, "and then head down to the shop."

You give a nod at this. That lunch on the train seems a long time ago.

The barn has been subdivided into partitions. Each has a

thin mattress, almost a pallet, on a wide ledge and there's a small chest of drawers with a Calor Gas lamp on top of it. It doesn't take more than a couple of minutes to sort your stuff out.

"Keep the bag with you, okay?" Jake tells you. "We'll find somewhere to stash the gear in the morning."

Halfway back down the path to the shop, you become aware of a figure walking over from the campfire. A teenage girl, you realise as she draws near, about your age at a guess.

"Hi," she smiles. "We saw you arriving and wondered if you'd like to join us. Thought that if you've been travelling all day, you'll probably be hungry."

"Wow, thanks," said Jake. "We were just heading to the shop, so that would be great."

He introduces you both as you walk over to the campfire.

"Pleased to meet you," says the girl. "I'm Emma."

It's smiles all around as Emma leads you to a trestle table loaded with metal trays of bacon, sausages, burgers, baked beans and fried bread. But little rings so false to your ear as forced geniality and it rarely plays out well.

"Have you travelled far?" she asks, as you load your plates.

"London," Jake tells her.

"Whereabouts? We live in Whitechapel?"

"We were staying in South Kensington?"

"Oh right, we have a branch in West 11 - Notting Hill - so I'm over that way a lot."

"A branch?" you ask.

"The Socialist Workers Party," she explains. "Mum and Dad run the local office."

She indicates a couple in their fifties, a doleful man in earnest discussion with a studenty looking youth and a short, wiry woman listening intently. We carry our plates over to where they're sitting and Emma introduces you to her parents.

"I'm Wilf," says her father, extending his hand, "and this is my wife, Frieda. Are you two down here on holiday?"

Jake nods, obviously deciding this is the simplest route to

take.

"And you?" he asks Wilf.

"Oh, we've been coming down to St Hannahs for donkey's years," Wilf tells him. "We hold a workshop here every Easter."

"Workshop?" You can't quite keep the confusion out of your voice.

"One of our core concepts is the necessity of continual revolution," states Frieda. "We use the dialectic to explore how that can be achieved."

You've learnt that answers which leave you more confused than enlightened are best left unpursued and so merely smile in her direction.

"Are you students?" asks Emma.

"No. Actually, we've recently been dabbling in the art world," you tell her, and in the corner of your vision Jake has shot you a look.

"Oh, you're artists?"

"No." You shake your head. "More the merchandising and distribution side of things."

"With a gallery?"

"Not really." You fix her with a smile. "Although lately, we have been exploring the potentialities of performance art."

"So what do you do, Emma?" asks Jake somewhat hastily, before she can respond to that.

"I'm still at school," she says. "Doing A-levels this year. But in my spare time, I work for a Claimants Union that Mum's set up."

"Claimants Union?"

You gather from Emma that a Claimants Union is a collection of volunteer social workers, solicitors and Citizens Advice Bureau staff, who process benefit and housing claims on behalf of those unable to cope with bureaucracy without some degree of hand holding. As she expands on this, your mind begins to wander. Your own journey through society's underbelly has left you with little patience for the symbiosis of do-gooders and professional victims.

How to go about finding a job down here? Try the Labour

Exchange first thing in the morning, perhaps. That girl at Reception seemed friendly enough, and she'll know what's what locally. That's probably the best place to start, and then...

Your thoughts break off as you become aware of them both looking at you expectantly.

"Sorry, I was miles away." You force a smile. "It's been a long day, which I think is catching up with me."

"Emma suggested going into town together tomorrow. To show us around."

"I've a couple of things to sort out in the morning." You hope you've pitched just the right note of regret into your voice for it to sound sincere. "But you two go and I'll wander down there later on to find you."

Before either of them can respond to this, you raise yourself up onto your feet.

"Sorry I'm not better company tonight," you tell Emma. "But I really am shattered."

Jake begins to rise, but you place a hand on his shoulder to gently push him back down.

"No, it's okay. You stay here, I'll see you later."

You're not surprised he doesn't put up much of an argument.

You're in your sleeping bag, reading by the light of the gas lamp, when Jake gets back about an hour later.

"I thought you'd be asleep," he said.

"I didn't want to cramp your style." You give him a smile. "She obviously fancies you."

"Really?"

There's an eagerness that's almost puppylike, never a trait likely to win fair lady, but, sensing an easy exit from the conundrum this relationship has become for you both, you plough on.

"She couldn't take her eyes off you." Coaxing someone into what they want to believe seldom requires much guile. "Trust me, girls know."

He sits down beside you, close but careful not to brush against you.

"So where are you off to in the morning?" *he asks.*

"The Labour Exchange," *you tell him.* "To look for a job."

He's silent at that and you pick your next words carefully.

"I'm starting to realise that I'm not someone who'd... flourish, in a Bohemian lifestyle," *you tell him.* "And to be honest, I doubt anyone does without money or family behind them." *You shrug.* "In the real world, free spirits have a tendency to be chewed up and spat out."

"I really can't see you in a suburban semi with two point four children."

"Well..." *You struggle for the right words.* "You don't need to be straitlaced to be straight, yeah? And not all jobs turn you into an automaton."

"So, what do you have in mind?"

"I've absolutely no idea." *You shake your head.* "Start looking for a job in the town and then put one foot in front of the other."

"I can let you have the cash for somewhere of your own to stay," *Jake tells you.* "A bedsit or maybe a chalet here, they probably..."

"Don't worry," *you break in.* "I'll find some live-in hotel work." *You hesitate.* "I really do owe you, I know that."

Jake seems to consider.

"We should get some sleep," *he says eventually.* "It's been a bloody long day."

And he's careful, you notice before closing your eyes, to turn away from you before undressing and slipping into his sleeping bag.

The girl in Reception studies you carefully.

"There's always hotel work in St Hannahs," *she tells you.* "Have you done it before?"

You shake your head, ready with the story you've concocted. But instead of questioning you further, she lifts the telephone and presses a single key.

"Dad, do you know if Mrs Nelson is still looking for staff?" *She listens to the reply and nods.* "Okay, thanks."

She gives you a brief smile and dials a number.

"Hello, could I speak with Mrs Nelson? It's Carol at Petroc..." *She covers the mouthpiece with her hand while she waits.* "Mrs Nelson owns Tregenna Bay Hotel, overlooking the harbour. It's the largest hotel in town. If you..." *She breaks off as you hear a muffled voice coming from the speaker.* "Hello, Mrs Nelson." *She pauses.* "We've a girl staying with us who's moved down here looking for work."

Carol listens and then glances up at you.

"Can I have your name?" *she asks and then repeats it into the phone. Listening, she scribbles on a notepad in front of her.* "Okay, Mrs Nelson, thank you."

Putting the handset down, she tears the sheet of paper from the pad and hands it to you.

"Mrs Nelson's expecting you at eleven o'clock," *she says.* "They're looking for waitresses and chambermaids. Waitressing pays more, because of the tips, but chambermaids live in."

"Right."

"If you're here for the season," *continues Carol,* "we could do you a deal on a chalet. It wouldn't be one of our better ones," *with a shrug,* "but tips would probably cover it. Living in might seem convenient, but what it actually means is that you'll always be available. And most of the hoteliers in town like to get their money's worth out of staff."

You stare at her and give a slow nod.

"Thanks," *you tell her.* "I really appreciate this."

You've rehearsed the story several times in your mind during the walk into town and now you listen to it fall from your lips almost flawlessly.

No, you've never worked, because since you left school you've had to look after your father, who contracted lung cancer five years ago. There were only the two of you, Mum died when you were a child. When Dad passed at the beginning of the year, you were too young to take on the council house you'd always lived in, while being too old for Welfare Services to assume any responsibility for you. So, you've decided to make a fresh start elsewhere.

Mrs Nelson makes sympathetic clucking noises at the appropriate moments, but her gaze remains steely. There's history behind those eyes... She's been had before, her expression tells you, and not just by itinerant maids of all work looking for a roof over their head. But if you've learnt anything over the past few months, it's how to read people. Sensing the interview drawing to a conclusion, and perhaps not a favourable one, you smile and make as if to rise.

"I do understand if you'd prefer someone with more experience," you tell her, "or at least to give the matter further thought. And I've other interviews today, so..." You extend your hand over the desk. "Thank you for seeing me and it's been very nice to meet you."

Mrs Nelson is suddenly hesitant, perhaps even wrong-footed, by seemingly having the decision taken away from her.

And you know she's only one route back to regaining control.

"We have been let down by an agency in the Midlands," she muses. "Two girls who were supposed to have started this week..."

She lets her voice trail off, staring at you.

"Shall we say a week's trial? We'll start you off in the dining room for breakfast and once that's cleared away, you can lend a hand with the rooms. Let's see where you'd seem to fit in best and take things from there."

"Thank you, Mrs Nelson." You aim for respectful rather than subservient. "I won't give you reason to regret this."

Her expression suggests that's very much still up in the air, but in the meantime has persuaded herself to display a certain generosity of spirit.

"It's a six-thirty start. You're staying at Petroc?"

"Yes."

"There are no buses at that time of the morning. You'll have

to walk over, I'm afraid, but several members of staff do drive by there. If you ask around tomorrow, you should be able to arrange a lift." She appears to consider. "If the position becomes permanent, you will be expected to live in. Would that be a problem?"

"Not at all," you tell her. Despite Carol's caveat, it would be one less thing to worry about and probably best not to be around when it dawns on Jake that it's conscription, rather than coitus, Emma the Red has in mind.

"Excellent." With just the slightest of smiles, Mrs Nelson rises from her chair. "We'll see you in the morning."

Arriving back at Petroc, Carol calls out to you from Reception.

"Mrs Nelson rang," handing you a slip of paper. "She asked if you'd give her a call."

Obviously she's had second thoughts. So, tomorrow the Labour Exchange...

"Where's the nearest phone box?" you ask.

With a smile, Carol lifts the telephone up onto the counter.

"As it's local, you can use this. But there's a kiosk on the main road, just by the bus stop."

Leaving you to it, she goes through into the back office.

The number you've been given must be a private line. Rather than being greeted by a receptionist, it's Mrs Nelson herself who answers.

"On reflection," she says, "it really is asking a lot of you to be travelling backward and forward from Petroc every day. If it makes matters easier, would you prefer to move into the staff annex today?"

"Yes..." You try to keep the surprise out of your voice. "Yes, that simplifies things quite a bit, actually."

"Mary, one of our kitchen staff, will be driving in this evening. I could call and have her collect you and your luggage from where you're staying. About six thirty?"

"That's brilliant," you tell her. "I really appreciate this."

"You're welcome."

Leaving the phone on the counter, you walk over to the barn, looking for Jake to explain what's happening. But he's not there and still hasn't returned by the time you've packed your things and are ready to leave.

'Found a job in a hotel, live-in and starting tonight,' *you scribble into your notepad.* 'Good luck with everything and don't worry about my share. As far as I'm concerned, we're straight.'

You tear it off, lay it on his pillow, pick up your bag and head back to Reception.

You see why they've started your day in the restaurant. Tregenna Bay follows the precept that an English gentleman is never served his breakfast. Instead, a variety of silver platters and dishes are placed on a long table immediately to the left of the dining room's entrance, from where the guests might help themselves.

You stand in attendance, dressed in a black blouse, skirt and tights with a frilly white apron at your waist. There's little to do but replenish the plates as they empty or grow cold, although remnants are simply reheated and brought back out again.

As the guests depart, you reset their table with fresh linen and arrange cutlery in precise alignment, carefully inspecting each piece for the slightest blemish.

Your own breakfast was at six thirty, taken with the commis chef, the kitchen porter and Debbie, the other waitress. The actual chef, you learn, won't arrive until preparations begin for lunch, his talents presumably wasted on such basic cuisine.

After that you were given a quick tour to be shown where everything is kept or goes, and the reason for there being two doors from the dining room to the kitchen was explained to you.

Left in, left out is the mantra you run through your head when approaching them from either side.

"There's at least one collision a week," the commis chef tells you. "Just make sure it's not you."

With breakfast finished and tables set for lunch, the white apron is discarded and Mrs Nelson takes you upstairs.

"We have guest rooms on four floors," she explains, "and there are two girls to each floor."

You learn that every morning the chambermaids are given a sheet listing that day's departures. As they finish each room, they use the internal telephone to inform Reception and then update that sheet with rooms whose keys have been handed in, the guests either departed or out for the day.

On the third floor, she introduces you to Emblyn, a girl perhaps a year or two older than you, who's busy stripping a bed.

"Before you finish," she tells Emblyn, "check how the second floor's going. Anne is by herself today."

"Yes, Mrs Nelson," says Emblyn. From her accent, you gather she's local.

Mrs Nelson leaves you to it and Emblyn gives a running commentary as you work your way through the room.

"Always start with the bed. Strip it if they're leaving, otherwise just make it. Hospital corners, know how to do that?"

Presumably the same as Cottage Home corners, but, to be on the safe side, you shake your head. Emblyn demonstrates, finally tucking neat little triangles under the mattress at each corner.

"Then a general tidy up. The more snobbish they are, the more messy their habits, is what you'll find. Give everything a quick polish, run the hoover over the carpet and then into the bathroom. Rinse the basin and bathtub, scrub the WC, change the towels."

She pauses.

"Most important of all, always knock before you go into the room. Even if the sheet says they're out, even if you can't hear anyone inside. And call out 'Hello' when you open the door." Emblyn shakes her head slowly. "You wouldn't believe some of the things I've walked in on."

You probably would, you reflect.

"And speaking of which, anything left behind goes in here."

"Left behind?"

She reaches down to the lower shelf of the trolley, lifts a cardboard box and takes out a skimpy pair of lace knickers and a suspender belt.

"We're supposed to hang on to whatever we might find after guests check out," she smiles, "in case they phone the hotel reporting it lost." She arches an eyebrow. "As if."

"So...?"

"We call it the 'cheap frills' box."

You laugh.

"What happens to it all?"

"End of the season, we divvy it all up between us. Considering there's not much in there that'd keep a chill off, it helps me and my Edward stay cosy through the winter nights."

Working together, the room is quickly finished. Emblyn buzzes Reception and updates her list.

"306 and 308 have checked out," she explains to you, "so we can do them any time, as long as they're ready for a two o'clock check in. 307's out, so let's get that done while we've got the chance."

Emblyn works briskly but without appearing rushed and it's a pace you easily fall in with. She displays less curiosity about you than you'd expect, but as the day goes on you realise you're probably one of a dozen girls she's seen come and go.

You're right about her being local. Emblyn's lived in St Hannahs all her life and this is the only job she's had since leaving school, three years ago. She's been married for a year, her husband's a fisherman and away at sea a lot more than she'd like, but, if they're ever going to get a place of their own, there's nothing to be done except grin and bear it.

It's no surprise to learn the quaint fishermen's cottages around the harbour have long ceased to house actual fishermen, most of whom live in small clusters of council houses, hidden away on the outskirts of town.

"It's all holiday homes these days," Emblyn tells you and you're surprised how sangfroid she appears about this. But she just shrugs when you press further.

"Tourism's what keeps St Hannahs going, and if you're local then you understand that. The only ones who really complain *about the visitors, calling them emmets and whatnot, are incomers, people from upcountry who've moved down here."*

By one thirty you've finished, and Emblyn is on her way home. Or rather, to the two-bedroom council flat shared with her husband's widowed mother.

"She's very nice," says Emblyn, "and I don't know what we'd have done without her. But it's not the same as having your own place, is it?"

No, you reflect, it's not.

CHAPTER ELEVEN

Amanda

The cab driver at the station taxi rank wasn't exactly enthusiastic when Amanda gave him the address, but, anticipating his chagrin at losing his position in line for a destination under a mile away, she already had a £20 note in her hand.

"I'm not expecting any change," she told him and he'd become positively chatty after that.

They headed towards the city centre but after less than a minute, turned left.

"Doesn't much look like a castle to me," Amanda said as they approached a sandstone outcrop, maybe a hundred feet high, with what appeared to be a Victorian manor house perched on the summit.

"The actual castle was destroyed by fire in the 1830s," the driver told her. "The rebuild went down a more contemporary route."

As they drove by, Amanda turned her head to stare at two caves at the foot of the mound, the entrance to each closed by a padlocked iron grill gate.

"Tunnels," said the driver, catching her expression. "Leading up to the top. In fact," he continued, turning right into the Park Estate through an open barrier against which a notice read *'No through route. Access only'*, "the whole city's built on a warren of them. If you know what you're doing, you can get from one side of Nottingham to the other completely underground."

The large, detached residences they passed were definitely more grand than Amanda had anticipated. Nineteenth century opulence so close to a city centre rarely survived twentieth century expansion, villas and mansions transformed into bedsit tenements for students and immigrants. But there wasn't a hint of that here, even the ornate streetlamps had a glisten to them.

"Just about all of these houses," the driver gave a nod of his head to one side, "have a passageway in the cellar leading to the tunnels. Well secured, of course, but it does make you wonder what they were getting up to back then."

It does indeed, thought Amanda, but she simply turned to him with a smile.

"You seem very knowledgeable on the subject," she said, and he shrugged.

"Local history's my thing," he told her. "I teach an evening class at the Poly, plus I'm researching a book. And this," he tapped the steering wheel with his fingers, "lets me pay the rent by working only when I have to."

They slowed to a halt outside a large townhouse. The driver reached into his pocket, took out a card and scribbled on it.

"If you need a cab later, that's the firm's number," he said. "My mobile's on the back." He gave Amanda a smile and another shrug. "If it's just to the station and I'm free, we'll take it out of the twenty."

"Okay, thanks." Amanda returned his smile, collected her shoulder bag and stepped out onto the pavement. As he pulled away, she took a moment to study the house.

A gravel path led up to a large wooden front door, oak by the look of it and lent a medieval flavour by a pattern of black iron bolts. A gate to the left had a sign which read *'Tradesmen and Deliveries'*, but, following the instructions she'd been given, Amanda walked over to the other side, where a flight of stone steps ran down to a basement entrance.

There was no bell, only a large doorknocker, an ornate lion's head which echoed surprisingly loudly. After a few seconds, Amanda heard footsteps from inside and the sound of a bolt being drawn back.

The door opened slowly and the figure standing there studied Amanda cautiously.

"DI Palmer," said Amanda, holding out her warrant card.

"Professional Standards. I'm here to see Helen Munro."

* * *

Once inside, the first thing to strike Amanda was that while Helen bore little resemblance to her famous sister, her father could have been Lee Munro's doppelgänger. John Munro had died the previous year, but as Amanda followed Helen along a narrow passageway into the living room, his presence was everywhere. Old posters depicted his role as pantomime dame in a variety of provincial theatre productions throughout the fifties and sixties, occasionally interposed with the rather more salacious persona of a nightclub drag act.

Ironic, thought Amanda, that should there ever be a film of his life, the best person to portray him would probably be his daughter.

In the living room, one wall was floor to ceiling framed photographs of an always smiling but - out of costume - strangely insignificant figure, posing with stars of the day whose heights he'd never quite managed to equal. All were signed with epithets of friendship or affection, yet somehow conjured a superficiality that Amanda couldn't help but feel matched their faded gloss.

"He knew absolutely everyone," said Helen, mistaking Amanda's lingering gaze for admiration. "But in our world, you either get the breaks or you don't."

No doubt she took comfort from telling herself that, thought Amanda, but for the most part we make our own luck.

A series of arrests, ranging from importuning in a public lavatory to acts of gross indecency, were probably responsible for putting the brakes on his career, although intriguingly none of these cases had actually come to court. But going through his file had proved a guided tour of a seedy postwar netherworld inhabited by denizens of both showbiz and politics, linked under the auspices of dubious charitable work. So, friends in high places, had guessed Amanda, with profligate tastes.

Not all memorabilia were John Munro's. A poster from

a production of Bernard Shaw's 'Man and Superman' listed Helen above the title and she featured in several framed film stills. Amanda recognised a few of these from her teenage years, mainly of the British horror genre that boyfriends had taken her to, she suspected, in the hope of having her clinging to them in fright. However, it seemed Helen's celluloid career hadn't progressed much further than decorative victim and there was nothing on display in which she appeared older than her mid-twenties.

And absolutely no evidence whatsoever of her sister's existence.

"Please, have a seat," said Helen, indicating an ornate but well-worn leather sofa.

"This is really very good of you," Amanda smiled. "Hopefully, it shouldn't take long."

"I honestly don't see how much help I can be." Helen sat opposite, shaking her head. "I've already told the police everything I know and again at the inquest. It's all in my statements."

"Well, it's now policy," lied Amanda smoothly, "to review, let's say, high-profile cases to determine if they could have been handled more effectively."

"Effectively?"

"The police are human, Ms Munro. We make errors, but there is a, we hope, change of culture in the air. If mistakes were made or we've been guilty of procedural error, then we believe that we should learn from them."

"Right," said Helen, dubiously.

Amanda reached into her bag, took out her notebook.

"It was you who found him?" she asked, uncapping her pen.

Helen hesitated, then nodded.

"Must have been quite a shock? Something like that?"

"I was aware Colin's inclinations were..." She shook her head. "Offbeat, shall we say, he made no secret of that, but..."

She slowly exhaled.

"You had no idea that's what he...?" Breaking off, Amanda looked at her quizzically.

"I don't think anybody did, really. I mean, this has always been a theatrical household, Mum and Dad rented rooms out to," she indicated the wall of photographs, "just about anyone who was up here for a season in rep and let me tell you, they ran to some pretty bizarre tastes. But, you know, the thing you learnt was that the more bizarre those tastes were, the less shy they were about them."

"Had you known Colin long?"

"Oh God, yes, absolute decades. From when he was a cub reporter on the *Evening Post*."

"He covered the theatre?"

"No, it was after a break-in here. He worked on the story. That's how we first met."

"A burglary?"

"I'm not sure what it was, to tell you the truth. It was all very creepy."

"Creepy?"

"It happened back in the early sixties. Mum, Dad and I had gone out to the Playhouse, but Eileen hadn't been feeling well, so-"

"Eileen?" interrupted Amanda. "That's Lee, your sister?"

Helen's lips tightened.

"Yes. *The Hendersons* had recently finished and she'd moved home." Helen shrugged. "During the series run - from the late fifties to sixty-three - she lived with our aunt in London and went to stage school there. After that she wanted to work in repertory, get some actual stagecraft under her belt, so she came back here hoping Dad would sort something out for her."

"Okay."

"Well, like I said, that night Eileen was out of sorts and so stayed indoors while the rest of us were out. When we arrived home, she'd gone to bed and so I went up to her room to make sure that she was alright. I opened her door without knocking, I mean we were in and out of each other's rooms all the time, and then..."

Helen broke off and took a deep breath.

"Sorry," she said. "Even all these years later, it still..."

She shook her head.

"Eileen was asleep on the bed, but someone was in there standing over her. A man dressed all in black and wearing one of those ski masks, you know, with only the eyes cut out?"

Amanda nodded.

"I'll never forget that stare. And Eileen just lying there, the sheets pulled back and in her nightdress, breathing softly..."

She raised her eyes to meet Amanda's.

"I started screaming. I screamed and screamed, then turned and ran out through the door. Dad was halfway up the stairs by the time I was on the landing. I remember telling him that there was a man in Eileen's room, but when we got back there, he was gone. The curtains were drawn apart, the window was wide open and, of course, Eileen was now sitting up in bed, totally terrified by all the commotion."

"Did they ever catch him?"

Helen shook her head.

"The police reckoned he'd shinned down the drainpipe - probably the same way he'd broken in - and was away into the night. But Colin covered the story for the Post and... Well, he played the pervy aspects of it down. It would've been really easy to have made a meal out of the whole 'child star escapes would-be rapist' angle - and presumably done his career no harm in doing that - but he didn't. There was an appeal for information, but he kept our names out of the papers and Mum and Dad never forgot that." She hesitated. "And Dad tried to help him out whenever he could."

"Help him out?"

"Back then, being gay wasn't easy." Helen shrugged. "Reputations could be ruined, thousands of men even sent to prison. But the theatre's always been very tolerant and Dad had contacts. There was a whole... freemasonry kind of thing going on, I suppose you could call it. People watching out for each other and opening doors. It was Dad who got Colin his first job on Fleet Street and his career took off from there. So, he'd been a family friend ever since."

"I see." Amanda was scribbling in her notebook.

"But I'll tell you something," said Helen and Amanda looked up at her. "Eileen was never the same after that night."

"In what way?"

"There was a..." She paused. "I know nothing was supposed to have happened, but they say that the mind often shuts traumatic memories out, don't they? Eileen was always distant after that. Whether she blamed us for leaving her alone in the house, or it was some kind of coping process that buried everything about that evening, but..."

Helen let her voice trail off.

"She moved down to London again almost straightaway. Dad had gone to all sorts of trouble to get her into local rep, called in a lot of favours, but she just wasn't interested anymore. She started getting involved with fringe theatre groups, playing in the back rooms of pubs or even old warehouses."

Helen couldn't keep the disdain out of her voice.

"Colin Savage," said Amanda. "Are any of his things still here?"

"No, I cleared his room before renting it out again, a carpenter at the *Theatre Royal*. The police had taken his computer and notebooks away and..." She broke off, staring at Amanda. "You know, you're not the first person to come here asking about his things. A friend of his turned up just when everything seemed to have died down, after the inquest."

"A friend?"

"Well, a couple, actually. I had met him two or three times before with Colin, so I knew they were friends from way back when. He said he wanted to... 'Create a more fitting testament to Colin's reputation', I think were the words he used. But I didn't have anything to give him."

"Do you have their names?"

"I can't remember hers. She must have told me, but everything was a bit," she shook her head, "haywire, at the time, as I'm sure you can imagine."

"Of course," said Amanda.

"She was European, Scandinavian I'd guess." Helen stood up and reached towards the mantelpiece. "But the chap..."

She picked up what looked like a business card and handed it to Amanda.

"In case I came across anything else, he said."

Amanda stared down at the inscription.

'Christopher Franklyn' it read.

"Is everything alright?" asked Helen, as Amanda continued to stare.

"Yes, I'm just..." Amanda gave a slow shake of her head. "Has he been in touch since?"

"No. In fact, I had been wondering about contacting him." Helen seemed slightly embarrassed and Amanda silently waited for her to continue.

"A letter arrived for Colin last week." Again that hesitation. "I had no idea if it might be important or not, so I thought I'd better open it. It was from a London company that supplied storage facilities. It said that the annual fee for a secure mailbox rental was due at the end of the month." She looked across at Amanda. "Whenever Colin had significant notes or research papers, he'd often mail copies of them to himself, here. As a kind of backup." She shrugged. "I suppose he also had a backup to the backup."

"Have you told anyone else about this?"

Helen shook her head.

"The thing is," said Amanda softly, "that letter is actually evidence."

"Am I in trouble?" asked Helen, biting her lip.

"You might have been if you'd sent it on to," Amanda went through the motions of reading the name on the card, "this Christopher Franklyn."

Amanda guessed that the delay was probably down to Helen Munro pondering how to monetise this snippet of information with Franklyn. With a mental shrug, she let that slide.

"But as the first person you've told about this is a police officer, then no, you don't have to worry."

Helen gave a deep sigh.

"You do still have that letter?" asked Amanda.

Helen nodded and rose to her feet.

"I'll get it for you," she said.

As the door closed behind her, Amanda sank back into the sofa and slowly shook her head.

Jenny

Just about the first thing Jenny Warwick did after taking up her post at Holy Trinity was to computerise the admin. As well as email and an appointments calendar, she ran a basic accounts package to stay on top of day-to-day expenses, desktop publishing for a monthly parish newsletter and a variety of word processing templates she could customise when responding to most issues raised by parishioners.

She'd even set up a simple database of those she dealt with on a regular basis, partner and children's names, interests and opinions. It didn't hurt to refresh your memory of what was what when dealing with a multiplicity of interlinked local committees. Jenny had managed a City hedge fund before changing paths, but the St Hannahs branch of the Womens Institute would have needed no lessons from her former colleagues when it came to Machiavellian intrigue.

However...

For her sermons Jenny always used a fountain pen and paper. Lines struck through, margin notes, a phrase restructured seemed to suggest an undertaking of serious purpose, whilst the scratching of an italic nib across the sheet, with its connotations of her schooldays, never failed to furnish a sense of comfort. The only child of loving parents, before cancer, before dementia...

Jenny didn't stockpile sermons the way she knew other members of the clergy did, an all purpose handy backup if time proved too pressing. She always set aside two hours on a Saturday to be at her desk and while she might have an idea of where she'd be going with things, she did her best to shy away from actual detail until she began to compose it.

She had no hard and fast rules regarding subject matter. If an event of significance was taking place in the world she'd often try to find some spiritual context, attempt to bring home to the congregation that however archaic the

Church frequently appeared, its relevance never diminished. Occasionally she'd get a bee in her bonnet about something or other and sound off on it and sometimes she'd simply let the Bible fall open wherever it may - a Judeo-Christian *homage* to the yarrow stalks - and work with whatever she was presented with.

But today....

Today, she did not have a single clue where to begin.

What it came down to was that most fundamental question of faith, often the first one a child asks once he or she's grasped the tenets of Christianity.

"*Why does God let bad things happen in the world?*"

If there was a comforting answer to that, Jenny had yet to hear it. '*As a test of faith*' certainly didn't cut it, unless you were one of those evangelists who believed He also squirrelled away fossils in the earth's substrata to weed out the doubters. '*That He does not cause bad things to happen, but allows us freedom of choice which can sometimes lead to negative consequences*', was another stock response which came across as a little too glib for its own good. Might wash if you only had the loving God of the New Testament to contend with, but what about that ill-tempered deity of The Pentateuch, always so ready with His frogs, locusts and boils?

'*God's ultimate plan is for us to learn and grow from our experiences and to come to know Him and His love and grace better,*' Jenny had once been told as a child and that might well be true, but there was little comfort there. Because the crux of it, she believed, was that life was hard, life was cruel, life was unfair and what had been self-evident to those generations who'd worked the land in all weathers or laboured in dark satanic mills, no one was buying that these days.

If there were any truth to Karl Marx's dictum that religion was the opium of the people, reflected Jenny, then cold turkey had been a bitch. Those same people have a need to believe and if you remove that which is genuinely profound from their lives, don't be surprised when they turn to pretty much anything else to endow with the same zeal. All well and good when life's happily ticking along, but just wait until something rips away the sticking plaster from that rent in your soul.

What Jenny was certain of was that her church would be full to bursting tomorrow. And that unlike a carol service, harvest festival or the sacraments, all eyes would be on her as more than some ritualised master of ceremony. And in those eyes, if the church were to have any meaning to this community, then it would be in the provision of solace and Jenny had to accept that in purely practical terms, she had only one job to do here...

So, have faith in where to begin.

She lifted her Bible, laid the spine flat against the surface of her desk and let it fall open. John, the most poignant of the gospels, chapter 11 and her eye moved down the page to verse 35.

Jenny stared for a few seconds and then, picking up her pen, copied it to the top of the blank sheet.

'Jesus wept.'

Amanda

"Can I ask you a question?" The cab driver's eyes met Amanda's in the rear-view mirror.

"Well, let's see?" was Amanda's dry response.

"Are you a reporter?"

"Why would you think that?"

"The place was swarming with them a couple of months ago. You know, after that journalist, Colin Savage, was found dead there." He paused. "Nothing like a bit of kink to get the public's pulse racing, right?"

"I'm part of the investigation looking into that," Amanda told him. "Just here to tie up a few loose ends."

"No surprise him living there," continued the driver. "That house has always had a reputation, at least for as long as I've been around. And the stories go back a lot further than that."

"Reputation?"

"It was built, as were most of the houses on the estate, in the mid-nineteenth century. Mostly for factory owners and the like - Nottingham's lace industry was a world leader at the time - but that house was first owned by a West End theatre impresario, who liked to indulge himself well away from prying eyes. They were the days when rank and money insulated you from just about anything short of murder and treason."

"I understood that in the sixties it belonged to John Munro," said Amanda.

"He didn't actually own it." The driver shook his head. "He was more of a glorified caretaker, although procurer would be closer to the mark, truth be told." In the mirror he smiled, but there was nothing amusing about it. "When I was a teenager, back in my mod days, he was always around the pubs and clubs, inviting kids there for parties. Those who went had some pretty wild tales to tell."

"So who does own the place?"

"A friend of mine - we're in the same historical society - once tried to find out. Like me, he's working on a book and thought it wouldn't hurt sales to spice things up with the odd bit of smutty tittle-tattle. Got nowhere, one shell company after another, disappearing off to the Cayman Islands via Jersey, and in the end he just gave up."

"It seems to be more of a boarding house these days," said Amanda. "Run by John Munro's daughter for visiting theatricals."

The driver shrugged.

"You know, the more you delve into history, the more some buildings seem to have a will - even a destiny, if that doesn't sound too fanciful - all of their own. Dig down into the stories and you'll see the same patterns repeating. I was reading the other day about the flat in London where Jimi Hendrix died. Well, turns out the same thing happened there to that American singer, Mama Cass."

"Perhaps it was owned by a record company. Who kept it for visiting musicians?"

"Maybe. But I'd think twice about spending the night there."

They pulled into the railway station's covered forecourt.

"Well," said Amanda, "thanks for the conversation, it was interesting."

"If you're ever back up here," he told her, "you've got my card."

Amanda reached into her bag, took out her wallet and passed over a £10 note.

"That's okay," he said. "I'll take it out of the first twenty."

"That was for the fare," she smiled. "This is a tip. And good luck with the book."

"I need you to run a small errand for me," says Mrs Nelson one morning, a few days into your career as a chambermaid. "The kettle at home is broken and I can't get away today. Would you collect a spare from the stillroom and take it over to Dennis at the house for me?"

"Of course," you tell her. Emblyn doesn't look too pleased about this, but Tregenna Bay is only half full at the moment and even by herself she'll have the floor done by lunchtime. You memorise the directions Mrs Nelson gives you and, with the kettle in a large shopping bag, set off along the coast road, noting the further you travel the grander the houses.

And, needless to say, your destination is at the very end.

A wide, sandy coloured gravel driveway loops around a sizeable decorative pond, before arriving at a facade that can't seem to decide between Baroque and antebellum plantation. Walking up the steps, you find the front door slightly ajar and so rather than pulling at the brass handle sunk into the wall, which looks more ornamental than functional, you put your head inside and call out, "Hello!".

Footsteps echo from what sounds a fair distance away. You recognise the figure that eventually appears as Mrs Nelson's son, who stops and stares at you in the doorway. Silently, you reach into the bag and take out the kettle. With a smile, you hold it aloft.

"Oh, right," says Dennis. "Could you bring it through?"

I could, you think, or you could just take it off me and do that yourself. But he has already turned and is walking away, so you follow him across the hallway, passing an imposing stairway sweeping up to the first floor, and through a door in the far wall.

The kitchen strikes you as being more suited to a small hotel than a home, but is probably warranted by the amount of entertaining you imagine goes on here. It leads into a dining room, from which French windows open out onto a terrace, spacious enough for half a dozen tables and chairs not to seem crowded.

"Would you like a coffee?" asks Dennis. Slightly surprised - you expected to be summarily dismissed once instructed where to leave the kettle - you nod.

"Yes, thank you."

Despite the presence of a very complicated looking coffee machine, he spoons Nescafé into two cups. You can't work out whether this means that as staff it's all you warrant or he doesn't know how to use it, but his smile as he turns back to you seems friendly enough.

"You're new, aren't you?" he asks. "How are you getting on?"

"Okay." You return his smile.

"Have you worked in hotels before?"

"No." You shake your head and he looks at you quizzically. "This is actually my first job," you tell him.

"Really?"

You repeat the story you gave to Mrs Nelson. At the end, he nods sympathetically.

"I'm sorry," he says.

"Thank you."

He is silent, filling the cups with boiling water and then gestures towards the terrace.

"Shall we have these outside?" he suggests.

Once again, you find yourself following him, wondering if five paces behind is his preferred status for women in general or just you in particular.

The view from the terrace is understated rather than breathtaking. The town and the harbour are out of sight around the headland, but the eye rolls easily across the sand dunes of the Burrows and on to the rolling Atlantic breakers beyond.

Casually he motions you to sit down, but you are, somehow, sensing something feigned about this manner of his. It has the air of hollow theatrics, learnt behaviour honed over formative years of how one dispenses gracious favour to the déclassé.

But he's not yet old enough, you reflect as you join him at a table, to understand just how much of a weakness that may prove to be.

"Is this your first time in Cornwall?" he asks.

"Yes," you tell him.

"But you seem to have made friends pretty quickly."

Something about his tone tightens the edges of your smile.

"I'm sorry?"

"I saw you in the town the other night." *He's staring out over the view, not meeting your questioning gaze.* "With some of the beats."

"Yes." *Your reply is slow and careful.* "I met them soon after I arrived here. At Petroc."

"Oh." *There's surprise in his voice and for the first time since you've sat down, he turns to look at you.* "They're staying there?"

"That's right. For the Easter holiday, down from London."

"Okay..." *Surprise has been replaced with uncertainty.* "It's only that most of them camp out in the Burrows or in the old army pill boxes along the beach."

You shrug.

"Just because someone has long hair, and they're more comfortable in jeans and a T-shirt than a suit, doesn't make them a dosser, you know?"

He shifts uncomfortably in his chair.

"Well, we've had a lot of trouble with them down here. Drugs, begging on the streets... You should be careful, it's easy to get tarred with the same brush."

"And whose brush would that be?"

He stares as you sip your coffee.

"And so you're okay with all of that, are you?" *He eventually breaks the silence.* "That kind of lifestyle?"

"I'm okay with any kind of lifestyle that doesn't hurt anyone else or push itself onto other people." *You shrug.* "Live and let live, right?"

"So, you believe in free love as well?"

"Do you believe in paying for it?"

Whatever reply might have been on his lips hangs in midair. You allow yourself a small smile at his consternation.

"Have you actually met any of them?"

"Sorry?" *shaking his head.*

"These beats that you're so judgemental about. Ever sat down and had a conversation with one of them?"

"No, of course not, I..." Under your steady gaze, his voice trails off. And then, suddenly, the young princeling has vanished and in his place sits a confused teenager.

"Would you like to?" Without giving him a chance to reply, you steam ahead. "There's a beach party on the Burrows tonight. Everyone's welcome."

His expression becomes even more uncertain.

"I'm not sure that..." he begins.

"Oh, don't worry," you break in. "I'll protect you."

Uncertainty remains etched on his face, but after a few seconds he slowly nods.

You suggest meeting at The Barque, a hotel and restaurant by the harbour, but Dennis says he'll wait for you in a shelter on the seafront, the one by the sandy lane that leads to the Burrows. Obviously he's nervous to be seen in your company, but you're amused rather than irritated by this.

You guess there'll be a lot more for him to be nervous about before tonight's over.

He's dressed in what he assumes would be suitable for the occasion - jeans, T-shirt, white plimsolls - and not made too bad a job of it, even if there's a crispness about it all more suggestive of undercover cop than dropout. You reach for his hand as you set out along the path. Initially he seems uncertain by the contact, but soon relaxes as the conversation turns to music, films and books. It's a twenty-minute walk over to where sand dunes meet the rolling surf and you're both surprised to discover shared tastes.

A large bonfire has been erected and is in the process of being lit. You introduce him to Jake and they exchange nods.

"Have you seen Emma?" asks Jake. "She said she was coming down here tonight."

"No," you tell him, accepting the joint he offers and drawing on it deeply. Sensing disquiet alongside, you pass it back to Jake who, picking up the vibe, simply smiles and walks over to a couple of girls who are dancing by the water's edge to a strummed guitar.

"Let's see if they want any help with the food," you say,

taking his hand again and leading him over to the bonfire.

"Don't you worry about getting hooked?" he asks.

"Sorry?"

"On reefers." His expression is stern. "A girl I was at school with started messing around with them and then couldn't give them up. Now word is that she'll do anything to get the money to pay for them."

Presumably with the bogeyman who lives under her bed, you think, but only shake your head slowly.

"Well, I'm always careful, you know, never too much at one time," you reassure him and before he can answer, ask the couple sorting out the food by the fire if they need help. They smile, say they're okay, and so you gesture over to where the girls are dancing.

"Let's go and listen to the music," you suggest.

The setting sun highlights two swaying silhouettes against the ocean background and so it's not until you're almost upon them you realise that while one of the girls is wearing either a bikini or bra and pants, the other is completely naked. And you know the exact moment he also realises this, as your fingers are suddenly held in a vice like grip.

You turn your head slightly to glance at him.

Dennis is staring at the girl, but the underlying impression is one more of ambivalence than lust. You're not that surprised, while aspects of sexual initiation are likely to prove more startling for girls than boys - an adolescent tumescence bearing no resemblance to the genitalia of infants they've tended or those Greek statues which allowed artistic license to alibi prurience - feminine mystique can also pack a few punches. You remember Peter telling the story of a famous Victorian art critic, whose wedding night encounter with a thicket of pubic hair soaked in menstrual blood so traumatised him that the marriage remained unconsummated for years, before finally being dissolved. Even today, magazines like Playboy still felt it necessary to reach for the airbrush...

So, it's no great stretch to suppose this remains uncharted territory for him.

"Shall we sit down?" you suggest and he releases your hand as you lower yourselves onto the sand.

"Do you have a boyfriend?" he asks, deciding he's more comfortable focusing on you than the gyrating figures at the water's edge.

You shake your head.

"Not at the moment," you say.

"I suppose you heard about me and Patty - it must be all over the hotel?"

"I've overheard a few things." You shrug, recalling staff gossip about the bossy little madam who you've noticed on occasions laughing too loudly in the bar. Mostly it went in one ear and out the other, but lately, you gather, there's been trouble in paradise. "I wouldn't worry too much, it'll sort itself out."

"Sort itself out...?" He stares at you. "What do you mean?"

Before you can reply, there is a commotion of sorts over by the bonfire.

"Good grief," you say, rising to your feet. "We're being invaded."

A dozen figures in army battledress have arrived, carrying crates of beer and plastic shopping bags. And Emma, you realise, is at the forefront of them.

With Kit, one of the beats staying at Petroc.

"We're late because the cops pulled me and Kit outside the store," she is telling Jake. "They were giving us a hard time and things were getting really heavy, when these guys came along and stopped it."

"Are you okay?" Jake asks her.

Emma nods.

"We'd tried to buy some food in the shop," she continues, "and the woman there refused to serve us. When we argued, she called the cops. They were trying to arrest us when these guys moved in." She turns to grin at the soldiers behind her. "'If you want 'em then come and get 'em', right? That's what you said?" Turning back to Jake, "God, you should have seen their faces."

Jake leans forward to shake the leading soldier's hand.

"Good to meet you," he says, and there are introductions all around.

The squaddies distribute bottles of beer and in return are passed a spliff, handled hesitantly at first, then less so on its second pass. Everyone mingles freely by the bonfire as sausages and bacon butties are served, but you can't help notice that while Jake's eyes are fixed on Emma, hers rarely leave Kit and it's hard to escape the notion that this isn't something that's going to play out well.

"Someone's coming," you hear and turn to look along the beach.

Two girls are approaching. One is tall and lithe, with long curly hair tumbling over her shoulders, the other almost elfin, an effect compounded by a pixie cut. You watch as Emma walks forward to greet them, embracing the tall girl. The other girl offers her hand and then Emma appears taken aback as she is pulled in close for a tight hug. You can't make out the words being exchanged, but alongside you sense Dennis stiffen.

"Is that Lee Munro?" he asks.

"Sorry?" Shaking your head. "Who?"

"Lee Munro - the actress." He turns to look at you. "From that TV show a few years back."

You shrug.

"I've never really watched much television."

One of the squaddies approaches the smaller of the two girls, leans forward, and whispers in her ear. Suddenly she laughs, places a hand on his shoulder and plants a kiss onto his cheek. The squaddie backs away, smiling.

"Bloody hell, it is her," he insists, and then hesitates. "What's she doing here?" he asks, almost plaintively. "And with these people?"

"Perhaps," you suggest, "because she gets treated like who she is, rather than who she's expected to be." You shrug. "Come on, let's go and find out."

"She was nice, wasn't she?"

"Hmm?" Walking home your thoughts are elsewhere,

speculating on the inevitability of the drama waiting to be played out within the Jake, Emma, Kit triangle. "Sorry?"

"Lee Munro." He smiles. "Not what you'd expect from somebody famous."

"And what about the soldiers?"

"What do you mean?" His expression becomes quizzical.

"Were they what you expected?" You shrug. "After all, they've been banned from every pub and restaurant in town, so you can't really have had a chance to form an opinion about them before."

"Nobody's banned them from..."

"Oh, come on," you break in. "The only reason they were at the beach was because all the bars they tried had 'a private function' on tonight." You pause. "I heard your mother on the phone yesterday, talking to the landlord of The Barque - saying 'if we give them an inch, they'll take a mile' and that there's always trouble wherever troops are stationed."

"Well, I think she meant..."

"Obviously not the same kind of 'trouble' you get from the beats, but trouble nonetheless. But guess what - kindred spirits tend to find each other and when they do, they stick together. And, thanks to the local police getting heavy-handed with Emma and Kit, what this town now has are dope smoking freaks with a military escort. How's that for trouble?"

Dennis comes to a halt, turns and stares at you.

"You know," he says eventually, "you have some funny ideas."

"So I've been told," is your dry response.

You begin walking again.

"Earlier," he continues, "before everyone started arriving and we were talking about Patty... You said something about not having to worry, that it would all sort itself out." He shakes his head. "What did you mean by that?"

"That she's not going to let a catch like you get away."

"'A catch like me'," somewhere between puzzled and bemused.

"Well, in her eyes, at least. Son of a local hotelier, scion to all that entails… Trust me, with Satan whispering in her ear, Patty's been looking out over the kingdoms of the world in all their splendour. And definitely not put up much of a fight."

"You don't even know her."

"She was in The Barque the other night." You shrug. "Ten minutes was enough."

He's suddenly uncertain.

"Who was she with?"

"There was a group of people, but it was some blond surfer who was all over her."

"Tony Richards." He gives a slow nod. "He was in the year ahead of us at school."

"Right, the popular kid?" You look at him and give another shrug. "He looked the type. Good at sports and everyone wants to be his friend, including the teachers."

"He's at university now, just home for the holiday."

"What's his family do?"

"His dad's a painter and decorator, his mum's a dinner lady at St Annes."

"Well, as I said. No problem."

"I don't understand."

"She's on shore leave," you tell him. "A last fling. Soon as this Tony's back at college, she'll be on your doorstep all teary-eyed, and with a sob story of how a break like that made her realise how much you meant to her."

He seems about to argue, but checks himself. You walk in silence for a while.

"So what am I in your eyes?" he asks, eventually.

"Difficult to say," you tell him. "We've hardly scratched the surface."

"Ten minutes was all it needed for Patty, apparently."

"She's shallow waters pretending to be deep. You've more bubbling away underneath than you even realise yourself… Or perhaps trust yourself to realise. And while I'm not exactly sure what that might be, I do know that your Patty, given the chance, would slowly suck it all dry." You let a smile play on your lips. "And not in a good way."

Now he really is lost for words.

You don't see each other for a while. Or rather, you see each other, but there's no contact other than a brief smile or an exchange of nods. The arrival of Good Friday, the day after your evening at the beach, heralds the beginning of the holiday season proper and the hotel is now fully booked. He's wholly occupied dealing with demands from guests which seem to serve little purpose other than to inflate self importance, while your days are filled with bedrooms frequently left in a state the sulkiest teenager would struggle to achieve.

But the beach barbecue has become a nightly event. Where the police might happily have gotten heavy-handed moving the beats along, they're displaying a marked reluctance to tangle with troops fresh from a combat zone.

Your evening shift finishes late enough for everything to be in full swing by the time you get down to the Burrows, where you mostly occupy yourself sitting by the fire passing around a spliff, reassuring Jake about Emma and enjoying the occasional amorous interlude in the dunes.

One new friend is Fiona, who is spending the holiday working in a local studio for an artist who's shortly to have her work shown on TV. She originally arrived with Aidan, an Irish art student also staying at Petroc, but on subsequent evenings she arrives by herself. There's a slightly nervous air about her, although friendly enough she makes it plain she's not open to advances by either beats or squaddies and usually seeks out your company when you're not otherwise engaged.

One evening you take a walk along the beach with her, sharing a joint. She has a boyfriend back home in Plymouth, she confides. They're at art college together, but things aren't working out. He wants to, well, go all the way and Fiona won't let him. Now she thinks he might be seeing someone else.

"I'm sorry about that," you sympathise.

Fiona becomes even more hesitant.

Since she's been at Joyce's studio, she's started to realise ... She breaks off and you walk in silence for a while, letting her find her own words.

"Joyce, she..." *Fiona shakes her head slowly.* "Joyce likes other women."

"Okay," *you say, careful to keep your tone neutral.*

"And I think I might, too," *she says.*

"Has Joyce, well, done anything that...?"

"No," *she interrupts.* "Of course not. It's only that actually realising that I..." *She grimaces.* "Oh, I don't know."

"You feel that perhaps you've finally found some place where you fit in?"

"Yes!" *She turns her head around to you.* "Exactly. It's not the, well, any of that, it's just... Like you say."

You nod.

"You should talk to her about it," *you tell her.*

"I don't have feelings for Joyce," *she says.*

"I know." *You shrug.* "But what you're experiencing now, she must have too, at some point. If this really is what you want, you're going to need steering through some choppy waters."

She slowly nods.

The next evening there is no sign of Fiona, but the following night she arrives with a slim, dark-haired girl and after she acknowledges you with a smile and a slight tilt of the head, they sit by the fire with eyes only for each other.

At which, with a sudden twinge of surprise, you realise you're almost envious.

The Friday following Easter weekend, you're on your way out of the hotel after your shift when it strikes you that the TV lounge is unusually crowded. Stepping inside, you realise they're watching the BBC broadcast about the local artist Fiona has been working with, Joyce Kelly. You hadn't realised she had such a reputation and the programme concludes with an interview with Aidan, who, you are surprised to learn, appears to be something of a rising star in the art world.

The end credits roll up the screen. You turn to leave, but find your way blocked.

"Patty came over to see me earlier," Dennis says softly. "To explain how much she's missed me over the last few weeks."

His gaze is steady and the slightest of smiles plays on his lips.

"Lucky you," you tell him. "Glad it all worked out."

"Would you like to go for a drive?" he asks.

You're tempted to make him work for it, but instead simply nod.

"Okay."

You guess the two-seater sports car has been a present, some rite of passage celebrated. You've never been in a convertible before and you like it, the wind in your hair and on your face. You suggest calling in at The Barque for a drink and note there's still a degree of ambivalence about his squiring you in public and that he can't quite mask a sense of relief at the pub's car park overflowing.

Okay, you reflect, perhaps it's time for a lesson in being careful what you wish for...

"Let's buy a bottle and go back to mine," you suggest.

"You're not allowed guests in your room," he says.

"Jesus, would you actually grass me up!" Smiling, you shake your head. "And technically, you're my boss and so you wouldn't be a guest... We could call it an impromptu inspection of staff premises."

You wait on double yellow lines outside the off licence while he buys a bottle of Bacardi, neither yours nor his spirit of choice, but the most acceptable compromise.

No one else appears to be home when you arrive at the staff annex, which further eases his uncertainty. You collect two glasses from the kitchen and climb the stairs to the top floor.

"I hadn't realised the rooms were so small," he says. He perches on the edge of your bed as you place the tumblers on the dressing table and half fill them.

"Is this your first time here?" you ask, sitting down alongside him and he nods. "It's actually okay," you continue. "It's not as though I have to live here, only somewhere to sleep, really."

He doesn't seem to be taking your words in.

"What you said about Patty." He's hesitant. "Is this something that, like, all girls would know?"

"What, that she's a gold digger? Nah!" A tight smile. "Most guys'd pick up on it, too." You shrug. "And be okay with that."

"Be okay with it?"

"At bottom, most relationships are transactions of some kind - beauty for wealth, sex for power, acquiescence for security. These days they've been ritualised to the extent it's easy for everyone to pretend that's not what's happening, but..."

You give another shrug and sip your drink.

"That's a very cold view of the world."

"The world's a very cold place... Unless, of course, you warm yourself with the self image of a modern day lady of the manor and all the privilege that would entail."

"So what you're saying is... There's never going to be any respect, is there?"

"No." You turn your head to stare at him. "No, there's not."

"I suppose you think I'm a fool?"

"No, more like someone who accepts that life is mostly about what we've decided we can live with. And I wouldn't think the worse of anyone for that."

He is silent. You finish your drink in one gulp.

"These Spring evenings get chilly quickly, don't they?" You're careful to keep your tone neutral. "I can either close the window or we could just climb into bed."

"I..."

You take the glass from him, place it down on the floor. Standing, you unbutton your dress and then step out of where it's fallen. He's wide-eyed as you reach around to unclip your bra.

"I haven't got a Durex," he says. "Do you...?"

"It's okay," you break in. "We won't need one."

"You're on the pill?"

"No," you tell him, pulling back the bedsheets. "We're going *to do other things."*

CHAPTER TWELVE

Amanda

"Any problems?" asked Amanda.

"Not really." Shravasti shook her head. "They started talking about a warrant, I said fine, probably take a few days and in the meantime I'd park a squad car by the front door, videoing everyone coming in and out." She shrugged. "It's a fair assumption that someone has a post box service for a reason. They were cooperative enough after that."

As Amanda expected, Sunday morning found the office deserted. The flat, cardboard backed A5 envelope Shravasti had collected during Amanda's train journey home sat on her desk, still unopened.

"And that's it? Nothing else?"

"That's it," Shravasti told her.

Amanda picked up the envelope, slid her thumbnail along under the flap and reached inside. She took out a 3.5 inch floppy disk, checked that was all it contained and gave Shravasti a smile.

"Looks like you're up," she said.

Shravasti slipped the disk into one of her work terminal's external drives and began typing. After a few seconds, the screen fill with what appeared to be nothing but gibberish.

Shravasti slowly shook her head.

"It's encrypted," she said.

"Can you break it?" asked Amanda.

"Without a key, no."

Amanda considered.

"Kendall told me that you first came to his attention by cracking open a drug dealer's PDA. Colin Savage doesn't strike me as someone who was particularly tech savvy, so I'd have thought-"

"I got into that Psion Organiser," Shravasti broke in, "because I could bypass the entry screens to access the data. Savage has used a program called PGP. What that does is to use a password to actually scramble the data itself, using 128-bit encryption. Even the most powerful mainframe computers would take decades to run through all the possible permutations"

"Shit," said Amanda.

"But you're right about one thing," Shravasti told her. "He doesn't come across as being naturally *au fait* with tech." She paused. "And that usually means a password is either something obvious or written down somewhere."

"All his stuff disappeared after his death," said Amanda. "This is literally everything we have."

"The only good thing about PGP," said Shravasti, "at least from the point of view of cracking it, is that you've an unlimited number of attempts. Some programs only allow you to try half a dozen times before locking you out forever or actually self destructing."

She began tapping away on the keyboard.

"And I can automate the process. I'll go through his file again to see if anything obvious leaps out, but in the meantime I'll run a script that exploits variations on the more common passwords people tend to use." She hit the return key and leant back in her chair. "It's often the case that..."

She broke off as the screen suddenly cleared and then presented a directory file listing.

"Is that it?" asked Amanda.

"'Password'," said Shravasti, slowly shaking her head.

"I'm sorry?"

"He used the actual word 'Password'," Shravasti told her. "But substituted fives for the letter S and zero for the letter O." She let a smile play on her lips as she turned to Amanda. "That's like having a foot thick solid steel front door, but with the key hanging on a string behind the letter box."

"So we're in?"

"We most definitely are in." Shravasti reached for a new 3.5 inch floppy and slipped it into another of her disk drives.

"What are you doing?" asked Amanda.

"First, second and third rules of dealing with data," said Shravasti. "Before all else, make a backup."

They sat in silence as the disk drives whirred and then Shravasti ejected the copy. Repeating the process, she handed the second copy to Amanda.

"You'd be surprised," Shravasti said to Amanda's quizzical stare, "or maybe not, to discover how easily inconvenient data can disappear. Put that somewhere safe, but hopefully we'll be able to forget about it."

She watched as Amanda slipped it into her bag.

"Okay," said Shravasti, turning her attention back to the screen. "Let's see what we have here."

Jack

Jack glanced at his watch and began to tidy his desk. Sunday lunch at Petroc was scheduled for three o'clock and Jack never liked coming back to unfinished business.

And especially today.

At the end of last year, Brian had talked to Jack about retiring. He'd no shortage of offers from leisure companies eager to add Petroc to their portfolio, but Brian wanted to sound out Jack and Carol about taking it over themselves. Jack had already given some thought to the future. He'd have his thirty in this year and that would qualify him for a two thirds salary pension. Few stayed on beyond fifty unless they chose to play politics and Jack's face had never fitted for that. But Brian's offer had still been something of a bolt from the blue.

Jack nodded to Tom on the front desk as he left the station.

"Back in a couple of hours," he told him.

In the car, Jack continued to turn Brian's proposition over in his mind. In truth, he and Carol had struggled to find a downside to it. As Brian pointed out, Carol was an only child, everything would go to her eventually and he wanted to leave more of a legacy than a fat bank balance. Even before the events of the last week, Jack and Carol had been planning on having a word with him after lunch today, but if ever...

His chain of thought was broken by Tom coming through on the radio. Jack listened for a few seconds and then braked heavily enough to be able to swing the car into a fast approaching Viewing Area. Flicking on the siren, he put his foot down as he headed back to St Hannahs.

And his, Jack quickly realised, wasn't the only siren converging on Trelawney Road.

He arrived to discover that Andy had beaten him to it and that the entire road had been taped off. A fire engine was pulling up and uniformed officers, none of whom he recognised, were piling out of a minibus. A police incident van was already parked at the bottom of the road.

As Jack stepped out of the car, the two civilians Andy had been speaking with turned towards him. Although one of them, noted Jack as he drew closer, definitely had that unmistakable air of the loftier echelons of CID about him.

"Sergeant Vanner?" As Jack nodded, he reached out his hand. "Detective Chief Superintendent Mason." He indicated his companion with the slightest tilt of his head. "Brian Leyton, environmental health."

"You're declaring a major incident?" asked Jack as he shook hands with Leyton. "In relation to what?"

"Initially, we're going with a suspected gas leak," said Leyton. "That usually gets everyone moving without panicking them too much." He paused. "We'll need to set up a temporary evacuation centre for the families. Where would you suggest?"

"The church hall," replied Brian automatically, his thoughts racing ahead of his words. "Sorry, *initially?*"

"Would you come with us, Sergeant?" asked DCS Mason, indicating the incident van.

Jack hesitated only slightly. The officers from the minibus were already walking up garden paths and knocking on doors. He turned to Andy.

"Liaise with Reverend Warwick, would you, about the church hall? Then head down there to see what's needed."

"Yes sir," said Andy and moved off towards his car.

Leyton opened the rear door of the incident van and the three of them climbed inside. A grey haired figure in a rumpled suit rose to greet them.

"This is Professor Martin," said Leyton. After shaking hands with the professor, Jack turned his quizzical gaze back to DCS Mason, but it was Leyton who spoke.

"The fatalities at the barbecue last week," he said. "Professor Martin's team have identified the cause."

"You're from Derriford?" Jack asked the professor.

"No." Professor Martin shook his head. "Porton Down."

Jack stared at him wordlessly. Porton Down was Britain's leading bio weapons research facility.

"When Derriford couldn't determine the pathogen, they sent samples to labs around the entire south of England," Professor Martin told him. "That's standard practice for incidents such as this. We identified it as the variant of a toxin known to be used by the Bulgarian secret service."

"*What!!!*" Jack didn't even attempt to keep the disbelief out of his voice.

"Once we knew what we were looking for, we found traces of it in an empty German schnapps bottle," Leyton told him, "that witnesses said had been added to the punch. Fingerprints on the bottle confirmed their statements. And now we need to get Professor Martin's people into the house without further delay."

"So…" Jack struggled to order his thoughts.

"In the meantime," asked DCS Martin, "what do you know about a Gillian Brown?"

Amanda

"I gather from Detective Chief Superintendent Thomas," said Kendall, slipping his coat off and folding it across the back of a chair, "that you've had a busy few days?"

"Yes, sir," said Amanda.

"Which you didn't feel the need to keep me in the loop on."

"As I understood things," said Amanda, "a multi-agency investigation into a potential national security issue arrived at the conclusion that no such issue exists." She shrugged. "A conclusion, by the way, that I agree with."

"I'm pleased to hear it," said Kendall, dryly.

"But as a serving police officer, still nominally in charge of a cold case unit and faced with prima facie evidence of unlawful killing, I don't believe I had any other option but to pursue further enquiries."

"Further enquiries…" Kendall took a breath. "And where exactly have those enquiries led you, DI Palmer? Do you have a name for your victim? Do you know who killed him? Do you even have motive?"

"The thing is," said Amanda, "we seem to be well beyond that now."

"Beyond that…?" Kendall shook his head.

"We need to make some decisions," Amanda told him. "Just the three of us. Which is why I asked you to come in."

Kendall looked across at Shravasti, who met his steady stare.

"Let's get some coffee," said Amanda, "and then we'll take you through it from the beginning."

* * *

It took about an hour to work through it all.

Amanda's meeting with Ronan Doyle, Shravasti's file on Robert Pascoe's inquest and Colin Savage's unseemly demise. Linda Thompson, Amanda's trip to Liverpool, what she'd learnt from Helen Munro, Shravasti's visit to Savage's post box service. The encrypted disk.

"I admit it's compelling," said Kendall, when they'd finished, "but standing back from it all, there's little more than speculation based on circumstantial…"

"Shravasti decrypted the disk," broke in Amanda, quietly.

She opened a folder and handed him the printout of a photograph. A large sepia print of seven people on a terrace, a sea view behind them. Four of the group were seated at a table, two with their backs to the camera. The three standing, two men and a young woman in what appeared to be some kind of military uniform, were all facing forward.

"This is…?" Kendall shrugged. "What, the nineteen thirties, I'm guessing?"

"Yes," said Amanda, "It's The Grange in St Hannahs. I recognised it because I was there the other day."

"So what exactly am I looking at?" asked Kendall.

Shravasti leant forward and touched one of the figures sitting at the table.

"Captain James Carrington, renowned veteran of the Western Front. He had the house built in 1921, the construction managed by," she tapped on one of the men standing, "Arthur Pascoe. Pascoe had been adjutant in Carrington's regiment during World War One and they'd been involved in a number of business ventures after the war. It was he who founded the estate agency which eventually passed to Robert Pascoe."

"That's who Alexander Beaumont's niece married, right?"

"Claudia, yes." Amanda nodded. "And Beaumont was Director General of MI5, correct?"

"Of course."

Amanda tapped another of the standing figures.

"Maxwell Knight," she said. "Director of Intelligence for MI5 throughout the thirties."

Kendall turned to stare at her and then back down at the photograph. With her finger, Amanda touched it three times.

"James Carrington, Arthur Pascoe, Maxwell Knight," she said. "And what they all have in common is being early members of British Fascisti. This country's first fascist party, founded in 1923."

"I..." Shaking his head, Kendall continued to stare.

"In itself," Shravasti told him, "that wouldn't have been too unusual. During the nineteen twenties, Mussolini had a lot of admirers in this country, including Winston Churchill. It wasn't until the early thirties, when the Nazis came to power in Germany and Moseley's Blackshirt thugs appeared on the streets of London, that they began falling away in droves. But what does make this notable is that ten years on, the three of them are entertaining," she placed her finger on one of the seated figures facing the camera, "Joachim von Ribbentrop, later German ambassador to Britain and," she slid her finger onto a seated couple with their backs to the camera, "according to Savage, the then Prince of Wales and Wallis Simpson."

Kendall didn't appear to move - or breathe - for the next five seconds. Then slowly he turned his head to face Amanda.

"Is there any corroboration of that?" he eventually asked.

"Photographic?" Amanda shook her head. "At least not here, but we'll come to that. Circumstantial? Plenty. Colin Savage was able to establish a date when everyone in that photograph could have been in Cornwall." She paused. "Apart from..."

Amanda pointed to the young woman in uniform.

"The thing about data," said Shravasti, "is that often its absence is as relevant as its presence.."

"I don't understand?" said Kendall.

"Sometimes you need to pay attention to what it isn't telling you." She tapped her finger on the young woman. "Not referenced anywhere in his notes."

"Well..." Kendall shrugged. "That looks like an army

uniform she's wearing, so I'd guess a driver. Maxwell Knight would certainly warrant one, maybe she'd been seconded from the ATS. Does it really matter we don't have her name?"

"Oh but we do have a name," said Amanda. "That's the point."

"But..." Kendall stared at her. "I thought you said there was no mention of her in Savage's notes."

"We have a name," said Amanda, "only because I was in Nottingham yesterday. That's John Munro, Lee Munro's father."

* * *

"After Savage's career nosedived," said Amanda, "he moved back to Nottingham, his home city. He and John Munro had known each other since the sixties. Munro was running a boarding house for theatricals there and, long story short, became Savage's landlord."

"What we have," Shravasti told Kendall, "are digital copies of Colin Savage's notes, drafts and scans of material collected by James Carrington. From the postmark on the envelope of the disk he sent to his mail service, it was backed up the day before he left for Cornwall."

"You're assuming this was how Savage got hold of that photograph?"

"John Munro died at the end of last year, so yes, an educated guess would be by going through his effects."

Kendall shook his head.

"Look, it's no great shock to learn the Windsors were fascist sympathisers," he said. "A whole wealth of stuff about that came out in the fifties. If there'd been a German invasion of Britain, Hitler intended to install Lloyd George as prime minister and put Edward on the throne." He shrugged. "It's why Churchill sent him off to be Governor of the Bahamas, to keep him well distanced from German influence. So, I really don't see this as an earthshaking revelation - during the war, maybe, but in this day and age..."

"The thing is," said Amanda, "Savage had most of his story already drafted before he headed to Cornwall. Where he told the Pascoes' he was working on a biography of James Carrington, giving him the excuse he needed to be digging around without raising eyebrows."

"For what, exactly?"

Amanda looked over at Shravasti, who opened a folder on the desk and took out half a dozen sheets of paper stapled together.

"This is the draft he'd completed before leaving for Cornwall," Shravasti told him. "You'll see that…"

"Just give me the bottom line," said Kendall.

"In 1944, a couple of months before D-day," said Amanda, "Carrington was arrested for his involvement with some scam involving petrol coupons. You can imagine how that would have gone down at the time, distinguished war hero and all. According to Savage, he asked Maxwell Knight, who by all accounts was now running what was pretty much his own little fiefdom within MI5, to get the charges dropped, play the national security card and it was a request that came with some thinly veiled threats."

"Of what, exactly?"

"That's what Savage was in Cornwall trying to find out. Because you could come up with a fair amount of speculation on that score." Amanda gestured to the photograph. "Cosy tête-à-têtes on the terrace with von Ribbentrop, which, however you chose to look at it, wouldn't have been that far short of treason. Maybe photographic evidence of more intimate encounters during the Windsor's visits, John Munro's reputation certainly lends some weight to that…" She shrugged. "Anyway, Knight agreed, told Carrington he'd fixed things with the magistrate to have the case thrown out of court when he turned up there to answer the charges."

Amanda paused to stare at him.

"But the morning Carrington was due to appear in court," she continued, "he was found on his balcony with a bullet in his brain. The official verdict was suicide, overwhelmed by the shame of disgracing his country at its time of greatest peril. But according to Savage he was murdered, probably by assets of MI11, who dealt with military intelligence security issues during the war."

"That is some accusation," said Kendall quietly.

"That was some threat he posed," said Amanda, "if Savage was correct and he does make a persuasive argument. But the thing is, Savage wasn't stupid. Like you say, accusations along those lines would have been earth shattering at the time, but half a century later…?" She shrugged. "From his notes, Savage believed he was onto something that would shake today's establishment to the core."

"But he gives no hint what that might be?" asked Kendall.

Amanda shook her head.

"Not when he was writing this draft." She looked over at Shravasti. "But we believe he had an idea of where he should go looking."

"And so that's what he was doing in Cornwall the week before he died?"

"From what Savage was telling his agent, he certainly didn't consider it a wasted trip." Amanda shrugged. "Given his track record over recent years that was met with a fair degree of scepticism, but in the context of everything else we've discovered, I'd say it's more than plausible he came up with something." She paused. "Something that not only warranted his silence, but to serve as an object lesson to other interested parties that worse things can happen to you in life than dying."

"I still don't see how this ties in with John Munro," said Kendall slowly. He picked up the photograph again and stared at it. "All we can establish is that he was at The Grange ten years previous to Carrington's death…"

With a shrug, he dropped it back down on the desk.

"If you read any biography pieces about John Munro," Amanda told him, "you'd gather that he spent the Second World War with ENSA. You know, entertaining the troops just behind the front line?"

"Okay?"

Shravasti lifted a glossy brochure from her desk.

"This is a guide for Aidan McShane's Cradle of Thorns exhibition at the Senara Gallery in St Hannahs. It includes interviews with those who posed for the paintings." She flicked through the pages. "Don Mayberry was the model for Pontius Pilate. According to Mayberry, he and Lee Munro were appearing in a production about to open at the National Theatre and wanted to work on their roles."

Shravasti stopped at the page she'd been looking for.

"*'We thought it best to get away somewhere for a couple of weeks,'* she read. *'Lee suggested St Hannahs because it was where she'd spent a lot of childhood holidays. Her father had been stationed there during the war and still had friends in the area.'*"

"We checked army records," said Amanda. "Turns out that until April 1944, John Munro was a wireless operator serving with the Royal Corps of Signals. At an RSS - Radio Security Service - station just outside of St Hannahs, which mainly functioned as a listening post for U-Boat Enigma traffic."

"For Bletchley Park?" asked Kendall and Amanda nodded. "So what happened in April 1944?"

"He was transferred out of the Signal Corps to ENSA," said Shravasti. "And promoted from corporal to Major."

"It's a credible assumption," said Amanda, "that he came into possession of a fair amount of leverage around that time and was probably better at covering his back than James Carrington. And I daresay that over the years, Colin Savage may have picked up a few conversational hints as to exactly what that might be."

Kendall considered.

"The problem is," he said eventually, "is that you don't have any original material to substantiate this." He shrugged. "There's no provenance with scans, is there? We all know how easily they can be faked."

"Do you believe they're fakes?" asked Amanda.

"I'm simply playing devil's advocate here," he told her. "And he'd have a pretty persuasive case. Assuming there ever was an inquiry, that this wasn't all swept away by the Defence of the Realm Act." He paused. "I take it that only the three of us are privy to this?"

Amanda and Shravasti nodded.

"So," asked Amanda, "where do we go from here?"

"We're a bloody long way from a thirty year old unsolved homicide, aren't we?" said Kendall, shaking his head. "Okay, if you had tangible proof, rather than the speculations of a bitter, discredited journalist, this would be a different ball game. One you could play fast and hard enough to have your backs covered. But as things stand, all you can do is push for further investigation and hope to Christ you've got this wrong, because if you haven't, well, look how that worked out for Savage."

"You're saying let it go?"

"I'm saying let it settle. If you are right, then they'll be eyes all over you, probably have been for the last week. We need to start covering tracks." He looked over at Shravasti. "Is there any way someone would be able to tell you've decrypted that disk."

She shook her head.

"No, sir."

"Okay. I'll contact Keith Venables. Inform him that as we were winding down our side of the operation, we came across a computer disk belonging to a journalist who'd been on the fringes of this case. It's encrypted, we can't get into it, do they want to try?"

"Hoping they'll assume we've lost interest," said Amanda.

"As long as no one goes rattling any more cages," Kendall told her. "And it's not like there's any urgency to this, even if your assumptions are true." He shrugged. "My money's still on the coroner being right about Savage, he wasn't exactly the most stable character, was he?"

He seemed to consider.

"DS Sule, could you give us a minute?"

"Of course, sir."

Kendall waited until the door closed behind her.

"I'm using the term '*we*' here, Amanda, but perhaps I'm getting ahead of myself. Have you given further thought to my offer?"

"Yes." Amanda nodded. "And it's very tempting. But part of me is now wondering if I couldn't get more done back where I was. Half a dozen retired detectives pulled in as and when I need them, poking around nooks and crannies everyone's forgotten about. Who knows what I might come up with?"

Kendall regarded her in silence, neither averting their gaze from each other.

"I believe that would be a massive waste," he said, eventually. "But I'll respect your decision, whatever it is."

He lifted his coat from the back of the chair.

"Goodnight Amanda," he said. "I'll look forward to hearing from you soon."

With neither word nor note, Dennis leaves in the night while you sleep.

You don't see him at the hotel the next morning, but as the day draws on, busy as it is, it becomes obvious something's amiss. A tight regime doesn't need much out of place to create a sense of unease and even way up on the third floor you catch the vibe, as Jake would have it.

You're finishing your last double, a very cornucopia for the cheap frills box, when a wide-eyed Emblyn sails into the room.

"You'll never guess what's just happened," she tells you breathlessly. Without letting slip you've a fair idea, you make a big deal out of giving her your avid attention.

At lunchtime Patty was spotted leaving the hotel crying, almost running down the steps. That was followed by an argument between mother and son loud enough to be heard in the dining room, before both departed in separate vehicles.

Returning to the annex, you shower, change and head over to the Burrows. You chat with Fiona and her new whoever-she-might-be for a while, deal with the persistent but friendly advances of one of the squaddies - which amuse more than annoy - and wheedle a spliff off Jake. You share it with Lee Munro and her friend Claudia, who have also become regulars down here. Kit and Emma, however, are more noticeable by their absence and you guess this isn't something that's passed Jake by.

You're genuinely sympathetic, but honestly don't get what he sees in Emma. She's attractive enough, if you're into that whole bluestocking on the edge of eruption cliche, but you've never seen politics as anything more than a puppet show, with whoever's really pulling the strings never emerging from the surrounding shadows. Far as you're concerned, whoever you vote for the government always gets in.

And so to see Jake nodding away like a little puppy dog around her is dispiriting, you thought he understood women better than that. If Kit has managed to get Emma's ankles behind her ears, it won't have been dialectical materialism that put them there.

You draw on the spliff, staring deep into the fire. Perhaps you should have a word with Jake. Sticking your nose into other people's relationships is a surefire way of getting it bloodied, but you've been through a lot together and, truth be told, are now starting to feel at least a twinge of guilt about that hefty push you gave him in her direction...

"Hello. I thought I'd find you here."

Dennis lowers himself down and sits cross-legged beside you.

"Hi." You turn to him and smile. "You okay?"

He both nods and sighs at the same time. You offer him the spliff and he hesitates before warily taking it from your fingers and raising it to his lips. He inhales slowly, then explodes in a coughing fit.

"Jesus!"

He makes to pass it back to you, but you indicate Claudia, sitting on his other side.

"Think of it as a bottle of port," you explain. "Always passed to the right."

"I'll try to remember," he grimaces, handing it to Claudia with smoke still escaping from his mouth, nose and possibly ears. As she smiles and delicately takes it from him, he turns back to you.

"Can we talk?" he asks.

"Patty came over to see me today," he says quietly. "I told her that things were over between us."

"I heard," you say. "Apparently, so did most of the hotel."

"Mother's not happy." He shakes his head. "She'd always hoped..."

His voice trails off, but it's not a silence you feel compelled to fill.

"Last night," he continues. "I'm really not sure what it was about." He turns to look at you. "Any of it."

"Well, it doesn't have to be anything more than what it was."

"It was pretty special. For me, anyway."

"Is that why you left in the middle of the night? Without a word? To keep it precious?"

"No, I ..." He stares, but your inscrutability is a skill long mastered. "I needed to think."

"What about?"

"You." He's suddenly on the edge of exasperation. "Everything you've said, the things you've done." He corrects himself. "The things we've done."

"And what conclusion did you reach?"

"That I've never met anyone like you."

"That makes me sound something of a novelty." You raise an eyebrow. "And don't all novelties eventually wear thin?"

"No." Shaking his head. "That's not true." He's suddenly cautious. "I really don't understand what's happening here - what last night meant to you?"

"What last night meant to me?" You consider. "Well, let's just put it down to being a heads up for ten years or so from now, when Patty - or some version of her - is spread out underneath you with her head empty of everything except the next dinner party or you're getting a tepid blow job because a certain piece of jewellery's caught her eye." You shrug. "To understand that there are other options, carte blanche if you did but know it, because the thing to grasp about the Pattys of this world is that they'll let an awful lot slide, so long as their particular boat doesn't get rocked."

"So that's it?" He's staring at you, shocked and unblinking. "It's over?"

"Over? I hadn't realised it had started." You turn to him with the slightest of smiles playing on your lips. "Okay, come on then. Squire me into The Barque and woo me in the Lounge Bar. Right now. Let the whole world rejoice in our love."

"I..."

"Or were you thinking more along the lines of the two of us heading over to the annex? And I'll bet you remembered to go by the chemists today, didn't you?"

He stares at you for perhaps ten, fifteen seconds. Then, with a shake of his head, he abruptly stands and, without looking back, *strides away.*

The next time your paths cross is an afternoon down by the harbour, where you join a gathering crowd. You recall an item on the TV news about a scheme to protect the beach by fastening some kind of boom across the harbour mouth and you watch as several sections are unloaded from a lorry and joined together by the water's edge. You see Claudia on the other side of the quay, talking to one of the squaddies. You give them a wave, but neither seems to notice you and so you decide to go over and say hello.

Then you spot Dennis standing just behind them, looking uncertain, and you realise he probably thought the wave was for him. Before he can react in any way, you turn and walk away.

You've not been down to the Burrows for the last few nights because you wouldn't be surprised to find him accidentally on purpose waiting to bump into you there. But that's stupid, you decide, you can't live your life always looking around corners. So, after you finish your next shift, you leave the hotel and start to make your way over there.

As you reach the edge of the dunes, two figures approach from the opposite direction and as they draw closer, you recognise Claudia and Lee.

"The place is deserted this evening," Claudia tells you. "There's no one there at all."

You join them for the walk back into town. Usually Lee is ebullient, chatting away ten to the dozen, but tonight she is almost taciturn. Seemingly thoughtful rather than unfriendly, she leaves Claudia to make most of the conversation.

She doesn't really break her silence until you reach The Barque.

"Fancy a drink?" she asks.

You decline with a smile, saying an early night wouldn't go amiss and you separate by the entrance. You're not sure exactly what dynamic is playing out here, but something certainly is and it's perhaps best left for the pair of them to resolve alone.

But you haven't gone twenty yards when you hear your

name being called. You stop and turn.

"Hi."

Jake steps out of the shadows.

"Hi," you reply.

"We need to talk," he tells you.

You hesitate and then shrug.

"Sure," you tell him.

The two of you begin walking along the quayside.

Your second taciturn companion of the evening, you realise.

"What's the matter?" you ask him.

Coming to a halt under a streetlamp, he reaches into his pocket and takes out a folded sheet from a tabloid newspaper. Silently, he hands it to you and after giving him a querulous stare, you slowly open it.

'Family mourns tragic loss' reads the headline. And underneath, staring out of the page at you, is Georgie.

Before you can take in a single word of the story, it seems the world is spinning around you. You're aware of Jake reaching out a hand to steady you and you use that pressure against your arm less for support than to reorient yourself, until everything becomes still again.

But even so, you seem to be incapable of making sense of the words in any coherent manner. Your eyes dart about the page, picking out random phrases - 'concerned friends broke down the door', 'a syringe was found by the body', 'drug use is reportedly commonplace amongst the Chelsea set', 'a post mortem revealed...'

You suddenly turn to one side and vomit. As you bend over, Jake holds you steady as it feels like every last morsel is being retched from your stomach and then, as you straighten, he offers a handkerchief.

"This is bullshit," he tells you, as you wipe your mouth. "Georgie never touched hard drugs."

Of course it's bullshit. 'I will get to the bottom of this,' almost the final words she spoke to you. Your mind is racing - the look between Peter and Sebastian the day that scout went missing, the licentious version of the book cover, the negatives, the

Polaroids...

Georgie had the Polaroids! Would whoever's behind this have found them? Would they assume...?

"I'm going to find out what happened," Jake breaks into your thoughts. "I'm heading back up to London - I've got contacts there." He seems to register either doubt or disbelief on your face. "No, seriously." He hesitates. "I can't tell you who, but..."

"Let's wait a bit." You reach out and gently take his hand. "Until we know the full story."

Are you and Jake loose ends? If he starts kicking up a fuss in London, you could well be. At the moment it's unlikely anyone could discover where you're working. In the chaos of the Easter holidays you've not yet applied for a National Insurance card and so the hotel is paying you off the books. But now you'll need to be out of there as soon as possible.

Not likely to be a problem, you reflect.

"If drugs are involved," you continue, "and they know we were staying at Linden Hall, don't you think the family might be looking for a scapegoat?" You pause. "I'm sure Miss Benfield will have a tale or two for them."

Jake takes a few seconds to consider before nodding.

"You're right," he says.

"Which means it's probably best to keep our heads down. Until we've an idea of what's what."

He stares at you.

"So, what do you want to do?"

"Let's sleep on it," you tell him. "And a few people did know we were coming to St Hannahs, didn't they? Look, maybe we should head on down to St Ives, sell the rest of your stash and take things from there?"

Jake nods.

"Okay, we'll decide in the morning." He forces a smile. "Come on, I'll walk you back."

It's a fitful night. You've hardly slept at all and just when you have drifted off comes an insistent banging on your door. Your heart leaps into your mouth for a second, before the realisation kicks in that anyone you'd really need to worry about will be a lot more subtle than this.

Dennis is standing there.

"Are you okay?" *he asks.*

The temptation to retort that you were fine until thirty seconds ago is curtailed by his obvious nervousness.

"Come in," *you tell him.*

He steps inside, then stares at you before quickly turning his gaze away. All you're wearing is a cotton vest and skimpy pants, which aren't revealing anything he hasn't seen before, but with a sigh you pick up a pair of jeans draped over the back of a chair and flop down onto the bed to pull them on.

"What's the matter?" *you ask, rising and zipping yourself up.*

"You've not heard?"

"All I've heard today," *you explain patiently,* "is a banging on my door."

"The soldiers have gone," *he says.* "They left yesterday."

Well, you think, that explains the deserted Burrows.

"Then in the middle of the night, the police raided everywhere."

You stare at him.

"Everywhere...?"

"The pill boxes by the beach, that old shack by the railway station, even the camping barns at Petroc. Police were brought in from all over the county, apparently. They loaded the beats into vans - the ones they didn't arrest - and dumped them on the Devon side of the Tamar Bridge."

You try to digest this.

"And while they were doing that," *he continues,* "someone swam out into the harbour and cut through the boom. The beach is six inches deep in oil now."

"So..."

"There's a lot of bad feeling in town this morning. Some of the local girls who've been hanging around with the beats are being *given a really hard time. And so..."*

He lets his voice trail off.

"And so you wondered if I'd had my head shaved and been paraded through the streets as a collaborateur horizontale?"

"It's not funny. The police are questioning everyone," he tells you. "About drugs. Sex parties out on the Burrows. Who was involved with all of that? And people are talking."

He's trying for righteous anger but, in light of the last twelve hours, all you feel is a wave of contempt. Georgie on a mortuary slab while he's wringing his hands over being caught with his dick out.

You walk over to the door.

"If you get pulled in," you say, slowly, "explain that you'd heard from one of the other chambermaids how easy I was. So, you let me take you down to a party on the Burrows, where you waited until I was out of it and then shagged me. Afterwards, you were so disgusted with yourself that you haven't seen me since."

He's staring at you open-mouthed.

"The cops won't have a problem believing that," you continue, "because that's exactly what they could imagine doing themselves."

"But what if you...?"

You let him flounder for a few seconds before opening the door.

"Unlike you, I can take care of myself," you tell him. "Now fuck off home to Mummy."

You slip into Petroc from the footpath over the hill, the route of your first arrival. You're half expecting a police presence but, if anything, the site seems quieter than usual.

The Camping Barn appears to have been ransacked, possessions strewn across the floor, sleeping bags turned inside out. Hearing a noise, you turn to see Carol, the girl from Reception, standing in the doorway holding a bucket and mop.

"Hi," *she says quietly.*

"Do you know if my friend's okay?" *you ask.*

"He wasn't here when the police came last night," Carol tells you. "But he hasn't been back today, either." She shakes her head. "Or if he has, I haven't seen him."

You recognise one of Jake's shirts laying on the floor, together with a copy of The Dharma Bums you remember him reading on the train journey down here. Obviously scooped up somewhere else, you guess, and hope that he managed to get rid of his stash first.

Well, he knows where to find you if he needs to and, after your conversation last night, also knows to keep his head down.

In the meantime…

You nod at the mop she's carrying.

"Need a hand?"

"Thanks." Carol smiles. "Have to get the whole place spic, span and shipshape by eighteen hundred hours."

"I'm sorry?"

"The army's on its way. They're being billeted here."

"I thought they left yesterday?"

"The British troops did." She shrugs. "Now the yanks are coming."

"Seriously?"

"US Army Corp of Engineers. There's a platoon arriving today. That's about forty men we've been told. Second Lieutenant gets a chalet, NCOs are in here, other ranks their own bivouac." She sighed. "Maybe the same again by the weekend - we're certainly going to have our work cut out."

"Does that mean you're looking for more staff?"

Carol gives you a curious look.

"Are things at…?"

Her voice trails off.

"Let's just say," you attempt to keep your tone as neutral as possible, "my removal is probably being orchestrated as we speak."

Carol grins.

"St Hannahs being what it is, I did hear…" She considers. "We could use another chalet maid and someone to occasionally cover the shop… Pretty antisocial hours, I'm afraid."

"That's okay, I'm used to that." You hesitate. "It needs to be casual, though."

"If it's just for the season..." Carol slowly nods. "Alright, five quid a week, cash in hand, live-in with meals. You'd be sharing a chalet with one of the other girls."

"No problem."

"Right. Well, let's get all this cleaned up, then we'll go over to Reception and sort you out."

Returning to Tregenna Bay that evening to collect your things, you're surprised Mrs Nelson isn't on hand to oversee your departure. You assumed she'd take a definite visceral pleasure in your living up to her worse expectations, but on reflection it's probably a scene that's played out too many times over the years to retain any real novelty for her.

"She and Dennis left earlier," says the chef, the most senior member of staff available to escort you from the premises. You're also here to pick up any wages due and are half expecting some argument over that, but he hands you the brown envelope before being asked.

"It's for the full week," he tells you. "Mrs Nelson said that's on condition you're gone tonight."

"Not a problem," you say. "I'll only need to get my stuff from the annex."

"Look, do you have anywhere to go?" he asks. "If you're stuck, the wife and I have a put u up in the living room. Until you sort yourself out."

"That's really kind of you, but I'm leaving town to stay with friends," you tell him. You appreciate the gesture, but if anyone comes around here asking questions the fewer people who know where you are, the better.

"Okay. Once you've packed, don't worry about bringing the key back. Just leave it in the room and I'll collect it later."

Over at the annex, it takes no more than a couple of minutes to gather your possessions and be on your way.

You must have read or seen a dozen tales where the last surviving gang member, or recently released jewel thief, has returned to retrieve the loot only to discover it's now under a car park or at the bottom of a reservoir.

So, you won't be making that mistake, you tell yourself, crossing the road to Holy Trinity Church. Because there are few places with a more reliable track record of immortalis *than the House of God. Whatever you may have become embroiled in, those negatives you stole from Peter remain your one ace in the hole. The threat of them finding their way into the public domain at your demise or disappearance means you can't allow them to be found either on you or in your immediate possessions.*

Assuming whoever might be coming knows you have them! Assuming they care!

You weren't sure if Holy Trinity would be locked after evening service. In a city almost certainly, but a Cornish town…

The door pushes open surprisingly smoothly, given its bulk. Your footsteps on the stone slabs echo as you make your way along the central aisle between both sets of pews. Only two others are in the nave, an elderly man seated at the front and a middle-aged woman three rows behind him. Both are still, heads bowed and neither registers your entrance.

Slipping into a row of pews on the opposite side, you adopt the same posture. You have no real plan here, only the skimpiest notions of what to expect and so this is likely to be little more than reconnoitre. You anticipate returning with screwdrivers, chisels and Polyfilla to take advantage of a loose tile or worn mortise joint.

Still with head bowed, your eyes dart about the building. Altar, lectern, a hymn board high on the wall. The old man slowly rises and shuffles out. What about the row in front of you? You've slipped the negatives into a narrow cellophane packet, there's no thickness to it at all. You could Sellotape it under the seat and come back tomorrow with brown paint to cover it over. The pews look centuries old, but how frequently are they maintained? Given a scrub and a varnish? It would be just your luck if…

The woman stands, bows her head towards the altar and leaves.

Straightening up, you begin a more methodical study of your surroundings. Your eyes keep returning to the hymn board screwed to the wall, you could have that down and back in place within minutes. There's the lectern, you wonder if the tubular pedestal could be hollow, if...

The Bible!

The lectern Bible is massive and you can see that however ornate the chain attaching it to the podium might be, it remains very much functional.

This is not something going anywhere soon!

You rise and walk over. The Bible must be eight or nine inches thick, bound in leather. Cautiously, you open it and as you do so notice the slightest of gaps appear between the spine and the inner bindings. With no hesitation, you reach into your pocket for the negatives and slip them into the space. They catch slightly, about halfway in, but then they're through and once fully inside you use a matchstick to work them perhaps an inch further down. You shut the Bible, then peering closely at the spine, open it again. There's no sign of your handiwork.

Satisfied, you close it one last time and head toward the main door. There's more than just a touch of irony to your smile as you step out into the night.

CHAPTER THIRTEEN

Sy

An airport lounge, figured Sy, was one of the very few places you never felt guilty about ordering a drink whatever the hour. Casinos might be another exception, but that was all they had in common. You'd never see a clock on the wall at *Caesars Palace,* but here it was all about time, watching the minutes tick down until you were through those magic doors by the gate to fly, fly away...

"Have you visited the States before?" Sy asked Carin, after the waitress brought their drinks and Kit had disappeared to find the men's room.

"Only the East Coast," she told him. "Over the years I've attended seminars, with a touristy day or two added on before flying home, but I've not been to California."

"It's almost another country," Sy told her. "I'm from what they call the Midwest, lived in LA since the late sixties and I've never lost that sense of still not being used to it all."

Carin smiled.

"Are you married, Sy?" she asked.

"Was," he said. "Several times. Until it finally sank in that Einstein's definition of insanity - repeating the same process while hoping for different outcomes - didn't only apply to bending space and time." Sy shrugged. "Just not cut out for it, I guess."

"I imagine that show business comes with a wealth of temptations?" suggested Carin.

"Well, that could be true of any workplace," said Sy. "But yeah, not a lot of jobs involve steamy scenes with the world's most beautiful people."

Then, as she gazed steadily at him, the nuance of her remark struck him. The three of them had spent the last couple of hours discussing - if things worked out - Kit possibly having to split his time between Amsterdam and Los Angeles.

Sy hesitated, but only for a second. He was too much a

seasoned pro to either backtrack or dig himself in deeper. You always ploughed onward.

"Kit was telling me," he said, "that you and he have almost thirty years together. What's your secret?"

"I think it's one of those mysteries," Carin told him, "that has to remain unfathomable to maintain its potency."

Smiling, Sy shook his head.

"So, just between the two of us," she asked, "how likely is all of this to come off?"

This time, still under that steady gaze, his hesitation was longer.

A few years ago Kit had sent a script - based on the true case of a novelist being sued for libel - to Lee, who'd forwarded it on to Sy with a note saying she'd be interested in doing it. To be honest, Sy couldn't see any money there, but was intrigued enough to check out the original novel and that he had been impressed by. So, he'd been lobbying studios and production companies to create a TV series around it, and dangling Lee as bait had generated sufficient interest to line up a few meetings. Kit was onboard to structure the narrative for the screen and act as script consultant. Okay, finder's fee maybe, for bringing it to them, but he did have a better understanding of the novel than anyone else they'd spoken with.

"I'd say fifty fifty," he eventually told her.

"Thank you," she said quietly. "I appreciate your..."

She broke off as Kit returned.

"What did I miss?" he asked, sitting down and registering their expressions.

"Life and marriage," Carin told him dryly.

"All done and dusted, I hope?"

"Just about. I was..." Carin registered Sy staring across the room and then turned her head to follow his gaze.

On the other side of the lounge, a fellow traveller was sliding in behind a table. Once seated, she reached into her bag to take out her cellphone.

"Cheers," said Kit, clinking his glass with Carin's, but Sy's attention was obviously still focused on the other table.

"Do you know her?" asked Carin.

Sy hesitated before shaking his head.

"For a second there, she kind of reminded me of someone," he said. "But no."

* * *

Like most of those whose profession is rooted where others seek pleasure or entertainment, Sy's outlook on life had a twist or two. Ever hoping to be impressed, but under no illusions as to how the magic weaved its spell, Sy gave literally everything his industry put out at least a cursory once-over, a stack of video tapes always waiting in his office was never lower than a foot tall. Sy's PA, Rachel, recorded every new show and attached notes to the ones she'd actually watched. Even when she was pretty dismissive - and Rachel had good instincts - Sy checked them out anyway and never fell more than a few days behind.

Because that's where the future's bread and butter would be coming from. Because contrary to popular belief, stars rarely arrive out of nowhere. Tomorrow's headliners were to be found today's sitcoms and cop dramas, the wacky neighbour's niece visiting for one episode or the witness to a drive-by too scared to talk. Blink and you'll miss them, until ten years later watching a late night rerun. *'Hey honey, do you see who that is!!?'*

Three decades in the business and Sy still couldn't tell you what he was looking for, just knew it when he did. Jimmy Cagney broke every rule of screen acting and for Sy's money was the most charismatic presence Hollywood's ever seen. Brando mumbled his way to greatness. The heart wants what the heart wants, the camera loves who the camera loves...

Sy almost missed *Belladonna* on its first run. Back then it was an independent production out of New Jersey, only being picked up by an East Coast cable outfit without a national franchise. *'This looks interesting'* Rachel scribbled on a photocopied piece from *Variety* she'd left on his desk and Sy saw straightaway what she meant. The show profiled present day female killers, ran reconstructions of their crimes.

What caught Rachel's eye was that it was being fronted by Kate Denver, a onetime reporter on the *Washington Post* who'd won a Pulitzer a few years back. Sy was familiar with the story - a life insurance scam being run on the elderly that had opened a real can of worms for the entire industry - because it was optioned for a documentary he'd put a couple of screenwriters up for and was still languishing in development hell.

The initial reaction to the show was that it seemed a pretty tacky project for someone with Kate Denver's kudos to be attached to, but that just piqued Sy's interest further. He had Rachel contact the production company for tapes of episodes aired so far and casting sheets for the rest of the series. Docudramas were fertile ground for the workaday talent on his books, with no regular weekly cast other than presenters, they came with a high turnover of available roles.

Sy got it from the start. Most TV tended to be downright dumb trying to act clever, but for all its luring the viewer in with a licentious beckoning finger, *Belladonna* was whip-smart. It's no mean feat to make the fact that angels and demons are actually few and far between in life compulsive viewing, yet *Belladonna* managed it. The narratives played out were as much about those betrayed by ideals to which they'd aspired as desires to which they'd succumbed and against all expectations the show became a sleeper hit.

After its first year, *Belladonna* had been snapped up by the WCN Network and production moved out to LA, where Sy had got to know Mike Weaver, the show's producer. Strictly business, but underneath the wheeling and dealing around the collective egos of talent they both in some fashion had to pander to, they liked each other. A few years ago Sy and Rachel somehow found themselves on the same table at the Emmys as the *Belladonna* party and Sy met Kate Denver and Mike's wife Gail, who worked as a researcher on the show. They made a good couple, Sy had thought, easy in each other's company and he hadn't been surprised to learn their silver wedding anniversary was only a few months away.

They'd stayed in loose contact since then, but when Sy spotted that *Belladonna* was missing from last year's Fall schedule and WCN were being uncharacteristically cagey about why, he'd tried to call Mike. The first couple of times he reached voicemail but after that there was only an automated *'the number you have dialled is not available'* message. Then a few days later WCN announced Mike's death.

Liver cancer at fifty-two.

Sy couldn't make the service, at an hour's notice he'd had to fly out to a location shoot in Florida to deal with the leading lady's meltdown over her body double for a nude scene - twenty five years her junior - somehow not being lithe enough. But Rachel had spoken at length with Kate and learned that not only had Mike been given a transfusion of infected blood after a car crash fucking decades ago, his wife was being treated with some experimental vaccine, had reacted badly to it and now it was looking touch and go whether she'd pull through herself. WCN, to their credit, put the show on hiatus while they waited to see how things panned out.

Well, Gail had made it, but from what Sy gleaned from various sources it had been a rough ride. And then a few months ago there'd been an announcement that *Belladonna* would be returning later in the year, with a feature length special in collaboration with the BBC. Sy guessed that must be why Gail was over here. The reason for his double take when he first spotted her was that she'd lost a lot of weight and it wasn't the kind of weight loss you complimented someone on.

Gail obviously hadn't seen him and he hesitated about going over. If he'd been by himself it would have been a no brainer, but introductions involve explanations and Sy guessed emotions would still be raw enough to shy away from the conjecture of strangers. He'd be in LA next week, maybe better to wait until…

Then, as a departure call came over the tannoy, the

decision was taken from him. Gail snapped her phone shut, dropped it into her purse and rising from the table headed towards the door.

Sy turned his attention back to Kit and Carin.

Faith

Ted had retreated to his study to catch up with emails and Faith was debating whether to wait for his return before pouring herself a glass of wine. She didn't exactly have a *rule* about drinking alone, just thought of it as a definite first step along that path between sociability and dependency. Although perhaps she could pop in to see if he wanted a snack to keep him going, maybe suggest something to wash it down with…

Mercifully, the doorbell emptied her head of all such thoughts.

Faith opened the front door to find Toni standing there. Silently, the two women embraced.

"Come in, Antonia" said Faith, quietly.

They sat across from each other in the living room. There were now dark circles under Toni's eyes and in the space of only a few days, her cheeks had become gaunt.

"How are you managing?" asked Faith.

Toni shrugged.

"Trying to keep busy." She shook her head. "That's what they say you should do, isn't it? Stay distracted. Bury yourself in work?"

"As part of a balance," said Faith, carefully. "But you have to grieve, that's the process which is going to get you through this."

"I know."

"How are the nights? I could give you something to help there."

Toni grimaced.

"I've never been good with sleeping pills. Everything's always foggy the day after. And I've things to do." She bit her lip. "Register the death, notify the bank, funeral arrangements…"

She let her voice trail off.

Do you want a drink?" Faith shrugged. "I was just

thinking about pouring myself a glass of wine?"

Toni seemed to hesitate.

"Actually," she said, "do you have anything stronger?"

"Sure. Whisky, gin vodka..."

"Whisky, if that's okay?"

Faith nodded, stood up and walked over to the drinks cabinet. After fixing Toni's drink, she decided against opening a bottle just for herself and mixed a gin and tonic.

"We've literature at the Medical Centre on dealing with the practicalities of bereavement," she told Toni, setting the glasses down on the coffee table between them. "Why don't I put together some..."

"I got into Dennis's computer this afternoon," broke in Toni, a glint in her eye belying the softness of her tone.

"I'm sorry?"

"I needed to get in touch with people about what's happened, the ones I didn't have contact details or email addresses for. He kept all that stuff on his laptop."

"Okay?"

"*God!*" Toni reached for her glass. "You live with someone for thirty years, think you know them inside out and..."

Breaking off, she took a gulp of whisky.

"Toni, I don't understand...?"

"I found things there! On his computer!"

Amanda

Whether or not a case ended well, the morning after the celebrations or recriminations Amanda had always been able to let it go. She'd grasped early in her career that there was only one golden rule.

Never dwell.

But this had been different. She cast her mind back to before setting off for Cornwall, when Kendall had offered her a place at NCIS. "*Ex police officers rarely do well in the intelligence community,*" he'd told her and gone on to speak of a binary mindset in a shades of grey world.

She'd shrugged that off at the time, but now she got it. Still wearing the dressing gown she'd spent the morning moping about her apartment in, she took her espresso through to the living room and flopped down onto the sofa.

She placed her cup on the coffee table, next to where today's newspaper lay folded from when she'd picked it up off the doormat earlier. Listlessly she opened it out, scanned the headlines and was about to turn the page when a piece at the bottom caught her eye. '*A sixty-two year old man is being questioned regarding historical sex crimes,*' she read. Alongside was the photograph of a clergyman, bishop or archbishop by his getup, guessed Amanda, but she was no expert. Then 'Full story pages 8 & 9' in bold print.

The report did in fact fully occupy two whole pages but, in the time-honoured manner of journalism when confident it has its teeth into a good story, it was fractured into numerous sidebars and appendages. A larger picture of, indeed, the bishop - Sebastian Vincent she learnt his name was - accompanied the main section, another section featured photographs of a girl in her late teens, early twenties, a poster child for sixties flower power by the look of her and one of a young lad in a boy scout uniform, faded with age. Yet another section featured a photograph which she did recognise, it was that children's author who'd died the previous week.

Amanda took a sip of coffee, sat up straight and began to work her way through the various threads.

* * *

Ten minutes later, she laid down the paper and considered.

Amanda knew better than most people how crime reporting worked and was under no illusions as to what a two-edged sword it could prove. She'd had cases where the press proved invaluable in solving them, others where they'd almost cost her career. But what she had learnt over the years was how to read between the lines.

This story boiled down to allegations that for the last three decades - at least - Sebastian Vincent and Peter Matthews had been running a child sex ring. The paper wouldn't have printed that without solid evidence, reflected Amanda and it was just too much of a coincidence that Peter Matthews had died only a week ago. Someone, she assumed, either no longer felt compelled to remain silent or had stumbled across something in his effects. In its way, the silence from Matthew's family was deafening, you'd expect the air to be thick with denials and threats of lawsuits.

Attributing the deaths of Lady Georgina Knowle and fourteen year old Keith Taylor to the pair - the former allegedly because of her suspicions, the latter as victim - appeared to be on shakier ground but Amanda guessed that if there were anything to the accusations, others would begin coming forward and that's what the paper was counting on. Victims of sexual abuse are rarely prepared to give evidence unless they expect to be believed and no longer fear for their safety. And once those criteria are met, just watch the floodgates open… This was going to run and run.

But to all intents and purposes, Peter Matthews had actually got away with it, hadn't he? And realistically, how long could Vincent have left to pay for what he'd done?

Amanda recalled her earlier reflections. In a career that

stretched over twenty years she could say with hand on heart that if she'd one guiding light, then that light was justice.

Albeit, natural justice.

Squeezed between old time coppers, recruited mostly from the armed forces with an ethos of fighting fire with fire and the new university educated technocrats, fast-tracked into the upper echelons with little grasp of street level *realpolitik*, she'd learnt to tread gingerly, walking a tightrope between today's corporate groupthink and yesterday's moral ambivalence.

That Carin Franklyn had killed 'Jake' she had no doubt, nor that Christopher Franklyn had been complicit. Probably done in a fit of rage, the rage perhaps justifiable, her actions not, but that should have been the business of a court of law. A court of law Amanda had failed to bring them before. And in reality, had no hope of bringing them before...

There was no clue to the identity of the victim, let alone a body. No witnesses, no provable motive, only the hearsay of a dead IRA informer and a catalogue of circumstantials that any half competent barrister would shred into confetti across the courtroom floor.

But Amanda *knew!*

She stared down at the newspaper and came to a decision. Whoever this Jake might have been - runaway deadbeat drifter more likely than not - he deserved justice and perhaps there was more than one way to deliver that.

She rose and crossed the room to a large dresser, where from a drawer she took out a writing pad and envelope. Seated again, in block capitals she printed, 'COLIN SAID YOU'D KNOW WHAT TO DO WITH THIS IF ANYTHING HAPPENED TO HIM. DON'T LET HIM DOWN.'

Amanda stared at the note for a few seconds before folding it around the disk Shravasti had given her. Again in block capitals, she printed Christopher Franklyn's name and address in Amsterdam on the envelope.

Franklyn would know full well he was playing with

fire here, but Amanda guessed hubris could be relied upon to override caution when it came to raising this poisoned chalice to his lips. If you can't bring the bad guys down, you can do worse than turn them loose on each other. And however this might play out from here on in, she was done with Christopher bloody Franklin.

Amanda picked up her phone and scrolled through Contacts until she reached Jim Kendall's number.

"Hello," she replied to his answer. "It's Amanda Palmer."

She hesitated only slightly before continuing.

"I've considered your offer," she told him.

Faith

"A child?"

Toni nodded.

"She's fifteen."

"So who...?" Faith broke off, staring at Toni.

"From what I can put together, it was some chambermaid. I remember her vaguely, or rather I remember her leaving us in the lurch when she left mid season. Had to go back home to Manchester she said, family emergency." Toni snorted. "Bloody family emergency, right enough."

They sat silently.

"And you're absolutely sure about this," asked Faith eventually.

"Oh, yes." Toni reached for her drink. "It's not like he's just making regular payments - and it looks from the bank statements there've been a few sizeable bonuses - she's sending him bloody photos and keeping him up to date with sport days and sodding school plays. Half the trips upcountry for hotelier conventions and trade exhibitions have alibied him going to see them." Toni's grip on her glass was tight enough for the knuckles to show white. "This isn't about atoning for some past mistake, Faith. This is a whole other life. A life that I'm not..."

Shaking her head, tears began rolling down both cheeks. There'd been years of IVF treatments, one disappointment following another and Faith could only guess how this must have stung.

"He loved you very much, Antonia," Faith said softly. "You can't let go of that."

"Really? And just how many more of them do you suppose there might be?" Toni finished her drink in a single gulp. "It's not like he didn't have form with chambermaids, is it? I mean, not counting myself, there was that bitch who totally fucked him over, leaving the pieces for me put back together…" She broke off to wipe her eyes. "I don't think he was ever right after her, to be honest. Some of the things he…"

Toni let her voice trail off.

"If this was another life," said Faith carefully, "it was one in which he's done the decent thing. Let's not take that from him." She paused. "Any idea what happened, how it started?"

Toni simply shook her head again.

Faith took their glasses over to the drinks cabinet and poured each of them a refill.

"And does she know?" asked Faith. "About what … About Dennis?"

"No." Toni shrugged. "At least I assume not."

"Then you have to tell her," said Faith. "Both of you need to understand what's what here."

Toni's lips tightened.

"You've also got to find out if the money being paid is down to a court order," Faith continued. "Because there'll be legal ramifications if it stops. You need to check with your solicitor to discover if there's a will you don't know about. If he's made provision for them in the event…"

"Oh God." Toni's mouth fell open. "I hadn't even thought of that. You mean I could lose…"

She broke off as Faith reached for her hand and squeezed it.

"Look, I'm only playing devil's advocate here," she told her. "But you'll need to be sure where you stand before you start making decisions, right?"

Faith nodded.

"Because it's not only what the legal position is. When all's said and done, you should also consider what Dennis would have wanted you to do." She paused. "But the first thing is to tell her what's happened."

"I've no idea what to say." Toni seemed on the brink of tears again. "Where the hell do you start?"

"The truth," said Faith. "That your husband has died, you've now discovered he's the father of her child and that you need to talk." Faith paused. "Do you want me to draft an email and then we can go through it together?"

"Yes," said Toni, biting her lip. "Thank you."

"First, I need to let Ted know I'll... That I'll be awhile." Faith rose to her feet. "I was about to see if he wanted a bite to eat. Could I get something for you?"

"I'm alright." Toni almost managed a smile. "Perhaps later."

"I'll only be a few minutes," Faith told her.

* * *

In the corridor outside, Faith took a deep breath.

The fact that she was so frequently the bearer of bad news should help in situations like this, but it never did. All too often she found her professional persona slipping into place when what the situation truly needed was the emotional empathy of friendship, however raw. Jesus, couldn't she simply have put her arms around Antonia and hugged her, instead of prattling on about bloody solicitors...?

But talk about bombshell. Making her way to Ted's study, Faith shook her head. *Who can ever guess what's really going on in any marriage?* The image of Claudia Pascoe at her dressing table came into her mind, the last person in the world you'd think would put up with what she must have gone through. Wasn't it William Blake who said that you never know what is enough until you know what is more than enough? Well bloody hell, Billy boy, you got that right...

She gave the study door a knock and as she pushed it open, Ted looked up from his laptop.

"Hi," she smiled. "How's it going?"

"Just finished." Ted sat back in his chair. "Who was that earlier?"

"Antonia."

"How is she managing?" he asked.

"Not good," said Faith, then shrugged at his quizzical expression. "It's complicated - I'll explain later."

"Okay."

"I thought you might be ready for something to eat, but..." She acknowledged the tracksuit he was wearing with a nod. "You off for a run?"

"Yeah, I need to blow the cobwebs away." Ted hesitated. "Unless you want me to stay?"

"No, I'll manage," she told him. "But look in when you get back, okay?"

"Sure," he nodded. Staring down at the screen, Ted gave the keyboard a final couple of taps and then flipped the lid shut. Rising from his chair, he smiled at her.

"Shouldn't be more than an hour, hour and a half. Do you want anything while I'm out?"

"No," she said, before adding, "Remember, all around Trelawney Road's still closed off because of that gas leak." She pecked him on the cheek as he passed by. "Be careful."

"Of course," he told her. "Always am."

The GIs catch you off guard. A shared language, together with immersion in a culture made so familiar by popular media, has lulled you into the misconception that there won't be any surprises here. But the first actual *Americans you meet don't so much belie your expectations as blow them clean out of the water.*

These boys - and boys they are, other than a few NCOs you doubt any are older than twenty - are as diverse a collection of humanity as can be imagined. There are swarthy, wisecracking New Yorkers, laid back tanned Californians, rosy-cheeked farm hands from the prairies and oh so cool black hipsters out of the South Side. You meet hardy souls from the Canadian border whose accents have never escaped their Scandinavian heritage, banter with southern drawls that conjure up visions of antebellum plantations and marvel at the precision of Appalachian grammar thwarting its hillbilly connotations. You've always been aware of the notion of the United States as a melting pot but find yourself singularly unprepared for the reality of that.

And they are unfailingly polite, as conscious of this cultural divide they're on the other side of as you are. In the shop they smile as you pick out the correct coins from their palms, totally baffled by pounds shillings and pence - 'LSD? You're shitting me?' - and struggle with the A and B buttons of a pay phone more with good humour than irritation.

You understand from a few guarded comments that fraternisation has been discouraged, but that soon flies right out of the window. Most evenings, after they've returned from the beaches, a barbecue is fired up and proves an irresistible draw for miles around. Inch thick hamburgers, crates of Budweiser, the latest hits from Motown, packs of Lucky Strike dispensed from an endless supply of cartons... Eventually Brian - Carol's father - has a word with the young lieutenant in charge and an arrangement is reached to ensure attendance is by invitation only. Guests now have to be signed in at Reception and be able to prove they're over eighteen years old.

Most of the girls you work with look forward to these nights, intent on making the most of this exotic flirting and flattery while it lasts. But you, still with a weather eye open for which way the wind might be blowing, mostly spend the evenings in your chalet with the proverbial good book.

And then, on one of those evenings, comes a knock at your door.

Answering it, you find the lieutenant standing there.

"Hi," *he says.*

"Hello," *somewhat cautiously.*

"I'm very sorry to bother you, Miss," *he continues,* "but I was asking at Reception if there was a library or maybe a bookstore nearby where I might lay my hands on something to read." *He flashes you a smile.* "The young lady I spoke with told me everywhere'd be closed right now, but that you were someone whose tastes ran beyond dime store romances."

You hesitate, then open the door fully for him. He steps inside and you indicate the dozen paperbacks stacked atop a dresser on your side of the room. He leans forward and examines the titles.

"Serious reading," *he says, raising an eyebrow.*

"For a chalet maid?" *you suggest dryly.*

"For anyone," *he tells you, straightening up and shaking his head. Then, turning to face you, he reaches out his hand.*

"Mike Weaver. I'm very pleased to meet you."

His grip is firm, but more reassuring than intimidating.

"I'm Abigail," *you say, almost losing yourself in what must be the deepest blue eyes you've ever seen.*

"So, Abigail," *he smiles.* "What's your story?"

EPILOGUE

"I'd have had you, you know? Until your mum got better. But that woman from the council, she said you had to go into care."

You and Maureen are sitting in the car, parked only a few streets away from the house, but right now you really don't trust yourself to be dealing with traffic coming at you on the wrong side of the road.

You'd left with little fuss or ceremony, explaining to the eldest daughter that it's all been a bit too much for Maureen and you're going to give her a lift home. A glance across the room to where Maureen was waiting in the doorway, holding her coat and visibly upset, would seem to confirm this. She'd quietly thanked you and would doubtless later reflect with her siblings on shared sorrow and the kindness of strangers.

And then you were gone, out of their lives forever with ridiculous ease.

"How did you recognise me?" you ask.

"I don't know, I just did." Maureen shrugs. "Maybe it was the way you were looking at those photographs... Still a lost little girl."

You're silent at that.

"It took a long while for your mum to get better," she says softly. "I didn't see her for years after... Well, that night." She sighs. "Then we bumped into each other in town. I was doing some shopping, she was with Gerald, her husband, although I didn't know that at the time. I said hello, but she pretended not to remember me. She said I must have mistaken her for someone else."

Maureen pauses for a second.

"I wasn't sure what to think, really. I was certain it was her alright, but given everything that had happened, I thought it best to let it go. Told her sorry, my mistake, and walked on."

Maureen opens her handbag, fiddles inside and brings out a handkerchief.

"Next day there was a knock at the door. I opened it and your mum was standing there. 'Hello Maureen,' she said, 'can I come in?'"

Maureen is twisting the handkerchief around her fingers.

"We sat down, had a cup of tea. She explained Gerald didn't know about her past. That she was a schoolteacher now, but it had taken her all this while to get things right with herself. She told me that she'd paid someone to try to find you, but you'd completely disappeared. He discovered you'd been sent to an Approved School at some point, because you were in need of care and protection, but from there on it was like you'd fallen off the face of the earth."

She's staring sideways at you now and you slowly nod.

"I moved abroad," you say, quietly.

"She said that if she'd been able to find you, then she'd have told Gerald everything. But what was the point of…?"

Maureen breaks off, dabbing at her eyes.

"Rocking the boat," you suggest dryly, "to no purpose."

"Anne and David had already come along," says Maureen. "Then Jane soon after."

You both sit in silence for a while.

"So, are you going to…?" Maureen's tone is cautious.

You exhale, slowly.

"What good would that serve." It comes out more of a statement than question.

"Where do you live now?" she asks.

"California."

"Are you married?"

"Was." You shake your head. "My husband died earlier this year. Cancer."

"Oh, I'm so sorry." She reaches for your hand, gently clasps it. "Do you have children?"

Another shake of the head.

"We tried," you explain. "In the end… Well, time just ran out."

She nods sympathetically.

You reach for the key in the ignition.

"Let's get you home," you tell her.

"Abby," she says and something in her voice makes you turn to look at her.

"I'm so glad you're alright." She gives the slightest of shrugs. "I never forgot you and I always wondered."

You force a smile and pull away from the kerb.

* * *

Is this a life you lost, is this a life that was stolen, or is this a life you've escaped? Is it for some kind of closure that you've travelled six thousand miles? Because if it was, there isn't even a hint of it here right now.

You sit on the edge of the hotel bed and consider. You're booked in for two more nights, not knowing how today would play out you left your options open. But cancelling won't be a problem and maybe you could bring your flight forward to tomorrow. It's not like there's anything for you here and you could be home in thirty-six hours.

You dial the number on the back of your ticket.

The airline puts you on hold, but when don't they ever? And what PR genius came up with the notion that music soothes the irritated breast.

As *'Your call is important to us'* is laid over the tinny melody, you pick up the TV remote and absently begin stabbing the 'P' button in search of a news channel. Every hotel chain has CNN, BBC and Sky numbered differently, but what they all had in common was having you work through a dozen telesales and home improvement shows to find one of them. You're about to give up when BBC News 24 appears on the screen.

"... although next week's eclipse will only be total along a swathe of the southernmost part of the UK."

"That's right, Jane," says her co-presenter, "and it's expected that..."

The music from your cell breaks off and in what is almost a single fluid motion, you mute the TV with one hand while raising the other back up to your ear.

"Hello," you say.

And then it starts over, obviously resetting itself on reaching the end of a loop. You stare at the phone in exasperation, so tempted to simply hang up. Or maybe try again in an hour's time.

Oh, *fuck it!*

Why not just check out and drive to the airport? And if you can't get your flight rescheduled, then board the first damn plane to LAX and write the loss off as the perfect ending to a shitty trip.

But had you truly expected things to be different? And to be honest, if resolution - or reconciliation - had been on the cards, was that genuinely something you'd have welcomed with open arms? The last few months have been such an emotional roller coaster, so much pushing away pain into the deepest recesses of your mind, has sublimation now become the *de facto* reaction to anything you're reluctant to face up to? You've sure as hell no recollection of actually weighing up the pros and cons of this journey before booking flights and hotels. And gee, look how swell that's turned out.

So let's head home, you tell yourself. Get your life back on track and start to...

Your thoughts break off as the TV screen fills with the image of a clergyman in ornate ceremonial robes.

It's a strange moment. Instincts honed by millions of years of evolution kick in, but, lagging so far behind the sensibilities of our modern lives, offer nothing more than a rush of adrenaline to wipe the mind clear of anything but outmoded notions of fight or flight, as hairs rise on the back of your neck...

You're not aware of pressing down your finger to unmute the TV, but the room is suddenly filled with sound.

"...when we spoke to the Bishop earlier," the presenter is saying.

As thought, comprehension, reason, cohesion and prescience return, they do so with a clamour, an absolute jumble of impressions are jostling for space inside your head.

If that was a recent photo he's aged well. You register the voice without taking in any meaning of words spoken, but that's what always resonates across the decades, isn't it, because voices never really change, do they?

The photograph on the screen is replaced with another, but you're prepared for this, sentences which passed you by a few seconds ago are reassembling themselves in the mind's cognitive wake.

You know exactly what's happened.

And you'd also know the face now on-screen, even without 'Peter Matthews, 1920 - 1999' superimposed below it. Seems time was kind to him as well…

"Peter and I were friends for over forty years," Sebastian is saying. "We initially met through our work with various children's charities…"

The music on your cell comes to an abrupt stop.

"Hi there. You've reached booking enquiries and are speaking to Melanie. How may I be of assistance?"

You look down at the phone almost uncomprehendingly, then click the red button and toss it onto the bed.

The TV screen now has your full attention, as you listen to Sebastian expand on what worthy efforts he and Peter have woven into their lives.

Maybe, you think to yourself, *if the fates have been kind, just maybe this won't have been a wasted trip after all…*

AFTERWORD

We hope you enjoyed Corrigenda, the third book in the St Hannahs series.

Like most independently published novels, its success is dependent on word of mouth recommendation rather then mainstream marketing. If you did enjoy it, an online rating or review would be appreciated.

The first two novels are *Amanuensis* (2020) and *Felo de Se* (2021). *Fascisti*, the fourth in the series will be published in 2024, followed by *Belladonna* in 2025.

ABOUT THE AUTHOR

Phil Egner

Phil was born in Nottingham in 1949.

During the late 1960s he was involved with a number of projects that had their genesis in the London counterculture and was a regular contributor to the underground press.

A career in software development followed, primarily as an IT contractor working in both the public and private sectors throughout the UK, mainland Europe and United States.

Home is now a Devon village, where his time is increasingly occupied with the St Hannahs series of novels.